Raves for *Midnight Rescue*, the Thrilling First Book in Elle Kennedy's Killer Instincts Series

"If you're looking for a chilling, hard-core romantic suspense loaded with sensuality, military camaraderie, and dry humor, why not arrange for a *Midnight Rescue*?"
—*USA Today*

"Talk about your kick-ass heroines. . . . Kennedy kicks off a gritty and thrilling new romantic suspense series with a heroine who is every bit as lethal as her hero. This launch novel sets up a reluctant partnership between two mercenary groups with deadly reputations: one all female, the other all male. The action is raw and deadly, and the passion sizzling. Romantic suspense just gained a major new player!"
—*Romantic Times* (4½ stars)

"Romantic suspense fans will want to get ahold of this book! . . . Elle Kennedy, please write faster!"
—The Book Pushers

"With its dark, edgy tone, passionate love story, and deadly protagonists, *Midnight Rescue* is a surefire win for fans of romantic suspense."
—Romance Junkies

"This was a very good romantic suspense. It had all the right elements that I look for in a book like this. The hot alpha men. The strong women they pair up with."
—Fiction Vixen Book Reviews

"Anybody looking for action, intensity, and passion will love this novel."
—The Book Whisperer

"With a large cast of colorful characters, multiple inter-_____ ted villains, *Midnight Res-*_____ vercoming the darkest, _____ Fans will be eager to see _____ her mercenaries."
_____ er, award-winning author
of the Edge series

continued . . .

D0951783

**Praise for Elle Kennedy
and Her Novels**

"A must read."   —Fallen Angels Reviews

"An undeniably erotic story. . . . The sex scenes are incredible and the characters are compelling . . . a great read!"
—TwoLips Reviews

"Wickedly entertaining."   —Joyfully Reviewed

"A top-notch tale."   —*Romantic Times* (4½ stars)

"Elle Kennedy makes her characters sexy, lovable, and realistic."   —Romance Junkies

"[A] heart-wrenching, sensual story that will make you laugh and cry as the characters come to life before your very eyes. . . . This is one emotional roller-coaster ride you don't want to miss."   —Long and Short Reviews

Also Available in the Killer Instincts Series

Midnight Rescue

Kennedy, Elle.
Midnight alias : a
killer instincts novel /
2013.
~~33~~0~~5227943572~~
sa   04/25/~~13~~

MIDNIGHT ALIAS

A KILLER INSTINCTS NOVEL

ELLE KENNEDY

A SIGNET ECLIPSE BOOK

SIGNET ECLIPSE
Published by New American Library, a division of
Penguin Group (USA) Inc., 375 Hudson Street,
New York, New York 10014, USA
Penguin Group (Canada), 90 Eglinton Avenue East, Suite 700, Toronto,
Ontario M4P 2Y3, Canada (a division of Pearson Penguin Canada Inc.)
Penguin Books Ltd., 80 Strand, London WC2R 0RL, England
Penguin Ireland, 25 St. Stephen's Green, Dublin 2,
Ireland (a division of Penguin Books Ltd.)
Penguin Group (Australia), 250 Camberwell Road, Camberwell, Victoria 3124,
Australia (a division of Pearson Australia Group Pty. Ltd.)
Penguin Books India Pvt. Ltd., 11 Community Centre, Panchsheel Park,
New Delhi - 110 017, India
Penguin Group (NZ), 67 Apollo Drive, Rosedale, Auckland 0632,
New Zealand (a division of Pearson New Zealand Ltd.)
Penguin Books (South Africa) (Pty.) Ltd., 24 Sturdee Avenue,
Rosebank, Johannesburg 2196, South Africa

Penguin Books Ltd., Registered Offices:
80 Strand, London WC2R 0RL, England

First published by Signet Eclipse, an imprint of New American Library,
a division of Penguin Group (USA) Inc.

First Printing, February 2013
10   9   8   7   6   5   4   3   2   1

Copyright © Leeanne Kenedy, 2013
All rights reserved. No part of this book may be reproduced, scanned, or distributed in any printed or electronic form without permission. Please do not partici-
pate in or encourage piracy of copyrighted materials in violation of the author's
rights. Purchase only authorized editions.

SIGNET ECLIPSE and logo are trademarks of Penguin Group (USA) Inc.

Printed in the United States of America

PUBLISHER'S NOTE
This is a work of fiction. Names, characters, places, and incidents either are the
product of the author's imagination or are used fictitiously, and any resemblance
to actual persons, living or dead, business establishments, events, or locales is
entirely coincidental.
   The publisher does not have any control over and does not assume any responsibility for author or third-party Web sites or their content.

If you purchased this book without a cover you should be aware that this book
is stolen property. It was reported as "unsold and destroyed" to the publisher and
neither the author nor the publisher has received any payment for this "stripped
book."

ALWAYS LEARNING   PEARSON

For my family

ACKNOWLEDGMENTS

This book was definitely a challenge to write, and it wouldn't have been possible without the invaluable assistance of my editor, Jesse Feldman, who whipped the story into shape with her astute comments and constant encouragement.

Special thanks to my research assistant and early reader, Amanda, for all her help and support; to readers Fatin and Heather, for their feedback, enthusiasm, and sheer awesomeness; and major high fives to my amazing circle of friends for letting me bounce plot ideas off them and talk their ears off, and for giving me pep talks whenever the writer's block settled in!

Chapter 1

"This is boring as fuck," Luke Dubois declared as he flopped down on the couch. His weight caused the cushions to bounce, which in turn woke up Trevor Callaghan, who was sprawled on the other end of the brown leather sofa.

Looking alert despite having just been jarred from slumber, Trevor tossed a crooked grin in Luke's direction. "Not every mission means hanging off a helicopter and shooting shit up, squid."

Luke bristled at the patronizing nickname—Trevor never failed to dis the navy, Mr. Army man that he was—but a part of him was actually happy to be insulted. It'd been far too long since he'd seen Trevor so lighthearted. When Trev had rejoined the team six months ago, he'd looked like a zombie. Scruffy, moody, dead inside. It had taken the man a year and a half to get over the loss of his fiancée, but he was finally on the right track. He'd cut his hair, burned the beach bum outfits, taught his facial muscles how to smile again. It was good to have him back, even if Trevor's leadership skills annoyed the hell out of Luke sometimes. If Morgan had made Luke team leader on this gig, they'd be storming Vince Angelo's club. But Trevor had always preferred the cautious approach. Also known as the *boring* one.

"This isn't even a mission," Luke countered. "All we do is watch."

A third voice joined the mix, this one boasting an Australian accent and a whole lot of scorn.

"Don't you even think of complaining, mate," Sullivan Port said as he strode into the living room in nothing but a towel. The white terry cloth, hanging low on the guy's hips, was way too small for that huge body of his. Sullivan was six-three, with broad shoulders and a heavy chest, and he constantly seemed to be strolling around half-naked. Maybe it was an Australian thing.

"*You* get to watch naked girls every night," Sullivan added. "*We* watch the building. Naked girls is my job. Tell me, how is that fair?"

Luke couldn't argue. Of all the men on Jim Morgan's mercenary team, Sullivan probably did have the greatest appreciation for the female form, and no matter where the guy was, he always managed to find a hot, eager girl ready for a lay. Not that Luke was hurting for female company himself, but Sullivan was a whole different league of player. Luke once watched a prostitute in Amsterdam offer to pay *Sullivan* to go upstairs with her. If Sully weren't such a cocky rub-it-in-your-face type, Luke might even call him his hero.

"Morgan is punishing me," Sullivan went on, crossing the parquet floor toward the kitchen. He disappeared behind the enormous refrigerator door, then reappeared with a beer bottle, towel flapping against his thighs as he returned to the living area. When he plopped down on the armchair across from the sofa, both Luke and Trevor shielded their eyes.

"Whoa, fix that towel, man," Luke ordered.

"Fix it?" Trevor echoed. "No, go put clothes on instead. For the love of God, this isn't a frat house."

Sullivan shrugged. "I like having a cold beer after a shower." He grinned. "If my cock makes you feel inferior, that's not my fault."

There, it was official. This was not a mission. When grown men started talking about each other's cocks, it meant things were bad.

Stifling a yawn, Luke focused on the wall of floor-to-ceiling windows flooding the loft with sunlight. He couldn't wait for the sun to set. Once that happened, the three of them could relieve Holden and D and get the hell out of this apartment, which was ironic because as safe houses went, this Tribeca loft might actually be the sweetest digs the team had ever used.

Three thousand square feet, the place boasted fourteen-foot cathedral ceilings, oversize windows, and an open-concept layout using wood beams and exposed brick. The kitchen was top-notch, spilling onto a formal dining room, and the luxurious living room offered L-shaped leather couches, overstuffed armchairs, and a massive stone fireplace. Not to mention the three enormous bedrooms, private terrace, amazing sound system . . . Morgan must have shelled out some big bucks to secure this place for the month.

Unfortunately, the novelty of this sweet loft was beginning to wear off. Luke was tired of sleeping all day. Pretty tired of doing shit-all at night too, but at least it beat being cooped up indoors. He wasn't made for indoors. He needed action. Excitement.

Battling another burst of impatience, he swiped a pack of Marlboros from the coffee table and headed for the glass sliding door that opened onto the terrace. He lit up, opened the door, and blew a cloud of smoke into the cool evening air.

"I'm serious," Sullivan insisted after taking a long swallow of his beer. "Morgan's pissed at me. There's no other explanation for why he didn't place me inside the club. Me and strippers go together like dingoes and babies. Dubois over here wouldn't even know what to do with a stripper."

"I watch," Luke replied. "That's all you can do with strippers." He took another drag, but the nicotine did nothing to eradicate his sense of restless boredom. "And you don't get to complain either, *mate*. You're the one who went off grid for six months. You asked for Morgan's wrath."

"You know I lose track of time when I'm sailing *Evangeline*." Sullivan's light gray eyes glazed over at the mention of his yacht. The guy was obsessed with his boat, had her name tattooed on his back and everything. Then he snapped out of it and frowned. "He didn't even let me stop at the compound first. I wanted to meet Kane's new lady. I bet she's real sweet."

Luke and Trevor nearly keeled over with laughter.

Sullivan shot them a blank look. "What?"

Wheezing, Luke bent over and gripped his side. Trevor wiped a tear from the corner of his eye.

"What?" Sullivan said again.

"Abby Sinclair is neither sweet nor a lady," Trevor said, still chuckling.

"But, please, can I be there when you call her that to her face?" Luke pleaded.

He pictured Sullivan trying that Aussie charm on Abby, and nearly broke out in laughter again. Abby would eat the other man alive. Sure, she cracked a lot more smiles these days, even laughed now and then, but she was still tough as nails. And truth be told, she still scared him just a little.

Downing the rest of his beer, Sullivan slammed the bottle on the table and got to his feet. He strode over to the sliding door, plucked Luke's cigarette out of his hand, and hijacked the thing.

Ignoring the scowl aimed his way, he took a few quick drags before handing the butt back. "Time to throw on some clothes." Sully tossed a look over his shoulder on his way to the corridor. "Unless you ladies want to see my dick again?"

"My eyes hurt when subjected to small things," Trevor called back.

The ring of a cell phone cut off Luke's resounding laughter. Trevor headed for the sleek dining table across the room and grabbed his phone. "It's Morgan," he said briskly.

About time the boss checked in. Morgan had decided this assignment was too boring for his taste, so he was back at the team's compound, "coordinating," as he liked to call it.

Luke hoped this call meant that things were finally starting to move. The team had been in Manhattan for four days now, and had absolutely nothing to show for it. They'd been hired by the DEA, of all agencies, to track down the whereabouts of Carter Dane, an undercover agent who'd gone off the radar. Dane's supervisors suspected a mole connected to the investigation had blown his cover, a likely scenario considering that Dane's last cryptic text to his handler had implied that someone had ratted him out.

At this point, the DEA had no clue as to whether the dude was dead or missing or who knew what. If there was a mole, any agents sent in subsequently could face the same fate as their missing colleague, so it was up to Luke and the others to find out what had happened to the guy. It wasn't the kind of job Morgan's operatives usually took on, but the boss had admitted during the briefing that someone had called in a favor.

Luke wished Morgan had just told favor-dude to shove it, but Jim Morgan was the kind of man who always paid you back. He was all about honor, which was one of the reasons Luke had signed on to work for the guy. The legendary former Ranger had recruited him six years ago, luring him away from the military to join Morgan's team of soldiers. Most of the others had already been on board, including Derek "D" Pratt, who'd apparently recruited himself by simply showing up on Morgan's doorstep one day and reporting for work. Sullivan was hired around the same time as Luke, but Ethan Hayes, the rookie, had joined them only three years ago. As a team, they worked like a well-oiled machine, and their reputation for getting the job done had spread over the years.

Luke would take a bullet for any of the men he worked with, and as far as the job went, he frickin' loved it. He reveled in the risk, the jolt of adrenaline he received from a particularly dangerous op. And the saving lives part. Sometimes the knowledge that he'd saved a life brought an even greater adrenaline rush than blowing things up.

Across the room, Trevor was muttering a whole bunch of

"yes, sirs" into the phone. When he hung up, his brown eyes looked grim.

Luke ducked out to the terrace to extinguish his smoke in the ashtray on the glass table, then returned to the couch and plopped down. "What'd he say?"

"Tonight you focus on a specific dancer. Livy Lovelace."

Sullivan reentered the main room in time to overhear Trevor's last words. "Livy Lovelace?" he echoed, laughing. "Say that five times. Total tongue twister."

Luke turned away so the others wouldn't see him gulp. Fuck, out of all the girls in that club, he had to focus on *her*? Livy Lovelace, or whatever her real name, was a goddess. The sexiest woman he'd ever had the pleasure of laying eyes on.

Lord, all that wavy chestnut brown hair spilling down her regal back . . . high, firm breasts tipped by dusky nipples . . . endless legs . . . bottomless moss green eyes. Just the memory of her got him semi-hard, and now he was crossing his legs so his buddies didn't catch *that* response.

Before this job, he'd firmly subscribed to the strip-clubs-are-sleazy philosophy, but the first time he'd seen the goddess dance . . . he'd sprung a boner. No other way around it. Watching her up on the stage, so vulnerable and so sexy at the same time, had been pure torture.

"Did Morgan say why to focus on her?" he asked, finally finding his voice.

"Whoever he's got on the inside thinks Lovelace might know something," Trevor answered, already heading for the hallway. "I'm gathering up my gear. We leave in five."

Sullivan, who'd changed into a pair of black trousers and a snug long-sleeve, bent down to unzip a duffel bag on the floor. He strapped on a shoulder holster, shoved a nine-millimeter Beretta into it, then reached for a black trench coat and shrugged it on.

Noticing that Luke was still on the couch, Sully shot him a puzzled look. "You coming or what?"

He smothered a sigh. "Give me a second."

Breathing through his nose, he willed away the annoying

erection straining against his zipper. Fuck. He couldn't even use lack of sex as an excuse for this juvenile reaction. He'd hooked up with a waitress at his favorite bar in Tijuana less than a week ago, and the sex had been damn good, so he definitely wasn't hard up.

But something about that dark-haired dancer totally got his blood going.

"Get off your ass," Trevor ordered as he strode back into the room in a getup similar to Sullivan's.

Releasing the sigh, Luke stood up. And hoped that neither of his teammates spared a glance at his crotch. When Sully hooted, it was clear his current state of discomfort hadn't gone unnoticed.

Giving his buddy the finger, he awkwardly marched out of the living room to get his gear.

"You're on after Cora."

Olivia Taylor shifted her gaze from her reflection in the mirror to see the Diamond Mine's newest dancer saunter into the busy dressing room. Candy Cane was the name she used, and the costume she'd chosen reflected it: a red-and-white-striped bustier with lace cups and a sheer mesh body, dental-floss G-string, and a garter with red lace trim. She wore crimson lipstick and pink eye shadow, which made her appear both innocent and erotic at the same time. Candy had been working here for only two months, but she was already a big hit with the customers. Even Vince was impressed with her, and the boss wasn't easily impressed.

As Candy flopped into a chair at the neighboring vanity table and began removing her makeup with a cotton ball, Olivia stood up and adjusted the straps of her dove gray satin cocktail gown. An exotic dancer in a cocktail gown—she didn't miss the irony of that. But Vince had ordered her to look elegant tonight. He insisted that the customers welcomed a break from the trash every now and then, that they longed for a taste of class. *And you, babe, are the epitome of class.*

Said the pimp to his whore.

Okay, that was a tad melodramatic. She was *not* a whore. But as Olivia gazed at her reflection, she didn't see the subtle makeup, elegant gown, and strappy heels. She saw the skimpy thong, the silver garter belt, and the glitter-dusted breasts that all those men out there were about to leer at.

Her throat tightened. God, she didn't want to do this anymore. Every night when she left the Diamond, she felt dirty. Dirty and exposed and so utterly drained it was a miracle she managed to drag herself out of bed in the mornings.

When a friend from NYU had hooked her up with this job last year, she'd told herself it was temporary. After her mother's cancer came back and the bills started piling up, Olivia's waitressing salary simply didn't cut it anymore. The rent needed to be paid. Her tuition. Her mom's latest round of chemo treatments. Groceries, phone bill, utilities. Seemed like there was an unending stream of *must-pay* in Olivia's life. The price was never right. It was high. Always high.

Shake her ass, count the bills in her G-string, and graduate. That had been the plan, except now there was no chance of that happening. Not if Vince Angelo had anything to say about it.

"You okay?"

She blinked away the tears threatening to spill over and pasted a smile on her face. When she turned her head, she found Candy staring at her. The concern in those blue eyes had Olivia averting her gaze, pretending to be fascinated with the chaos around her.

The huge dressing room had twenty makeup stations, costume racks against one wall, a luxurious bathroom, and a bank of lockers at the far end of the room where the dancers stored their belongings. All around her, girls were dressing or undressing, chatting with one another or into their cell phones. They were in their twenties or thirties, came in all shapes, sizes, and races, and most of them were here for the same reason as Olivia: money.

Across the room, one of the other dancers, Heaven Monroe, was busy applying makeup to her gaunt face, but Olivia doubted any amount of beauty products could rid the girl of that gray pallor. Heaven was a junkie, had been for as long as Olivia had worked here, and for the life of her, she still couldn't figure out why Vince kept the girl on.

"Olivia?" Candy was still eyeing her.

"I'm fine," she lied. "I just have a bit of a headache. I'm worried the spotlight will only make it worse."

"You sure it's just a headache?" Candy reached for an elastic band, tied her long blond hair into a ponytail, and rose from her chair. "Every time I look at you, you've got the saddest expression on your face. What's going on with you?"

Uh, other than the fact that our boss covered up a murder for me?

She hastily broke eye contact again. Candy seemed like a nice woman, but confiding in her wasn't an option. Vince had eyes and ears in every inch of this club.

"I said I'm fine." Her tone came out sharper than intended, but it got the job done.

With a wounded look, Candy slunk back to her station. An apology bit at the tip of Olivia's tongue, but before she could voice it, the door swung open and Vince walked in.

"Evening, ladies," he announced in that silky-smooth voice of his. "Give me and Livy a minute, okay?"

Not a single dancer so much as protested. Even those in a state of undress obeyed the boss, filing out of the room without a word. When they were alone, Vince stepped closer, his dark eyes softening as he looked at Olivia.

The mere sight of him made her nauseous. The fact that he was actually quite handsome made it even worse. In his mid-thirties, Vince Angelo was Italian to the core, with slicked-back black hair, shrewd brown eyes, and a gym-toned body forever clad in tailored suits. He was constantly on the receiving end of appreciative female attention, but Olivia knew better than the women who checked Vince out.

And she didn't appreciate a damn thing about him.

"You look beautiful, babe."

"Thank you," she murmured.

Another step closer. His arm came out as if he wanted to touch her, but then he dropped it to his side and smiled ruefully. "Fuck, babe, don't look so sad. We got good news yesterday, remember?"

We? No, *she'd* received good news. *Her* mother was in remission. But Vince had a habit of acting like they were in this together. A sliver of anger pierced her, but she forced her expression to remain neutral. She couldn't let him see the anger. It would only provoke his own ire, and Olivia knew quite well what happened when Vince got angry.

So she mustered up a smile and said, "I know. It's just hard to be hopeful. The cancer already came back twice before. I don't know how long the remission will last this time."

"If the disease returns, we'll deal with it."

The way you dealt with that customer's body? she almost blurted out. She stopped herself, though. A part of her still hoped that if she never mentioned the attack, Vince might forget about it. Release her from the debt she owed him. But she wasn't naive enough to give much credence to that hope. Whether she liked it or not, she *did* owe him. For paying her tuition, and for taking care of her staggering medical bills, not to mention her mother's. She hadn't asked him to do any of that, but he had, and now he owned her.

"Come here, let me hold you for a moment," Vince said huskily.

He opened his arms. Olivia hesitated before stepping into them. *Play along. It won't be forever. You'll find a way out soon.*

A way out. God, she dreamed of that every night. The salary Vince paid her went toward rent, bills, and groceries, but her tips went directly into her escape fund, and since Vince didn't monitor those, he had no idea how much she'd already managed to save. She'd definitely amassed a decent amount this past year. But not decent enough. If she'd been on her own, she would have skipped town months ago, but no way would she leave her mother behind. That just made things more difficult, though. She couldn't uproot her mom unless she had a job to support them both with. Kathleen was still recovering, still required the epoetin injections to help her produce the red blood cells that her damaged kidneys denied her body.

Starting fresh in a new city required money. Starting fresh in a new city while having to pay for expensive medical treatments? They'd end up living on the streets.

Her best bet was to finish school first. She had one more semester, and then she'd have a degree in hand and a better chance of landing a higher-paying job and supporting her mom. Hopefully a scholarship to law school would be in the cards too, and she could always take night classes if need be.

Vince wouldn't follow her once she was gone. He would find a new pet to obsess over, a new girl to control.

Or at least that's what she kept telling herself.

When it came to Vince Angelo, she truly didn't know how far he would go to get his way. What she did know brought a tremor of fear.

Vince stroked her hair and held her tighter. The buttons of his pin-striped suit jacket rubbed against her chest, irritating the bare nipples beneath her satin dress. He cupped her chin with both hands, his dark eyes searching her face. "I've been patient with you, haven't I, Olivia?"

She nodded.

A smile tugged on his full, sensual lips. His lips were the only soft thing about him. Everything else was hard, sharp. Eyes like a hawk, handsome but cold features chiseled out of stone.

"I saved you," he went on, pride creeping into his voice. "I know we haven't spoken about it in a while, but I just wanted you to know that everything I did that night, I did for you. Because I love you."

Her voice wobbled. "I kn-know."

Inside, she was seething. For her? How had any of it been for her? She'd wanted to tell the police the truth, but while she'd been in surgery, Vince's goons had dumped the body, and their boss had spun the police a tale about how Olivia hadn't seen her attacker. When the cops had backed off without so much as taking her statement, it wasn't hard to figure out that Vince must have paid somebody off. By then, he'd also paid every outstanding debt she'd owed, officially placing her in *his* debt.

"And that's why I'm waiting," Vince said, his soft words jerking her from her thoughts. "I know who you are, babe. You're not the kind of girl a man just screws. You're the one he marries and screws."

Gee, how romantic.

"I'll wait as long as I have to, Liv. I *respect* you. That's why I'm letting you continue your schooling. That's why I allow you to live with your mother rather than push you to move in with me."

She wanted to scream. Wanted to slap that handsome face of his, rip his hair out by the roots. *Letting* her? *Allowing* her? Wow. And he truly believed that he loved her.

"I'm an honorable man," he finished, gently tracing her jaw with his index finger. "A patient man. And it brings tears to my eyes knowing that you're untouched and saving yourself for me."

Now she wanted to gag. Telling him she was a virgin had been a last-ditch effort to hinder one of his early seduction attempts, and to her shock, it had actually worked. After the attack, when he'd hinted that she could repay him with a fuck, she'd almost thrown up. Instead, she'd played the innocence card, and so far it had served her well. But how much longer? She knew his imaginary honor and supposed patience wouldn't last forever, which made it all the more imperative to prepare for her escape.

Before he decided to take her to bed without her consent.

"Your honor is my favorite thing about you," she said in a shaky voice.

A knock rapped against the door, and Cora Malcolm poked her head into the dressing room. Onstage she was Coral Holliday, but to Olivia she was simply Cora, the pretty redhead who sat beside her in nearly every lecture hall. Cora had been the one to set her up with this job, but these days Olivia wasn't feeling so grateful.

"You're on, Liv," Cora announced. Her cheeks were flushed, and sweat coated a pair of perky bare breasts that bounced as she sauntered over to her station.

Vince leaned down and planted a kiss on Olivia's cheek. "Go on, babe, turn them on, get them nice and hard."

Said the honorable prince to the love of his life.

She choked down a hysterical laugh and headed for the door, feeling Vince's eyes burning into her back. In the corridor, she drew air into her lungs, blinked away some more tears, and attempted to regain her composure. After a year of this, she still couldn't shake the sick feeling in her belly. It wasn't nerves; it was shame. She hated dancing for the customers out there, feeling all those hungry eyes on her. Her own desperation had brought her to this club, but it wasn't desperation keeping her here. Now it was fear. Vince had made it painfully clear that he wouldn't be happy if she quit dancing—not before the wedding, anyway.

And she knew better than most what Vince Angelo did to people who made him unhappy.

Chapter 2

A man could get lost in those eyes. They reminded Luke of the Spanish moss growing in the bayou back home, a lush earthy green that left you feeling calm and sated. And she had incredibly long eyelashes. Probably those fake stick-on kind, but if they were real, then *damn*. It didn't escape him that he was sitting here ogling the dancer's *eyes*, while all the other sleaze buckets around him were staring at her breasts. Not that her breasts weren't as spectacular as her eyes. Because they were.

Luke shifted in his seat and took a long swig of his beer. There was something extremely disconcerting about having a hard-on while surrounded by a bunch of other men. He'd never understood the appeal of strip clubs. Why look when you could touch? It didn't take much effort to walk into a bar, find a willing female, and touch the night away. Looking *sucked*.

Or maybe it didn't. He had to relent as the stunning brunette on the main stage began grinding against a silver pole.

Focus.

He drew in a breath and heeded the voice in his head. Morgan might have ordered him to keep an eye on Livy Lovelace tonight, but that wasn't the only task at hand. He'd paid the extra cover charge to get into the roped-off VIP lounge, which was up on the second floor and offered a perfect line of sight to the stage below. The VIP area boasted a smaller stage with a counter around it, where a voluptuous blonde in a white corset was dancing for a couple of high rollers. A lot of hair tossing, pelvic grinding, and hip jerking going on, but Luke was more interested in the happenings on the main floor.

He rose from the comfortable padded armchair and strolled up to the railing, his gaze sliding over the activity below. Scantily clad waitresses rushed from table to table, while half-naked dancers worked the room, making conversation with customers, sizing them up as if to calculate how much dough they could score from a particular mark. Luke ignored the females, studying the men instead. He examined, discarded, moved on to the next.

Carter Dane's face was imprinted in Luke's memory, but he saw no sign of the missing DEA agent. Not among the customers, nor the various bouncers and staff moving through the club. If Dane was here, then he must be in the restricted areas: the employee section in the back or the upstairs management offices. If he *wasn't* here, then he was probably dead, which was beginning to seem likely.

Dane had been ordered to buddy up to Vince Angelo as a means of reaching the agency's real target: Ric De Luca. The Diamond Mine was nothing more than a glorified washing machine—De Luca laundered his money and ran his drugs through there. And if Luke were a betting man, he'd go all in on the wager that Carter Dane's cover had been blown. De Luca was too smart to let just anyone infiltrate his organization, no matter how outstanding the person appeared on paper.

Okay, he concluded, no Dane in sight. Poor dude was probably six feet under or chained to a cement block at the bottom of the Hudson. But until they had confirmation, the team couldn't pack up and leave.

Draining his beer, he signaled the waitress for another, then watched the beautiful dancer finish out her performance. The slinky cocktail dress she'd sauntered out in lay in a puddle of satin on the floor. The heels were gone too, but she still wore a silver G-string and a garter belt jammed full of bills.

The waitress returned with his beer. This time he sipped slowly. Couldn't afford to get hammered on the job.

When he felt a pair of eyes boring into him, he realized the waitress hadn't left. She stood next to him, watching the stage. "She's good, ain't she?" the top-heavy blonde drawled.

"Beautiful," he heard himself say.

The music died, and his goddess was rewarded by deafening applause and lewd shouts. He noticed the waitress moving away and cleared his throat. "How much for a private dance?"

She giggled. "I don't do that. I just wait tables."

He hooked a thumb at the stage below. "I meant with her."

Disappointment flashed in the blonde's eyes. "That one's expensive."

"How much?" he asked again.

"A hundred out on the floor. Five hundred in the VIP rooms."

Luke whistled softly. Five hundred to get the goddess alone? Pretty damn steep.

On the other hand, he pictured her beautiful face, the heart-stopping body, and decided it could actually be considered a bargain. Ignoring the waitress's amused expression, he pulled out his wallet and did a quick count.

"Arrange it," he said, his voice coming out gruff.

"You got it, big spender."

As she flounced off, Luke released a heavy breath. What the hell was he doing?

What you were asked to do. Investigating.

Well, sure. Morgan *had* ordered him to pay closer attention to the stripper, hadn't he? Nothing closer than a lap dance.

A few minutes later, the waitress returned and gestured for him to follow her down the wide spiral staircase. With the blonde taking the lead, they wove through the tables scattered around the main room, past several curtained alcoves and the hallway he'd noticed staff members coming in and out of. Didn't go near the second spiral staircase, which intel told him led up to the management offices, including Angelo's. Luke suppressed his disappointment. Ah well. The opportunity to snoop around would present itself eventually.

They went beyond the bar area, stepping into a shadowy corridor lined with half a dozen doors on each side. The waitress led him to one at the end of the hall, where a dark-skinned bouncer with massive shoulders stood guard. The behemoth's sharp gaze pierced Luke.

"No touching," the bouncer said curtly. "We'll be watching. You touch, you're out."

"Yes, sir." He appreciated the warning. It told him that the folks at the Diamond Mine didn't fuck around. Someone was looking out for his girl's safety.

Your girl?

The girls, he mentally amended. The bouncers looked out for the girls who worked here. *All* of the girls. Not just the one who got his blood going.

The big man opened the door for him and Luke stepped inside, surprised by the tasteful interior of the VIP room. He'd expected a strobe light and tacky decoration, but instead found a plush leather couch in a semicircle shape, walls draped in red velvet, and an old-fashioned-looking light fixture emitting a romantic glow.

"Drinks are free," the bouncer barked, nodding to the wet bar by the couch. "Livy will be in soon."

As the door shut behind him, Luke bypassed the bar and sat down. He studied the room, immediately pinpointing the locations of the three security cameras. Did they pick up sound too? He'd get Holden to check it out later, but right now it meant he couldn't be too direct in his fishing expedition. If Livy Lovelace had any information about the missing DEA agent, he'd have to use some subtle digging to pry it out of her.

He was considering pouring himself a drink after all when his goddess sauntered into the room.

The saliva in his mouth turned to sawdust. Oh boy. The woman wore nothing but that silver thong and garter combo she'd stripped down to onstage, and her bare breasts, high and round, gleamed in the dim lighting of the room. Jeez, she was even more gorgeous up close. Smooth golden skin. Movie starlet face. And tall, he realized, as she walked toward him, hips swaying.

He opened his mouth to say something—*Hello* would probably have been a good start—but no words came out. His vocal cords had turned into limp spaghetti noodles.

She didn't speak either. Just advanced on him like a wary jungle cat, green eyes locked with his. When she was standing a foot away, Luke saw her face change. Gone was the wariness. The tension in her jaw eased. And she went into seduction mode.

"Hey there," she murmured. "Mary said you like the way I dance."

Mary? Right, the waitress. Luke still couldn't remember how to talk, but he managed a quick nod. Her voice was not what he'd expected. It was husky, throaty, with a musical lilt to it.

"Not much of a talker, I see." She tossed her long chestnut hair over one bare shoulder and smiled wryly. "All right then."

Music began to pour out of the speakers mounted on the walls. It was some slow, jazzy beat, but he paid no attention because really, how could a man pay attention to a *song* when the sexiest woman on the planet was climbing onto his lap? With one fluid motion, she straddled his thighs, her breasts inches from his face, swaying softly as she moved to the music. The scent of her flooded his nostrils. Surprisingly sweet, with a hint of lemon and quite possibly strawberries. Fuck, he was suddenly really hungry.

And horny. Incredibly horny as the goddess ground her lower body against him, her green eyes slitting sensually as she danced for him. On him. Whatever.

Luke kept his hands at his sides, battling the impulse to reach up and touch her. Each time she rubbed her pelvis against the aching ridge in his pants, he wanted to grab her by the hair and bring her down for a kiss. He sat there, trying not to move a muscle, but the erection throbbing down below didn't want to cooperate. It strained against his zipper, jerking each time the goddess's warm mound made contact with it.

Raw mortification slammed into him when he realized he was about two seconds away from coming. Holy shit. He hadn't come in his pants since the ninth grade, when he and Lisa Hamilton had been dry humping on her parents' couch. Well, no way. He wasn't fourteen anymore. He was thirty frickin' years old.

Knowing the only way he could derail this attraction was by making conversation, he said the first thing that popped into his head. "So, have you always wanted to be a stripper?"

She went off-rhythm, a startled look entering her eyes. Then she laughed, a short burst of sound laced with incredulity. "Yes, every little girl dreams of being a stripper," she replied, shaking her head in amazement.

Luke felt his cheeks go hot. "Sorry. Dumb question."

She continued to dance, raising her arms over her head and letting her long hair tumble down her shoulders. His cock jutted up again, so he blurted out another inane question. "What'd you want to be then?"

Her movements were disrupted once more. Irritation flashed across her face before she sighed. "A teacher. I love working with kids. But that never panned out. I'm at NYU now, majoring in poli-sci. Taking a lot of pre-law courses to prepare for law school."

Luke hid his shock, but evidently not too well. "Not what you expected to hear from a stripper, huh?" she said knowingly.

"No," he admitted. He studied her beautiful face. "Do you like it? Pre-law, I mean?"

"Yes. Now quit talking and enjoy the dance."

She leaned forward and pressed her breasts to his face. A nipple darted past his mouth and he clamped his lips shut before he did something stupid—like lick it. His erection, depraved asshole that it was, continued to plead for attention.

"I like hearing you talk," he said. "You've got a nice voice."

You've got a nice voice? Oh, brother.

She surprised him again. "So do you. Is that a hint of the South I hear?"

"New Orleans, born and raised," he confirmed.

Her eyes twinkled. "A Cajun boy. Do you speak French?"

"Sure do."

"So do I."

All right, this woman just kept tossing out the curveballs. He'd been expecting a giggling airhead and he'd gotten a French-speaking pre-law student who liked kids.

Never judge a book by its cover, man.

Her dancing had slowed into an awkward kind of grinding, a hint that he wasn't the only one distracted by the conversation. "I went to New Orleans once when I was a kid," she said, absently dragging her palms up and down his arms. "We stayed in the French Quarter. It was lovely." She tilted her head. "Are you in Manhattan on vacation?"

"No, I just moved here actually," he lied.

"How do you like it?"

"It's a beautiful city." His gaze strayed to the perfect pair of breasts he was at eye level with. "The people are really . . . nice."

Her lips twitched. So did his cock.

"Yeah, some of them," she said vaguely.

He decided it was time to do some of that delicate digging. "How do you like working here?"

Her expression went shuttered. "Good people, great pay" was all she said.

Luke furrowed his brows. It had been almost imperceptible, but he could've sworn he'd glimpsed a spark of fear in her eyes before her guard shot up. But why? What could she possibly be afraid of? All he'd asked was whether she liked her job.

Before he could dig any deeper, the music faded and a male voice crackled out of an intercom over their heads. "Time's up. Take a bow, Livy."

Luke saw relief flicker on her face as she climbed off him.

"Can I see you again?" he burst out before she could leave.

"Said the lap to the dancer."

He shot her a quizzical look. "What?"

"Nothing." She sighed. "It's this thing I like to say when I— Forget it." She stepped toward the door.

"I mean it. I want to see you again," he told her retreating back. "Maybe take you out to dinner?"

She slowly swiveled around. And stared at him.

Oh, for fuck's sake, of course she doesn't want to see you again. He realized she probably got asked that every other second, from every other pervert who came to ogle her tits.

"Dumb question," he said again.

"Yes, it was," she said quietly.

And then she was gone.

Taking a breath, Luke staggered to his feet. Damn. What had he been thinking? He'd been ordered to keep an eye on her, not ask her out to dinner.

But it wasn't his dim-witted request that troubled him. Or her rejection. It was the fact that when the words had slipped out of his mouth, he'd completely forgotten about the mission. He hadn't asked her out to gather information. He'd done it because—God help him—he'd actually wanted to see her again.

On the roof of the low-rise across the street from the Diamond Mine, Trevor lowered his binoculars and reached for the water bottle at his side. He took a quick sip, then ran a hand over his close-cropped hair and sighed. Although he wasn't about to admit it to the others—the team leader had to lead by example, after all—this gig really was too tedious for his liking. Surveillance was boring as hell, especially after the last couple of missions the team had taken on. Rescuing the relief workers in Ethiopia, the kidnapped executive in Johannesburg. The thirteen little girls in Luis Blanco's Colombian prison . . .

As usual, the memory of *that* particular assignment caused his thoughts to drift to Isabel, the undercover operative he'd teamed up with during the Colombia job. He'd been thinking about her a lot these past six months. Too much, probably. But hell, it was hard not to. He'd been a total shit for leaving things the way he had. The woman had saved his life, and instead of thanking her, he'd lashed out, blamed her for making him face his issues.

Funny, but the anger he'd been consumed with all those months ago had completely evaporated. Now when he thought of Isabel Roma, he was overcome with gratitude. He'd walked away from that mission with an important piece of knowledge—he *didn't* want to die. Once, maybe, but not anymore. Isabel had helped him see that.

And he'd yelled at her like a toddler throwing a tantrum and left her in a hospital room to recover from a bullet wound she'd suffered while saving *his* life.

"You're a real asshole, Callaghan," he muttered to himself.

Yep, he sure was. He could still make amends, though. After this job was over, he was in line for the vacation time Morgan pushed on his men to prevent them from burning out, and Trevor was thinking of sticking around in New York. Isabel had mentioned she had an apartment here, so maybe he could finally work up the courage to contact her. Unless she was out in the field, carrying out whatever task Noelle, the queen of assassins, had charged her with. In that case, Noelle would probably know how to reach her . . .

He contemplated picking up the phone and calling Isabel's boss, then shuddered. Maybe he'd ask Morgan to make the call. The boss didn't seem to be frightened by Noelle.

He was jolted out of his thoughts when Sullivan's voice crackled in his ear. "The kangaroo's leaving the Outback. I repeat, kangaroo's leaving the Outback."

Trevor grinned. He'd rather shave his legs than say it

aloud, but he really had missed that crazy Australian. Missions were always more fun when Sullivan was around.

Reaching for his field glasses, he focused on the strip club. Sullivan had positioned himself in the outdoor patio of the pub next door, directly in the line of sight of the club's entrance. Sure enough, Luke had just exited through the double doors. Trevor zoomed in closer, noticing that the dark-haired man looked a bit dazed.

He frowned. The plan had been for Luke to remain in the club until closing time, but a glance at his watch showed that only a few hours had passed since Luke had gone in. Since they'd determined this was a low-risk job, the eyes on the outside had no radio contact with Luke, so they had no way of knowing the reason for his early departure until he told them.

On the street below, Luke stepped to the curb, zipping up his Windbreaker against the early October chill. He paused at the crosswalk, then bounded across the street, disappearing into the alley separating Trevor's building from the adjacent one. He was coming up here, then. Something must have happened in the club.

The only telltale sign of Luke's arrival was the faint creak of the fire escape. Then utter silence. Again, not something Trevor would say out loud, but those SEALs had definitely perfected the art of *stealth*. Luke didn't make a single sound as he made his way up to the roof, and when he appeared out of nowhere like a damn ghost, Trevor almost jumped.

"What happened?" he demanded.

Luke shook his head, frazzled. "I got a lap dance."

"Oh." He arched a brow. "Okay."

Without elaborating, Luke bent down and unzipped the backpack next to Trevor's gear, rummaging in it until he found what he was looking for. Popping the earpiece in, he clicked it on and said, "Holden, you read me?"

Since they were all wired in, Trevor heard Holden McCall's response. "Yeah. What's up?"

"Call D to take your place. I want you to head back to

the apartment and use your computer magic. Find out everything you can about one of the dancers. Livy Lovelace."

"Is that the order, Trev?" Holden said briskly.

Trevor appreciated the other man's deference to his authority on this job. "Yeah. Do it."

There was a crackling sound, then radio silence. "What's going on?" Trevor asked, shooting Luke a puzzled look.

"I don't think Dane's in that club, man. If he is, then he's hiding away upstairs or somewhere in the employee area."

Luke reached into his jacket pocket for his Marlboros. He lit one up, the orange tip glowing as he sucked hard, then exhaled a cloud of smoke into the night air.

Huh. The guy was definitely on edge.

"I can go back in," he added. "Try to get past those mammoth bouncers and snoop around, but I'm thinking we go about this another way."

"The dancer."

"Yeah." A crease dug into Luke's forehead. He took another drag. "Something about her triggered an alarm. I asked her how she liked her job, and she just shut down. I swear, she even looked scared."

"That's rather flimsy."

"Look, I can't explain it, but my gut is telling me Morgan's informant was right. This dancer knows something."

"About the missing agent?"

Luke made a frustrated noise. "I don't know. Maybe. But she warrants a closer look."

Trevor snorted. "Another lap dance perhaps?"

"No. Fuck, not that kind of look. But I think we need to find out more about her."

Trevor wasn't entirely convinced, but he'd learned to trust the instincts of the other men on the team. A soldier's gut feeling was often the most valuable weapon in your arsenal. "Fine. We'll find out more." He cocked his head. "You'll go back in tomorrow night, then?"

Luke sighed. "That might be a problem."

*   *   *

Olivia had just buttoned up her jeans and was reaching for her red wool peacoat when Tony, one of Vince's personal guards, appeared in the doorway. "Boss wants to see you upstairs," he informed her.

With a submissive nod, she followed the tall man out of the dressing room. Truth be told, Vince's bodyguards terrified her. Tony, Mikey, and Sal. All three were Italian, tight-lipped and scowl-faced. And they were always armed, no matter what. Before the attack, she hadn't understood why the owner of a strip club needed his own protection squad, but Vince had insisted it was simply a precaution. He was a wealthy man and wealthy men needed to watch their backs, he'd told her.

She knew better now. Vince Angelo was much more than the owner of a strip joint. In the last six months, she'd seen several men being carried out of the upstairs offices, bruised, beaten, usually bleeding. And the men who came by to meet with Vince a few times a week, with their olive coloring and slick business suits . . . they weren't door-to-door salesmen, that was for sure.

Mafia.

She quickly forced the thought away. The less she knew about what Vince was really up to, the safer she'd be. She'd realized months ago that she couldn't count on anyone else to get her out of this mess. The cops couldn't be trusted—they were frequent visitors to the VIP lounge, not to mention Vince's office, which led her to deduce that he had more than one officer in his pocket. She had no friends she could turn to. Her mother—well, Olivia refused to involve her in any of this.

So really, she didn't need—or want—to know the details of Vince's business activities. She simply had to bide her time. Make him believe he had her undying gratitude for taking care of that dead body, make him believe she desired him the way he did her. In a few more months, she'd have her degree and enough money to leave town with her mom, and then she could put all this bullshit behind her.

She followed Tony up the spiral staircase, exhaling a

breath of relief when the bodyguard took up his post at the top of the stairs, leaving her to walk the rest of the way alone.

The management quarters occupied half of the second floor, but she'd only been inside Vince's office and the one belonging to Melinda, the club manager. At the end of the corridor was a sinister metal door that led to the rear offices, but she had no clue what really lay beyond it. Supposedly storage and administrative space, though she didn't quite buy that.

Vince's office was a massive room with glass windows that overlooked the club below. When she walked in, he was sitting in the plush leather chair behind his huge mahogany monstrosity of a desk.

"I heard you caught the eye of a VIP tonight," he said without preamble. His brown eyes narrowed with displeasure.

"Yes, a man requested a private dance," she replied carefully.

Vince crooked a finger at her. "I want you to see something."

Swallowing, Olivia rounded the desk and tried not to cringe when Vince pulled her into his lap. He angled the computer monitor so she could see it, then typed a command on the keyboard. To her dismay, the security footage from the VIP room she'd danced in earlier popped up on the screen. He fast-forwarded her entrance and the beginning of her dance, then pressed PAUSE.

Olivia stared at the monitor. Her own face stared back. The amusement in her eyes, the curve of her mouth, was unmistakable.

"You're laughing." Accusation rang in his voice.

She had been, hadn't she? That was when the customer had asked her if she'd always wanted to be a stripper.

"You're *laughing*," Vince said again.

Olivia opened her mouth, but he grabbed her chin, keeping her jaw locked. "Were you turned on?" he demanded. "Did you get wet when you were humping his thigh?"

She gave a wild shake of her head.

Vince's grip tightened. He forced her to look at the screen again. "Then why do you look like you're having such a delightful time, Olivia?"

Her heart thudded, a spurt of fear erupting inside her. When Vince released her jaw, she took a breath and said, "I was pretending. That's what I'm paid to do."

He relaxed. Slightly. "Pretending."

"Y-yes. You trained me, remember? You taught me what to do, showed me how to adapt to each customer's needs." Her words popped out rapidly, one after the other. "He was a talker. So I talked to him. I only did what you taught me to do."

His expression softened, but she still glimpsed the traces of fire in his eyes. She had to calm him down. Placate him. The last time she'd "upset" him, he'd reciprocated with a black eye that no amount of makeup could cover up. She refused to let that happen again.

Olivia let her shoulders sag, deciding to play the one card that always seemed to work in her favor. Innocence.

"I can't believe you think I was enjoying myself," she whispered, making her bottom lip quiver. Summoning the tears was easier—she constantly felt like crying in this man's presence. "I was just doing what you told me."

It worked. Almost instantly the anger vanished, and Vince reached out and wrapped his arms around her trembling shoulders. "Aw, fuck, babe, don't cry. I'm sorry. I didn't mean to upset you." He stroked her back in circular motions. "You know I'm a proud man. I don't like the idea of anyone other than me bringing a smile to those beautiful lips."

Olivia buried her head against his neck and tried not to breathe in the scent of his overpowering cologne. *Soon, Liv. Soon you'll be free of him.*

At the sound of a knock, Vince released her, and she almost keeled over in relief. He patted her knee as a signal for her to rise, then turned to the door as another one of his bodyguards entered the office.

"Cora's waiting to see you, boss."

"Good, send her in. And walk my girl out to the car, Mikey."

"Yes, boss."

As her heartbeat reverted to a normal tempo, Olivia followed Mikey downstairs, waving good-bye to a few members of the waitstaff. Mikey stuck close as he escorted her to the parking lot, and despite the uneasiness that Vince's guard evoked in her, she appreciated his presence. Each time she walked across this parking lot, the memories hit her hard and fast.

The pain shooting through her scalp as the customer dragged her by the hair. The odor of garbage and urine in that dark alley. The cold steel pressed against her flesh.

Scream and I'll slash your throat.

Gulping, she banished the grisly images and followed Mikey to her car. Gone was her rusty old Impala—after the attack, Vince had given her a brand-new BMW with heavily tinted windows. Every time she drove the car, she felt like vomiting.

"Have a good night, Liv," Mikey said curtly.

"You too," she murmured.

He waited until she was safely in the driver's seat before stalking back to the club. Olivia's hands shook as she stuck the key in the ignition. God, that had been close. Handling Vince Angelo was like walking a tightrope; one misstep and she risked taking a tumble—and there was no net to catch her. Fortunately, tomorrow was her day off, and she couldn't wait for the reprieve. Vince never bothered her on her nights off—it was almost as if he forgot she existed once she left the vicinity of the club. Out of sight, out of mind—and thank God for that. It only added fuel to her hope that he'd forget about her once she left New York. He *had* to.

Yet as she drove away from the club, she had to wonder, what if he didn't? What if she ran, and he came after her?

What if she could never be rid of him?

Vince Angelo prided himself on being a patient man, but it was getting harder and harder not to claim the woman he'd loved for nearly a year now. A tender expression graced his face as he watched Olivia leave with Mikey. Olivia. Even her name was elegant, as elegant as the beauty it belonged to. She'd stolen his heart the day she'd interviewed for the dancing position. Even back then he'd known she was different. Special. *Worthy*.

And that worth was the only reason he'd held back for so long. Women like Olivia Taylor deserved to be respected, worshipped. A more brutish man would have just taken her, but Vince was no brute. He was a perfect gentleman, just as Olivia was a perfect lady.

Rage bubbled in his gut as he remembered what the punk in the alley had done to her. Some women deserved to be raped, some even asked for it, but the mere notion of anyone taking his Olivia by force made him want to shoot something. Yet something beautiful had stemmed from that ugly night. Olivia had finally opened her heart to him. Sure, she'd put up some resistance at first, reluctant to let him in. She hadn't wanted preferential treatment, or to trigger the other girls' jealousy by dating the boss, but he'd worked his magic and eventually she'd come around. Realized just how much she needed him.

"You wanted to see me?"

Cora's hesitant voice drew him out of his reverie. He beckoned for the redhead to sit on the chair in front of his desk. After she was settled, he leaned forward and clasped his hands together. "I'm sending you to dance at a private party tonight."

As he'd expected, Cora's fair face turned an annoying shade of gray. "But . . . you said I wouldn't have to do that again. You know what happened last time, Vince."

He waved a careless hand. "That was unfortunate, yes, but this is different. The customer who requested you is an important client and a distinguished businessman."

She chewed on her lower lip. "I . . . don't know. I don't know if I can find a babysitter for Katie on such short notice."

"Doesn't your mother watch the kid for you?"

"Yeah, but Mom has to work the graveyard shift to-night." She nibbled on her lip some more.

"Tell her to call in sick. You can give her twice what she'll make tonight out of your earnings. Two G's, babe. Two fuck-ing grand for an hour of dancing." Vince grinned. "Olivia only got a grand when she danced for him last month."

Cora lifted her head, her pale blue eyes flickering with indecision. "You sent Olivia to him?"

"I told you, he's a good guy."

The girl went silent again, raising Vince's hackles. You'd think she'd be a bit more grateful, the little bitch. He'd hired her when no other club would—B-cups weren't that popular with the customers, after all—and he'd kept her on even af-ter she'd completely fucked up several performances. Well, if he was being honest, he'd kept her on only because Cora had been the one to refer Olivia to him. But still. He could have fired the stupid twit a hundred times over.

"Okay," she agreed, pushing strands of hair out of her eyes. "I'll do it."

"Great. Go find Tony—he'll drive you to the client's hotel."

After Cora left the office, Vince reached for the phone on his desk and punched in a number. "Tony," he barked when his bodyguard answered. "Cora's on her way down. I want you to give her something to relax her. Can't have her sobbing like a fucking newborn again. De Luca's guests were very insulted the last time." His tone hardened. "Make sure it doesn't happen again."

Chapter 3

"So, her name's Olivia Taylor. Twenty-five years old, born in Arlington, Virginia." Holden McCall closed his laptop and set it on the coffee table, resuming his recitation from memory. "Her father, Eddie, was a marine. He died in a car accident when Olivia was ten—going way over the speed limit, lost control of the car, and slammed into a telephone pole. The mother, Kathleen, was a teacher, moved them to Brooklyn when Taylor was twelve."

Luke waved his hand. "Can you skip to the relevant shit?"

Holden shot him a menacing scowl. For a moment there the man resembled Morgan, their prickly, unsmiling boss, mercenary extraordinaire. Not surprising. Holden was as serious as the boss, a black-haired man with intense charcoal gray eyes that rivaled Morgan's intense blue ones. He was older than most of the guys too, late thirties or so, and the only one who wore a wedding ring. Luke had yet to meet Holden's wife, Beth, but it was clear her husband worshipped the ground she walked on.

It was also clear that Holden didn't appreciate being interrupted, so Luke decided to back off. "Sorry. Continue," he mumbled.

Along with possessing the most impressive set of hacking skills on the planet, Holden also had a photographic memory, and he was apparently determined to give them a play-by-play account of Olivia Taylor's life.

The name lingered in Luke's mind like a woman's perfume. Olivia Taylor. He had to admit, he liked it a lot better than Livy Lovelace. And he found himself liking her even more as Holden continued spitting out details.

"Mom taught junior high at a private school in New York. Held the job for four years, until she was diagnosed with breast cancer." Holden's voice grew serious. "She had a mastectomy—Taylor was sixteen at the time. She dropped out of high school during her junior year and got a job at a fast-food joint to help out her mother."

"The mom didn't get any assistance from the marine corps?" Trevor piped up from his perch on the other couch.

"I'm still looking into that. All I know is that the mom used the life insurance to pay her medical bills. I haven't finished following the financial trail yet, but it looks like the Taylors hit some tough times. Eddie Taylor made several bad investments, then the house in Virginia burned down—"

"Arson?" Luke asked, furrowing his brow.

"Electrical issue. Apparently an electrician told Eddie Taylor in no uncertain terms that the place needed to be rewired, but he ignored the advice. Insurance wouldn't pay up since the homeowner had neglected to fix the problem. Anyway, that's irrelevant. So the family was broke, Kathleen had breast cancer . . ."

"And Olivia dropped out of school to help her mom," Luke said, hoping the others couldn't hear the crack in his voice. What was it about that woman that got him feeling all gooey inside? She was a stripper, for fuck's sake.

And a pre-law student.

Fluent in French.

Drop-dead gorgeous . . .

"Kathleen went into remission after the surgery, and Olivia went back to school," Holden continued. "She was a semester from graduating when the cancer returned."

Luke ignored the ache in his heart.

"Kathleen's remaining breast was removed. Olivia held

three jobs to pay a second round of hospital bills. She got her G.E.D., applied to NYU." Holden sighed. "Thirteen months ago, Kathleen's cancer made an appearance for a third time."

Trevor let out a soft whistle. "Shit, the mom is one tough broad. Double mastectomy, twice out of remission, and still hanging on."

"And in remission for a third time now," Holden said, "according to the hospital records I hacked into. They got the good news a few days ago."

Smothering an impatient groan, Luke reached for the Starbucks cup on the table and took a long swig of coffee. "When did she start stripping?"

"A year ago." Holden shrugged. "She was waitressing at the time, but I'm guessing on her wages she couldn't afford tuition *and* a new round of medical bills."

"What's her connection to Angelo?" Trevor asked.

"I'll let Morgan tell you that part." Holden was already punching a number into his cell phone. He placed the phone in the center of the table, and a moment later, Morgan's commanding voice boomed out of the speaker.

As usual, Morgan got right to business. "So my informant just phoned in—"

"How's my dog?" Luke interrupted, earning himself an annoyed frown from Trevor.

But the boss just chuckled. "Busy. Abby's teaching him some new tricks."

"*What?* No. Get Bear away from her. My dog is not an assassin."

Morgan's tone turned sarcastic. "She's making more progress with that mutt than you hacks are with this gig." There was a soft expletive. "Anyway, you were right to suspect the dancer. Our source tells me that Olivia Taylor is Vince Angelo's girl."

The blast of jealousy that hit Luke in the chest was most certainly unwelcome. He couldn't help it, though. The thought of that gel-haired slimeball putting his hands all over Olivia's delectable curves made him want to hit something.

"They don't see much of each other out of the club," Morgan added, sounding perplexed. "Can't figure that one out. But apparently she spends a lot of time in his office, and my source says she glimpsed them kissing once. He also bought her a car, a shiny new Beemer."

"So if we want to get to Angelo, it might be worthwhile to do it through Olivia Taylor," Trevor mused.

"Look, it's been six days and we've got no leads on Dane's whereabouts," Morgan said, his voice hard. "At this point, I don't care what it takes to get the fucking job done. So it's your show, Luke. Go back in and pump Taylor for information, see if she knows anything about Dane, if she saw him at the club, heard his name mentioned."

"That won't happen," Luke answered. "She won't talk to me, not at the club, anyway. To her, I'm just another horny loser who wants to see her tits. Only way she'll trust me is if she sees me as a normal guy. A guy she could go on a date with."

Morgan's sigh slid out of the speakers. "If that's the case, I should have sent Ethan."

The boss had a point—Ethan Hayes was the boy next door; he practically oozed "normal guy." But the idea of Ethan spending time with his goddess made Luke grind his teeth.

"I can get close to her," he said in a steely voice. "But I'll need to make contact outside the club."

"Fine. Do it." Morgan's curse reverberated through the room. "Just find the missing agent so we can wash our hands of this bullshit. Government agencies are a total bitch to deal with."

"Any progress on the mole angle?" Trevor spoke up.

"The DEA can find their own moles" was Morgan's harsh response. "We were contracted to find out what happened to Dane. That's our focus."

"And the girl on the inside—she came up with nothing in regards to Dane?" Trevor asked with a frown.

"She says there's no trace of him, but there are areas in the club that are restricted to her."

"How did you get someone in place so fast, anyway?"

"I have my ways." A typically vague answer from the boss. "Anyway, she hasn't seen Dane. He might be there." Morgan paused. "Or he might not."

Gee, how fucking encouraging. Luke stifled another groan, once again wishing they'd never taken this job. As far as he was concerned, this was the DEA's mess to clean up. They were the ones who'd sent in an undercover agent to gather intel on Ric De Luca's drug-smuggling rackets. Luke was no Mafia expert, but he was pretty sure the Mob didn't take kindly to strangers sticking their noses into its business. Apparently this had been a deep-cover job; Carter Dane had been cozying up to Vince Angelo for more than a year. But Angelo worked for De Luca, and according to the dossier they'd compiled, Ric De Luca possessed razor-sharp intelligence. He'd sniff out a rat in a heartbeat, no doubt about that.

Which meant that Carter Dane was probably dead. Or who knew, maybe his cover had been so good and he was now so deep in De Luca's organization that he couldn't get out. The agent had broken off contact two months ago. The DEA had tried handling the matter on their own before finally admitting defeat and hiring Morgan's team last week, but Luke and the guys weren't making any damn headway either.

"If Olivia Taylor knows something about Dane, I'll get it out of her," he announced.

"Good." Morgan hung up without another word. Words like *hello* and *good-bye* weren't part of his vocabulary.

Reaching for his coffee, Luke drained the cup and glanced at Trevor. "Tomorrow I start tailing her."

The other man nodded. "The rest of us will keep watching the club." He gave a wry smile. "And trying not to rip out our hair from boredom."

"Weren't you the one who gave me a whole lecture about how not every mission was gonna be exciting? Hypocrite."

Trevor sighed. "That I am. You were right. This sucks."

Not anymore, Luke almost said. But he bit his tongue. It was probably best if he didn't let the others know just how interesting this job had become.

"Liv?"

Olivia quit tiptoeing through the bedroom when she heard her mother's voice. She'd been trying not to wake her mom as she'd gathered the clothing strewn on the weathered hardwood floor, but now she approached the bed, putting down the laundry bag and sitting on the edge of the mattress. She took her mother's hand and squeezed it. Tried not to cringe when she noticed the skinny arms poking out of Kathleen's sleeveless white nightgown.

"I was just getting the laundry," Olivia said. "You should go back to sleep. You look exhausted."

The chemo had really taken its toll on Kathleen Taylor this time. Her bald head looked painfully grotesque, especially now that it was covered with brown stubble as her hair began to grow back. Her cheeks were hollow, green eyes sunken in her skull. And so thin. So frail. It was hard to believe that the woman lying in this bed was only forty-six years old. She looked two decades older, a remnant of the vibrant, strong woman Olivia remembered from her childhood.

But she was alive. That was all that mattered. Her mom was the only family she had, the only person she could depend on, and seeing her like this made Olivia want to cry.

She's in remission, came a gentle reminder.

Yeah. And maybe for once—God, just once—she'd stay that way.

"I'm tired of being cooped up inside," Kathleen said in a weary voice. "I was thinking of taking a walk today."

Olivia tightened her grip on her mom's hand. "Maybe tomorrow," she said firmly. "Right now, you need to recover your strength. These last treatments were stronger than the others, all that poison being pumped into your body. Dr. Hopkins said you can't overdo it."

"She also said I wouldn't live to see my fortieth birthday."

"She was wrong about that," Olivia conceded. "But not about this. I mean it, Mom. You've got to take it easy for at least a few more weeks."

Kathleen's eyes turned sad. "Don't talk to me about overdoing it. You've been working double and triple shifts at the restaurant. *You're* the one who needs to rest, honey."

"I'll rest when you're back on your feet." Squaring her shoulders, Olivia let go of her mother's hand and stood up. "Now, I'm going to the Laundromat to do two weeks' worth of laundry. And you'd better be in this bed when I get back."

Without waiting for the argument she knew would come, Olivia waved a breezy good-bye and hurried out of the bedroom with the laundry sack slung over her shoulder. In the hall she stopped and took a deep breath. God, how much longer could she keep lying? When her mom was in the hospital, it had been easier to hide the truth from her—that Olivia had quit the restaurant twelve months ago and now took off her clothes for money. But with Kathleen in recovery ...

You're almost out of there. Three more months and you'll have your degree.

With a shaky exhale, she headed for the minuscule living room of their tiny two-bedroom apartment and plucked her purse off the couch. In the closet-size front hall, she shoved her feet into a pair of Uggs, picked up the two heavy laundry bags, and left the building.

It was chilly out and she hadn't bothered with a coat, but the Laundromat was only a block away. She had no desire to drive the BMW Vince had given her. She only took it to and from work, just so he could see how much she valued his generosity. That she got nauseous each time she slid into its leather interior was something she'd keep to herself.

She took off at a brisk walk, lugging her bags and thinking what a pitiful sight she probably made. Her jeans were frayed and riddled with holes, her brown boots clashed with her purple off-the-shoulder sweatshirt, and her hair was a tangled mess, twisted into a bun atop her head. She felt like a total slob, but the hobo getup sure as hell beat the shiny, see-through crap she wore every night.

Whether she liked it or not, her looks brought her a ton of perks—tables at packed restaurants, a job application being moved to the top of the pile—but she'd never wanted to use them to get ahead. She wanted to earn her way with her intelligence, her skills, and it shamed her that, as of late, she'd had to rely on her appearance to make things happen. Sure, she could pretend it was her dancing that won over the customers, but she knew it was her face and her body that convinced those men to open their wallets.

When she walked into the Laundromat five minutes later, the place was empty save for a harried-looking mother with two young girls clinging to her legs. The woman shot Olivia a frazzled smile, then resumed the task of sorting a pile of laundry. Olivia did the same, then shoved a bunch of quarters into two machines and flopped down on a plastic chair to wait. She'd planned on studying for her upcoming midterms, but when she reached into her oversized purse in search of her economics textbook, she realized she'd left the book at home.

"Wanna see my doll?"

She lifted her head and saw the two blond girls skid to a stop in front of her. The question had come from the younger one, who couldn't have been older than four.

"Fiona, get back here!" the girl's mother ordered. "Don't bother that poor woman."

"It's okay," Olivia called. She looked at the little girl, whose hair was arranged in two adorable braids. "I'd love to see your doll."

The older girl, ten or so, rolled her eyes. "Don't touch it. It's covered with jam."

Yep, it sure was. Olivia smothered a grin as the toddler held up a ratty doll with floppy arms, a knot of red hair, and a jelly-smeared white face. "She's beautiful. What's her name?"

"Steve," the little girl said proudly.

She choked back a laugh. "Steve. That's an interesting name."

"It's a boy's name," the older girl grumbled. "I think it's dumb."

The remark led to a discussion about gender-appropriate monikers, followed by the toddler's insistence that Olivia *must* be told the name of every doll, stuffed animal, and toy the kid had ever owned in her short life. The children's mother kept shooting Olivia looks loaded with gratitude, but she truly didn't mind entertaining the kids.

If anything, being around the girls brought a pang of longing to her heart. She'd always dreamed of following in her mom's footsteps and becoming a teacher. She would've loved to teach at the elementary-school level—interacting with younger kids came so naturally to her, and she knew without a doubt that teaching would bring her great fulfillment. Unfortunately, it wouldn't pay well, not unless she lucked out and managed to land a position at an elite prep school where her salary would come out of the pockets of the wealthy parents and donors.

Teaching might be her passion, but law was a far more practical career choice. It might take longer and more work to get there, but the payout was bigger in the end.

Trying not to second-guess the choices she'd made, Olivia focused on the two girls in front of her. She was laughing about something the older girl said when the door swung open and heavy footsteps sounded behind her. Reflexively, she turned to scope out the new arrival.

And felt all the blood drain from her face.

The customer from last night had just walked in.

She immediately swiveled her head back to the girls, hoping he hadn't spotted her. But oh God, what if he recognized her? It was bad enough that she'd been grinding half-naked on top of the guy last night. Having him glimpse her outside of the club was too embarrassing to contemplate. What if he mentioned the lap dance? In front of the *children.*

She snuck another peek at him, and her heart skipped a beat. Holy hell—why hadn't she noticed yesterday how attractive this man was? Actually, with his chocolate brown eyes, messy dark hair, and ruggedly handsome face, *drop-dead gorgeous* was a more apt description. And his broad chest and bulky shoulders radiated strength and masculinity, something she'd completely overlooked when she'd been grinding away on his lap.

She did, however, remember the endearing awkwardness that he'd exuded and the trace of a Southern accent in his husky voice, which was unusual in and of itself—normally the men she danced for morphed into one faceless blur.

Swallowing, she tried to pay attention to the two girls chattering away in front of her, but it was difficult. From the corner of her eye, she saw the hottie from New Orleans heading toward an empty washing machine. Which happened to be right next to hers. Oh, and look at that, her loads were done, both machines coming to a halt as the cycle ended. She decided to stay seated and pretend not to notice.

Little Fiona squashed that game plan. "Your stuff is done!" the girl announced.

The children promptly darted back to their mother, who was stacking a pile of neatly folded clothes in a big wicker basket. A minute later, the trio made for the door, waving to Olivia as they exited the Laundromat.

Oh great. Now she and the hottie were all alone.

Gritting her teeth, Olivia stood up. She ignored the guy, who was shoving a stack of T-shirts into her machine's neighbor. Only T-shirts. Like fifty of them. And they were all white as snow and looked pretty damn clean. Okay then.

Keeping her back to him, she removed her wet clothing and shoved it into the dryer. Once that was whirring away, she carried the second wet load to the counter and began putting aside the items that couldn't go in the dryer.

"Do I know you from somewhere?"

The deep voice made her jump. Gulping, she slowly met his eyes and feigned ignorance.

"No, I don't think so." She ducked down. Treated the laundry in front of her as if it was the most fascinating thing she'd ever seen.

"You sure?" Her peripheral vision caught him tilting his

head, pensive. "Wait. You work at the Diamond Mine. We met last night."

She glanced over again. Acted as if recognition had dawned on her. "You," she said with mock surprise. "What are you doing here?"

He arched a brow. "Laundry, same as you." After a moment, he extended his hand. "I'm Luke Dubois, by the way."

She reluctantly leaned in for a handshake. The second their palms made contact, a shiver shimmied up her spine. He had big hands. A man's hands, rough and calloused and warm to the touch.

"Olivia Taylor," she replied, her voice doing an annoying little wobble.

"Olivia. I like that better than Livy Lovelace."

"I'm pretty sure any name is better than Livy Lovelace," she said dryly.

"You're probably right." The corners of his dark brown eyes crinkled in amusement, and then he flashed her a cocky grin. "So, Olivia. How 'bout another lap dance?"

Trevor woke up with a start when his ass started vibrating. Groaning, he fished his cell phone out of his pocket and sat up. Morgan's number flashed across the screen.

"Did I catch you at a bad time?" the boss asked after Trevor grunted out a hello.

"I was sleeping."

"Where are the others?"

Trevor rubbed his eyes. "D's crashing on the living room couch. Luke's tailing the dancer, and Holden and Sully are watching the club."

"So you're alone."

Wariness circled his gut. "I am. What's going on?"

"You're rendezvousing with our informant in an hour."

"The girl on the inside?"

"Yep. She's got some new information, potentially about Dane."

Trevor frowned. "And she couldn't just tell you when you spoke?"

"The call got disconnected." He could practically hear Morgan's scowl of displeasure. "She sent a text, though. With an address, a time, and a quick note about sending someone to meet with her."

"This sounds like a trap," Trevor said flatly.

"If it were, I wouldn't be asking you to handle it." Morgan's next words rang with confidence. "She's legit. Trust me. I'm texting you the address now."

As Morgan hung up, Trevor shook his head in bewilderment. Would it kill the boss to offer a few more details? Like the informant's name, for Christ's sake?

Hell, of course it would. Jim Morgan played his cards close to the vest. Always had and probably always would.

Trevor rose from the king-size bed and went into the private bathroom. As team leader, he'd commandeered the master bedroom, despite the grumblings of the other men. The memory made him grin. It felt good to be back in the game, exchanging insults with the boys and kicking some ass again.

This time last year, he'd been nursing a vodka bottle in his condo, staring at a framed photograph of him and Gina, taken in Hawaii. Where he'd proposed to her.

That memory brought an ache to his heart, but not the bone-deep agony that used to slice into him whenever he thought of his fiancée. It had taken a long time, but he could finally think about the woman he'd lost without wanting to put a bullet into his head. Definitely progress.

After he took a leak and splashed some water on his face, he strode out to the living room. D was sprawled on the sofa, but sat up the second Trevor entered the room, alert as a hawk.

Of all the men on Morgan's payroll, D was the only one Trevor didn't know very well. What he did know was kind of terrifying. Derek Pratt had been Delta at one point, then moved on to some covert agency that didn't seem to have a name and of which D never spoke. His training was top-notch, his instincts spot-on, and he could kill a man in the blink of an eye. Everything about the guy screamed *lethal*.

The shaved head, coal black eyes, huge shoulders, and abundance of tattoos. Trevor had never seen the man smile, but Kane and Luke both swore that he was capable of it. He thought they were full of shit.

"What's up?" D asked in that gravelly voice of his.

"Go back to sleep," Trevor told the other man. "Morgan's got me running an errand."

"Need backup?"

"Nah. I'll be fine."

D lay back down and closed his eyes. Just like that, end of conversation.

With a wry grin, Trevor swiped his nine-millimeter Sig off the granite counter in the kitchen and slid it into his shoulder holster. He shrugged into a black wool coat and pulled the collar up, then left the apartment.

Outside the building, he breathed in the crisp afternoon air, only to inhale the exhaust of a passing taxi. He grimaced, the bustle of the sidewalks and blaring car horns confirming what he'd already known. He was *not* a city person. His condo in Aspen was tucked away in the mountains, far from the noise and people and bullshit. Though really, he probably ought to sell the place. It had been Gina's home too, and now that he was making a conscious effort to work through the loss, it might be good to start fresh.

But not here. He didn't find the Big Apple the least bit appetizing. Too big and far too loud.

He pulled out his cell phone and entered the address Morgan gave him into the GPS app. Sweet. Only a fifteen-minute walk. He'd way rather trek it to SoHo than sit in some stuffy cab.

He headed west on Canal Street, still contemplating the notion of selling his place in Colorado. He could always move into Morgan's compound. God knows it had enough bedrooms, and it would be nice having the team around. That way, when his thoughts turned dark—which they still did every now and then—the company could distract him. He tucked the idea away as he turned on Sixth Avenue and headed north, pausing to check the GPS again.

The girl's apartment should be over on the next block. He passed a corner store with a display of Halloween costumes in the front window, then crossed the street and walked until a converted warehouse building with ivy-covered brick walls came into view.

He climbed the front stoop and scanned the intercom mounted on the wall, then keyed in the numbers 2-3-2.

A static-ridden female voice wafted out of the speaker. "Who is it?"

"Your three o'clock," he answered as per Morgan's instructions.

"Come on up."

The building didn't have an elevator, so he headed for the stairwell, which was surprisingly clean and smelled like pine. On the second floor, he emerged into a wide corridor with a gleaming hardwood floor. Huh. The place was a lot nicer than it looked from the outside. Apartment 232 was at the end of the hall, and he was about to knock when the door swung open and a pretty blonde with big blue eyes appeared in the doorway.

He didn't recognize her at first.

Not until she spoke, and that warm, melodic voice met his ears. "Hey, Trevor."

He swallowed. "Hello, Isabel."

Chapter 4

As Olivia gaped up at him, her expression a combination of shock and disgust, Luke held up his hands in surrender. "I was kidding about the lap dance," he assured her. "Just trying to ease the tension."

She wrinkled her forehead. "Tension?"

Sighing, he hopped up on the counter and rested his hands on his knees. "Last night you were dancing on top of me half-naked. Today we're doing laundry together. I don't know about you, but I find it pretty damn awkward."

After a moment she laughed. "Yeah, it's awkward all right."

She went back to separating her wet clothing into two piles. Luke gulped when he noticed her pick up a pair of lacy red panties. Fuck, did they have to be lace? He was a total sucker for lace.

He rapidly looked away, focusing on the woman instead of her underwear. Too bad she was as tantalizing as her panties. Some men preferred their women dolled up, high heels and skimpy dresses and all that shit, but he'd choose a pair of faded, ratty jeans over a short skirt any day. It was always sexier when a woman wore clothes that actually covered her up—it got you thinking about all the fascinating possibilities that lay underneath.

But he got the feeling that it was impossible for Olivia

Taylor *not* to look sexy. Even now, with her hair up in a haphazard twist and the purple sweater that kept sliding off one shoulder, she was dazzling. Yep. He was totally dazzled.

Stop thinking with your dick. Remember who she is.

His shoulders tensed. Right. This was Vince Angelo's girl. He needed to remember that.

Though for the life of him, he couldn't figure out how a woman like her had fallen for Angelo's smooth lines and dark, reptilian eyes. It had only taken Luke five minutes in her company to decide that she was much more than some stripper airhead. She was funny and serious and smart, and not the kind of girl he'd picture with a guy like Angelo.

Then again, five minutes of talking—during a lap dance—didn't mean shit. Maybe she had a thing for slick Italian mobsters.

Well, that's why he was here. That's why, when he'd seen her walking into the Laundromat, he'd ducked into a store and bought a fuckload of T-shirts just so he'd have a reason to be here. The reason was simple—find out what Olivia Taylor knew.

"No school today?" he asked, trying to sound casual.

She shook her head. "No classes this week. Midterms start next Wednesday."

"You've got a lot of studying to do, then."

"Yep." She continued to divert her gaze. "Do you live around here?"

"A few blocks away," he lied.

She nodded. "So. Are you following me?"

Yep.

And so was that thug with the shaved head and black trench coat, the one who belonged in a *Godfather* flick. Luke had spotted the goon five seconds after beginning his tail on the dancer, which made his own task more difficult, since he then had to evade both Olivia and her watch guard. Luckily, Angelo's man had proven to be totally incompetent, so focused on his target that Luke wasn't even on his radar.

Nevertheless, he made a conscious effort to angle his face

away from the front window. He didn't want the goon getting a good look at him or snapping a photo, though if that happened, no biggie. Sully could always take his place as the eyes inside the club. And the Australian wouldn't have a single complaint about it either.

Pretending to be perplexed, he said, "Of course not. Why would you think I'm following you?"

"It's just . . . I've danced for hundreds of men, and this is the first time I've ever run into one of them outside of the club." Suspicion laced her throaty voice, but she kept her head down, fiddling with her clothing.

"Maybe none of those other men do their own laundry."

A laugh burst out of her mouth. "Yeah. Maybe."

"Rest assured, I'm not some sick stalker."

"That's exactly what a sick stalker would say," she pointed out, but the doubt on her face had eased. She still didn't meet his eyes, though.

"You know, it's common courtesy to look someone in the eye when you're having a conversation with them," he said lightly.

She stiffened. Her sweater fell over her shoulder again, revealing a flash of golden skin. Then she looked up and sought out his gaze. "I'm sorry. I'm being rude, aren't I?"

"Perfectly understandable." He shrugged. "We've already established that last night's lap dance is the big uncomfortable elephant in the room."

"Do you do it often? Get lap dances, I mean."

"Honestly? No. Yesterday was my first."

She looked surprised. "What made you ask for one then?"

Luke knew he had to tread carefully. He had to be a normal guy. A man she could confide in. "I was curious."

She raised one delicate brow. "Curious."

"I'd never had one before, and I'm a firm believer in the try-anything-once philosophy."

She smiled, and something shifted in his chest.

Vince Angelo's girl, he swiftly reminded himself.

"A risk-taker," she said knowingly.

"You don't know the half of it." He flashed her a grin. "I can probably go on for days about all the dangerous things I've done."

Instead of the "Oooh, tell me more" he'd expected, Olivia remained silent and her expression lost its playful light. Even worse, he could've sworn he saw a flicker of annoyance in her eyes before she carried her things to the dryer.

"Not a fan of danger?" he asked.

She spared him a pithy glance over her shoulder. "Not really, no."

When she didn't elaborate, he could see all his hard-earned progress flying right out the window. Damn it. The daredevil stories usually worked like a charm. Chicks *loved* a man who flirted with danger.

But apparently not this one.

He mulled it over, then opted for a different approach. "So there's no room for risk in your life? You're forever playing it safe?"

She turned to face him with a coy smile. "No, I take risks. Last week I ordered a double cheeseburger at McDonald's instead of a regular old cheeseburger."

Luke laughed. "How'd that work out for you?"

"I had a stomachache all night." She shrugged. "See? Taking risks is overrated."

"Sometimes," he agreed. "But sometimes you've got no choice. Like, wouldn't you do something risky or dangerous if it meant helping someone you cared about?"

Olivia seemed to ponder that. "Yeah, I would."

"See?" he said, mimicking her. "Risk-taking can be necessary at times."

"I guess." She sauntered back to the counter. "So what's the riskiest thing you've ever done for the sake of helping someone else?"

"Faced down a pack of wild dogs with nothing but a stick," he revealed.

"Really?"

"Yep. That's how I rescued my mutt."

"I'm intrigued," she said, waiting expectantly.

"Well, there was this pack of dogs roaming the streets a few years back. It was New Orleans after Katrina, so a lot of strays were wandering around."

The word *Katrina* plugged up his throat like a wad of gum, but thankfully Olivia didn't seem to notice. Swallowing, he went on, trying to maintain a casual tone. "Anyway, I was leaving a bar one night when I heard a scuffle in the back alley. Got out there just in time to see the pack circling this poor mutt. He was another stray, from the looks of him—scrawny, rib cage jutting out, and his hind leg was broken. An easy meal for the pack. The poor thing looked so pitiful I couldn't *not* save him."

Olivia looked fascinated. "So you fought off the other dogs."

"Yep." He rolled up the right sleeve of his black button-down and held out his forearm to display the jagged white scar there. "That's how I got this. One of the dogs got hold of my arm, but then I got hold of that stick, and they scurried the fuck out of there."

"And the mutt?"

"Me and him both got rabies shots, the vet fixed him up, and we've been best friends ever since."

That got him another smile. His chest felt kind of hot.

"So were you involved in the relief efforts after the hurricane?" Olivia asked.

He knew it was an innocent question, but he couldn't control the way his shoulders stiffened, or the sudden tension in his jaw. Crap. Why had he brought up this damn subject to begin with? He'd wanted to get a conversation going, but now, as memories of Katrina blew through his head like the gusts that had blown his city apart, he regretted opening his big mouth.

"Yeah, I was involved," he answered noncommittally. "I'm big on helping people."

She slanted her head. "Okay, tell me another story then. Other than a stray from New Orleans, who else have you helped?"

Painting himself with a heroic brush wasn't exactly Luke's cup of tea—more like Sully's style—but since he was the one who'd opened the door to this discussion in the first place, he couldn't really complain.

Besides, with her green eyes shining and her exquisite face dancing with amusement, Olivia looked so fucking gorgeous that Luke would have given her any damn thing she wanted, including the clothes right off his back.

But he settled for a story instead.

Isabel hadn't anticipated the thrill that shot through her body when she laid eyes on Trevor. She'd been trying hard not to think about him these past six months—and failing miserably at it. Now here he was, standing in front of her, and she couldn't deny that his presence affected her.

"So you're Morgan's girl on the inside," Trevor said, his deep voice containing a wry note. "I don't know why I'm surprised. I should have known."

She gestured for him to enter the apartment. "He contacted me two months ago," she admitted. "Right after Carter Dane went AWOL."

"Two months ago?" He looked surprised. "The DEA didn't call us in until last week."

"Officially. But Morgan's friend at the agency asked him to unofficially look into Dane's disappearance right after it went down. Morgan asked me to gather some intel. He knew you guys would eventually be contracted so he figured he may as well have someone in place ahead of time."

"And didn't say a word about it to any of us. Again, not a surprise."

Trevor's tall, muscular frame dominated the narrow front hall of her apartment. He was bulkier now, had definitely been working out since he'd been dragged out of retirement for that Colombian job. He looked good. Really good. Dark hair in a short style, wool coat snug against his broad shoulders, black trousers emphasizing his long legs. But it was his whiskey brown eyes that snagged her attention. They were completely devoid of the overwhelming grief she'd glimpsed that day in the hospital, when he'd ripped into her for saving his life.

It was strange—they'd spent only a short amount of time together, yet after they'd gone their separate ways, his chiseled face had continued to flash through her mind, the memory of his baritone voice a constant nuisance. She'd found herself thinking about him so frequently that she'd started begging Noelle for assignments. She'd thrown herself into a stream of undercover gigs, using them as a distraction, but each time she returned to being Isabel Roma, the memory of Trevor Callaghan returned too.

She wondered what that meant.

At the same time, she wasn't sure she wanted to know.

"Do you want something to drink?" Isabel asked as she led him into the cozy sunken living room.

"No thanks." He glanced around. "So this is where you live."

"Told you it was small." She followed his gaze, seeing everything through his eyes. The only furnishings in the living room were a pair of tall bookcases, a plump yellow couch, and a square pine coffee table with a stack of take-out menus on it.

Trevor turned to face her. "I like it. It's you."

She drifted over to the couch and sat down. "How so?"

"Straightforward. Warm."

After a beat, he sat down next to her. Not that he had any other option. The sofa was the only place to sit in the room. She'd never cared much for material things, and her apartment showed it. Her bedroom boasted nothing but a bed and a big wicker chair that she tossed her clothes on. The kitchen had a table and one chair. The spare bedroom sat empty. The sparse surroundings didn't trouble her, though. She was hardly ever here anyway. In fact, she'd spent more time in this apartment these last two months than in the past five years combined.

"So," Trevor began awkwardly, "how've you been?"

"Busy. You?"

"Same."

"Morgan said you're back to work full-time."

"Yeah. Being in the middle of the action has helped a lot." His throat worked as he swallowed. "Isabel, about that last day in Bogotá, I—"

"In the past," she cut in. Before he could press the subject, she hurried on. "Let's just focus on this job, okay? I think Carter Dane is alive."

That got his attention. "What makes you say that?"

"I overheard Angelo talking on the phone last night. My presence is never required in his office, so I sweet-talked my way up there, told his bodyguard I desperately needed to talk to Vince about my performance. His door was ajar, and I caught the tail end of his conversation. I don't know who he was talking to, but it was about Dane."

"What did he say exactly?"

"That sooner or later they—I assume the DEA—will start looking for Dane, so it would be best to get rid of him before that happened."

Trevor's features hardened. "The agency was right, then. Dane's cover was blown."

"That's what it sounds like."

Suddenly those brown eyes were pinning her down with a sharp look. "Did Angelo see you at the door? Does he suspect you were eavesdropping?"

"I don't think so." She grinned. "Candy Cane isn't the sharpest tool in the shed. I play her off as dumb when I'm around Vince."

"Unfortunately, Angelo *is* sharp." Concern hung from his deep voice. "I'm going to recommend that Morgan pull you out of there."

Isabel's heart did a little flip. Last time they'd worked together, she'd been the one watching out for Trevor, doing her damnedest to make sure he didn't get himself killed. The role reversal was unexpected.

"I'll be fine," she assured him. "Angelo didn't suspect a thing. He just ushered me into his office and sat there rolling his eyes in boredom while I babbled on about this new routine I want to try out." She leaned back, toying with a strand of her hair. "In all honesty, the man doesn't seem to notice or care about any of the dancers. He's only got eyes for one."

"Olivia Taylor."

She nodded. "He's obsessed with her."

"Does she return the sentiment?"

Isabel pondered that. She was a seasoned operative, yet she couldn't quite figure Olivia Taylor out. Onstage, the dark-haired dancer exuded sex and sin. In the dressing room, she was subdued, jumpy even. Shadows haunted the woman's eyes, but the reason for those shadows remained a mystery, even after two months of working with the girl.

"I don't know," she admitted. "Something is definitely troubling her, and I'm not certain, but I swear she flinched one time when Angelo touched her. Other times, she smiles at him like he's the love of her life."

"What's your gut telling you?"

"That she's scared of him," Isabel said flatly. "That he's got her under his thumb, and she doesn't want to be there."

Trevor went silent for a second, then gave a decisive nod. "Then we go with your gut."

A rush of warmth spread through her. Oh, this was bad. It was obvious that whatever bond she and Trevor had formed in Colombia still existed. She'd hoped time would have severed it.

She cleared her throat, steering the discussion back to safe ground. "I'll continue keeping my eyes and ears open, but Olivia needs to be watched. Morgan said Luke's trying to get close to her?"

"Yeah. And the rest of us are still on the club."

"Abby too? Morgan didn't say."

"She's at the compound—mandatory break."

Isabel grinned. "Abby's not a fan of mandatory anything."

He grinned back.

Six months ago, smiles from Trevor Callaghan appeared about as often as Halley's Comet. Now they seemed readily available. God, he *had* changed. She wondered if he still struggled with the nightmares.

Their eyes met again, and a frustrated groan left his lips. "I don't care if it's in the past," he blurted out. "I still need to apologize."

"Trevor—"

"I acted like a total ass, all right? When you saved my life, I was so fucking pissed. I was ready to die, Isabel. I *wanted* to die."

"I know."

He let out a breath. "I lashed out at you and you didn't deserve that."

"No, but I understood where it was coming from."

It had still hurt, though. That's probably why his presence was so unsettling to her now. She was thirty-two years old and thought she'd reached a point in her life when nothing and no one could hurt her. Her family's Mafia background had made her childhood unorthodox, not to mention unbearable, and she'd lived through too much heartache, too much bullshit. Truth was, her easygoing charm was nothing but a practiced facade. Inside she was hardened.

Trevor's callous parting words and cold accusations had punched a hole in her shield, and it troubled her that he'd gotten close enough to be able to do that.

"I've been thinking about you a lot," he confessed. "I wanted to call so many times and tell you how sorry I was, but I kept chickening out."

That brought a wry smile to her lips. "I could've called too, but you told me to stay out of your life."

"I'm a bastard."

"You *were* a bastard," she corrected. "You seem better now."

"I am." He swallowed again. "I let her go."

She didn't need to ask who he was referring to. Gina, his dead fiancée. The woman who'd haunted his dreams and given him a death wish. "That's good," she said quietly.

He cleared his throat. "Isabel—"

"I'll keep digging at the club," she said abruptly, getting

to her feet. "And I think trying to befriend Olivia will be on my to-do list as well."

The moment had passed. Trevor snapped back into business mode. "I want you to start checking in with me. Keep Morgan in the loop, but I want a check-in every four hours."

"That seems a little excessive."

His dark eyes met hers. "Humor me."

Luke Dubois was the most fascinating man Olivia had ever met. By the time her laundry was washed, dried, and folded, she actually felt reluctant to leave the Laundromat. Luke had been entertaining her with stories for the past hour and a half, but to be honest, she was more interested in the man than his words.

He was incredibly intelligent, funny as hell, charming without even trying. And blatantly masculine. When he'd stood up to transfer his clothes into the dryer, she'd realized just how huge he was. Six-two at least, without an ounce of fat anywhere on that big, sexy body of his. She kept sneaking peeks at him, pathetically intrigued by the thick forearms he'd revealed when he'd pulled up the sleeves of his button-down, the unruly dark hair that curled under his ears, the thin white scar bisecting his left eyebrow.

But when she found herself staring at the curve of his sensual mouth and wondering what his kisses would feel like, she knew it was time to go.

Cutting him off mid-sentence, Olivia reached for a neatly folded stack of sweaters and said, "I should get going. My mother's waiting for me at home."

"Here, let me help." He grabbed one of her empty sacks and began to fill it with folded items. Then he shot her a sideways look. "You live with your mom?"

She nodded. "I was on my own a couple of years ago, but then she got sick so I moved back in to help her out."

"Is she still sick?"

"She's in remission now. For the third time."

"She must be a fighter."

Her throat tightened. "She is. She's . . . God, she's the

strongest woman I've ever known. I wish I was half as strong as her."

Luke's voice was rough. "You seem pretty strong to me."

Before she could stop it, the memory of the attack in the alley flew into her head. The customer's black eyes flashing in fury, his fists coming down on her face.

A wave of sickness swelled in her stomach. She'd tried to be strong that night. She'd kicked, scratched, punched, but the more she'd tried to strike out, the deeper the serrated blade had dug into her neck.

Just as quickly, her nausea was replaced by a blast of anger that burned a path through her body. She *had* been strong. She'd fought for her life that night. It was afterward that she'd become weak. She'd allowed herself to be weakened when she'd let Vince pay her bills, when she'd let fear keep her under that man's control.

"Hey. Olivia, look at me."

A pair of hands cupped her chin. She looked up and found Luke staring at her in concern.

"What's wrong?" he asked.

His hands were so warm. And strong. She wanted to sink into his palms. No, she wanted to bury her face against the wide expanse of his chest and pretend that everything was all right.

Were you turned on? Did you get wet when you were humping his thigh?

She shrugged Luke's hands off and took a step back. What the hell was she thinking? She couldn't touch this man. She couldn't even be around him. If Vince's temper could be provoked by an innocent lap dance, how would he react if he discovered she'd been hugging some stranger in a Laundromat? And Olivia didn't doubt that he would discover it. She'd only been half-serious when she'd asked Luke if he was following her, but when it came to Vince, she wouldn't be surprised if he'd sent a guard to keep tabs on her. Over the past six months, the hairs on the back of her neck often tingled when she was out of the apartment, as if she were being watched.

"Nothing's wrong," she murmured. "I just have to go."

Her hands shook as she started shoving clothes into the second laundry bag, not bothering to be gentle about it. She would just refold everything when she got home. When she locked the door behind her and shut out the world.

"Can I see you again?" Luke's dark eyes followed her hasty movements. "Maybe we can go out for coffee?"

"That's not a good idea," she said sharply.

A crease carved into his forehead. "Why not?"

"Because I have a boyfriend." The nausea returned. Vince would be happy to hear her say that. As far as he was concerned, she'd become his "girl" the second he'd rescued her in the alley.

Luke's wariness seemed to deepen. "Oh. Well, I don't see why we still can't share a cup of coffee as friends."

Friends? She wanted to laugh. And what would happen when Vince Angelo found out she was *friends* with the man whose lap she'd danced on?

"Not a good idea," she reiterated.

When he looked ready to protest, she set her jaw. "My boyfriend is on the possessive side. He doesn't like me talking with other men, or hanging out with them."

He raised one dark brow. "And you're fine with that?"

Irritation and panic shot through her. "It's none of your business what I'm fine with." She quickly tightened the drawstrings at the top of each sack. "Look, it was nice chatting with you, Luke. You seem like a good guy, okay? But I don't need any friends."

"Olivia—"

"I have to go."

Without so much as a backward glance, she hurried out of the Laundromat, her breath coming in gasps. She practically sprinted down the street, dodging a group of boys in private school uniforms and nearly knocking over an elderly woman exiting a bakery. She suddenly wanted to burst into tears. And why shouldn't she? She was weak, right? She was too terrified to even talk to another man because Vince might find out.

She came to a halt in the middle of the sidewalk, a streak of fury soaring inside her. No. She was *not* weak. She was being *smart*. Vince might have gotten his slimy hooks into her, but she would soon sever the rope of control he'd wrapped around her. She could have packed up and run a long time ago, which was exactly what her father would have done. But guess what—Eddie Taylor had been a rash fool. Her mom might sing her dad's praises, but Olivia had figured out at an early age that her father wasn't the big hero Kathleen claimed he was. He'd blown all their money on high-risk investments and get-rich-quick schemes. He'd been reckless, diving into dangerous situations without a single thought for the family waiting for him at home.

Well, Olivia was not reckless. She was practical. There was no way she could support herself and her mother without finishing school. Sure, they could flee now, before she got her degree, but how would she pay the rent? How would she pay for her mother's medication? And what happened if Kathleen's cancer came back? What happened if the bills piled up again?

So screw reckless. She could keep Vince at bay for another three months. She would suck it up and dance at the club. She would play the virgin card and hope Vince respected it. And then she would get the hell out of this city and never look back.

"For fuck's sake, you'd think she's never had a cock inside of her," Vince remarked as he stared in disdain at the sobbing idiot on the queen-size bed.

The man next to him shared his disgust. Marco Bianchi was an enforcer for Ric De Luca and a trusted player in De Luca's inner circle. He'd been assigned to monitor the private party that had taken place in this hotel room last night. Vince wished De Luca had sent somebody else, someone he could slip a few hundred to in exchange for keeping quiet about this.

On the bed, Cora was shuddering and quivering like a

bitch in heat, tears streaming down her freckled face. She was drowsy, her blue eyes glazed, but the smack was leaving her system and the memories of what she'd done last night were making her wail like a squawking infant.

Fighting a rush of annoyance, Vince approached the bed and slapped the bitch in the face. She wailed even louder.

"Shut the fuck up," he snapped.

"You . . . y-you said I only had to dance."

"People say a lot of things." Ignoring her, he turned to De Luca's man, pasting on an apologetic expression. "She's high maintenance."

Marco's cold eyes took on a surprising glint of humor. "Most whores are."

"I'm not a whore!" Cora cried.

Vince continued to ignore her. "But she performed well? Our associates were pleased?"

The enforcer nodded. "Very pleased. She only started with this bullshit when she was coming down."

And who said drugs were bad? Vince had long ago realized that shooting the girls up was a surefire way to gain their cooperation.

"The boss wants a sit-down tonight," Marco added. "He'd like to discuss the upcoming shipment."

"I'll be there," Vince promised.

After Marco left the room, Vince crossed the off-white carpet and returned to the bed. He sat down at the edge of the thick gold duvet and stared at the redhead, who was shaking like a leaf. Then he glanced around the suite, absorbing the expensive furnishings, the floor-to-ceiling windows that offered a view of the city skyline. Cora's crying annoyed him. She was a dumb single mom with a pile of student loans—when the fuck would she ever have the opportunity to stay in such a lavish suite? He resented her ingratitude.

Nevertheless, he drew her into his arms. She was still one of his girls, and he had a duty to comfort her. He stroked her hair without interest, wishing she'd just shut up already.

"It couldn't have been so bad." He clucked as the red-head's tears stained the collar of his black silk dress shirt.

"Th-there were th-three of them." Her voice was muffled. "They . . . they . . . made me do things that . . ." She trailed off, a new series of shudders wracking her body.

Vince sighed. "They were important clients, Cora. We need to keep important clients happy."

Ric De Luca demanded it, and Vince had no problem arranging it. And to think, fifteen years ago he'd been nothing but a twenty-year-old punk selling drugs on the street corner. The son of a pair of piss-poor losers, smarter than everyone around him yet unable to climb out of the gutter he'd been born in. All that changed when Ric De Luca had taken him under his wing. He'd started off as a drug runner, the lowest on the totem pole. Now he was thirty-five years old with cash to spare, another one of those blessed to be part of the inner circle. Number six man for the head of one of the Five Families. The most powerful family. Number six, but that would change too. As long as he kept De Luca happy, his star would continue to rise.

So big deal if he had to send some whores De Luca's way to entertain the man's associates. Dancer. Whore. Didn't make a difference. He supposed he could always prowl the streets and find some regular old hooker to do the job, but De Luca expected class, and the Diamond was known to employ only the most beautiful girls.

Even now, with snot pouring out of her nose and her eyes puffy as marshmallows, Cora was breathtaking. The associates had wanted her the moment they'd seen her dance, and Vince had obligingly given her to them.

"They liked you so much they even gave you a bonus," he told her. "Instead of two grand, you're getting five."

Out of his own pocket, he might add. But shutting this one up was worth the extra dough.

She pulled back, her tear-streaked face red and swollen. "How can I ever look my daughter in the eye?" she stammered. "What would she think if she . . . if she knew what I . . ."

Vince smothered an annoyed groan. It was either that or give in to the urge and smother this bitch with a damn pillow.

"I won't do it again." Cora spoke in a fierce whisper. "I won't. You can't make me."

He patted her head. "If that's what you want. You won't have to work another private party."

Unless they ask for you again.

Still trembling, Cora wiggled out of his embrace and stumbled to her feet. "I want to go home. Take me home now."

Her demand irked him, but since she hadn't insisted that he take her to the police station, Vince simply nodded and stood up. "If that's what you want," he said again.

Chapter 5

The rest of the team was already holed up in a back booth when Luke walked into the diner later that afternoon. He'd been watching Olivia's building until now, but after hours of inactivity, it became obvious that she wouldn't be venturing out again. When he'd reported in, Trevor had ordered him to come for a briefing, and he had to admit the team leader had chosen a good place for it. The diner on Hudson Street was one of those greasy spoons that reminded Luke of his favorite haunt back home. Lou's Bacon. He'd always thought it was a dumb-ass name for a restaurant, but Lou did fry up some damn good bacon.

At the thought of home, he made a mental note to give his mother a call. Ellen and Vanessa were probably impatient to hear from him too, which brought a trickle of guilt. Shit, he'd been a bad son and brother these past six years. Hadn't visited, hardly ever called. But he knew his mom and older sisters understood. Him on the other hand? He would never understand why the three of them had decided to stay in New Orleans, why they'd chosen to remain among the ghosts instead of trying to forget.

Luke banished the memories attempting to surface and walked across the checkered floor. The booth was a huge red-vinyl monstrosity, but even so, it was a tight squeeze for four mercenaries. Trevor, D, and Sullivan, already tackling their food, grunted out hellos when Luke slid in next to the team leader. A waitress walked up to take his order, then flounced off.

"We think Dane's alive," Trevor said through a mouthful of scrambled eggs.

Luke swiped a french fry off D's plate, earning himself a stony glare. He popped the fry in his mouth and glanced at Trevor. "Morgan's source?"

"Yeah. She overheard Angelo on the phone telling someone that they needed to get rid of Dane before people started looking for him."

He experienced a burst of satisfaction. Finally. He'd been starting to think that maybe Carter Dane didn't even exist and the DEA was just fucking around with Morgan. "So what are we thinking? He's being held somewhere?"

"That makes the most sense," Trevor answered. "While he was undercover, he went to the club almost every night to buddy up to Angelo, but we've been watching the place for almost a week, and Dane is nowhere in sight."

"If Dane's a captive, then this job just became an extraction," D said in his raspy voice.

"We need to find out where they're keeping him," Sullivan piped up, sucking on the straw sticking out of his chocolate milk shake.

Luke didn't comment on the shake. Everyone else had ordered coffee, but he'd never seen Sullivan Port drink anything you'd call normal. At a bar, while the other men ordered beers, Sully ordered the most obscure cocktail on the menu. At diners, it was apparently milk shakes. Luke wondered what the guy sucked down on his yacht. Probably some weird coconut shit Sullivan had concocted himself.

"Can the source get the location?" D demanded.

"She'll try, but her cover's too new. She might get lucky, but she thinks we'll have better luck using Olivia Taylor." Trevor turned to Luke. "What's your take on her? How close is she to Angelo?"

"Close," he said, struggling to keep the derision out of

his voice. "She said she's got a boyfriend. I'm assuming she meant him."

Trevor looked pleased. "Then there's a chance she knows something. Keep doing what you're doing—get close to her."

He shook his head. "She won't talk to me. The second I even mention the club, or going out for coffee, she shuts down." He remembered the way she'd sprinted out of the Laundromat as if the damn bogeyman was chasing her. "She's scared of him. Big-time scared."

"That's what our source thinks too," Trevor said with a frown.

"She said he's possessive," Luke added. "He doesn't like her talking with other men."

"She's a mobster's girlfriend." D spoke up, his black eyes flickering with irritation. "And she shakes her ass in a G-string for dirty old men."

He stiffened. "So?"

"So stop acting like she's some quivering virgin. She's not a victim. She knows exactly what goes on in that club. Her man runs drugs and beats the hell out of dealers who piss off De Luca." D shrugged. "I don't give two shits if she's scared. She chose to be in this position when she decided to bang Angelo."

Anger crept up his spine. D was a heartless bastard on a good day, but this was just fucked. "And if he beats the hell out of *her*?" Luke said coolly. "She deserves that?"

"When you willingly get involved with bad dudes, you pay the price."

"How do we know it was willingly? I've spent time with her. You haven't."

"You got a lap dance. Whoop-dee-doo. What exactly did the feel of her pussy rubbing against your leg reveal, bro? Are you sure it wasn't telling you that she's just some airhead stripper who's screwing her Mafia boss?"

Luke's jaw tensed. "Trust me, she's not an airhead. And she's not some gangster's moll either." She was a woman who entertained a pair of little girls while their exhausted mother washed their clothes. A woman who dished out change for a homeless dude on her way home.

"And I'm not kidding," he went on. "She's terrified of something. She doesn't want to be in that club, and I don't think Angelo is her boyfriend by choice."

He finished in an angry rush, just as the waitress approached the table with his order. The huge bacon, egg, and sausage combo didn't look so appetizing anymore. The others had fallen silent, except Sullivan, who was sucking the last bit of milk shake from his glass.

"What do you suggest we do?" Trevor finally asked.

"Find out how she became Angelo's girl." Luke released a breath. "My instincts are telling me he's got something on her, that she's in trouble."

"Fine. I'll get Holden on it." Trevor paused. "And if you're right, and she's in some kind of trouble, then what?"

"We use her. Bring her over to our side."

D barked out a laugh.

"I'm serious. I think I should tell her the truth about who I am."

The team leader looked unenthused. "You want to blow your cover?"

"It could be the only way. She won't date a customer or share her secrets with a stranger. End of story. But if she knows I'm one of the good guys, she might agree to help."

"*If* she's an unwilling player like you believe," Trevor pointed out. "If she's not, then—"

"Then you've just announced to Angelo that he's under surveillance," D cut in, annoyed. "And that we're looking for Dane."

"It's a risk," Luke conceded. "But I'd rather go with my gut than your paranoia."

D scowled, ready to argue, but Trevor held up his hand. "Let's see what Holden comes up with. If we find any evidence to suggest that Angelo has some kind of hold over Taylor, we'll consider using her."

Luke knew that was all he was gonna get at the moment.

At least Trevor was willing to explore the idea that Olivia might be caught up in something beyond her control.

The tête-à-tête officially came to an end when D got up abruptly. "Come on, bro," he growled at Sullivan. "It's our watch."

Sullivan frowned, but when the team leader gave him a nod, the big Australian followed D toward the door. After they were gone, Luke slid into D's seat so that he was facing Trevor. "Is it just me, or has he gotten even more volatile?"

"It's not just you."

His appetite returning, Luke reached for his plate and dug in. He chewed on a piece of bacon, watching Trevor with growing wariness. Something seemed to be bugging the guy, judging by the tension in his jaw.

"What?" Luke said between mouthfuls. "Did something go down?"

The other man shook his head. "Nah. It's nothing."

They didn't say a word for the next five minutes, as Luke polished off his meal. Yep, Trev was most definitely perturbed about something. So was he. But he hadn't realized how perturbed he actually was until he'd set down his coffee, opened his mouth, and something unexpected popped out: "I want to fuck her."

Trevor's mouth fell open.

It suddenly occurred to him that he was in the vicinity of one of the world's last remaining gentlemen. "I mean, have sex with her. Make love to her, whatever."

"I know what fucking is," Trevor said dryly. "I'm more perplexed by why you felt that was something you needed to share with me."

"I know, it's TMI, but—"

"WTMI."

"What's the W—oh, *way*. Yeah, way too much. But you're team leader, so I figured I owed you full disclosure."

Mr. Team Leader wrapped his fingers around his coffee mug. "You want to sleep with Olivia Taylor."

He swallowed hard. "Yes."

"Okay." A beat. "Is this going to be a problem? Mission-wise?"

"No."

Trevor's brown eyes bored into his own. "You sure about that?"

"It won't be a problem." He suddenly felt uncharacter-istically exasperated. "She's hot, all right? She's super hot and my body reacts to her, but my cock has nothing to do with my gut. There's more to her story. I feel it. And I be-lieve she will help us find Dane if she knows we're the good guys." He slugged down the rest of his coffee. "She might have referred to him as her boyfriend, but she doesn't want him to be."

"Whether that's true or not, the fact is she's still tangled up with the bastard."

"Which puts her in the best position to gather intel. I've been to the club a dozen times and haven't come up with shit. Morgan's source is inside too, and she—"

"It's Isabel."

Luke blinked. "What?"

"Morgan's source. It's Isabel." Trevor picked up his mug, tipped his head back, and drained his coffee. "She's under-cover there."

"For real?"

Trevor nodded.

"My favorite chameleon," he said with genuine delight. "Damn, and I didn't even recognize her. I've seen every dancer in that place. Who is she?"

"Candy Cane."

Well, *damn*. Luke pictured the curvy Candy Cane, with her long blond hair and delectable ass. Then he went pale. Aw, shit, he'd seen Isabel Roma's tits. How could he ever look her in the eye now?

"I can't believe she didn't say anything to me," he grum-bled. "We're e-mail buddies."

Trevor's jaw dropped. This time he was the one blurting. "For real?"

"Sure." In fact, Isabel Roma was probably the only

woman Luke had ever maintained a platonic relationship with. They'd totally hit it off when she'd helped them with the Colombian job last year. Even did some target practice together on the compound. The woman was pretty damn impressive with a rifle.

He cocked his head. "Didn't you keep in touch with her?"

"No," Trevor admitted.

"Even after she took a bullet to save your sorry ass?"

Trevor's expression darkened. Without responding, he yanked out his wallet, dropped two twenties on the table, and rose from his seat. "I'm heading back to the safe house to brief Holden. You keep tailing Olivia until we know more."

Trevor left, and Luke found himself in an empty booth. Well. Apparently he was the buzz kill of the day.

After her rendezvous with Trevor, Isabel went to the Chinese place over on the next block to grab some dinner. When she waltzed back into her apartment a half hour later, she found Noelle sitting on her couch.

Nearly dropping her takeout bag, Isabel gaped at her boss, then recovered and smiled uneasily. "Funny, I don't recall ever giving you a key."

"You didn't."

Well, of course. The queen of assassins didn't need silly things like keys. Isabel suspected her boss had an arsenal of weapons and tools underneath her clothing, although it certainly didn't show. Tight leather pants encased Noelle's legs, an even tighter black tank hugging her torso. She must be hiding her gear beneath her leather jacket, but that was pretty tight too. Ah well. Isabel wasn't about to ask how she got in, and Noelle sure as hell wouldn't tell her.

The boss looked fierce this afternoon. Fiercer than usual. Her blue eyes were narrowed with displeasure, and she tapped her red-manicured fingernails against her thighs.

Isabel sighed. "All right, let's have it. I'm ready."

The blonde was on her feet in a nanosecond, bearing

down on her. "Did I give you permission to work a job for Jim Morgan?"

"I didn't realize I needed permission. I'm on vacation, remember?" She sidestepped Noelle's approach and headed for the coffee table.

She set her takeout bag down, then flopped on the carpet cross-legged and began removing the white cardboard food containers. After seven years of working for Noelle, she'd learned that the best way to defuse the woman's wrath was to ignore it.

Sure enough, Noelle dialed back the rage, but her beautiful face still glittered with disapproval. "You know what you do on vacation, Isabel? You go to a beach. Get a tan. Fuck a cabana boy."

Isabel stuck her plastic fork into a container and speared some spicy noodles. "I've got fair skin. I burn easily."

"But no," Noelle continued as if Isabel hadn't even spoken. "You decide to do some undercover work for Morgan."

"He asked for my assistance. What can I say? He appreciates my skills."

It didn't escape her that she possessed a skill set that couldn't exactly be considered normal. Her expertise didn't involve numbers or computers or whatever it was that normal people did. What she excelled in was transformation. She could alter her appearance with whatever means necessary—makeup, padding, clothes—but becoming a different person was more than just using the tools at your disposal. It meant a new way of walking, talking, thinking. Facial gestures, body language, changing your entire mental outlook to convey a distinctive persona. Funny how nobody had ever really trained her for that. Stepping into a new role came as naturally as brushing her teeth in the morning. And she was good at it.

Probably, she supposed, because she'd spent her entire childhood and adolescence wishing she were somebody else.

"Morgan doesn't appreciate shit," Noelle scoffed. "He's using you."

Isabel chewed, swallowed, and shot her boss a pointed stare. "You went to him for help when Abby was missing."

Given the tightness of her jaw, Noelle was evidently grinding her teeth together. "I had no other choice. And trust me, I don't sleep at night, knowing I owe that man a favor." She sauntered back to the couch and lowered herself on the cushions, crossing her leather-clad legs.

Isabel still couldn't figure out how someone so graceful and heartbreakingly beautiful had grown up to be a ruthless killer. Call her a coward, but she was kind of scared to ask Noelle that question.

"Then call this job your repayment," Isabel said, reaching for a carton of chicken in black bean sauce. "Tell Morgan he's receiving my services now in exchange for his help with Abby."

"Damn right I'll tell him."

"So there you go. Now you can sleep at night again, and all is right in the world. I even forgive you for breaking into my home."

Noelle's blue eyes flickered with scorn and a touch of bewilderment. "How is it that you're able to take everything in stride? Does nothing piss you off?"

"Getting pissed off requires too much energy." She popped a piece of chicken into her mouth. "I prefer to use that energy to get the job done."

"Morgan's job," Noelle muttered. "Don't even *think* about joining his team. I mean it. I already lost Abby to that son of a bitch."

"That drives you crazy, doesn't it?" Grinning, she reached into the brown paper bag and pulled out a can of Sprite. She popped the tab, then took a sip and eyed the other woman over the rim. "Why are you really here, Noelle? I don't believe you hopped a plane to New York simply to bitch at me for taking on a little side gig."

Those midnight blue eyes became veiled. "I had some business to take care of. Figured I'd stop by while I was in town."

"What kind of business?"

Noelle just stared at her. Well, okay then. Not that Isabel was surprised. Her boss happened to be the most secretive person on the planet.

"Sorry I asked." With a shrug of her shoulders, Isabel gave up on receiving an answer and ate some more noodles.

"Out of curiosity, does your sudden desire to help Morgan out have anything to do with the fact that Callaghan is back in action?" Noelle drawled.

She lifted her head and leveled a stare of her own at her boss.

After a beat, the deadly blonde laughed. "Sorry I asked."

When Olivia showed up at the Diamond Mine the following evening, Tony intercepted her before she could reach the dressing room. "Boss wants you in his office," the bodyguard announced.

A tremor of panic moved through her body, growing stronger when she realized there could be only one reason why Vince would demand to see her.

He knew she'd been with Luke yesterday.

Her heart thudded as she followed Tony upstairs, her brain already working through various excuses. *He followed me to the Laundromat. I was caught off guard, Vince. I swear, I tried to tell him to get lost, but he kept pushing and—*

"There she is."

Vince's warm greeting interrupted her frantic thoughts. He was behind the desk again, but rose when she entered the office. His expression revealed no anger. Just pleasure.

Her heartbeat slowed. This wasn't about Luke, then.

Unless Vince was toying with her, playing nice until he went in for the kill . . . She dismissed the thought. No, that looked like genuine joy sparkling in his eyes.

"I've got something for you," he said, his tone containing that tease of anticipation a lover used when he was about to present you with something special.

Her panic all but disappeared when Vince extended a velvet jeweler's box in her direction.

Olivia eyed the gift with uneasiness. "What is it?"

"Open it."

After a second of reluctance, she accepted the box and carefully opened the lid. A flash of silver winked up at her. No, not silver. Diamonds. Resting on the box's black velvet bed was a sparkling diamond tennis bracelet accented with white gold.

"Wow" was all she could think to say.

"Five carats," Vince said smugly.

Now she said, "Oh." Five carats. Of diamonds. On a silly bracelet. She was about to insist she couldn't accept it, but the practical side of her objected. She could probably sell this thing for a huge chunk of change.

So she met his eyes, feigned delight, and breathed, "Thank you." *For helping me bankroll my escape from you.*

His gaze shone with pleasure. "You like it?"

"I love it. Will you help me put it on?"

She started to lift the bracelet from its box, but Vince reached out and snapped the lid. He promptly tucked the box into the inner pocket of his Armani jacket. "You can't wear it when you dance, babe. Diamonds and G-strings don't complement each other. I'll hold on to this until tomorrow night."

A spark of panic returned. "What's tomorrow night?"

Displeasure glittered on his face. "Have you forgotten?"

Olivia quickly searched her mind. Tomorrow night. A Thursday. October eighteenth. What was special about October eightee—

"It's our six-month anniversary," Vince snapped.

Said the kidnapper to his hostage.

"Of course it is," she answered, donning a playful look, as if she'd known all along and had only been teasing him. "I just can't believe you remembered."

"I remember everything. You know that."

Yep, and she also knew he wasn't referring just to his knack for remembering dates.

Message received, asshole.

Olivia managed a smile. "So what are we doing tomorrow?"

"Dinner. At my place." His tone brooked no argument.

She choked down a wave of sickness. His place? She'd never set foot in his Midtown penthouse. Oh God. That could mean only one thing. He expected her to sleep with him tomorrow. A million excuses burned through her brain, everything from *I have my period* to *I'd rather slit my wrists*. But she knew some blood between her legs would only turn him on even more, and the wrist-slitting thing . . . well, he'd probably be the one handing her the razor if she refused to fuck him.

"S-sounds lovely," she stammered.

He stepped closer and dragged his thumb along her lower lip. His eyelids grew heavy, his features taut with arousal. "It's what we've both been waiting for." He gave her butt a little pat. "Now get downstairs and change."

Hiding her terror and disgust, she forced herself to exit the office with calm steps rather than breaking into a dead run. God, she had to find a way out of this. She couldn't sleep with that man. She felt nauseous just thinking about it.

She hurried downstairs and wandered into the busy dressing room, making a beeline for the bathroom. Inside, she approached the double sinks, flicked on the faucet, and splashed cold water on her face. She was so distracted that she didn't even notice Cora come up behind her until the redhead's face appeared in the bathroom mirror.

Olivia turned around, concern washing over her. "Cora, hey. You startled me."

Her friend didn't answer. Waves of hostility radiated from Cora's body and her expression burned with stark fury. It took Olivia a second to register that the hostility was directed at *her*.

"Cora," she said again. "What's going on? Are you okay? Oh God, did something happen to Katie?"

"Leave my daughter out of this!"

She blinked in confusion. "What the hell is going on? What's wrong?"

"What the fuck do you care?" Cora hissed. "You fucking slut. You're the one who should have gone last night!"

"What?"

"He told me how much you liked it the first time. Why did he have to send me?"

Uh. All right. She had no clue what the other woman was talking about, but it didn't sound good. At all.

"I don't know what you think I did, but—"

Pain slashed into her cheek. Olivia raised her palm to her face, stunned. Cora had *slapped* her.

She took a step forward, but the redhead edged away. Her cheeks were flushed with anger, her hand shaking wildly as she lifted it to point an accusing finger. "Don't come near me."

"Cora—"

"I thought you were my friend, but you're *not.* You're no better than all the other sluts in this whorehouse."

"What are you *talking* ab—"

"I thought we were friends! That's why I got you this job, so I'd have someone to watch my back, someone who gave a shit about me. But you don't. You never did, did you?" A maniacal laugh spiraled out of the girl's mouth.

Gulping, Olivia dared to approach the hysterical redhead. She reached out her hand, only for Cora to slap it away as if she'd been stung by a hornet.

"Don't touch me," Cora growled. "I only came to tell you what you could do with your *friendship.*" She stumbled toward the doorway. "And tell that sick motherfucker he can shove his five grand up his ass. I'm going to the cops."

Chapter 6

From the bathroom doorway, Olivia watched with wide eyes as Cora stormed out of the dressing room. Her mind reeled from confusion, and her cheek still stung from that slap. What the *hell* just happened?

What had Vince done to her friend?

Snapping out of her stupor, she charged across the room.

"Bad idea, Olivia."

She spun around and spotted Candy in the process of lifting a tube of lipstick to her mouth. Dumbfounded, Olivia met the dancer's blue eyes. "Why is going after her a bad idea?"

"It's not the time. The boss won't appreciate your interference."

She bristled. "What makes you an expert on Vince?" Without waiting for an answer, she took another step toward the door. "Cora needs a friend. She needs me."

"She needs to calm down," Candy corrected, reaching for a flat brush and dipping it into a container of cream-colored powder. As if she had no care in the world, the dancer began applying her makeup, her voice gentle and oddly comforting as she went on. "Whatever happened with her and Vince, they need to work it out amongst themselves. You'll make it worse if you get involved."

"Why?"

"Because Vince likes you meek. Doesn't he, Olivia?"

She remembered the last time she'd talked back to him, and the right side of her face experienced a phantom pain. She hadn't been able to open her eye for days.

"Whatever you're doing to control him, keep doing it," the blonde advised. "Stay off his radar."

Off his radar? She almost laughed. She was the *only* thing on that bastard's radar.

"Why are you saying this?" Unable to help it, she glanced up at the camera mounted in the corner of the ceiling.

Candy's eyes met hers in the mirror. "I'm just trying to look out for you."

Olivia noticed for the first time that Candy Cane's blue eyes were far sharper than she'd realized. Shrewd. Warm. The dancer couldn't be older than thirty or thirty-one, but she exuded a maternal aura that made Olivia want to launch herself into Candy's arms and let the other woman comfort her, the way her mother used to do before she got too weak for even the gentlest of embraces.

"What does he have on you?"

The out-of-the-blue inquiry slammed into her like a punch to the gut. "Wh-what?" she sputtered.

"I'd like to be your friend, if you'll let me. You can talk to me."

"I don't know what you think is going on, but—"

"The shadows in your eyes," Candy replied. "I still see them."

The temptation to confide in the woman was so strong she nearly blurted out every last detail, but then her mouth snapped shut. For all she knew, the dressing room was wired for sound and Vince was listening to every word. This was a trick. Vince must have put the dancer up to this. He'd caught on to the charade and now he was using Candy to extract a confession from her. So he could punish her.

"Then you're seeing things," she said coldly. "Because the only thing Vince has is my heart." With that, Olivia ended the conversation by marching toward the rack of costumes and keeping her back to Candy.

Several minutes later, Olivia's suspicions were confirmed when she passed by the woman's station and spotted Candy texting on her BlackBerry.

Checking in with Vince and typing out every word that had just been exchanged, no doubt.

Friend, her ass.

Nothing beat New York pizza. Trevor couldn't deny that as he wolfed down the last slice of the extra-large pie he'd devoured all by his lonesome. Man, he was piling on the carbs lately, but then again, he was burning them just as fast now that he'd begun working out again. It felt good to be at the top of his game.

Wiping his mouth with a napkin, he glanced at D, who was standing by the railing staring at the skyscrapers in the distance, then at Luke, who was smoking a cigarette on the other side of the table. Although they'd been on the terrace for the past hour, the conversation had been scarce, and Trevor was kind of grateful for the silence.

He couldn't get Isabel off his damn mind. Which was nothing new, seeing as he'd had Isabel on the brain for the past six months.

Yet now that he'd seen her in person, his preoccupation with the woman disturbed him on a whole other level. His reasons for wanting to contact her had been purely about making amends, and that was exactly what he'd done earlier—as much as she'd let him anyway. So theoretically speaking, she shouldn't be on his mind anymore. He'd apologized. She'd accepted. End of story.

Except it didn't feel like anything had ended—it felt like the beginning of something, and he had no clue what to make of that.

Swallowing a sigh, he tossed his napkin in the pizza box and closed the lid. He was just reaching for his bottle of Bud Light when his phone chimed to signal an incoming text.

Speak of the devil.

"Morgan?" Luke asked, leaning forward to stub out his cigarette in the ashtray.

Trevor shook his head. "Isabel."

"What does she have to say?"

"See for yourself."

He tossed the BlackBerry to Luke, who peered at the display and read the text aloud. "Vet Cora Malcolm. Something fucked up happening at this club."

Luke's resulting frown matched Trevor's, who was wishing Isabel had been more forthcoming with the details. They already knew Angelo ran drugs out of that upstairs suite of his, so what other fucked-up thing could be happening over at the Diamond Mine?

D left his place by the railing and joined them at the table, plopping his big body in a chair. Their resident asshole hadn't said much to anyone since he'd made his position clear at the diner, but that didn't mean shit considering D didn't say much on a good day.

"Who's Cora Malcolm?" D demanded.

"Good question." Rather than go inside to find the dossier Holden had compiled on each of the dancers, Trevor opted for the easy alternative. He dialed Holden's number and put the phone on speaker.

Holden's brusque voice came on the line a second later. "What are you, a mind reader? I was literally about to call you. I think I have the answer to—"

"Hold that thought," Trevor cut in. "First, who's Cora Malcolm?"

Mr. Photographic Memory didn't let them down. "One of the dancers. Stage name's Coral Holliday."

"Coral?" Luke echoed. "Yeah, I remember her. Redhead, small breasts, long legs."

"Any idea why she might merit vetting?" Trevor asked Holden.

"No clue. She's a single mom, NYU student, keeps her nose clean. She didn't raise any red flags for me. Anyway"—the man sounded impatient—"forget about her for now. I think I figured out the deal with Angelo and Olivia Taylor."

When Trevor made out the sound of typing, he had to

roll his eyes. "You're supposed to be watching the club, McCall. What the fuck did you bring your laptop for?"

"I do know how to multitask, *Callaghan*." A few more clicks sounded on the extension. "So listen, I was following the money trail and I hit pay dirt."

Since Holden had the tendency to drone on for hours, Trevor leaned back in his chair and got comfortable.

"This April, Olivia was admitted to St. Francis Hospital. I hacked into her medical report—sounds like she got beat up pretty bad. One of her cheekbones was fractured and collapsed in her face. A surgeon came in to fix it, put some plates and screws in there to repair it."

D looked extremely interested. "Angelo roughed her up?"

"I don't think so. One of the bouncers at the club filed the police report. Tony Moretti. He claims a customer dragged Olivia into an alley and started pounding on her. This Tony showed up in time to stop the attack, but the perp ran off. Olivia's medical bills were paid in full—by Angelo. He also covered all her outstanding debts and bought her the Beemer."

When the line went silent, Luke spoke up in a sharp tone. "What are you thinking, Holden?"

"That a three-hundred-pound bouncer wouldn't just let a would-be rapist run off," Trevor said grimly, voicing Holden's thoughts.

"You think Angelo killed the customer?" Luke asked.

"Yep. And then he covered it up, dumped the body, and lied to the cops," Holden hypothesized.

Luke cursed under his breath. "That makes sense. And Olivia . . . she probably saw him do it and didn't tell the police. Or maybe she tried to tell the truth, and Angelo threatened to kill her too."

D snorted. "Or she stood by and let it happen, then high-fived Angelo when it was done."

That D's first instinct was to think the worst of Olivia Taylor was as predictable as Luke's impulse to think the best of her. Trevor had worked with both men long enough to know the way their brains worked, and so he wasn't surprised when the bickering started.

"I don't think she's in cahoots with Angelo," Luke said evenly.

"Shocking," D muttered. "The beautiful, misunderstood stripper *must* be a victim in this, right?"

"Why do you immediately assume she isn't?"

D exhaled an annoyed breath. "Whatever. It's all good. You can go all Sir Galahad and chase after the damsel in distress. I'll be here, ready to save your ass when your virginal damsel tries to tear your throat out."

Trevor released a breath of his own, ready to run interference, but Luke ended the bicker fest by standing up. "I'm going back in," he announced. "It's time we figured out whether she's a player in this game or a victim."

Chapter 7

Olivia's breath caught in her throat as she entered the VIP room and found Luke Dubois inside. When she'd been told five minutes ago that someone had requested a private dance, she'd felt like running out of the club and throwing up behind the Dumpster. The confrontation with Cora had lingered in her mind all night, leaving her so on edge it was a miracle she'd managed to get up onstage and pull off a decent performance—working that pole took a lot more skill than people knew.

Normally she walked into the VIP room with dread, already making an effort to mentally detach herself, but tonight her pulse sped up and her palms went damp. He was back. And as gorgeous as ever.

As she strode toward the couch, she tried to pretend that the sight of him didn't affect her. That those thick, muscular legs encased in worn blue denim and the hard chest beneath his long-sleeved shirt didn't do a thing for her. But her traitorous body betrayed her, and her heart beat faster and faster the closer she got to him.

"Hey," he greeted her, his gaze focused on hers.

You'd think after all this time at the Diamond she wouldn't feel embarrassed waltzing around half-naked, but she did, even more so now that she'd spent time with Luke outside the club. And now here she was, standing in front of him topless, and she couldn't help but wish that he was see-ing her like this under different circumstances.

But that was just crazy. She might be attracted to the man, but nothing could ever come of this attraction. Getting involved with Luke—with anyone, for that matter—was a risk she couldn't afford to take.

"Hey," she answered.

Their eyes locked.

Olivia cleared her throat. "I thought you only tried things once."

"I had to make an exception." His voice sounded a bit hoarse. "It was the only way I could see you again."

Ignoring a tiny spark of pleasure, she closed the distance between them. "I guess I didn't make myself clear yester-day."

"I don't give up that easily, darlin'."

His Southern drawl flared up. Her pulse went off-kilter again.

And then the music started.

Olivia's throat ran dry. God, she couldn't do this. She couldn't straddle that big, strong body again. Maybe if she hadn't spent time with him yesterday, maybe if he hadn't made her laugh with all those stories, then she could treat him like any old customer and do her job.

As she hovered over him, hesitating, she became excru-ciatingly aware of the cameras pointed right at her. Vince would review this footage. He'd see her standing there like a deer in the headlights. He'd punish her for making him look bad in front of a customer.

Taking a breath, Olivia started to dance.

She heard Luke's sharp intake of breath. When she looked into his eyes, the heat she saw in them floored her. Quickly, she spun around. Okay, no eye contact. Eye con-tact was a bad idea.

Instead, she moved into the triangle created by his open legs, keeping her back to him as she undulated her hips to the rhythm of the music. Bending her legs, she placed her palms on his knees for support, lowered herself onto his lap, and rotated her hips in a circular motion. She nearly keeled over when she felt a thick ridge pressing into her bottom. Her cheeks scorched. Oh God, he had an erection.

Of course he does. Look at what you're doing to him.

Breathing deeply, she arched her back so that her long hair was flung into his face.

"Olivia."

She blocked out the sound of his husky voice, refusing to turn around. If she did, he'd surely notice that her nipples had puckered into two tight buds. He'd surely see the signs of arousal on her flushed skin.

"Fuck, this isn't right."

He sounded so tortured that she caved in, needing to see his eyes. They were filled with reluctance. Disappointment.

"What do you mean?" she heard herself whisper.

"It's not right," he mumbled. "I don't want to pay to see you. I don't like knowing that it's the only reason you're even in here with me."

She gulped. When she realized she'd gone still, noticed that the music continued to pound from the speakers, she shimmied closer and straddled him, jutting her breasts as she sank onto that bulge in his jeans.

"Can we please just stop talking?" she said, her throat tight. But she knew what he meant. This *wasn't* right. He was the first man she'd been attracted to in who knew how long. The only man who'd ever made her feel all pathetically tingly when he smiled at her.

"No," he choked out. "We can't. I came here to talk."

She brought her breasts toward his face, rolling her hips. Maybe if she ignored him, just did her thing until the music ended, he would let it go. Stop pushing for . . . for whatever it was he wanted from her. A date. Coffee. Friendship. It wasn't in the cards, no matter how hard he pursued her.

Averting her eyes, she trailed a finger along the curve of his jaw, then leaned forward and blew seductively on his ear. He flinched as if she'd shot him. The erection pressing against her core seemed to thicken.

"Goddamn it," he growled. "Stop distracting me."

She stared at his hands, which were palm-down on the couch on either side of his thighs. He lifted them slightly, as if he wanted to touch her, but then he flattened them and groaned. "I came here to help you, Olivia."

Her gaze darted to the camera aimed at them.

"No sound," he said quietly. "I checked."

Checked? How?

As his expression turned fierce, it suddenly occurred to her that she had no idea who this man even was. She didn't know what he did for a living, why he'd moved to New York. She knew nothing except that her heart skipped a beat at the mere sound of his smoky voice.

"We don't have much time, so I need you to listen to me, and listen carefully." When she went motionless, he groaned again. "No, keep doing . . . what you're doing. Angelo's watching, isn't he?"

Olivia knew her eyes had gone as wide as saucers, but she didn't disregard his order. She kept up with the grinding, all the while wondering what the hell was going on. His easy-going charm had transformed into urgency, his face burning with intensity.

"I lied to you," Luke admitted. "I wasn't here the other night for a lap dance. Frankly, if it was up to me, we'd be doing this in the privacy of a bedroom, no cash involved, just two people who seriously want to turn each other on."

Olivia's lips parted in a startled O.

"We've been watching Angelo. My team and I."

Now her jaw fell open. She quickly slammed it shut, hyperaware of the camera pointed at her.

"We've been watching you too, and I think I know what's going on with you, Olivia. The attack in the alley—something happened that night, didn't it?"

Her heart hammered against her ribs. "Why . . . how . . ."

"Angelo's not your boyfriend, is he?"

"I . . . I don't know what you're talking about."

"Whatever he has on you, I can help you," Luke said in an impassioned voice. "I lied to you about who I am and why I'm here, but I'm not lying about this. If you're in trouble, we can help. But we need your help too. We need you to—"

The music died.

As the bouncer's voice blasted out of the intercom, ordering her to take a bow, panic constricted Olivia's chest. She was too stunned to move, uncertain as to whether she'd imagined everything Luke had said or if this was some sort of trick, just another way Vince was toying with her or testing her loyalty.

"Fuck." Luke's tone became more insistent as he rattled off a series of numbers. "That's my cell number. Memorize it. Quick, Olivia." He recited the numbers again, twice. "Say it back."

She stared at him, dumbfounded. Then she stumbled off his lap, knowing that one of the bouncers would come storming in if she didn't.

"You can trust me," Luke said softly. "I'm one of the good guys, darlin'. If you need help—"

"I don't need help," she sputtered.

Resignation filled his brown eyes. "I know you're scared of him. I don't blame you. He's dangerous, and you *should* be scared of him. But I promise you, I can help you."

She took a panicked step to the door, but his voice stopped her.

"Did you memorize that number, Olivia?"

Without turning around, she whispered the seven digits.

"Good. Then call me when you're ready. Anytime, darlin'."

The endearment had just exited his mouth when the door flung open and a scowling bouncer named Bobby appeared.

"This gentleman giving you a hard time, Liv?" Bobby asked gently.

She gave a wild shake of the head. "What? No. No, he's not. I just feel a little under the weather." Shock continued to spiral through her body, making her muscles go limp, which only gave credence to her sudden bout of illness.

Looking concerned, Bobby stepped forward and took

her arm to steady her. "Come on, let's get you to the dressing room. You do look a bit pale."

Olivia refused to look over her shoulder as the bouncer half carried her out of the room, but she could feel Luke's gaze burning into her back. Later. She would absorb everything he'd told her later. Right now, she had to pretend everything was fine, a game plan that only increased in importance when she and Bobby entered the dressing room to find Vince pacing the floor. He must have dismissed the other girls again—he was alone in the room.

His eyes snapped in her direction when she walked in. "Leave us," he said to Bobby.

As the big man disappeared, Olivia sank into the nearest chair and gathered her composure.

Vince loomed over her, his features livid. "What the hell happened? Bobby said a customer was upsetting you."

She lifted her head, finding the courage to meet his eyes. "That wasn't it. I got light-headed during the dance, that's all."

Doubt clouded his perfectly sculpted face. "Lightheaded."

"Yeah." She made a show of rubbing her temples. "I suddenly felt really sick. I almost collapsed on that poor customer. I think I scared him."

Vince slid down to his knees in front of her. "Screw the customer. I'm more worried about you."

The concern in his voice might've been sweet if she hadn't known exactly who this man was. "I'm fine," she said in a tired voice. "I think I'm just coming down with something." Inspiration streaked through her. "I don't know if I'll be up for anything too action-packed tomorrow night."

"Don't worry, we'll take it nice and easy, babe. I know we've got you scheduled for the afternoon shift, but fuck it. Spend the day at home tomorrow, and you'll feel good as new by the time evening rolls around."

Well, it had been worth a try. Looked like she'd have to find another way to keep from sleeping with him. On their anniversary.

Vince leaned closer, the stench of his strong cologne making her stomach roil. "I was worried when Bobby called me down."

"I'm fine," she insisted.

"Good."

And then his mouth touched hers and she was *so* not fine. It was the briefest of kisses, just the brush of his lips, but it brought bile to her mouth.

Pulling back, she massaged her temples again. "Yeah, it's probably a good idea that I don't come in tomorrow. I'm sure Cora would be willing to—" She halted, the memory of Cora's breakdown flooding her head. "She was here earlier and she totally freaked out on me. She said—"

"I know all about it, babe." Vince's smile was a tad condescending, and he ruffled her hair as if she were a five-year-old. "Cora and I straightened everything out."

Olivia studied his face. "You did?"

"Yeah, it's all good. She was just pissed off that Candy was taking all her shifts." Vince shrugged. "Don't worry about it. We reached an agreement."

"Oh. That's good." *If it was true.* But she could tell by the vague lilt in his voice that he'd lied to her. She'd known Cora since freshman year and she knew the other woman wouldn't have freaked out over losing a few shifts. Something else had happened. Something bad.

He's dangerous.

Luke's words buzzed through her head. Luke. Was that even his name?

Standing up, she headed for the bank of lockers. "I need to get home."

She heard him approach her from behind. Cringed when his arms wrapped around her. "That's a good idea. Make a cup of tea, get in bed, and get some rest, my love."

My love. It was the first time he'd ever called her that.

"And you'll feel all better tomorrow." His breath fanned over her neck, making her skin crawl. "Just in time to celebrate."

*   *   *

This felt like a date.

It wasn't, though. Of course it wasn't. And yet as Isabel stretched her sore legs on the carpet and watched Trevor devour the leftover Chinese food he'd pillaged from her fridge, she couldn't help but feel that it was. A date, that is.

But it wasn't.

"You should be team leader on this one," Trevor mumbled between mouthfuls.

She raised a brow. "Is that a job offer?"

"No. Well, kind of." He chewed slowly, then reached for the can of Bud Light on the table and popped the tab.

He swallowed a sip of the beer, drawing her gaze to his strong, corded throat. And no, she hadn't ducked into that corner store to buy a six-pack because she'd known he was stopping by after her shift at the Diamond. She'd had a legitimate thirst for beer. At three in the morning.

God, she was such a loser. A thirty-two-year-old loser who had no business enjoying this man's company. She couldn't even count the reasons why getting involved with Trevor would be a bad idea.

"What do I know about the Mafia?" he continued. "I'm a soldier, not an investigator. Put a gun in my hand and tell me what to shoot? No problem. But ask me to figure out where the Mob is stashing an undercover agent? I don't even fucking know where to begin."

She sighed. "I'd like to say you've come to the right place and claim to be some kind of expert on the subject, but truth is, I didn't get too far when I worked the organized-crime unit."

His brown eyes sharpened. "You went undercover in De Luca's outfit twice."

"And came up with nothing. Twice. De Luca tolerated me because of my father, but he sure as hell didn't trust me. He was trying to marry me off to his oldest son and the fact that I wasn't interested didn't help in the trust department."

"You must have uncovered something. How they run their operation, where they conduct their interrogations."

"Nothing," she reiterated. "I have no clue where they'd be holding Dane."

"What about your father?" Trevor asked. "You said he's in prison, but maybe he can—"

"No."

He instantly backed off, probably because the tone of her voice brooked no argument. Her flat-out refusal lingered in the air. She drew a calming breath, hoping to ease the sudden pounding of her heart.

"I'm sorry," she said. "I didn't mean to snap at you."

"It's okay."

"I won't involve my father. I can't. He might be locked up in a federal penitentiary, but don't think that means he's safe. If anyone in the organization so much as suspected him of being a rat . . ." She trailed off. Pulse kicked up another notch.

"I get it." Trevor's voice was soft, husky. "I'm sorry. I shouldn't have even suggested it."

Silence fell over the living room. Seemed like there was always some kind of baggage cluttering up the space between them. But hell, at least Trevor was honest about his crap. She, on the other hand, played everything so cool. Just the daughter of a former mobster. No biggie. Sure, she'd once told the bureau, she'd *love* to try to bring down the people who'd sold her dad up the river. *Love* to punish those who'd had her brother murdered.

So strong, wasn't she? Strong, not-a-care-in-the-world Isabel Roma. And that was the crux of the matter, the reason why getting close to anyone was a bad idea.

Because she could put up that tough and happy-go-lucky front for only so long before the exhaustion set in.

"Hey. Isabel. What's going on?"

She inhaled. Collected all the jagged little pieces of her composure, putting the mask back together. "Nothing," she said with a careless wave of the hand.

Trevor didn't look convinced. A deep crease cut into his proud forehead, and those whiskey brown eyes flickered with uneasiness. She got the feeling he could see right through her, and she didn't like it, not one damn bit.

She briskly changed the subject. "Olivia will help. I'm sure of it."

"Olivia left the club hours ago and still hasn't used the number Luke gave her."

"She's scared. But desperate. The desperation will work in our favor." Isabel stood up and began collecting the empty food containers. "She's a smart one too. If she comes on board, she'll get us the information we need. And while she does, I'll be at the club, watching over her and—"

His hand covered hers.

She nearly dropped the takeout boxes. Trevor swiftly freed them from her grip, tossed the containers back on the coffee table, and encircled her clenched fists with his hands, his long fingers dragging over her knuckles.

"I'm sorry I mentioned using your father for information," he said hoarsely. "It was a stupid idea."

"I told you, it's no big—"

"Deal?" he finished. His lips twisted wryly. "Nothing's a big deal for you, is it, Isabel?"

She was acutely aware of his touch, the warmth of his fingers. The scent of him infused her senses, some spicy masculine aftershave that tickled her nostrils.

Yep, this silly attraction was getting way out of hand.

She broke the physical contact and tackled the garbage again. "I feel bad kicking you out, but it's almost four and I'm dead on my feet." She flew past him, heading for the steps that led from the sunken living room up to the kitchen. "Can you let me know when Olivia contacts Luke?"

He didn't answer, so she paused on the top step and risked a glance in his direction. The look in his eyes stole the breath right out of her lungs. Loaded with heat, soft with tenderness.

"Of course," he finally said. "You'll be the first person I call."

*   *   *

By the time noon rolled around, Olivia was no closer to dragging herself out of bed, even though she'd been lying in it for a good twelve hours. She'd barely slept—just slipped in and out of restless slumber, tossing and turning until the covers were nothing but a tangled ball at the foot of the bed. Her NYU T-shirt clung to her chest, damp with the sweat that had been coating her skin when she'd woken up an hour ago from that paralyzing nightmare.

She'd dreamed that she was in bed with Vince and being stabbed by sharp needles of pain as he thrust into her violently, over and over again, refusing to stop even as she pleaded for mercy. Good chance the nightmare would become reality tonight. Actually, forget chance. It was a certainty. There was only one outcome. Only one way to celebrate their *anniversary*.

Unless . . .

"It's a trick," she muttered to herself.

Sitting up, she swung her legs over the side of the bed, refusing to let herself believe that Luke Dubois—if that was even his name—could actually help her. He may have sounded sincere last night, but the more she thought about it, the more she realized just how suspect all this was. Some charming stranger starts frequenting the Diamond Mine out of the blue, claiming he can rescue her from Vince's clutches? Yeah, and the tooth fairy leaves glitter-dusted surprises under children's pillows.

This was another test. Vince gauging her loyalty, making sure his sweet virgin was on the up-and-up.

She headed into the bathroom and cranked the shower faucet, then pulled her T-shirt over her head and climbed into the stall. The warm water coursed down her body but did nothing to ease the chill in her bones. She couldn't fight the troubling feeling that something terrible was about to happen, like dark clouds gathering and moving, preparing for a torrential downpour. Vince had been watching her so closely lately, and the patience he'd displayed over the past six months had begun to dwindle. And now Luke had entered the picture, claiming to be one of the good guys.

A laugh slipped out of her throat, bouncing off the tiled walls. Spinning around, she dunked her head under the spray and smoothed her wet hair out of her face. The good guys. There was no such thing. Not in her life anyway.

Olivia reached for a bottle of body wash, expelling all thoughts of Luke Dubois from her mind. A few minutes later, she rinsed, shut off the water, and reached for her pink terry-cloth robe. She proceeded to go through the motions. Brushed her teeth, applied moisturizer to her face, brushed her hair, got dressed. But the mundane activities couldn't distract her from the noose of dread slowly winding around her neck.

She couldn't do it. She couldn't have sex with Vince tonight. She was already taking off her clothes for money, lying to her mother about her job, pretending to feel something for a man who disgusted her, but she had to draw the line somewhere.

And whoring herself was something she absolutely could not do.

You're no better than all the other sluts in this whorehouse.

As Cora's words echoed in Olivia's head, confusion swept through her. She remembered the savage glint in her friend's eyes, and that feeling of foreboding returned, another black cloud positioning itself over her head. Why had Cora snapped like that? What had Vince done to her? Only Cora could answer that, and Olivia promptly decided to disregard Candy's advice. She had to see Cora and find out what had happened. Today.

Squaring her jaw, she left the bedroom and followed the corridor to the kitchen, where she found her mother standing by the stove, lifting a stainless-steel kettle from one of the burners. Kathleen wore a tattered plaid robe, her bald head gleaming in the sunlight that streamed through the small square window over the sink.

Olivia instantly went to her mom's side and took the

kettle from her. "You shouldn't be moving around," she said firmly. "Sit."

Kathleen offered a tired chuckle, but did as she was told. Settling on one of the plastic chairs around their shabby kitchen table, she rubbed her weary green eyes and said, "You slept in. I can't remember the last time you did that."

"Me neither." She prepared two cups of tea and joined her mom at the table. "I had a long night."

"Oh, honey. I wish you wouldn't take on so many extra shifts. We're not ... the bills ... how bad is it?"

She thought about the debts Vince had so eagerly erased, the hospital bills, tuition ... he even paid their rent now. Bad? Well, no, because technically they didn't owe anybody a damn penny. But *bad*, because she owed Vince Angelo something entirely different.

"We're in good shape," she said vaguely. "Don't worry about a thing, okay? I'm taking care of it."

"You shouldn't have to."

"Mom—"

"You're twenty-five years old, Liv. You've got such a bright future ahead of you, the potential to do wonderful things and put your mark on this world." Shame filled Kathleen's eyes. "You shouldn't be taking care of me."

She reached across the table and clasped her mother's frail hand. "That is *exactly* what I should be doing."

"Not at the expense of your own happiness."

Tears clouded her vision. "You're alive. That's what makes me happy."

"Olivia—"

She stood abruptly. "I'm going to the pharmacy to pick up the refill for your prescription, and then I've got a few more errands to run, but when I come back we'll take that walk, okay?"

Her mother stared at her with such sorrow that Olivia wanted to sob. "All right," Kathleen said in a weak voice.

"Did you give yourself the injection?"

"Not yet. I'll do it when I finish my tea."

"I can wait and—"

"No, you go out and take care of what you need to take care of. I'll be fine, honey."

Swallowing the lump in her throat, she walked over to plant a soft kiss atop her mother's head. The stubble there tickled her lips, making her throat tighten again.

"I'll be back soon, Mom."

She took a few more sips of tea, then set the mug in the sink and left the room, grabbing her coat and purse from the front hall. The second she stepped out of the building, she breathed in the surprisingly warm air and let it fill her lungs, but the tightness in her chest refused to be alleviated. She was relieved to be out of the apartment. Relieved, and so incredibly ashamed of that. It took every ounce of energy she possessed to remain strong for her mother, to hide the overwhelming fear that continued to shudder through her in spite of her mother's remission.

She was going to lose her. She would nurse her mom back to health and then what? The cancer would return. It always did.

Sooner or later, it would claim her mother's life.

And Olivia would be all alone in this world. Alone and exhausted.

Throw yourself a pity party, will ya?

The mocking voice snapped her into action. She sucked in a breath, reached into her purse for her car keys. Yeah, she was being whiny as hell lately, wasn't she? This wretched situation with Vince was messing with her head.

The BMW he'd bought her was parked in the small lot at the rear of the building, and she rounded the brick wall, her sneakers crunching on the gravel as she headed for the car.

Olivia made a quick stop at the pharmacy to pick up her mother's prescription, then drove south toward Brooklyn. She'd visited Cora's apartment only once, but she remembered the general area and knew she'd recognize the building if she saw it. Fifteen minutes later, she reached Cora's neighborhood and slowed the Beemer, driving until she spotted a one-way street that looked familiar. Yes, there it was. The redbrick warehouse had been converted into lofts, and the corner unit featured a black iron balcony with a string of Christmas lights along the railing. Cora had laughed about how her daughter refused to let her take those lights down because Katie liked to pretend it was Christmas year-round.

Confident that she had the right place, Olivia miraculously found an empty spot on the street and parallel-parked her way into it. She hopped out of the car and darted across the street toward the brick building. On the front stoop, she scanned the wall for Cora's apartment number, then hit the intercom button and waited.

No answer.

She buzzed again. Nothing but static greeted her.

There were a ton of reasons why Cora might not answer. She could be out with her daughter, or at the library studying for midterms, or shopping for groceries. Yet Olivia's instincts were humming, ordering her not to give up until she got into that apartment.

Sighing, she reached into her purse for her phone. She'd just pulled Cora's number from her contact list when the big metal door on the stoop swung open and a guy with shaggy red hair and a multitude of facial piercings came out. He didn't spare her a glance as he strode off, and Olivia quickly ducked through the door before it slammed shut.

Cora would probably be pissed at her for strolling into the building like she owned the place, but she didn't care. She couldn't erase the memory of Cora's ravaged eyes from her mind, and that humming continued to wreak havoc on her body as she rode the elevator to the top floor. Something was wrong. She couldn't put her finger on it, but she *felt* it. And it only got worse when she walked up to Cora's front door. Metal, like all the others in the building, but Cora's was painted bright yellow and the apartment number had been scrawled on it in pink marker, courtesy of Cora's daughter.

Unable to control the apprehension trembling through her body, Olivia knocked on the door.

It swung open.

She froze. Okay. Something was definitely wrong.

"Cora?" she called out.

No response.

Gulping, she stepped across the threshold. A beeping noise caught her attention. She moved deeper into the loft, following the high-pitched sound to its source—a cordless phone handset announcing that Cora had two new messages.

The apartment was one of those open-concept designs with exposed ductwork and weathered hardwood floors. The living room was tucked off to the right, the kitchen to the left. There was one small bedroom in the back that belonged to Cora's daughter, as well as a narrow iron staircase leading up to the sleeping platform that Cora used.

Olivia remembered her friend telling her that the apartment belonged to Cora's grandmother, who now lived in Florida and was subletting the loft to her granddaughter. The place was clean and cozy, littered with children's toys, textbooks, and framed photos of Cora and Katie.

Taking a breath, Olivia walked toward the staircase, her sneakers squeaking against the floor. "Cora?" she called again. She didn't expect an answer, and didn't get one.

A feeling of dread crawled up her spine. Nothing about this felt right.

The stairs creaked as she made her ascent. Her heart thudded. Okay, she was just being silly. Cora obviously wasn't home. She'd probably taken her kid to the park and forgotten to lock up and the latch on the front door was defective or something. She would undoubtedly return any minute and tear into Olivia again, this time for breaking and entering.

She relaxed as she reached the top step. Nothing to worry about. That weird hum in her body didn't mean a damn thing. Cora would come back, and the two of them would straighten everything out and—

The thought died when she poked her head into the sleeping area and found Cora.

Chapter 8

Vince's cell phone went off in the middle of his fitting, startling the salt-and-pepper-haired tailor who had his hands and a measuring tape on the inseam of Vince's Armani trousers. Stifling a groan, Vince marched out of the dressing area and into the master bedroom. He'd tossed his phone on the king-size bed and it took him a second to spot the black Motorola camouflaged by the black silk sheets.

Flipping open the phone, he glanced at the display and saw the number for the guard he'd posted on Olivia. "What is it, Rocko?" he barked.

"They found the body."

Satisfaction swept through him. "When?"

"About a half hour ago. Your girl called it in."

His shoulders stiffened. "What the fuck you talking about?"

"I tailed her to Brooklyn after she left the pharmacy. She went up to Malcolm's apartment and ten minutes later the cops showed up."

"Olivia spoke to them?"

"Yes, sir. They took her statement while the coroner rolled the body out. They just finished up with her now."

His eyes narrowed. "They taking her in to the station?"

"Don't think so."

"Good. Stay on her."

"Yes, sir."

Vince disconnected the call, dialing another number as he stalked back to the dressing suite. "We're done for today, Lou," he told the little old man. "Come back Sunday to finish taking the measurements."

"Of course, Mr. Angelo." The tailor began gathering up his supplies.

Vince promptly forgot about the man and strode in the direction of his study. The room was bigger than most people's apartments, boasting a commanding desk and a big leather chair, mahogany bookshelves and a stone fireplace he could walk into without ducking. He settled behind the desk as Mikey's voice cracked in his ear.

"Yeah, boss?"

"The cops found Cora Malcolm's body. How clean was the scene?"

"Spotless."

"They'll be coming to the club." He rubbed his clean-shaven chin. "We'll play it surprised. No, we had no idea she was that deep into the shit. Suspected, but didn't know for sure."

"Got it, boss."

Vince ended the call and leaned back in the chair. He didn't look forward to the questioning, but he knew his boys at the station wouldn't give the case too much scrutiny. Just another stripper junkie losing the battle with addiction. Whole thing would blow over in a matter of days.

He did wish Olivia hadn't been the one to find the body. Clearly she hadn't bought his everything-is-fine speech. His chest went rigid as the implication sank in. She hadn't trusted him. He'd specifically told her that Cora had been handled, and she'd still gone to the bitch's apartment today.

Because she's got a good heart.

The reminder loosened his tense muscles. Yeah, perhaps he ought to cut her some slack. Olivia's heart was too big for her own good. She'd simply been making sure her friend was all right. That was the kind of woman she was, and one of the reasons he loved her so much.

Something else suddenly dawned on him. "Goddamn it," he muttered.

His girl had just seen a dead body.

The anger returned in full force, clawing at his gut like a hungry animal. Fuming, he cursed that bitch Cora. Her death was about to throw a wrench in all the careful plans he'd arranged for this evening.

Sure enough, when he dialed Olivia's cell and heard her voice, he knew making love to his woman tonight would not be on the agenda.

"Vince?" she croaked.

"Hey, babe. Just calling about tonight," he lied.

She made a sniffling sound. "Oh God, Vince. I just . . . Cora . . ."

He injected some heavy-duty worry into his voice. "Livy? What's going on? Are you okay?"

He only half listened as Olivia told him what had happened in a voice that cracked with shock and grief. She sniffled again, and his hands clenched into fists. That motherfucking Cora. Fucking bitch had reduced his woman to tears. It made him want to have her killed all over again.

"Babe," he interrupted, "calm down. Where are you now?"

"Sitting in the car."

"Can you drive home or do you need me to come and get you?"

There was a soft sob. "I can drive."

"Good. Get yourself home." Before she could respond, he added, "I'll be right there."

Olivia felt like she'd fallen through a hole into a frozen lake. Her body wouldn't stop shaking, her palms were so cold they felt like two ice cubes, and shivers kept trembling up and down her spine. She knew she was in shock, but she'd resisted when the cops who'd questioned her outside of Cora's apartment suggested she go to the hospital to get checked out. Because what, the nice people at the hospital were going to give her a prescription for grief? A drug that would erase the horrible images swarming her mind like hornets?

Her fingers trembled as she shut off the engine of the BMW. She was surprised that she'd managed to drive home, but she knew if she hadn't, Vince would have insisted on picking her up. Bad enough that he was coming over, but he'd hung up before she could protest. So now, instead of entering her building, she grabbed her purse and the pharmacy bag, got out of the car, and leaned against the hood to wait for Vince. He'd never come over to her place before, and she did *not* want him going upstairs. She didn't want him anywhere near her mother.

She rubbed her cheek where Cora had slapped it. God, why hadn't she gone after her yesterday instead of listening to Candy? Now it was too late to make amends. Too late to do a damn thing.

Cora was dead.

Overdose, the paramedics had said grimly.

Olivia blinked back tears. She kept seeing her friend lying there on the bed, one slender arm flung over the side of the mattress. The needle marks on the inside of her elbow, the bluish tinge to her pale skin. Drug paraphernalia had littered Cora's bedside table—hypodermic needles, beige powder on a crumpled piece of tinfoil, a spoon. It had been a scene right out of *Trainspotting*. A ghastly tableau starring a pretty young girl who'd always dreamed of being a lawyer.

An overdose. It still struck her as . . . wrong. Cora was a single mom, for Pete's sake. She'd had Katie at sixteen and spent the next six years working her butt off to balance job, school, and motherhood. Cora would never do drugs. She hated them, or at least that's what she'd always maintained.

But how well had Olivia really known the girl? They'd shared a few classes, sat side by side in lecture halls, crammed in Bobst Library together. ~

And they both danced at the Diamond Mine . . . where half the girls were junkies.

She wasn't a junkie.

Olivia clung to that, but the uncertainty persisted. Maybe

Cora had been shooting up for years. It wasn't like they were best friends—Cora was too busy raising a six-year-old, and Olivia had rarely spent time with her outside of work or school. She certainly hadn't told Cora about the attack in the alley, so was it unreasonable to think that maybe Cora had kept her addiction on the down low?

Oh God. Olivia couldn't stop thinking about those eyes. Those lifeless blue eyes, wide open and bloodshot.

Cora's mother was going to be devastated. And Katie. God, that little girl had just lost her mother. Luckily, Katie had been spending the afternoon with her grandmother today, according to the officer who'd gotten in touch with Cora's mom. And Olivia had no idea where Katie's father fit into the equation. From the meager details Cora had provided, she knew the guy had left after Cora got pregnant at sixteen and hadn't been heard from since.

The purr of an engine caught her attention. She turned her head and saw a Lincoln Town Car pull into the parking lot. The windows were tinted, but she could make out Vince's driver, Paul, through the windshield.

Her "boyfriend" had come to "comfort" her.

Olivia gathered her composure as the back door opened and Vince slid out from the leather interior. He wore his trademark black pin-striped suit, this one paired with a wine-colored dress shirt and burgundy alligator loafers that probably cost more than her tuition. His dark eyes softened at the sight of her, his full lips pursing in concern.

"C'mere" was all he said.

Stifling a sigh, she walked into his outstretched arms and let him embrace her. Vince cooed unintelligible bullshit in her ears as he held her, stroking her hair, rubbing the small of her back. Her body felt cold again, but for a different reason now.

"Oh, Jesus, you're freezing, babe." He grasped her hand and ushered her toward the Town Car. "Let's sit in here. C'mon, Livy."

They settled in the backseat. Olivia inhaled the scent of his overbearing cologne, a pungent, spicy odor that permeated the car. She tried not to breathe, but then he moved closer and it was all she could smell.

Vince cupped her chin with his palms. "I'm sorry you had to go through that."

Tears pricked her eyelids. "I still can't believe it."

"Me too. I mean, I had no idea she was shooting that shit. You think you know someone . . ." Vince shrugged. "This really screws up our anniversary plans, doesn't it?"

The annoyed glint in his eyes said she hadn't misheard him. Unbelievable. One of his dancers had *died* and he was ticked off that it put a damper on his *dinner* plans?

Olivia almost gagged—until his exact wording registered in her brain. Wait, was she getting a reprieve? Relief exploded in her chest, then fizzled when she realized she was getting ahead of herself. He hadn't conclusively said the happy celebration was being postponed . . .

With a stroke of inspiration, she looked up at him, doe-eyed. "I think we should celebrate another night, Vince."

A muscle twitched in his jaw. "I figured you'd say that."

"It's just . . . If I give myself to you tonight, I'll see her face the entire time." She blinked again, letting the tears fall, then blinked harder so they'd stream down her cheeks. "That's not fair to you, and it's not fair to Cora's memory. I need . . . I need to mourn her. She deserves that."

She was laying it on pretty thick and feared he'd see right through it, but to her surprise, he chuckled softly. "Remind me to introduce you to my *nona*. That woman still mourns my grandfather and he's been dead ten years." He leaned in to kiss her. "You won't make me wait ten years, will you, babe?"

"Never," she whispered, resisting the urge to wipe her mouth with her sleeve to erase the taste of him.

Vince seemed pleased by her answer. "Do you want me to stick around? I have a meeting, but I can cancel if you'd like me to stay."

"No." She spoke a little too quickly. When his eyes flashed, she hurried on. "I think I want to lie down for the rest of the evening. This is . . . it's too much to absorb, you know?"

His features relaxed. "I understand." He slid over to open the door. The gold ruby-studded ring on his fourth finger winked as the afternoon sun streamed into the backseat. "I'll walk you up."

"You don't have—"

He silenced her with a hard kiss. "I don't *have* to do anything. I *want* to make sure my girl gets upstairs all right."

Olivia got out of the car without argument.

Vince kept a possessive hand on her shoulder the entire time, and although she wanted to object, he escorted her up the three flights of stairs and didn't release his grip until she'd opened her front door. With a tender expression, he bent down and kissed her again, this time dragging his tongue over her lower lip before pulling back.

"Get some rest, my love."

Olivia let out a breath of relief after he was gone, but the second she entered the apartment she realized she'd forgotten her purse and her mother's prescription in Vince's car. Damn it.

Gritting her teeth, she dashed out into the hallway and glimpsed Vince's retreating back at the top of the stairs. His heavy footsteps thudded as he made his way down. She was about to call after him but the sound of his voice stopped her. His irritated words echoed from the stairwell.

"Yeah, it's taken care of."

She instinctively closed her mouth. Judging by the long pause before he spoke again, he was on the phone.

"Nah, it can't be tied back to the club," he said after a moment.

Unable to stop herself, Olivia crept down the corridor. At the landing, she kicked off her sneakers, then continued barefoot down the stairs, her pulse quickening as Vince's voice reverberated in the stairwell.

"The bitch was going to the cops—what other choice did we have? Yeah . . . whatever . . . I don't give a shit what De

Luca says about it. He's the one who keeps demanding my girls fuck his associates. The bitch wasn't into it."

Olivia felt all the blood drain out of her face.

A smug note entered his smooth voice. "It was an overdose. No one's gonna question it." A pause. "How about this, motherfucker—you worry about the shipment, I'll worry about my bitches . . . What? I don't give a damn . . . There's a lot of money riding on this deal. Take care of it."

Silence. Then a muffled curse as he hung up the phone.

Olivia halted, sagging against the cement wall. She suddenly felt light-headed, shock and horror coursing through her body, her heart beating dangerously fast. When she heard a door slam below, she jumped, startled out of her paralysis. Damn hands were trembling again, but she managed to fumble in the pocket of her coat for her cell phone. She nearly dropped the thing, then took a breath to steady herself and dialed Vince's number.

"You okay, babe?" he barked into her ear.

She swallowed. "I'm fine. I just realized I left my purse and prescription in your car."

"Good thing you caught me—I'll have Paul bring your stuff up." He sounded like he didn't have a care in the world. Like he hadn't just confessed to *murder* in her fucking stairwell.

"Thanks." She hung up before he could say another word. The sound of his voice had made her stomach churn, and she was precariously close to throwing up. Or worse, passing out.

Breathing deeply, she hurried back upstairs and waited outside the apartment door. A minute later, Vince's driver appeared, her purse and shopping bag dangling from his meaty hand. She forced a polite smile as he handed her the items, waited for him to leave, then whirled around and flew into the apartment. She couldn't control the persistent pounding of her heart, the clammy fingers of shock clawing up her spine.

She shut the door. The phone fell from her grip and clattered onto the faded blue carpet in the minuscule front hallway.

Black dots swam in front of her eyes, causing her to sink down to the carpet. She rested her head between her knees. Desperately tried to calm down. She couldn't pass out. She couldn't fall apart.

Oh God, Cora's *eyes*.

Gasping for air, Olivia curled her hands into fists and slammed them on the floor. *Get it together. Pull yourself together.*

Okay. Okay, she could do this. Sucking in a deep breath, she willed her heart to beat at a regular pace. Banished the panic constricting her chest. Forcibly pushed the memory of Cora's lifeless body from her mind.

And then she grabbed the phone she'd dropped and dialed the number she'd been ordered to memorize.

Luke was taking a catnap in the guest room when his phone rang. Eyes snapping open, he lunged for the phone, the way he'd been lunging every time the damn thing went off. Except this time, the number on the caller ID didn't belong to Trevor or any of the other guys.

Feeling a flicker of hope, he pressed a button and brought the phone to his ear with a quick "Yeah?"

A tiny pause. Then, "Luke?"

Relief spilled through him at the sound of her throaty voice. He'd been starting to think she wouldn't call, that his hurried explanation during their last encounter hadn't been enough. Hell, he'd seen the doubt and suspicion flashing in her green eyes. She hadn't believed or trusted him.

But she'd called.

"Olivia?"

"Yes, ah, it's me. I . . . Is the offer still on the table? You helping me, I mean?"

He instantly picked up on the desperate pitch of her tone. "Are you all right?"

"I'm fine." An anguished breath filled the line. "Actually, no. No, I'm not fine. I'm *so* not fine."

"Tell me what happened."

Silence greeted his ear. It lasted so long he thought she'd

hung up, but when he pulled the phone back and looked at the screen, the seconds were still ticking away on the display. "Olivia?"

"Cora's dead."

Luke's shoulders tensed. "What?"

"Cora. She's . . . She works at the club with me. She's one of the other dancers. No, she's more than that. She's — *was* — my friend. And she's dead. I found her body an hour ago."

He remembered Isabel's insistence that they check out Cora Malcolm, her claim that something fucked up was going on at the Diamond. Looked like she'd hit the nail on the head with that one.

"How did she die, Olivia?" he asked gently.

"The cops said it was an overdose. God, her face . . . and her eyes . . ." Her voice shook. "He did it. Vince did it."

Luke froze. "What are you talking about?"

"I heard him. He said it was taken care of. He had her killed." Olivia made a tortured sound, then began talking so fast he could barely keep up. "He was making her sleep with customers and she must have refused. Yesterday she told me she was going to the cops, but I didn't know why, but now I know, and I feel sick. He had her *killed*."

"Olivia. Calm down, darlin'."

He heard a sharp inhale on the other end, followed by a ragged exhale. "I'm sorry. I just can't . . . I can't stop thinking about her eyes. Cora has a little girl, Luke. Katie. She's only six years old and now . . . now . . ." Abruptly, her tone changed, hardened. "I shouldn't have called. I don't know what I was thinking. If Vince finds out—"

"Do *not* hang up. I'm glad you called, okay? I'm really fucking glad you called." He hesitated. "If what you're saying is true, then you're in danger. Does Angelo know you overheard him?"

"No. No, he didn't see me."

"Good." His grip tightened on the phone. "We need to meet. We need to talk face-to-face."

"We can't," she whispered. "I think he's having me watched."

"He is," Luke confirmed. "Where are you now?"

"At home."

"Good, that's good. I can be at your place in twenty."

"But—"

"Angelo's man won't see me," he assured her. "I can get into the building, no prob—"

"No," she interrupted. "My mother is home. She can't be around for this. I can't involve her in this."

Shit. He scanned his brain for another option and came up short. "All right. I won't come to you. We'll figure out an alternative. I'll call you back, okay? I'm going to talk to my team and I'll call you right back."

Silence.

"Olivia?"

"I'm here," she whispered.

"Stay put, darlin'. I promise you, I'm going to help you."

He hung up without a good-bye, then sprinted into the main room. Trevor and Sully were sprawled on the leather couches, watching the Giants clean up the field with the Eagles on ESPN, while D stood by the sliding door smoking a cigarette. Holden was the only one monitoring the Diamond at the moment; now that they'd determined Carter Dane had probably been taken captive, they'd eased up on the club surveillance.

"Olivia called," Luke announced. "We're meeting with her."

Everyone snapped to attention. "Her apartment?" Trevor asked.

"No. She lives with her mother, doesn't want her involved. It has to be somewhere else."

"And how do we know this isn't a trap?" D spoke up, his tone laced with irritation. "How do we know she didn't tell Angelo what you two talked about last night?"

"Because Angelo just offed her friend."

Every eyebrow in the room shot north.

"Cora Malcolm is dead," Luke said grimly. "Olivia found the body, and then she overheard Angelo say he's the one who took care of the girl. Now she's scared shitless. We need to bring her in but Angelo's got one of his goons watching her. Once she steps out the door, the man will follow her." He paused in thought. "We need to get her somewhere private, maybe get a decoy in place—" Isabel. They could use Isabel.

Trevor must have read his mind. "Already on it," the team leader said, reaching for his phone.

Thirty minutes after speaking to Luke, Olivia left her building and stepped onto the concrete stoop, making a conscious effort not to give her surroundings much inspection. But as she descended the steps, the nape of her neck tingled, which told her that Vince's thug was nearby. On the sidewalk, she pulled up the hood of her sweatshirt but didn't tuck her hair into it. Luke had ordered her to wear a red sweatshirt, blue jeans, and white sneakers, and he'd stressed that her hair needed to be loose. She adjusted the hood so that her long brown tresses were visibly hanging out, then shoved her hands in the front pocket of the sweatshirt and started to walk.

Her legs felt like Jell-O, her heartbeat was erratic, and no matter how many times she tried reassuring herself that everything would be okay, she was still a bundle of nerves.

Cora was dead.

No, Cora had been *murdered*.

As her pulse took off in another irregular gallop, she swallowed hard and forced her legs to move. Luke had sounded so confident on the phone, so sure that this meeting would go off without a hitch, but she refused to underestimate Vince. He might be a sleazebag, but he was smart.

On a whim, she came to a halt by a bus shelter and sent Vince a quick text message. *Going to light a candle for Cora. Will be home in a few hours.* Short and sweet. She pressed SEND, then resumed walking, annoyed that she was checking in like some clingy girlfriend. But she knew Vince would appreciate the gesture—and it would get him off her back, give her a reason not to answer if he called.

Her hands began to shake, so she laced her fingers together, keeping her head low as she sidestepped a businessman talking loudly into his cell phone. It took three blocks to reach her destination, and when she finally approached the huge granite steps of St. Mary's church, she was starting to reconsider this entire thing.

Could she trust Luke? *Should* she?

Hearing Vince speaking so casually about Cora's death, listening to him admit he'd arranged it . . . it had sent a blast of fear straight to her bones. Her first instinct had been to call Luke, and when his husky voice had filled the line, the urge to confide in him, to trust him, had been so strong.

But what if her instincts had led her astray? Luke Dubois had already lied to her once. He'd pretended to be just some guy curious about lap dances. What if he was still pretending? Making her think he'd help her, only to sell her out to Vince?

You can still turn back.

She stared at the towering red doors of the church. Swallowed again. Then she remembered Cora's overdosed body on that bed, pictured the big blue eyes of Cora's little girl, now an *orphan*. And she firmly pushed down on the door handle.

She hadn't been inside a church since she was a kid, back when her mother had been teaching at St. Matthew's Catholic Academy. Back when her mother had been healthy.

Now here she was, surrounded by endless rows of glossy brown pews. Statues of Jesus and Mary graced the space, and across the room a majestic altar sat on a raised platform in front of an ethereal wall of stained glass. Looking around, she couldn't help but remember all those times she'd begged God to help her mom. She'd thought her prayers had been answered after the first remission. After the second one, her faith had taken a hit. By the third, she'd given up on the divine.

Choking down her bitterness, she headed toward the confessional booths. A narrow doorway stood to the right of the confessionals, and though there were no signs warding her off, she felt as if she was trespassing as she moved across the threshold. She kept expecting a priest to pop up and reprimand her, but the corridor was as quiet as the rest of the church. She followed it to its end, turned right, as Luke had instructed, and walked until she spotted the emergency door he'd indicated would be there.

She glanced around to make sure nobody was in sight, then pushed the door open. She emerged in the back alley between the church and the chain-link fence that bordered the elementary school in the distance. Just as Luke had promised, a black Range Rover awaited her in the alley.

Heart thudding, Olivia rounded the vehicle and slid into the passenger seat.

Luke sat behind the wheel, and the rush of relief that flooded her body had her sagging forward. He instantly reached out and touched her shoulder. "You okay?"

She shook her head as she met his eyes. He looked calmer than ever, all business in his olive green cargo pants and black bomber jacket. His dark hair fell onto his forehead as he leaned toward her, his expression shining with gentle reassurance.

"I know you're scared, darlin', but just take a deep breath. You look like you're about to pass out."

He was right. She was dizzy as hell. As she drew much-needed oxygen into her lungs, his scent filled her nose. Subtle aftershave and masculine spice. Nothing like the overpowering stench of Vince's Obsession for Men, or whatever the hell he used. At the thought of Vince, her breathing went off-kilter once more, and she had to start again. Long inhale, slow exhale.

After most of her panic had dispersed, she sought out Luke's gaze. "Feel better?" he asked gruffly.

She managed a nod.

As Luke shifted gears, she shot an alarmed look at the back door of the church. "What if the man who's following me goes inside and sees I'm not there?"

"But you are there," Luke said lightly. "Trust me, it's taken care of."

Again with that *trust me*. But why should she? She had no idea who this man really was, and although a thousand questions ran through her mind, she couldn't get her vocal cords to function properly. Instead, she leaned back and closed her eyes, thinking of her friend's dead body in that loft. Luke must have sensed she was too overwrought to talk, because he didn't say a word as they drove away. At one point she opened her eyes and noticed they were heading west, nearing Broadway, and then her lids fell shut again and she continued with the deep breathing. Everything was going to be fine. She would tell Luke everything, and he would help her.

God, he *had* to help her. Because she simply couldn't stomach the idea of returning to the club tomorrow night and seeing Vince. Looking into his eyes, all the while knowing he'd had Cora killed.

When the car finally came to a stop, Olivia saw that they were in an underground parking garage. Her legs felt weak as she stepped out of the vehicle and breathed in the odor of motor oil and car exhaust hanging in the cavernous space.

"Elevator's this way," Luke said quietly, holding out his hand.

After a second's hesitation, she took it, and the warmth of his fingers spread into her cold flesh. She gripped his hand as if it were a life preserver, following him toward a door at the far end of the parking garage. They stepped through it, then into the elevator in the fluorescent-lit space. Without letting go of her hand, he pressed the button for the third floor.

They rode up in silence. When the doors dinged open, Luke led her down a carpeted hallway. He kept his hand on her shoulder the entire time, just as Vince had done earlier, only Luke's touch was soothing rather than suffocating. Strong but gentle.

"Everyone's inside," he told her as he opened the door and gestured for her to enter.

Olivia was taken aback by the luxurious surroundings. The apartment offered endless ceilings and huge windows with a breathtaking view of the city skyline. There was a gourmet kitchen to the left, featuring granite counters, stainless-steel appliances, and frosted tiles. It spilled out to a dining area with a mahogany table that seemed big enough to seat thirty, and a living area with L-shaped leather couches, an array of stuffed armchairs, and a humongous flat-screen TV screwed into one of the walls. The place was incredible, ten times the size of her apartment and most certainly expensive. The cost of it would probably make her faint.

A handsome dark-haired man wearing gray trousers and a black turtleneck sat in one of the armchairs. On the couch was a second, equally handsome man in faded jeans and a white wife-beater, running a big hand over his close-cropped blond hair. A third male loitered by a door leading out to a massive brick terrace—he was smoking a cigarette, his broad back all she could see.

Wary, she looked from Luke to the others, then started noticing a bunch of other details. Like the butt of a weapon poking out from the smoker's waistband. The collection of handguns on the coffee table. The fact that none of these men wore badges or resembled law enforcement personnel in any way.

Fear shivered up her spine. Had coming here been a mistake? She'd naively assumed that Luke was a cop, or an undercover agent, or at the very least military, but even though he moved like a soldier, she didn't get an official feeling about any of this. Especially when the man at the terrace door turned around, and she found herself staring into a pair of coal black eyes that glittered with danger.

"Who are you people?" she blurted out.

Luke wasn't surprised that the sight of D succeeded in wiping away all the color on Olivia's cheeks. With that cold gaze and predatory way of moving, Derek Pratt was capable of scaring anybody shitless, even people who knew him. It didn't help that the massive arms coming out of his black muscle shirt were covered in tats. The guy was a head-to-toe menace, and Luke instinctively stepped closer to Olivia in a protective move.

But hell, she seemed to need it. Wound tighter than a drum, her long slender body radiating fear. When he'd seen her back at the church, the look in her eyes had nearly done him in. Frightened, shocked, and bewildered. Just like she was now.

Actually, add *suspicious as hell* to that list, which was evident when she spun around to meet his eyes. "You guys aren't cops, are you?"

"No."

"Military?"

"Most of us are former military."

"What the hell does that mean?"

And oh yeah, the color returned to her face, staining her silky cheeks rosy red. Despite her I-want-answers-*now* glare, she was still a fucking knockout. Those incredible green eyes, cosmetic-model cheekbones, lush mouth. Even her dark brown eyebrows were stunning, thanks to that graceful arch of theirs.

Across the room, Trevor rose from the armchair and headed toward them. "We're private contractors," he explained. "I'm Trevor."

Olivia stared at Trev's outstretched hand before leaning forward to shake it. "Private contractors," she echoed dully. "Soldiers for hire?"

Trevor nodded, then gestured to the others. "Blondie over there is Sullivan, and the mean-looking one is D. And Luke you know, of course. Come on, sit down. You look like you're about to collapse."

Moving as if she was in a daze, Olivia allowed Trevor to lead her to the couch, where she flopped down next to Sullivan. Luke bit back a burst of annoyance, but the fact that she'd accepted Trevor's suggestion to sit without so much as a protest bugged him. Or maybe it was the way she'd relaxed at the sound of the other man's voice.

When his chest got hot and tight, he realized he was actually jealous. The entire ride over here, Olivia had been tense as shit, her expression blank, her fists pressed into her knees. But now, a couple of words from Callaghan, and she calmed down. Then again, he'd seen it happen before. Trev might not lay it on thick the way Luke or Sully did when it came to females, but the man exuded a quiet strength that women went wild for.

Luke's spine went rigid. Well, fuck that. For some reason, he felt possessive about this woman, and he didn't want anyone but him reassuring her.

Striding toward the couch, he shot Sullivan a look that said, *Go sit somewhere else.* The Australian raised a brow but got up without a word.

Luke promptly claimed the seat. "Tell us exactly what went down today," he told Olivia.

She shifted, angling herself so that she was facing him as well as the others. "Last night one of the dancers... Cora..." Pain flashed through her eyes. "She showed up at the club and pretty much freaked out at me. She implied that Vince had made her do something, something awful, but she stormed out before I could get any answers. So today... I went over to her loft to check on her, to see if she was okay..." She trailed off, shaking her head in distress.

"And you found her body." Trevor filled in the rest of her sentence.

Olivia turned toward his voice, giving a small nod. "The paramedics said it was an overdose. Heroin. But Cora never used drugs... She hated them... She... God, it didn't make any sense. But then Vince came by to comfort me—"

That stupid streak of jealousy reappeared. Damn it, he didn't like the idea of her with Angelo. Ever since he'd seen her dance that first time, he'd started to think of Olivia Taylor as *his.* Total caveman bullshit right there, but he couldn't help it. And he didn't like it.

When he realized Olivia was still talking, he forced his head back into the game. "He said it was taken care of, and something about Cora not being into it, and—"

Trevor interrupted by holding up his hand. "Let's slow down. Tell us his exact words, as much as you can remember."

She released a shaky breath. "He was telling someone

that *it*—I'm assuming he meant Cora's death—was taken care of, and that it wouldn't be tied back to the club." She paused in thought. "He said they didn't have a choice because Cora was going to the cops, and then he mentioned a name . . . De something . . . De Luca."

Luke exchanged a quick glance with the others, who were all frowning.

"You sure it was De Luca?" Trevor spoke up.

"Yeah, that was definitely it. Vince said that he didn't care what De Luca thought about it because De Luca's the one"—her voice cracked—"who asks Vince to send him girls. So that . . . so that his associates can . . . have sex with them."

She fell silent, torment etched into her features.

"Anything else?" D barked. His tone was far from gentle. Or understanding.

Olivia flinched at the harsh demand. "Ah, something about a shipment. He said there was a lot of money riding on it, and he told the person on the other end to worry about the shipment, and said that he would worry about his . . . his bitches."

Now her face was overcome with shame. Was that how she viewed herself? As another one of Angelo's bitches? For some messed-up reason, Luke felt the impulse to yank her into his arms and stroke her hair or some shit, but he rooted himself to the couch.

"So . . . what do I do now?"

Her voice sounded so small and forlorn that Luke's heart squeezed. Fuck it. Without looking at the others, he took Olivia's hand and gripped it tightly. "Now you tell us how you got tangled up with Angelo in the first place." He hesitated. "Angelo killed the customer who attacked you, didn't he?"

Her mouth fell open. "What? No. *I* did."

Chapter 9

Luke's eyebrows shot up as Olivia's confession hung in the air. "*You* killed him?"

She nodded, looking more than a little stricken.

As surprise continued to ripple through him, he exchanged a look with Trevor, who looked equally startled. So much for their theory about Angelo murdering a man for Olivia.

"Do you want to tell us what happened that night?" he asked, injecting some gentleness in his voice.

After a second of reluctance, Olivia released a ragged breath. "I was leaving the club after my shift. It was late, and one of the bouncers offered to walk me to my car, but I foolishly said no. There weren't any PCs that night—"

"PCs?" Trevor cut in, wrinkling his brow.

"Problem customers," she clarified. "It was a pretty tame night, and I thought I'd be fine. I had my whistle on me—every dancer at the Diamond has one. The girls call it a rape whistle. But it didn't do a lick of good when I got jumped from behind. I dropped the whistle, and the next thing I knew, this man was dragging me into the alley next to the club."

Luke's gut flooded with anger. "Did you know the guy?"

She gave a quick nod. "I recognized him from the club. He would come in a few times a week, but he never caused any problems or raised any red flags."

From his spot by the door, D spoke up in a bored voice. "What happened in the alley?"

Olivia's voice wavered. "He had a knife, and he . . . tried to rape me. I was struggling, fighting back, but that only made him angrier, so eventually I quit fighting and pretended to surrender. That made him happy." Her lips tightened. "He said as a reward for my submission, he'd be gentle."

Luke resisted the urge to slam his fist through the wall.

"So I waited for him to"—she looked uncomfortable—"unzip his pants, and while he was, um, you know, pulling it out, I made a grab for the knife. I only managed to nick him before he batted the knife out of my hand, and that just infuriated him even more. He . . . beat me. Pretty fucking badly. I don't know how I was able to stay conscious, but I did, and while he was pounding at me with his fists, I got hold of the knife again." Now her voice steadied, growing hard. "I stabbed him. In the throat."

Silence crashed over the room.

Well, damn. Pride welled up in Luke's chest, along with a sick sense of satisfaction that the man who'd tried to hurt Olivia had paid for it. Dearly.

As he glanced at the others, he noticed that Trevor and Sullivan looked as gratified as he felt and were nodding their approval. Hell, even D looked impressed.

"What happened afterward?" Luke asked.

She hesitated, but when he gave her hand a gentle squeeze, her posture relaxed, her mouth opened, and a whole lot of details came spilling out.

She told them about how Angelo and his guards had come to her rescue, how they'd dumped the body of the man she'd killed, took care of the cops while she was in the hospital. By the time she finished explaining how she'd ended up in Angelo's clutches, Luke was ready to clock something. Sully and Trevor didn't look pleased either, donning matching scowls when Olivia described waking up at St. Francis two days after the attack to find Angelo at her bedside. Telling her he owned her now.

Owned her. Like she was a piece of prime real estate, or another one of his expensive suits. Classic case of abuse, right down to the characteristics she described. Angelo's control, his sick sense of entitlement, the superiority complex and possessiveness.

"Did he ever hit you?" Sullivan asked carefully.

She started to shake her head, but then a resigned light entered her eyes. "Once when I insisted I could pay my own tuition, and another time because I made him look bad in front of a customer by refusing to do a private dance."

Outrage bubbled in Luke's gut, congealing into hard knots. The thought of Vince Angelo laying a hand on this woman made him want to grab that Glock from the coffee table and empty a clip into Angelo's chest. Violence against women had always made him see red, ever since his sister, Ellen, had wound up in an abusive relationship that lasted for years. But Ellen had gotten out of that hellhole with the help of her family. Olivia was still living in hers.

"Why didn't you skip town?"

D's cold inquiry hung in the air, bringing another flicker of sorrow to Olivia's eyes.

"My mom was sick," she said softly. "I couldn't leave her, and she was in no condition to be uprooted. Money is an issue too. I can barely afford two train tickets, let alone a new apartment, Mom's medication . . ." She swallowed hard. "I thought we'd have a better chance at starting fresh if I got my degree. That way I could land a higher-paying job. And I've been saving money the past six months . . ." She trailed off.

Luke didn't like the defeated look on her face. Leaning closer, he searched her eyes and asked, "Do you want this son of a bitch out of your life?"

She nodded.

"Then he'll be out of your life. We'll make sure of it." Probably presumptuous, throwing the *we* in there, but he'd seen Trevor's and Sully's expressions during Olivia's story, and knew they'd be on board. As for D, well—

"And you'll return the favor," came D's raspy voice,

which only confirmed Luke's thoughts. D wouldn't do a damn thing without getting something back from Olivia.

She looked over at D. "What does that mean?"

Trevor quickly took control of the conversation before D could respond with some tactless comment. "Here's the thing, Olivia," he said gently. "We need your help too."

She shifted warily. "To do what?"

"We were hired to find someone. An undercover agent who went missing two months ago. Sully, grab me that pic of Dane."

Sullivan headed for the kitchen counter and rummaged around in the file folder sitting on it. He extracted a photograph, then walked over to hand Olivia the photo.

Luke instantly saw the recognition dawn in her eyes. "You know him?" he said sharply.

"That's Kyle. Kyle . . . I can't remember his last name, it started with a B, I think." She stared at Carter Dane's average features and short black hair. "He came to the club a lot, usually hung out in Vince's office or the VIP lounge. Vince said Kyle was a business associate."

"He's DEA," Trevor revealed. "When was the last time you saw him?"

She mulled it over. "I guess . . . it's been a while actually. He could have showed up on my days off or when I was in the dressing room, but it's definitely been a couple of months since I saw him." Her gaze landed on the photo again, and her sensual mouth twisted in a frown. "You want me to help you find him."

"Yes," Luke said simply.

The frown deepened, almost a scowl now. Her shoulders stiffened, then sagged. "Of course you do. Nothing comes free, does it?"

She spoke in a flat tone, as if she truly believed that people weren't capable of helping each other out of the goodness of their hearts. He supposed he didn't blame her. Vince Angelo hadn't helped her out of kindness—he'd done it so she'd be indebted to him. And those doctors who'd treated her mother's cancer, maybe they'd been genuinely happy to do it, but at the end of those treatments there'd still been a price tag.

Everything about Olivia's body language communicated weariness, from the way she hung her head as if her neck could no longer support it to the way she unclasped her hands and let them fall to her sides. But then she surprised him. Rather than tell them to go to hell, she lifted her head and focused on Trevor. "What do I have to do?"

Luke answered for the team leader. "Dig. Use your connection to Angelo."

"Get into his office and snoop around," Trevor added. "See if you can find anything relating to Carter Dane—a location, a lead, anything that might help us find him."

"There are cameras in Vince's office," Olivia pointed out.

"If you can get in, they'll be taken care of," Luke answered.

Her eyebrows lifted in challenge. "If it's so easy, why don't you go in yourself?"

"Because if it all goes south, it'll be hard to explain away my presence. Or it could turn into a gunfight or something equally unproductive. The last thing we want to do is alert Angelo that he's being watched. We'll come up with a reasonable explanation that you can use if you're ever caught upstairs."

When she nodded in resignation, he reached for her hand, and found her fingers cold and shaky. "We won't risk putting a wire on you, but we'll get you a secure phone," he assured her. "You'll stay in contact with us, and anytime you're in the club, we'll be right outside, ready to storm the place if you say the word."

He moved his thumb in a soothing motion around the center of her palm. "You won't be alone, darlin'. And if you do this, you'll be helping us put Angelo out of commission once and for all. He'll never hurt you or any of the other girls again."

That got her attention. The steel that entered her gorgeous green eyes brought another spark of pride. He remembered her saying how she wasn't half as strong as her mother, but clearly that was bullshit. Olivia Taylor might not be battling cancer, but she'd been living in her own personal hell for a long time now, suffering right along with her mom. Even now, with that son of a bitch Angelo and his obsession to contend with, she was still holding her ground, refusing to be knocked down.

Damned if that wasn't sexy.

"When's your next shift?" Trevor asked.

"Tomorrow night. Oh, and Vince won't be there. He meets his investors every Fri—" She stopped, bitterness washing over her face. "Well, the investors thing is probably a lie. I don't know who he meets, but I do know he won't be there tomorrow."

"Good. That's good." Trevor checked his watch. "We need to wrap this up and get you back to the church before Angelo's goon gets suspicious."

"How will I get in touch with you?"

When Luke noticed she was looking at him and not Trev, warmth spread through his body. "We'll work it out, find a way to get you that phone. Don't worry, we'll come up with some kind of system. But Trevor's right, you've gotta go back now."

"Can I use your restroom before we go?"

"Of course."

As Olivia stood up, D took several menacing steps toward her. Luke shot to his feet, but the other man didn't get too close, halting when he and Olivia were about six feet apart.

"Have you fucked him?" D asked with his typical callousness.

She faltered. "Wh-what?"

Now the guy just sounded annoyed. "Have you fucked Angelo?"

"No."

Although D's totally inappropriate line of questioning ticked him off, Luke couldn't help letting out a breath of relief.

"Will you do it if it's the only way to get information?"

Luke's head snapped in D's direction. "For Christ's sake, man—"

"No," Olivia cut in, her tone as sharp as a blade. "I won't."

D shook his head. "Let's hope it doesn't come to that, then. Otherwise you'll be pretty fucking useless to us."

Olivia's green eyes burned. "Where. Is. The. Restroom."

Sullivan spoke up. "Down the hall, first door on the left."

Without a word, she spun around and disappeared into the corridor.

Setting his jaw, Luke turned to D and said, "You're a real asshole, you know that?"

The other man shrugged. "Just wanted to know how far our new operative will go to complete her mission."

Surprisingly, Sullivan was first to respond. "You didn't have to be such a jerk to her, mate. She's been through a lot."

"And this isn't her mission," Luke reminded him. "In fact, I feel like a total shit telling her we'll only help her if she helps us. If it were up to me—"

"You'd be playing hero and saving our little damsel," D finished, equally cold.

Luke advanced on D, going nose to nose with the guy. D stared him down. The angry throb of his pulse made it look like the red and black snake circling his neck was undulating, pulsating.

"What the fuck is with you?" Luke demanded. "I know you're a surly son of a bitch, but lately you've been a straight-up pain in the ass."

"Give it a rest." Trevor came out of nowhere and shoved himself between the two men. Planting a hand on D's chest, he gave their resident asshole a firm push and said, "Go take a walk."

D raised his dark brows. "You giving me a time-out, sir?"

"You bet your ass I am. Now go."

A second. Two. And then D marched out of the apartment without a backward glance.

"Shit," Trevor said softly.

"Shit is right," Sullivan concurred.

"I'll talk to Morgan about it."

Luke shook his head, half bewildered, half pissed the fuck off. He had no clue what was up D's ass, but right now he didn't care. They had more important things to worry about—and with that thought, he realized Olivia had been in the bathroom for way too long. Sighing, he stepped toward the corridor and said, "I'm going to check on her."

When he reached the door, he heard the sound of running water. He figured she was washing her hands, but the water kept flowing. And flowing. Frowning, he rapped his knuckles against the door. "Olivia? It's me. Open up."

After a long delay, the door creaked open. He took one look at her face and pushed his way into the washroom, firmly closing the door behind him. Olivia's cheeks were stained with tears, which she swiped at with the sleeve of her red sweatshirt as if trying to destroy the evidence.

"Look," he said brusquely, "ignore D, okay? He's not exactly Mr. Social, and everything he said was out of line."

When he reached out for her, she backed up until her hip bumped into the porcelain sink. "This isn't about your friend," she choked out. "I'm just . . . the sex thing . . . God, I'm scared I might actually have to do it."

Luke moved forward and planted both hands on her slender hips before she could wiggle away. "Nobody is asking you to sleep with that bastard."

Her expression exhibited a whole lot of misery. "Vince is. And he's not asking. He's expecting." An incredulous laugh popped out of her mouth. "He wanted to do it tonight. He says it's our anniversary. But Cora screwed everything up for him by dying. You should have seen how annoyed he looked that our special evening was ruined."

He slid one hand up to her face and touched her cheek, rubbing his thumb over her damp skin. "How have you managed to avoid it so far? The sex thing, I mean."

Another laugh, this one bordering on hysterical. "I told him I was a virgin and that I was saving myself for the man I married."

Luke couldn't help but feel proud. "Smart."

"Not smart enough." Her gaze darkened. "He's getting impatient, and the marriage thing doesn't seem to matter anymore. He was ready to screw me tonight, married or not." When Luke stroked her cheek again, she leaned into his touch. "I don't know how much longer I can hold him off. I don't know how much more I can take."

Since she wasn't balking at the physical contact, he took a chance and pulled her into his arms. She stiffened, then sank into the embrace. The top of her head reached his chin, which was a nice feeling. At six-two, he usually towered over women, but Olivia was tall herself. They fit well together, and he liked the feel of her warm, willowy body against his.

Lecherous bastard that he was, he found himself getting hard, an erection thickening and straining against his zipper. He tried shifting away, but Olivia must have picked up on his body's transformation because she suddenly gazed up at him, her lips parted in surprise.

"Sorry," he said gruffly. "Close quarters, beautiful woman pressed against me. My body is confused."

A shadow of a smile lifted the corner of her mouth. "I appreciate the honesty."

"Yeah? 'Cause it usually gets me into trouble."

She tilted her head to meet his eyes. "Thank you, by the way."

"For what?"

"I was pretty much falling apart earlier. Finding Cora, realizing Vince did that to her . . . I was a mess. And then I called you, and I felt . . . better. Safer."

She swept her tongue over her lower lip, probably just to moisten her dry mouth, but God help him, he grew even more aroused. His hands, of their own volition, caressed the small of her back.

Her breath hitched. "Luke . . ." There was a chord of uncertainty in her voice.

His hands froze. "I'm sorry. I didn't mean to—"

"No, it's okay, I—"

"I really want to kiss you right now."

She blinked. "What?"

He backpedaled as fast as he could. "Sorry, it just came out. Sometimes I forget there's this brain-to-mouth filter that—"

Her mouth slammed into his.

Holy fuck.

She was kissing him, full-on mouth-to-mouth, her tongue sliding through his surprised lips and robbing him of breath. Despite the shock reeling through him, his male instincts snapped into action—hands slid down to cup her bottom, tongue thrust out to tangle with hers. The kiss was deep and forceful, all sex and desperation without an ounce of tenderness. Olivia's hands clawed at the front of his shirt, bunching up the material as she stood on her tiptoes and molded her lips to his.

It ended as quickly as it had begun. He was drowning in the sweet taste of her one second, watching her back away from him the next. Her cheeks were flushed, her chest heaving as she took a breath, and when their eyes met, she looked startled. And aroused.

"I didn't mean to do that," she murmured.

He had to grin. "I'm not complaining."

An expression he couldn't decipher flitted across her face. It might have been disappointment, but that didn't make sense considering she was the one who broke that ridiculously hot kiss.

"We should go," she said, taking a step to the door. "I've already been gone long enough."

Trevor watched as Olivia darted toward the back door of St. Mary's, her red sweatshirt and dark hair disappearing through the doorway. She hadn't said much during the drive over, probably because she'd been expecting Luke to be with her, and not some man she'd just met. And yeah, he probably should've let Luke play chauffeur—the guy hadn't been thrilled to be sidelined—but Trevor couldn't pass up this opportunity. Call him a loser, but he wanted to see Isabel again, even if it was only for a quick briefing.

The back door swung open once more, and for a second Trevor thought Olivia had returned. Then he blinked, and realized he was looking at Isabel. As they'd arranged, she wore a red hoodie, blue jeans, and a pair of white sneakers. Hair the same shade as Olivia's chestnut brown hung loose and cascaded down to her chest, and Isabel's fair skin matched the dancer's golden tone. At first glance, Isabel Roma was Olivia Taylor, and it wasn't until she slid into the passenger seat and fixed those pale blue eyes on him that Trevor noticed a difference.

Isabel truly was a chameleon, and a damn good one. He'd seen her in action when they'd gone undercover together in Bogotá. Her alter ego, Paloma Dominguez, was a Brazilian heiress with a lust for life, oozing sex and mischief and without a single inhibition. She was so convincing in the role that Trevor had been certain she *was* Paloma—until they returned to their hotel every night and Isabel's laid-back disposition and outspoken approach made an appearance.

"Hey," she said in that melodic voice of hers. She pushed down the hood of the sweatshirt, lifted her hands to her hair, and began pulling out little brown bobby pins, which she tossed into the cup holder between them.

"Hey," he answered.

One last pin popped out, and then she removed the wig.

"The color's spot-on," Trevor remarked. "Just had it lying around the apartment, huh?"

Her smile was sardonic. "I own a lot of wigs."

Those six words spoke volumes. It dawned on him that although they'd spent an entire week together all those months ago, he hadn't once asked her if she liked her work. He knew she'd worked for the FBI before joining up with Noelle, but he'd never thought to ask why she'd gotten into undercover work to begin with. If she liked it. If becoming different people brought her a sense of fulfillment.

"Did everything go okay?" he asked.

"Smooth sailing. Angelo's man came inside after about thirty minutes. I didn't turn around, but I felt his eyes on me.

I think he got bored watching me kneeling in front of the altar, because he left a few minutes later." Confidence lined her tone. "Don't worry. As far as that thug is concerned, Olivia was praying for her friend's immortal soul the entire time."

"Good." Shifting the gears, Trevor steered the Range Rover out of the lot and made a right turn. From the corner of his eye, he saw Isabel rummaging around in her purse. She removed a tube of clear liquid and some cotton wipes, flipped down the sun visor, and began removing the makeup from her face.

"Thanks for stepping up on such short notice," he added as he merged with traffic.

"Not a problem."

His peripheral vision caught a blur of motion and he glanced over in time to see the hoodie slide over her head, leaving her in a snug white tank top. The bra beneath it was black, one strap falling onto her shoulder. Man, she had the prettiest skin. Smooth and creamy, and it looked soft to the touch.

As she readjusted the strap, she fixed him with a wry look, and he knew she'd caught him staring. The air in the vehicle seemed to get real hot, real fast, and the tightening of his groin caught him off guard. He might not be the broken mess he'd been six months ago, but it still surprised him to discover he could get turned on by a woman who wasn't Gina.

"So Olivia's going to help?" Isabel asked, breaking the awkward silence.

He nodded. "She'll be at the Diamond Mine tomorrow, and she's agreed to snoop around. I guess I don't need to remind you to—"

"Watch over her?" she filled in. "I'm on it. I won't jeopardize my cover, though. We might need Candy Cane before this is over."

"Just be careful when you're at the club, and try not to draw any undue attention. If Angelo decides to send you to one of those private parties . . ." He didn't even bother finishing the sentence. Besides, his throat had suddenly gone dry. He knew Isabel was perfectly capable of taking care of herself, but the thought of Angelo whoring her out was distressing as hell.

"I knew something was up," she said quietly. "When Cora Malcolm came stomping into the dressing room . . . I should have tried to help her."

The despair on her face startled him. Keeping one hand on the wheel, he reached over and touched her knee. "You couldn't help that girl. You would've compromised your cover, Iz."

Surprise flared in her eyes, which made him realize this was the first time he'd used the nickname. It was weird—last time this woman had been around, she'd had him in a constant state of discomfort. Troubled by the attraction he felt toward her, annoyed by her frequent attempts to draw him out of his guilt-induced shell. But now . . . now he felt utterly comfortable. Soothed by her presence.

And *she* was the one shifting in discomfort.

"Trevor—"

"Have dinner with me," he said roughly.

Her eyes widened. "What?"

"Dinner," he repeated. "Not tonight obviously. But when this job is over."

When she didn't respond, an atypical pang of insecurity tugged at his insides. This was the first woman he'd asked out since Gina died, and now he wished he'd kept his mouth shut. Isabel's reluctance was written all over her beautiful face.

"I don't know," she finally said.

They reached a stoplight and he used the opportunity to shift around so he could face her. "No pressure, Isabel. Just a nice dinner between . . ." Between what? Friends? Coworkers? Neither of those labels seemed to fit, but it was way too soon to consider *potential lovers*. Truth was, the idea of starting up a relationship with another woman made his palms go damp.

"You gonna finish that sentence?"

Isabel's dry voice jerked him from his thoughts, and the car horn that blared an instant later only punctuated the fact that he was putting way too much thought into this.

He accelerated and drove through the intersection. "Dinner between friends," he said with a faint smile. "That's probably the right thing to say, huh?"

"Maybe. But what's the *true* thing?"

A heavy breath rolled out of his chest. "I have no idea," he admitted. "The only thing I do know is that I've been thinking about you a lot over the past six months. I'm not sure what it means, but . . . but damn it, I want to find out. Don't you?"

Isabel raked both hands through her blond hair, her straight white teeth worrying her bottom lip. For the first time since he'd met her, she seemed less than poised. Which was odd, because he'd come to associate her with infallible composure and an awe-inspiring ability to take everything in stride. That her uncertainty should startle him only reminded him that he'd never truly taken the time to dig deep with this woman.

Sighing, Isabel laced her fingers together on her lap. "How about we talk about this when the job's over? Let's just finish this thing and deal with the rest later."

Disappointment swelled in his stomach, but hey, at least she hadn't shut him down outright.

"Sounds like a plan," Trevor murmured, all the while trying to convince himself that her less-than-enthusiastic reaction didn't bother him in the slightest.

Olivia and her mother shared a light dinner of rice and steamed vegetables. It was all Kathleen's delicate stomach could handle, yet for Olivia, it was a challenge to keep the food down. Ever since she'd come home from her clandestine rendezvous, she'd kept expecting Vince to show up accusing her of espionage. By the time eight o'clock rolled around, she'd decided that probably wouldn't happen, but her stomach was still tied in knots. Maybe she'd been naive, but when she'd gone to Luke for help, she'd figured it would be immediate. As in, right now. As in, let's whisk you out of town and send you to safety.

Instead, she'd foolishly agreed to spy on Vince, which meant going to the club tomorrow night and pretending everything was fine and dandy.

"Liv?"

She found her mother's concerned green eyes probing her face. "I spaced out. What did you say?"

"That I'm so sorry about your friend. I wish you hadn't been the one to find her like that."

Olivia swallowed. "I wish that too."

Although she'd told her mother about Cora, she'd omitted most of the details, including the fact that Cora had been murdered. Her stomach churned again, this time from guilt rather than nausea. Soon she wouldn't be able to hide the truth anymore; when the time came for them to leave town, she'd have to tell her mom everything, and that wasn't something she looked forward to.

Kathleen scraped back her chair and staggered to her feet. "I think I'll turn in now." She paused. "Unless you'd like some company."

She shook her head. "No, it's all right. You need the rest, and I was going to draw a bath anyway. Plus I really need to start studying for midterms. I'll flunk out if I don't pull it together—I haven't even made study notes yet."

"You'll do just fine. You always do," Kathleen said proudly.

"I hope so," she murmured.

Her mother shuffled toward her. "I love you, sweetheart," she said as she reached down to smooth Olivia's hair off her forehead.

"I love you too, Mom."

Her heart squeezed painfully as Kathleen left the kitchen with slow, heavy steps. It would take a while for her mother to regain her strength, but last time she'd bounced back much faster. Kathleen's kidneys were in bad shape after this last round of chemo. And her heart was weak . . .

Olivia quickly derailed that scary train of thought and

rose from her chair, gathering up their empty plates and carrying them to the sink. She left them there to soak, then headed for the bathroom. As she filled the tub and rummaged around in the cabinet beneath the sink for some bubble bath, her thoughts drifted, floating into territory she so didn't want to deal with right now. Territory that involved Luke. And his team of soldiers. And—

Voilà—the memory of the impulsive kiss they'd shared in the bathroom.

What were you thinking?

Uh-huh. What *was* she thinking? Agreeing to spy on Vince was stupid enough, but kissing Luke? That had *Terrible Idea* written all over it. In permanent marker.

It figured, the first man she'd been attracted to in forever was precisely the kind of man she didn't want in her life. She couldn't deny Luke's charm and intelligence, and maybe if he'd been a lawyer, or an accountant, or hell, worked the drive-thru counter at Mickey D's . . . But no, he was a soldier for hire. A mercenary. A man who no doubt loved danger and had no problem diving headfirst into any situation, no matter how risky.

Well, she had no desire to get involved with someone like that. She'd decided a long time ago that when she got serious about someone, it would be a man who lived and breathed *normal*. Nine-to-five job, stable, levelheaded, and most important, reliable. No bad boys for her, thank you very much.

And Luke Dubois was a bad boy from head to toe.

Not to mention a damn good kisser . . .

Her cheeks went hot as she remembered the feel of his lips, the spicy taste of him, the tongue he'd skillfully thrust into her mouth. The kiss might have been unexpected, rushed even, but he'd known exactly what to do. And she couldn't even fault him for it, because *she'd* initiated it.

She, the ever cautious Olivia Taylor, had thrown herself at a man she barely knew, and hours later, she still didn't know why she'd done it.

Sighing, she got into the tub, just as the cell phone she'd

left in the pocket of her hoodie started to ring. With a groan, she leaned over the tub, splashing water onto the tile floor as she stuck out her arm and fumbled for her sweatshirt. She yanked on the sleeve to drag it closer, then pulled out her phone. UNKNOWN CALLER.

In spite of herself, her heart did a little flip.

And yep, Luke was on the line when she said hello.

And of course, that honesty she was growing accustomed to made a quick appearance. "So why'd you kiss me?"

She lowered her body into the hot water and rested her head on the edge of the porcelain tub. "You know, I was just asking myself the same question," she admitted grudgingly.

His husky laugh tickled her ear. "What'd you come up with?"

"I'm leaning toward temporary insanity. Or shock. A friend of mine did die today." Her insides clenched at the memory.

"I really am sorry about that," he said. "I know what it's like to lose someone you care about."

She sank deeper into the bubbles, the warm water lapping over her breasts. "Who did you lose?"

"My dad." His voice was hoarse. "Six years ago in Katrina."

Her breath caught. "Oh. I'm sorry, Luke."

"It's cool. I've worked through it. So do you really speak French?"

The abrupt change of subject startled her. Then she laughed. *"Avez-vous pensé que je restais de cela?"*

"Nah, didn't think you were lying. I just wanted to judge your accent." He laughed. "Where'd you learn to speak it?"

"From a patient at St. Francis. She was from Paris, and she and my mom shared a room." A lump rose in her throat. "Spanish I learned during the second hospital tour, from one of my mom's nurses."

"Sounds like you've spent a lot of time in hospitals," he said softly.

"Yeah. Yeah, I have."

"At least it gave you time to pick up some new languages."

It took her a second to comprehend that he'd spoken in perfect Spanish. And God help her, but her heart leapt again. "You're obviously skilled in the language department yourself," she remarked.

"I do okay." She could practically see him shrugging those broad shoulders of his, and wondered if he treated everything in life so casually.

"Can I ask you something?"

"Anything." No hesitation on his part.

"I want to know about Vince." Olivia leaned her head against the white-tiled wall. "What am I dealing with here, really? Is he . . . he's Mafia, right?"

"Yes."

She swallowed. Couldn't say she was surprised, though. She'd suspected it the moment Vince covered up the customer's death. "Is he a big boss or something?" she asked, suddenly realizing she had zero knowledge about the inner workings of the Mob.

"Not quite. That honor goes to Ric De Luca and the other four bosses. They call the shots, and each one of them gets a piece of the pie. Right now there're five families operating in New York—De Luca operates in Manhattan, Brooklyn, and Queens."

"And Vince works for De Luca."

"Yep. Our man Angelo is a soldier, which is a member of the crime family but not a shot-caller. Soldiers work for the boss, who usually gives them a racket to run—"

"Racket?" she echoed. "Like an illegal business?"

"Right," he confirmed. "In Angelo's case, it's drug dealing. The Diamond is a front for it. Vince oversees the operation, and in return he has access to the family's influence and connections, and gets a cut of the profits."

"So the club is illegal?" She gulped as she had a mental picture of herself being carted off in handcuffs.

"No, the club itself is legit, and on the surface Angelo is an upstanding citizen. Pays his taxes, liquor licenses and permits up to date, runs a clean place."

"But under the surface, he's a drug dealer," she said dully.

"That's always been Vince's bread and butter," Luke said in a matter-of-fact tone. "He started dealing when he was a teenager, and even back then he was an arrogant bastard—he muscled in on De Luca's territory, but the boss didn't kill him. He must have seen promise in young Vince, because he took him under his wing."

"And put him in charge of the club."

"Yep. They launder money through it, and that's where the drugs are cut and bagged, then distributed to the low-life dealers who sell the shit on the street."

She shook her head in amazement, sending drops of water everywhere. "Why don't the cops just raid the place and arrest Vince then?" Her knowledge of the law quickly kicked in. "Let me guess," she said before he could reply. "There's not enough evidence for a warrant."

"And De Luca's got half the police force in his pocket," Luke added. "Nobody's gonna touch him, and that means nobody touches Angelo."

Shifting in the tub, she rested her feet on the faucet, then tipped her head back and stared up at the ceiling. God, what a messed-up world they lived in, where people like Vince did whatever the hell they wanted and the cops turned the other cheek, happy to do it as long as they had some cash to line their wallets.

A hiss filled the extension. "Are you in the bath?" Luke demanded.

Heat suffused her face. "Yeah. Why?"

"So you're naked."

Olivia couldn't help but laugh. "That's what usually happens in a bathtub. Or do you keep your clothes on when you bathe?"

"No, I don't keep my clothes on." He sounded frazzled. "And I don't do baths. I shower. Baths take too long."

"And you're the kind of guy who can't waste time, right? You need the action."

"Pretty much." There was a suggestive pause. "You don't like action?"

She grinned to herself. "You're incorrigible."

"And you're beautiful."

Olivia was flustered. "What?"

"You're beautiful," he said gruffly. "You know that, right?"

"I know that the water's getting cold and my skin is starting to prune," she said lightly. "So we should probably say good night."

He cleared his throat. "Okay. Cool." Another pause. "Olivia?"

"Yeah?"

"I . . ." He uttered a soft curse. "Be careful tomorrow."

The phone trembled in her hand. "I will."

"And remember, if anything goes wrong, if you feel like you're in the slightest bit of trouble, we'll be right outside the club. You're not in this alone anymore. You've got people looking out for you now."

The lump in her throat got so huge that she could barely squeeze out a single word. But she managed two. "Thank you."

Chapter 10

Vince checked the Cartier watch strapped to his wrist and cursed under his breath. He had to leave now if he wanted to make it to the meeting on time, and as much as he'd like to stick around until his girl showed up, he didn't want to piss off the boss. De Luca didn't take kindly to tardiness. Vince didn't like it much either, but when Olivia had texted she'd be late for her shift tonight, he'd decided to let it slide. He knew she was still grieving—hell, she'd been praying for that bitch Cora's soul for more than an hour at St. Mary's yesterday. Rocko had been bored to tears, but Vince wholly approved of Olivia's visit to the church. Her indifference toward religion had always annoyed him, good Catholic boy that he was. He'd planned on working on her after they were married, but evidently all he'd needed to do was rub out some whiny whore for Olivia to rediscover her faith.

Things were changing. She was opening her heart to him, he could feel it. These last couple of days, she'd made an effort to reach out to him, and it made his fucking heart sing. He'd never enjoyed the dominant way he treated her, but Olivia was too strong-willed for her own good. Sometimes the only way to keep the strong ones in line was with a solid backhand. Didn't mean he liked hitting her, though. Violence was reserved for your mistress, not your wife, and he had every intention of making Olivia Taylor the latter.

Truth was, he was tired of trashy women. Before he'd met Olivia, he'd dated strippers or groupies looking to become Mafia wives, women who cracked their gum and teased their hair and expected him to lavish them with gifts. Olivia didn't expect or ask for anything, which in turn made him eager to please her. Nevertheless, it was about time she started thinking about pleasing *him*.

Remembering that he still needed to grab the club's monthly earnings report to show to De Luca, he left his office and headed for the door leading to the back rooms. He'd just slid through it when his cell rang. A glance at the caller ID had him rolling his eyes. Erik Franz. A stupid name in Vince's opinion, but the man it belonged to didn't seem to mind it.

Vince barked out a response. "Have we taken care of our problem yet?" He entered the file room and flicked the light switch.

The beat of hesitation told him the answer. "We had to move him."

"Move him where?" Vince snapped as he marched toward a tall filing cabinet across the room. "And why?"

"The boss had other uses for the warehouse."

Vince clenched his teeth. "Why am I only finding out about this now?"

"I just found out myself. But don't worry—the new location is secure."

"Give me the address."

As Franz rattled off the info, Vince extracted a monogrammed fountain pen from the inside pocket of his jacket, then rummaged around on the table next to the cabinet for a notepad. He scribbled down the address, ripped the paper from the pad and shoved it in his pocket.

"The truck's showing up Tuesday night," he reminded his associate. "So this needs to happen then. The body will provide a nice distraction for the DEA and keep them busy while we slip the shipment in under their noses."

"They'll be distracted," came the reassuring reply. "We'll keep him alive for a few more days, and then come Tuesday, an anonymous tip hits their switchboard." Franz chuckled. "They'll be relieved to get Dane back—even if it's in a body bag."

Vince's Town Car wasn't in its designated parking space when Olivia arrived at the club. Good. So he'd stuck to his weekly schedule, which meant he wouldn't show up here until at least midnight. That's when he normally wrapped up his "investor" meeting.

A part of her wished she hadn't asked Luke about Vince's criminal dealings. She'd known he was involved in shady activities, but last night's phone call had been an eye-opener. Drugs, money laundering, the Five Families. Those were things you saw in movies, not real life, and now that her eyes were open, she wished she could just slam them shut again.

The lowlifes she'd seen being hauled out of Vince's office bloody and beaten were drug dealers. Those mysterious rooms up on the second floor were probably where Vince and his goons stored the drugs they distributed. And the girls—Cora . . . Heaven . . . the countless others who walked around with needle marks on their arms—Vince had probably given them the drugs himself. Hooked them. Turned them into zombies so he could pimp them out to important clients.

It made her sick. And angry. God, she was angry, not just at Vince but at herself too, for foolishly putting herself in this position. If she'd never applied for a job at the Diamond Mine, she never would have met Vince. She never would have been assaulted in that alley. And she wouldn't owe that man a damn thing now.

Olivia got out of the BMW and headed inside, wishing like hell she could just turn around and drive far, far away. But she'd promised Luke she would dig around, and if she wanted his assistance, she had to follow through.

And now that she'd given it more thought, it was almost better that Luke and his men were private contractors. That meant he could help her pull off a good old disappearing act. No official channels or witness protection or anything that would leave a trail. If Luke had the kind of connections she suspected he did, she and her mom would be able to start a new life somewhere Vince Angelo would never find them.

But first things first. Dig.

She kept to a relaxed pace as she headed down the rear corridor toward the dressing room. Luke had texted her during the drive over—three words: *We're all set*. She wasn't sure what that meant, but she hadn't wanted to text back, especially since he'd mentioned something about getting her a secure phone. But how? Was he just going to drop by and slide a cell phone into her G-string?

When she opened her locker and spotted a black backpack on the bottom shelf, she realized that Luke Dubois was far more resourceful than she'd given him credit for. The bag didn't belong to her, but she immediately knew where it had come from.

Shooting a surreptitious look around the crowded room, she bent down and unzipped the backpack. It contained a few items of clothing, a pair of jeans, some tank tops, a cardboard tampon box—nice touch, she had to admit—and a bag of Doritos. She shoved her hand deeper, rummaging around the base of the bag until she connected with something hard and slender. Without daring to turn around, she fished out the cell phone, startled to find it was the exact model and color as her own BlackBerry. Swallowing, she slid it into the pocket of her jeans.

As she stood up and unbuttoned her coat, she felt someone watching her. She turned, saw Candy's blue eyes fixed on her, and frowned. She remembered the way Candy had grilled her the other day, and made a mental note to tell Luke about it. Candy Cane definitely couldn't be trusted.

Olivia hung her coat in the locker, stowed her purse on the top shelf, and then left the room, ignoring the mindless chatter of the other girls. In the hallway, she took the new cell phone out of her pocket, opened up the contact list and blinked in surprise when she discovered it matched the list from her real phone. How on earth had they transferred her contacts into this thing? She scrolled down and found two new entries, one labeled L, the other T. Luke and Trevor. She highlighted Luke's number. Just as she pressed SEND, Bobby strode into the corridor, his huge pecs doing a little jiggle beneath his black muscle shirt.

"Evening, Liv," the bouncer said.

"Hey, Bobby." She covered the mouthpiece. "I'm just checking in with my mom." When Luke's voice sounded in her ear, she put on a chirpy voice. "Hey, Mom—yeah, hold on a sec." Turning back to Bobby, she said, "Is Vince around?"

The big man shook his head. "Friday meeting."

"Oh, right." She uncovered the mouthpiece. "Mom? Yeah, I'm here."

Bobby marched off, giving an awkward wave as he continued down the corridor. She waited until he was out of earshot, then said, "Luke?"

"You found the phone."

"Duh. Now what?"

There was a short pause. "Did you just say 'duh'?"

"Yes." She rolled her eyes to herself. "And then I said *now what*?"

"Get in position by the stairs. I'll tell you when it's clear."

"Okay. Should I . . . are we hanging up?"

"No, keep me on the line."

Holding the phone to her ear, she left the hallway and stepped into the club, letting her eyes adjust to the barely-there lighting. The place was packed, like it was every Friday night. Every table on the main floor was occupied, and by the stage, a group of rowdy frat boys were whistling and shouting as one of the dancers, Georgia, strutted her stuff. When she removed her bra and twirled it around with her index finger, the club went wild.

Olivia shifted her gaze, studying the waitresses as they rushed by in their micro-minis, the bouncers positioned all over the vast room. Her eyes landed on the pair of spiral staircases. One led to the VIP lounge, the other to the management offices. She edged toward the farther staircase, keeping her eyes on the crowd. When she reached the foot of the stairs, she leaned against the iron railing and waited.

"All right, darlin', the hallway's clear," Luke announced.

"How do you know that?" she hissed. "What if I run into one of Vince's—"

"It's clear," he repeated. "Trust me, we're looking at it right now."

"You are? How?"

He ignored the questions. "Move, Olivia. Stay casual. If someone follows you up, tell them you needed a quiet place to talk on the phone."

Taking a breath, she ascended the stairs and sure enough, the hallway was deserted. As her heart thudded, she walked as casually as she could in the direction of Vince's office. The double doors were shut, but when she pushed on the handle, she found them unlocked. Without risking a backward glance, she slid into the room, shut the doors, and let out a shaky exhale.

"Okay, I'm in."

She looked around, not feeling very hopeful. There was a reason Vince didn't lock his door—other than the desk and computer, the office was bare. No filing cabinets, no shelves, just miles of smooth parquet, expensive art on the walls, and a pair of cushioned visitor chairs.

"What should I look for?" she whispered into the phone.

"Anything and everything. Try the computer first, but I doubt he keeps anything of value in there."

Olivia made her way to the desk and sank into Vince's leather chair, cringing when the overbearing scent of his cologne wafted into her nose—his chair reeked of it. She reached for the mouse and the computer screen came to life. A box demanding that she enter a username and password popped up.

"It's password-protected," she said in dismay.

"We figured. Don't bother trying to crack it, just go through the desk, see if anything looks suspicious."

Sighing, she put the phone on speaker, set it on the desk, and got to work. The drawers were unlocked, but they con-

tained nothing but some pencils, paper clips, a pack of matches.
She yanked open the bottom drawer and found a leather ledger that looked promising, but when she flipped open the cover, she saw only blank papers inside.

A few minutes later, she'd been through the entire desk and found absolutely nothing incriminating.

"There's nothing here," she announced.

Luke's disappointment reverberated over the line. "Shit."

She paused in thought. "Should I look behind the paintings and see if there's a safe or something?"

A deep laugh tickled her eardrum. "And if you find one? You brought your safe-cracking tools, right?"

"Are you making fun of me?"

"Just a little."

She bristled. "I'm glad this is so entertaining for you."

Luke instantly went serious. "It's not. I'm sorry."

"You're forgiven. Now what?"

"Now you get out of there. We knew that finding anything of value in the office would be a long shot, but we had to try."

"So that's it? You don't need me to snoop anywhere else?"

"Not tonight."

Not tonight? Annoyance and fear shot up her chest and vied for her attention. She'd have to go through this *again*? Sneak up here, put her neck on the line, risk getting caught by Vince?

As unhappiness rippled through her, she left Vince's office and stepped into the hallway, but rather than go downstairs, she lingered in the hall. Torn.

"What are you doing, darlin'?"

She glanced to the left, her gaze drawn to the heavy metal door she'd seen Vince and his goons coming out of so many times before.

Luke wanted something of value? Well, chances were, that something was right behind that door.

"I should investigate the back rooms," she murmured without moving her lips.

"No, you shouldn't," came his sharp reply. "Get downstairs, Olivia."

She stayed rooted in place. "But that's probably where he handles all the drug stuff, right? He bags it up and the dealers come and get it?"

Silly as it was, her words brought to mind the image of rooms filled with floor-to-ceiling piles of heroin. And then, in a flash, those pictures were replaced with the very real scene she'd stumbled on in Cora's apartment. The brown powder. The spoon and the syringe and Cora's blank eyes.

Ignoring a burst of pain, she clenched her teeth and said, "If you want something incriminating, it'll be back there, Luke."

"This wasn't part of the plan. If you're caught, it'll be impossible to explain why you're there."

"I'll figure something out."

"Olivia—"

"I can't do this again," she cut in, desperation rising in her throat. "I told you I'd snoop around, but this is too damn stressful and I only plan on doing it once. I'm already up here, so why not check it out?" She paused in hindsight. "Is there anyone there? Can you see on the cameras?"

"I see forty dudes with machine guns."

"Seriously?"

He swore loudly. "No. But—"

"Will the cameras pick me up?"

"No, but—"

She lifted her chin in resolve. "Then I'm going back there."

Chapter 11

"What the *fuck* is she doing?" Holden muttered from his seat.

Luke followed the other man's gaze and let out a few choice expletives. He and Holden were in the guest room that Holden had dubbed Command Central. There were five computers on the oak corner desk, the floor was littered with cables and wires, and a couple of fax machines and scanners sat on a thick shelf above the desk.

Three screens displayed the live feed from the Diamond Mine's security cameras, while a fourth showed the loop that Holden had created. With some serious tricks that Luke still didn't understand, Holden had substituted the loop for the live footage, so anyone monitoring the footage in Angelo's security booth was seeing what Holden wanted them to see—an empty office, empty corridor, empty back rooms.

The back rooms that Olivia was determined to get to.

He wasn't sure if she was brave as fuck or crazy as hell, but there was no stopping her. On the live screen, Olivia walked through the big metal door. She promptly appeared on the next monitor, standing in the corridor.

"She gets caught, it'll be hard to justify her presence there, man," Holden said in a low voice.

"I know." Which was precisely why they'd asked her to poke around in Angelo's office only.

"I'm going to try this door first." Olivia's quiet voice emerged from the speaker. The monitors flickered, changed location, and then she stood in a brightly lit room full of filing cabinets.

Luke watched as she tried opening one of the drawers. Though he couldn't see her face, he heard the frown in her voice when she reported in. "Locked. Let me try the others."

She did a quick sweep of the room, but none of the cabinets opened. "You know," came her throaty voice, "you should have taught me how to pick locks if you wanted me to be of any use."

He couldn't help but grin. "I'll teach you some other time. Now get your ass out of there."

"No, wait." She bent over a table by one of the cabinets. "This is Vince's pen," she murmured. "He must have been in here . . . Yeah, I think he wrote something down." She paused, her spine curving as she hunched closer. "There's an impression on the paper, left over from the sheet above it. Hold on, let me see if I can read it."

Luke knew there was no point in arguing with her. Something he'd discovered tonight? Olivia Taylor was as stubborn as a damn mule.

From the rattling sounds that filled the line, he could tell that she was riffling through the contents of the desk drawer. When her hand emerged, he spotted a pencil between her fingers.

"I knew those Nancy Drew mysteries I read as a kid would come in handy," she murmured.

Luke stifled a laugh, then followed the hurried movement of her hand as she shaded over the impression on the notepad.

"One sec . . . okay, I've got an address," she hissed. "One seven eight Concord Avenue, unit thirteen. Or maybe it's one seven five. I can't tell if it's a five or an eight. But the street is definitely right, and so's the unit number."

Luke glanced at Holden, who was already typing the address into one of the computers.

"Good job, darlin'. Now take the paper with you and get out of there."

He heard a ripping sound and noticed Olivia tucking something into her pocket. To his overwhelming relief, she made a beeline for the door, except rather than head back to the main hall, she merely moved to the next doorway.

"Damn it, Olivia. Get out of there. The address is enough."

"More than enough," Holden concurred, turning away from the screen. "We're looking at an industrial area with a shit ton of abandoned warehouses and apartment buildings on the verge of demolition. Any one of those sites would be the perfect place to stash a hostage."

"Did you hear that?" Luke said to Olivia.

"Yes," she replied.

"Good. Now get out."

"All right."

Her easy agreement brought another rush of relief, but the feeling didn't last long. Olivia had just taken a step when Holden said, "Company."

Luke shifted his attention to the other monitor and fought a burst of alarm. Two stocky men in black suits and with an indecent amount of gel in their hair were marching toward the metal door.

"Olivia," he said sharply. "Hide. *Now*."

On the screen, she seemed to freeze, and then there was a blur of movement. Her long brown hair whipped around her as she dove into the doorway she'd been lurking in front of. The picture changed quickly, revealing another dark room.

The second monitor showed the two new arrivals striding down the corridor. Heading directly for the room Olivia was in.

"Fuck," Luke muttered. "Find somewhere to hide, damn it!"

Olivia raced toward an open door on the other side of the room. She poked her head in. "It's some kind of storage room," she said, her voice barely above a whisper.

His heart lodged in his throat as he watched her dart

through the narrow doorway. They had no visual on her anymore, but he heard soft rustling, a creak, and finally her voice. "Luke?"

"You hidden?" he asked roughly.

He scarcely heard her soft reply. "Yeah."

"Don't make a single sound, darlin'."

The two men entered the room. One flicked on a light as the other headed toward a steel cabinet.

Frowning, Luke studied the long worktable in the middle of the room, which was covered with grinders, strainers, digital scales, some discarded baggies, and other paraphernalia he couldn't make out. Man, the bastards had balls. They were milling the shit right out of the club, storing it, packaging it. Angelo must truly believe himself to be untouchable.

Olivia's quiet breathing filled the line and Luke held his breath, praying that the goons wouldn't go near that shadowy doorway. They didn't. The taller of the two, an olive-skinned thug with a shaved head, leaned against the cabinet as his buddy unlocked it.

"Shipment's coming in next week," the tall one said. "Boss wants us to oversee it."

The second goon reached into the cabinet, his voice muffled. "Tell the rest of the crew." He straightened up with a rectangular felt pouch in his hand.

"For the girls?" Shaved Head asked, gesturing to the zippered pouch.

"Yeah. Get-together at Rodriguez's tonight. The boss is sending a few party favors." The guy tucked the small bag in his coat pocket. "And we're in charge of making sure those party favors aren't party poopers."

"Rodriguez." Shaved Head made an annoyed sound. "That Mexican bastard? I fucking hate catering to those spics."

"The Mexicans are good to the organization, so we're good to the Mexicans." The goon pulled another pouch out of the locker and tossed it to his buddy. "The boss wants the girls relaxed. H for the junkies, E for the ones who need a little loosening up."

The two men left the room. Luke waited until they descended the staircase to the main floor before he addressed Olivia. "They're gone, darlin'. Now get the fuck out of there."

"You swear too much" was her faint reply.

He couldn't help it. He laughed. Which earned him a strange look from Holden. "I'll work on my potty mouth if you work on following orders," he promised her.

A pale-faced Olivia reappeared on the monitor. Luke could tell she was rattled. He wished he could be there with her, or at the very least outside the club, but Trevor had ordered him and Holden to handle the security issue, claiming Olivia might feel safer if Luke was the one talking her through it. He wasn't sure it had worked, though. She didn't look too great, her features drawn and ashen, her spine stiff as she moved through the second floor toward the stairs.

When her voice came on the line again, he expected to hear fear, panic even, but to his shock, she sounded pissed off. "Did you hear what they said?"

"We heard," he confirmed with a sigh.

"There's another one of those private parties tonight. The girls are going to be drugged." She sounded horrified. "He's getting them stoned so a bunch of perverts can screw them without any trouble."

"I know." His chest felt heavy.

"What are we going to do about it?"

Beside him, Holden's eyebrows shot up. He and Luke exchanged a wary look.

"We're not going to do anything," Luke said carefully. "We weren't sent in to mess with Angelo's drug business. We're here to find Dane. Nothing less, nothing more."

"I see." Her voice was tight, her disapproval evident.

The security cameras on the second floor belonged to a different feed than the ones in the actual club, so Luke couldn't see her on the monitors anymore, which meant she'd gotten downstairs in one piece. He wished he could observe the expression on her face, but suspected he wouldn't like it.

"I have to get ready for my shift," she said flatly. "I assume I'm done playing Nancy Drew for the night?"

"Yeah, but—"

She hung up.

Cursing, Luke pocketed his cell phone and rose from his chair.

"She's pissed," Holden remarked.

"No kidding." He slashed a hand through his hair, trying to pin down the source of his frustration.

He understood Olivia's anger—listening to those goons talk about "loosening up" the girls had triggered a spark of fury in his own gut. But their hands were tied here. Carter Dane was their top priority. Their *only* priority.

Still . . . he really didn't like the idea of Olivia being disappointed in him. And he got the feeling she totally was.

"I'm getting the club's security feeds back online," Holden said, his fingers moving over the keyboard. "I'll start on the address after that. We'll need to do some recon before we raid the place."

Luke made for the door. "I'll join up with the guys. Olivia needs to be watched twenty-four-seven. If Angelo even suspects she's digging around in his biz . . ."

"Luke."

He stopped, glancing over his shoulder. "What is it?"

"Our job is to find that agent."

His jaw hardened. "I know."

Holden turned back to the monitor. "Just thought you needed the reminder."

Isabel was in the middle of a sexy spin up on the main stage when she spotted Olivia descending the spiral staircase. Even with the spotlight doing its best to blind her, she could see the paleness of the other woman's cheeks, contrasted with the heated look in her eyes. Huh. Olivia looked pissed off, but Isabel pushed the observation aside and focused on the task at hand. Extending her leg, she rested her heel against the metal pole then ran her fingers up her leg from ankle to thigh, tossing her hair over her shoulder as she moved her head to the music.

She wondered why Olivia was all riled up. Hopefully Trevor would update her when she checked in.

On second thought, maybe she'd just call Luke to find out. Ever since that uncomfortable conversation in the car yesterday, she'd been trying to distance herself from Trevor. Even now, the thought of him brought on some serious agitation, causing her to lose her rhythm.

For Pete's sake, get it together.

Stifling a sigh, she worked the stage, shimmying out of her bustier, slow, sensual, making the men beg for it. When her breasts were finally exposed, she wiggled toward the end of the stage, dancing down to her knees and leaning forward so the frat boys sitting front-and-center could shove bills underneath her lacy red garter. One-dollar bills. Cheap bastards. When she'd worked undercover at that strip club in Paris, she'd walked away with fifties and hundreds. You couldn't knock the stripper life—if you were good, some customers were good right back.

She made a lot of eye contact with the boys, shooting each one a wicked smile as she worked her way back to Heaven. She and Heaven were doing a dual set tonight, which involved a lot of girl-on-girl grinding and the occasional kiss if the crowd demanded it. The other dancer was high as a kite, dark circles under her eyes covered up with makeup, but the girl was a pro. Heaven didn't miss a beat as she hooked one leg up and around Isabel's hip and threw her head back in mock ecstasy.

Isabel went through the motions. A headache was forming at her temples. The boys in the crowd shouted out catcalls. Someone let out a sharp whistle that made her head pound even harder.

She was beginning to work the pole again when a familiar face caught her eye.

Fuck.

Fuck.

Marco Bianchi was weaving his way through the crowd.

Isabel immediately whirled around, raised her hands above her head, and rolled her hips, giving the crowd a nice view of her ass.

Shit. She'd glimpsed several of De Luca's men in the club before, but never one she was well acquainted with. Marco worked as an enforcer for the big boss himself, a bodybuilder/steroid type who crammed his huge body into expensive suits and packed enough firepower to start a small war. It had been eight years since she'd last seen him, but she could pick the guy out of any lineup, and he could probably do the same to her.

Unfortunately, this latest disguise, albeit tacky and over the top, was close to her true appearance. Aside from the hair extensions she'd used to give her that ass-length tousled look, she hadn't altered her looks to play Candy Cane. Which meant Marco simply needed to take a good hard look and he'd recognize her as Isabel Roma. Daughter of the man who'd sacrificed himself for the organization. Sister of the man whose brains De Luca had blown out.

As her pulse raced like a thoroughbred, Isabel concentrated on the performance, keeping her head turned, offering nothing but a fleeting profile to the crowd. Her peripheral vision caught Marco heading for a table to the right of the stage, where a group of Latino men were tossing back tequila shots. The enforcer bent down and the group started whispering. One of the men lifted a hand, pointing an index finger at the stage.

Isabel's heart lurched. Holy hell, were they pointing at her?

Ignoring the panic surging through her, she risked another quick look in Marco's direction. His Latino buddies were guffawing now. One of them pointed to the stage again, then reached down and cupped his crotch.

Her spine went rigid. Was this related to one of those private parties? Was that how it worked? De Luca's buddies saw a pair of tits they liked, and Vince delivered those tits to a hotel room?

She said a silent prayer that the tits in question didn't

belong to her, because for Isabel, self-preservation came first no matter what. Some of the other operatives who worked for Noelle did whatever they had to for the sake of the mission, but using sex to get the job done was not part of Isabel's professional code. She would pull out of a job before spreading her legs for a bunch of horny scumbags.

When the set finally came to an end, she swallowed a sigh of relief and sprinted off the stage. She and Heaven headed for the dressing room, neither saying a word as they walked over to their lockers. They were the only ones in the room, and when footsteps echoed from the hallway, a wave of uneasiness swelled in Isabel's belly.

Sure enough, a big man appeared in the doorway. Not one of the bouncers, but Mikey, Vince's number one bodyguard. Mikey was straight-up thug in his dark suit, the bulge of a weapon beneath his coat, a goatee circling his unsmiling mouth.

"The boss needs you to work a party tonight," he announced.

She glanced at the oversize leather purse hanging off the top of the locker door, then reached for it, her teeth sinking into the insides of her cheeks. Well, looked like this job had just come to an end. She quickly assessed how long it would take to grab the Beretta from her purse. Three seconds tops. Hopefully she wouldn't have to shoot her way out of the place, but that might be the only—

"You hear me, Heaven?" Mikey growled. "Your services are needed."

Isabel's hand froze. From the corner of her eye, she noticed Heaven's already pale face go even paler, and then the other dancer turned around to nod at Mikey. "Let me just get dressed," the girl said in a wooden tone.

"Car's waiting out front," the man barked before leaving the room.

Isabel drew in a breath, letting her limbs relax. Finally, she looked over at Heaven. And her breath caught again. God, the girl was just . . . not there. Heaven was one of the prettier girls at the club, tall and willowy with layered ash-blond hair and enormous blue eyes. She could have been a model, probably would've been crazy successful too, but the track marks on her arms said it all. The girl was too far gone, a junkie with dead eyes and hollow cheeks and no way out.

"You okay?" Isabel asked softly.

Heaven shrugged and reached for a fuzzy blue sweater. She put it on over her bare breasts, then grabbed a pair of hip-huggers from her locker and pulled them up her long legs.

"Heaven . . ." She impulsively put her hand on the girl's arm, finding Heaven's skin hot to the touch. "You can get help, you know. You don't need to keep poisoning yourself."

The blonde shrugged again.

"I'm serious, sweetheart. I know addiction is tough, but if you don't kick it now, it'll kill you."

"Maybe I'm already dead," Heaven said gloomily. "Or maybe I'm just a lost cause."

She slammed her locker shut and stalked off, her high heels clicking against the floor tiles.

The sag of Heaven's shoulders brought an ache to Isabel's heart. Yeah, maybe the girl was right. Maybe Heaven truly was a lost cause.

"Damn shame," she muttered to herself.

She slipped into her coat, then slung her purse over her shoulder. The Beretta stayed inside the bag, but Isabel got the sinking feeling that one of these days she might actually need to use it.

Chapter 12

When Olivia walked into her bedroom several hours later, she found Luke sleeping on her bed.

Yep, he was asleep on her *bed*. Just sprawled there on his back, long legs and scuffed black boots hanging off the edge of the mattress, one arm crooked behind his head.

Although she was startled, she didn't cry out, because for some reason a part of her wasn't all that surprised to find him here. After she'd hung up on him earlier, she'd pretty much expected to see him tonight. She got the feeling Luke wasn't the kind of man who enjoyed being dismissed, and yeah, maybe giving him the dial tone had been unnecessarily harsh, but at that moment she'd been too ticked off to consider telephone etiquette. His cavalier attitude toward the fact that Vince was doping up strippers had annoyed the hell out of her.

The second she shut the door behind her, Luke's eyes popped open, making her wonder if he'd even been sleeping at all. Either that, or he possessed the ability to snap out of slumber in a nanosecond and manage to look utterly alert.

As she approached the bed, his voice came out in a low drawl. "What part of 'get the hell out of there' didn't you understand, Olivia?"

She frowned at him, grateful that her mom was sound

asleep across the hall. This was the first time she'd ever had a man in her bedroom, and Kathleen would be full of questions if she knew Luke was here. Which raised the question of *how* he'd gotten in undetected in the first place.

"I climbed the fire escape," he said, as if reading her mind. "And your window was unlocked. You should invest in a security alarm, darlin'." The lazy voice sharpened. "Now answer my question."

Scowling at him, she crossed the hardwood floor and approached her dresser. It was kind of awkward having Luke in her private space. Not that her bedroom was overflowing with feminine secrets. If anything, the room revealed her to be the most boring person on the planet—bed, closet, chest of drawers, and a stand-up floor mirror with a picture of Olivia and her mother tucked into the top corner.

"Do we have to do this now?" she grumbled. "It's three in the morning and I'm exhausted. I want to get ready for bed."

She heard the covers rustle and turned to see him slither up to a sitting position. "Then get ready for bed," he said in a silky voice. He propped his arms behind his head with an indifferent expression. "It's not like I haven't seen it all before."

Good point. But his remark still irked her. She pretended it didn't and began undoing the buttons of her thin cardigan sweater. When his breath hitched, she experienced an odd sense of satisfaction. Ha. Mr. Indifferent wasn't so indifferent anymore, was he?

Smirking, she shrugged out of the sweater and tossed it aside, took off her black camisole, and then undid the side zipper of her knee-length suede skirt. She was wearing a pair of black thigh-high stockings underneath, which looked silly paired with the boy-cut yellow panties with the smiley face on the crotch.

"I'm totally digging the undergarments," Luke said, his sultry eyes moving from the yellow panties to the strapless wisp of black lace covering her breasts.

She frowned again. "Just get it out of your system, okay? But don't yell, because my mom's sleeping."

"Fine." He scowled. "What were you thinking? I told you to check Angelo's office—and just his office. You had no business going to the back rooms."

"I was carrying out *your* business. You wanted me to snoop, so I snooped. I don't get why you're so upset." She reached for the butterfly clip holding her hair up and yanked it out. As her long brown tresses cascaded down her back, she finger-combed them and shot him a stony look.

"I'm upset because you could have been killed."

Before she knew what was happening, Luke had hopped off the bed and barreled toward her, the muscles of his rippled chest bunching and flexing. In his snug black long-sleeve shirt and olive green camo pants, he looked downright predatory, yet at the same time sexy as hell. Her heart did an involuntary flip, and when he touched her face with one big hand, her heartbeat went Formula 1 on her.

He gripped her chin, forcing eye contact. "When I give you an order, you follow it, Olivia. If those two dudes had caught you . . . Fuck. This isn't a game."

She stared into his liquid chocolate eyes, stunned by the genuine concern she saw in them. "I know," she said. "And I am sorry. But there was nothing in Vince's office, so I figured I might as well keep snooping since I was already up there." She paused. "I don't think I can do that again, though. My heart was pounding like crazy the entire time. I'm not cut out for espionage."

When Luke smiled, she knew he was no longer pissed at her.

"Oh, and speaking of espionage," she added. "I think your team should investigate one of the dancers. Her name's Candy Cane and I'm pretty sure she's spying too. On me, that is."

An odd look floated across his face. "Candy Cane," he repeated.

"Yeah. I'm serious—I think Vince asked her to watch me, and I don't want her to become a problem."

"We'll look into it" was all he said.

"Thanks." She hesitated. "I really am sorry I didn't follow your orders. The opportunity was there and I took it, you know? And damn it, but I just want to bring Vince down."

"I know." His thumb grazed her bottom lip. "Still, you can't take chances like that. Leave the taking-down-Vince part to us."

She bristled at that, stepping out of his grip. "But that's not your endgame, is it? All you want to do is find that missing agent. The drugs, what Vince is doing to the girls, stopping him—that's not part of the mission."

"No," he admitted. "And that's not something you can fix either, darlin'. You need to focus on staying alive. If you want out of this messed-up situation you're in, you've got to look out for yourself."

Olivia knew he was right. Hell, since the attack, her only goal had been to get out of town and away from Vince Angelo. But things were different now. Was she supposed to forget that Vince had killed Cora? That he was sending her coworkers out to sleep with his criminal pals?

"You're not a cop," Luke continued. "You're not going to single-handedly bring Angelo down, no matter how hard you try." He shook his head. "I've got a friend who infiltrated De Luca's organization *twice* and the Feds still couldn't put the bastard away. These people are smart— that's how they've stayed in business for this long. Nothing you or I do is going to change that."

She sighed. "I know."

"So look out for yourself. If the address you found pans out, this could all be over by tomorrow." He stroked her cheek again, and she let him. "Once we find Dane, I'll get you out of here. Both you and your mother."

"How?" she whispered.

"Depends on how you want to go about it. You want new identities, you'll get 'em."

"And if I want to remain Olivia Taylor?"

"Then we'll whisk you out of town, set you up somewhere, and arrange for round-the-clock protection in case Angelo tries to follow you."

His earnest words floored her. Yes, she was risking her neck by spying on Vince, but Luke's offer seemed above and beyond what he ought to be doing for her. She went quiet as she let it all sink in, until she felt his gaze burning into her and realized she was standing there in her underwear.

She cleared her throat. "I should put something on."

"Or not," he replied with a faint smile.

Olivia moistened her dry lips. "What exactly did you think was going to happen when you showed up here tonight?"

He shrugged. "I was going to lecture you for disregarding my orders."

"And after the lecture?"

His eyes skimmed down to her chest then moved back to her face. "I didn't plan that far ahead."

A laugh slipped out. "I really do love the honesty."

She studied his gorgeous face, and a jolt of attraction rippled through her. Jeez, she seriously had to get that under control. This man, charming as he might be, was not someone she could ever have a future with.

"How's this for honesty?" Luke said abruptly. "I want you."

Pure heat engulfed her body, turning into an inferno when she looked at his groin and saw the unmistakable bulge of an erection.

"And I think you want me too," he added, raising one brow as if expecting her to contradict him.

"There might be a spark between us." Her tone was grudging.

"Darlin', that spark is burning so hot we're about to burst into flames."

Yep, there were flames licking at her skin, all right. And her nipples had puckered, straining against her lace bra. As their gazes locked, the air in the room grew thick, crackling with tension.

"I don't have sex with men I've just met," she murmured.

He rested his hands on her hips, the warmth of his touch searing her flesh. "Would you consider making an exception?"

It became difficult to breathe. God, she wanted this man so badly she couldn't think straight.

But she couldn't succumb to temptation without thinking it through first. She'd always been cautious when it came to relationships, probably because she'd spent her entire life listening to her mother defend a man who hadn't deserved it. Kathleen had married Eddie Taylor after knowing him for less than a month; Olivia would never be that foolish. And she wasn't going to be foolish now either. Luke Dubois was a mercenary making a pit stop in her life before he moved on to his next adventure. She couldn't let herself forget that, even if his mere proximity did make every inch of her body tingle.

"If we do this . . ." She swallowed. "It won't lead to anything permanent. You know that, right?"

"I don't do permanent." His words were gruff.

"You're not allowed to fall in love with me," she continued gravely. "And I'm not going to fall in love with you."

Luke offered a dry grin. "Any more ground rules you'd like to set?"

"No. I think that's it."

"Thank God."

And then his mouth came down on hers.

The kiss was pure domination. He simply took what he wanted, thrusting his tongue into her mouth as his hands tangled in her hair and his lower body slammed into hers. It caught her off guard, the skill with which he kissed her, the way he moved his hips to position his erection right against her. Yet there was something thrilling about that skill too. This was a man who knew precisely what to do, whose toe-curling kisses promised that the hottest sex of her life was on the horizon.

Olivia gasped when his hands moved to her chest. He cupped her breasts through her bra, then growled and tore open the front clasp.

She wrenched her mouth away. "Did you just rip my bra apart?"

"I'll buy you a new one," he rasped.

"Said the caveman to the—"

He cut her off with another kiss, and a blast of heat scorched her skin. She was dizzy with desire, battling a level of arousal she'd never known before in her life. Everything about this man drove her wild. His scent, the feel of his calloused palms on her breasts, the taste of his lips as they devoured her mouth. She might not be the virgin Vince believed her to be, but she wasn't some sexual vixen either. Her hands trembled as she touched Luke, her fingers tingling as they stroked the dark stubble covering his strong jaw.

She yelped when he cupped her bottom and lifted her up against him. Instinctively, she wrapped her legs around his waist, her arms around his neck, and held on tight as he carried her over to the bed and lowered them both onto the mattress. Their tongues dueled again, while his hips continued to thrust and release, teasing her into sheer oblivion. Moisture pooled between her legs and she spread her legs farther apart, sliding her hands down to his ass to bring him even closer. With a groan, he ground harder, moving his mouth to her neck, his tongue and teeth teasing her feverish flesh.

Olivia's body was on fire. She was close to orgasm—and Luke was still fully dressed, for Pete's sake. Her hands took on a life of their own, fumbling with the buttons of his shirt, dragging the material off his broad shoulders. He helped her out by whipping the shirt onto the floor, the black wifebeater he wore underneath quickly following suit.

The sight of his bare torso made her moan. He was absolutely spectacular—golden skin, perfect sculpted muscles. She explored the planes of his chest, running her fingers over hard sinew, precisely defined pectorals, washboard abs. He had a few scars, a puckered one under his right nipple, a long white one on the curve of his hipbone, the one he'd acquired on his right arm while fighting off that pack of dogs. A tattoo covered his left bicep, an old-school clipper ship with billowing sails, and she traced it with her fingertips before pressing her mouth to the center of his chest, her tongue darting out to savor the clean, salty taste of him.

"Christ, you're beautiful," he muttered, gazing down at her with heavy-lidded eyes.

His hands found her breasts, squeezing, fondling, and when his fingers tugged on her nipples, she cried out in delight, stunned by the shock waves that rocked her body. His hips continued to move, the friction making her mindless with lust. She writhed beneath him, ready to beg him to take his damn pants off when the tension in her body suddenly snapped and an unexpected orgasm pounded into her.

Biting her lip to stop herself from shouting her release out to the world—and her mother—she arched her back and shuddered as the climax sizzled through her like wildfire.

When she finally crashed back to earth, Luke's dark eyes were focused on her face. "Did you really just come?" he demanded, his voice a cross between a growl and a groan.

She let out a ragged breath. "Uh-huh."

"Fuck, that's hot." He ground his pelvis into her. "Do it again."

A laugh flew out of her mouth. "How about you take off your pants and we'll see what happens."

His hands shot down to his waistband, deft fingers unbuttoning it, pushing down his zipper and—a cell phone rang.

"You've got to be kidding me." The sheer distress in his voice made her laugh again.

She was about to suggest that he ignore it, but he was already off the bed and yanking the phone out of the breast pocket of his discarded long-sleeve. He cursed as he lifted the phone to his ear. "Yeah?" Another curse. "Yeah, I'll be right there."

As a wave of disappointment crested inside her, Olivia propped herself up on both elbows. "You have to go?"

"Trev needs me on recon." His gorgeous features remained taut with passion. "Damn it."

Although his reluctance to leave made her heart skip, the practical part of her kicked into gear, intensifying when

Luke's gaze fixed on her bare breasts. Her nipples were practically saluting him, puckering even more when he swept his tongue over his bottom lip.

God, what was she doing? Ground rules aside, this was still a really bad idea. She wasn't a fling girl. She didn't do casual. And Luke Dubois was casual to the bone.

That phone ringing . . . hell, it was probably a blessing in disguise.

"Don't even think about it," he said softly.

She blinked. "What?"

"Don't second-guess it." He flopped down on the edge of the bed. "This isn't over. Just postponed."

"Unless the interruption was a sign that we shouldn't do this," she countered. "A sign that we should end this before it even starts."

He laughed, slow and sexy. "Darlin', the only way this is ending is with me buried inside you."

Well, damned if that didn't nearly make her climax again.

With a lopsided grin, he bent down and brushed his lips over hers. As their mouths met, he grazed her breast with a lazy finger, tweaked her nipple, and just like that, any notion of practicality flew out the window.

When Luke's boots landed on the pavement beneath the fire escape, Sullivan was waiting for him by the ladder. Decked out in all black, Sully leaned against the brick wall and scanned Luke's disheveled appearance with dancing silver gray eyes.

"Surveillance ain't so boring anymore, is it, mate?"

He tried to conjure up a decent comeback and failed. He couldn't deny it, either. His hair was a tousled mess from Olivia's fingers running through it, and his cock was like a slab of marble, which had made his descent down the fire escape pretty damn painful.

"I'm here to relieve you," Sullivan added when Luke didn't take the bait. His gaze dropped to Luke's crotch. "Not that kind of relief, though."

"Gee, not even a hand job? I thought we were friends."

"You're not my type."

"Really? Because I'm pretty sure that *everyone* is your type—as long as they get you off."

The Australian just grinned. No denials on his part either. Sullivan was the consummate ladies' man, but it was no secret he'd done dudes too. It didn't make a lick of a difference to Luke. The guy could screw whomever he wanted, as long as it didn't affect the mission. Jim Morgan demanded only two things of the team—show up and back each other up. And Sullivan *always* had Luke's back.

"Anyway, team leader's waiting," Sullivan said. "I'm covering Olivia while you mates scope out the address she got us. Depending on what you find there, we might need to bring in the contractors. Morgan's got them on call."

Luke raised his eyebrows. Morgan had eight permanents on the team—well, nine now, with Abby coming on board—but he had a dozen other soldiers on call, men they turned to when missions required more bodies. Every last contractor was a solid asset to the team, but Luke didn't know any of them all that well, which made him uneasy. He really fucking hated having strangers watch his back, even with Morgan vouching for them.

"Let's hope it doesn't come to that," he said, smoothing his hair down. "Where you setting up?"

"Building across the street. Don't worry, mate, anyone comes near your girl, I'm on it."

"She's not my girl." He fixed Sully with a hard look. "That said, any harm comes to her, and I'll put a bullet in your knee."

"My knee? That's kind of a random place."

"Would you prefer I put one between your eyes?"

"Yes." Sullivan scowled. "You blow my knee out, how will I play rugby?"

Luke snickered. "Right. I forgot about your thriving rugby career." He clapped Sully on the shoulder. "Make sure she stays safe. I'm heading out."

He made a move toward the SUV parked in one of the visitor spaces, but Sullivan's voice stopped him.

"Milk."

He turned around with a frown. "What the hell are you talking about?"

"It'll help with the blue balls." Sullivan grinned. "Not that I get rebuffed often, but when it happens, drinking milk eases the ache. So does jerking off, but since we're sharing a room I'd rather you chug some milk."

"Thanks for the tip." Rolling his eyes, Luke got into the Range Rover and started the engine. A glance in the rearview mirror showed Sullivan darting around the side of the building, nylon backpack hanging off his shoulder.

As he navigated the deserted streets of the East Village, his thoughts drifted to Olivia, and he suddenly had to ask himself what the hell he was doing. He was always up for casual sex with a gorgeous woman, but he'd never screwed around on the job before. Being a former SEAL, he knew how to separate business from pleasure. Stay focused, get the job done, and do the pleasure thing during shore leave. Women were a distraction, and distractions could be deadly when your ass was on the line. His military career might be over, but the same philosophy applied to mercenary work—mission first, fun later.

This attraction to Olivia Taylor was getting out of control, and he was starting to suspect it went beyond a simple case of lust. She was smart, funny, and far sweeter than any of the women he'd hooked up with in the past. Strong as hell too, which was a huge turn-on. Not many women would have the guts to gather intel on a drug-dealing mobster, and Olivia's staunch determination to investigate those back rooms still floored him. She might not consider herself strong, but she had nerves of steel. And he wanted to get to know her better. He wanted to hear about her childhood, and her college classes, and her fucking hopes and dreams. How messed up was that?

Not that he was a commitment-phobe or anything. He was happy indulging in no-strings affairs and one-night stands, but he planned on settling down eventually, if he found the right woman to do it with. He'd just figured the right woman would be someone more like him — adventurous, bold, easygoing. Olivia was too cautious, too serious for him. And he could sense that she longed for security, normalcy.

Well, she wasn't gonna find that with him. He was too reckless for his own good. He lived on a private military compound with a bunch of soldiers, an ex-Mafia housekeeper named Lloyd, and a slobbering mutt. Oh, and one of his best friends was engaged to an assassin. Could anyone really call that *normal*?

Smothering a sigh, he pulled into the underground garage of the safe house. When he neared the reserved parking space, he spotted Trevor leaning against one of the concrete columns, a duffel bag by his feet and an impatient expression on his face. The second SUV wasn't in its spot; D and Holden must have already left for the address Olivia had given them.

Luke let the car idle, waiting for Trevor to toss the duffel in the back and slide into the passenger seat. While the other man buckled up, Luke punched the address into the nav system.

"All good with Olivia?" Trevor asked as they drove off.

"Yeah. She's safe and sound at her place. Nobody gave her any trouble at the club after her shift ended."

"Good."

Stopping at a red light, Luke opened the compartment in the armrest and grabbed his smokes. He shook out a cigarette, lit up, and rolled down the window. "So what happens if we case the place and confirm Dane is there? Do we extract him tonight?"

"No. Tonight we assess, see what kind of perimeter they've set up, how many guards are posted, that kind of shit."

Luke took a deep drag. "More watching, then. Yay."

"I spoke to Morgan. He said Abby's gonna try to make our job easier. She's still got contacts in the CIA, so she's calling in a favor to see if they can get us satellite images of the place, maybe use thermal imaging to get a sense of how many bodies we can expect to find inside."

"I can't imagine De Luca putting a full crew on this," Luke commented as he exhaled a cloud of smoke out the window. "This is an industrial area. He won't want to draw too much attention."

The prediction proved to be correct—when they neared the area in question, they found it utterly deserted. Killing the headlights, Luke drove along the gravel road, scanning the derelict buildings and nondescript warehouses. Most of the buildings dealt with commercial goods, and tall chain-link fences closed off several of the lots. The warehouse they were looking for stood at the very end of the strip, featuring a weathered sign that labeled the place as a carpet depot. It was a large square structure, two stories high with no windows, steel doors, and a loading dock. A few abandoned forklifts littered the pavement, but the unmarked white van parked by the recessed bay hinted that the place wasn't totally abandoned.

Luke drove right past the warehouse and turned left at the end of the road. He slowed in front of a crumbling brick building, but the glimmers of candlelight slicing out of various boarded-up windows told him there were squatters inside. He kept driving, eventually coming to a stop on a gravel lot behind a furniture warehouse.

He and Trevor got out of the car, quickly gathering up their gear. Guns slid into waistbands and shoulder holsters, earpieces went in, rifles were locked and loaded. Trevor reached for his earpiece and said, "We're here. You guys set up?"

D's voice crackled in Luke's ear. "I'm covering the back."

"I've got the west entrance," Holden said.

"Eyes and ears open, boys." Trevor turned to Luke. "Get positioned by the east entrance. I'll take the front and the loading dock."

They went their separate ways, each one disappearing into the shadows. Reaching into his back pocket, Luke pulled out a black wool cap and shoved it on his head, then put on a pair of leather gloves. There was a chill in the air, and his breath left puffs of white as he wove through the various lots toward the warehouse. He hopped a fence, his boots making no sound as they landed on the gravel. To the east of the warehouse stood a vacant mechanic shop that had seen better days. It was a sprawling one-story building with the doors chained up, but the rusted metal roof would provide good cover. Securing his rifle over his shoulder, he approached the side of the garage and found a half-gutted gray van on the pavement. He glanced at the van, then up at the flat roof, fifteen feet up. The exterior cinder-block walls rose about a foot above the roof, parapet style.

Rubbing his hands together, Luke vaulted onto the roof of the van. There was a creak of metal. He froze. Waited. Nobody came storming out of the next building. Good to go. He secured his footing, then rose to his full height on top of the van, which brought him to nearly eye level with the roof. Quick as lightning, he leapt from the van to the wall. As his hands connected with the edge, he hoisted himself up and crawled on his belly toward the other side of the roof.

When he was in position, he murmured, "East entrance covered."

And then he fixed his gaze on the neighboring warehouse and prepared for the long night ahead.

They reconvened at the apartment at nine the next morning, all except Holden, who'd stayed behind to monitor the warehouse. After spending the entire night casing the place, Luke was convinced they were onto something. There were only six guards patrolling the property, but they'd been armed to the teeth—AKs, M16s, M4s. Heavy-duty shit. They had to be protecting something damn important, but Morgan's intel said De Luca didn't use the facility for his drug operation, so that meant a different kind of merchandise was being held there. A missing DEA agent perhaps . . .

Problem was, they still had no idea what to expect if they raided the place. Only six men were posted on the exterior, but who knew how many guards they'd find inside the warehouse.

Fortunately, that question was answered once Trevor got Morgan on speakerphone. Luke, Trevor, and D settled on the couches for the briefing, and Holden and Sullivan were conferenced in while each continued to man his respective post.

"Abby got us the intel," Morgan announced. "She's on the line."

"Hey, boys." Abby's voice slid out of the speaker.

"How you doing, Sinclair?" Luke drawled. "I hear you've been teaching my dog some new tricks."

"I have." She gave a dry laugh. "Bear can now rip someone's throat out on command, and we've been working on sniffing out explosives. I set C4 around the compound but your mutt's detection skills suck. You should've started training him a long time ago."

He shook his head, even though Abby couldn't see him. "You are the most terrifying person I've ever met," he informed her. "And I swear to God, if one of your bombs blows up my dog, I'll kill you."

"I'd like to see you try."

And they both knew that wasn't gonna happen. He had no desire to mess with a former assassin, not even one as hot as Abby.

Trevor leaned forward. "Did you get in touch with your CIA guy?"

"Sure did," she answered. "I just e-mailed you some satellite images. According to my source, you're looking at eight guards. Looks like they patrol the building in teams of three, with five on the inside. Of the five, two watch the front door, two guard the back, and one's posted on the second story. My guy said there might be someone else, a static target near the second-floor guard. Heat signature's fucked up, but it could be a ninth body."

"Dane," Trevor guessed.

"That's my bet. I think the upstairs guard is posted outside the room where they're holding Dane." There was some shuffling on the line. "Gotta go. Lloyd's serving brunch on the terrace. Good luck, boys."

Morgan's voice replaced Abby's. "Come up with an extraction plan," the boss ordered. "If you have need of the contractors, call me and I'll set it up."

After the boss disconnected, Luke looked at Trevor, then D. "What do we think?"

"Eight men? No problem," D said with a shrug.

"Eight men with assault rifles," Trevor pointed out.

"Assault rifles, yeah," D agreed, "but that's it for security. No trip wires, no alarms, no motion sensors."

"No cameras," Holden piped up from the speakerphone.

"Cakewalk." Sullivan's voice chimed in.

"Yeah, maybe. Or we're walking into a trap." Trevor pursed his lips. "Let me study the images Abby sent and we'll go from there."

The briefing came to an end, and both Luke and D stood up. As D stalked off toward the rear of the apartment, Luke glanced at their team leader. "I'm going to crash for a few hours, and then I'll take over for Sully with Olivia."

Trevor nodded. "Tell her to ask Angelo for a few days off. If she's serious about getting out of the city, she needs to be ready to skip town at a second's notice."

Chapter 13

Olivia hesitated outside Vince's office the following evening, trying to collect her composure before she knocked. She'd caught a glimpse of him when she'd walked into the club twenty minutes ago, but he'd been in deep conversation with two of his bodyguards, and then the three of them had hurried upstairs as if something big was going down. She wanted no knowledge of that, though. Ever since she'd overheard those two thugs talking about drugging the girls, she'd been battling rage and horror. She knew she shouldn't be surprised that Vince was pulling shit like that, but she couldn't comprehend it. The bastard was pumping heroin and Ecstasy into those girls' veins, all so they'd be compliant and sleep with Vince's Mafia pals. What kind of person did that?

At least this would all be over soon. The voice mail Luke had left on her phone this morning had sent hope soaring through her. The address she'd found looked promising, and tonight his team would hopefully find the agent they were looking for. She'd held up her part of the bargain, and now Luke would return the favor. He would help her get away from Vince.

But who would help the girls she left behind?

She shoved away that troubling thought and knocked on Vince's door. When he shouted out an impatient "Come in," she took a breath and stepped into his office.

"Do you have a minute?" she asked.

His brown eyes lit up. "For you? Of course. Come here, babe."

She walked over to him. Didn't even flinch when he pulled her onto his lap and leaned in for a quick kiss. "Sorry I wasn't around last night," he said. "My meeting ran late."

"Everything okay with the investors?"

"It's all good. Nothing for you to worry about." He stroked the side of her neck, then frowned when he felt the thin chain around her throat. The frown transformed into a happy smile as he lifted the chain and saw the dangling silver cross, studded with small diamonds. "You're wearing it."

Olivia mentally awarded herself a gold star. Vince had given her the necklace when they'd first started "dating" after the attack. She hardly ever wore it, but after her visit to St. Mary's, she'd dug the chain out of the bottom of her jewelry box. That way if he questioned her visit to the church, she could claim to have rediscovered her religion.

"Cora's death reminded me how important faith is," she said demurely.

Vince beamed. "Good girl."

She noticed he didn't even address the *Cora's death* part, but that didn't surprise her.

"So what do you need?" he prompted.

"I was hoping I could take the next few days off."

A cloud of suspicion darkened his eyes. She'd expected that—he always got agitated when she brought up something he didn't approve of. "Why's that?" Vince asked sharply.

"It's my mom. She's not doing too great after this last round of chemo and I need to be at home to take care of her."

"You said her hair's growing back."

She bristled, biting back a nasty remark. Right, because that meant everything was A-OK. All the poison that had been pumped into Kathleen's veins hadn't hurt her at all, because, hey, her hair was growing back.

"It is, but that doesn't mean she's better," Olivia replied, trying to keep her voice calm. "The treatments hit her hard. The fatigue is worse than ever, she's anemic, her immune system is shot. And don't get me started on the kidney damage." She sighed. "It'll take a while before she's fully recovered."

"Oh, baby."

The sympathy on his face made her nauseous. She didn't know why he bothered pretending to care. They both knew he was a megalomaniac who cared only about himself.

"I need to be home right now," she maintained. "Mom just came down with a cold, and I'm worried that if I'm not around to make sure she rests and takes care of herself, it'll turn into pneumonia. That's what happened a few years ago, and she nearly died."

Vince fell silent, but his eyes never left hers. His distrustful expression returned, and she could see his brain working, as if he was trying to figure out whether to grant her the request. She prayed he would.

And that the price of it wouldn't be too high.

Her prayers went unanswered when he opened his mouth and said, "And what about our celebration, Olivia, or have you forgotten about that?"

She swallowed. "I haven't forgotten. I'm . . . looking forward to it."

His hand moved back to her neck, fingers curling over her flesh. It was a gentle touch, but not an idle one. His fingertips skimmed over the hollow of her throat as he spoke in a low voice. "I've waited a long time for you."

"I know," she whispered.

He found her pulse point and pressed the tip of his finger into it. "I'd like to think it'll be worth the wait." He slanted his head. "Will it be worth the wait, my love?"

"Yes."

"Prove it."

Queasiness washed over her. God, was this it? Was sleeping with this man the price she'd be required to pay for her freedom? Luke had told her to ease Vince's mind, to ask for a couple of days off and act like nothing was out of the ordinary, but she doubted he'd meant for her to have sex with the guy.

She swallowed again, pretty close to gagging—until it occurred to her that Vince had to be bluffing. He *had* waited a long time. Six months had passed since the attack in the alley, and in those six months he'd used tender persuasion and seductive words to bend her to his will. But she hadn't bent. And even though his advances had grown more persistent, and more frequent, he continued to stress that their first time would be special.

A quickie on his desk? With the music pounding from below and the chance of being interrupted?

No, he wouldn't allow that.

As Vince continued to stroke her neck, she met his eyes and decided to call his bluff.

"I wanted it to be special," she murmured, "but you're right. The waiting is becoming unbearable."

Surprise flared in his eyes. "What are you saying?"

Rather than answering, she pressed her lips to his. Acid shot up her throat, but she willed it away, feigning a moan when Vince's tongue pushed into her mouth. He made a satisfied sound, snaking his arms around her waist. His tongue was wet and insistent, slithering in and out of her mouth like an eel.

He won't go through with it. He won't.

She felt the evidence of his arousal poking into her butt. Taking shallow breaths, she shifted on his lap and reached for the waistband of his trousers. "Promise to be gentle," she whispered into his lips, while her hand fumbled with his zipper. "I heard it hurts the first time."

The breathy remark worked like a charm. Vince swiftly covered her hand with his, stilling her ministrations. He was breathing hard, his handsome face twisted in agony, as if putting a stop to this was pure torture. "Oh, babe," he muttered, leaning his forehead against hers. "You are ... extraordinary."

She blinked innocently. "I am?"

His breath warmed her chin. "I won't take you like this.

No matter how much I want to shove my dick inside your tight pussy, it can't be like this."

Jeez, were these the kind of sweet nothings he whispered in the ears of his bedmates? If so, no surprise he was still single.

She sighed with mock disappointment. "But—"

He silenced her by pressing his finger against her mouth. "It's going to be special," he vowed.

Said the rapist to his victim.

"But it won't be tonight," he finished. "Not here, and not like this."

"Then when?" she asked, holding her breath.

His features grew agitated. "This will be a busy week for me, babe. I've got important meetings lined up, but it'll all settle down after Tuesday."

Olivia released the breath. "Wednesday then," she said eagerly.

He gave her an indulgent smile. "Someone's getting excited." He ran his fingers over her cheekbone. "Wednesday it is, my love."

Luke instantly knew something was wrong when Olivia stormed into her bedroom. He was lounging on her bed again, but she didn't seem surprised to find him there. She also didn't seem very pleased. Without a word, she began pacing the hardwood, her muscles stiff beneath her dark blue jeans and black V-neck sweater.

"What's wrong?" he asked, keeping his voice low in case her mother was still awake. He'd heard Kathleen puttering around the apartment earlier, but fortunately she hadn't come into her daughter's bedroom. He was always a big hit with mothers—they found him downright charming—but he doubted Olivia's mother would be charmed if she discovered a strange man in her home.

He was probably an idiot for sneaking in through the window again. What he ought to be doing was keeping watch outside the building like Trevor had ordered him to, but Olivia Taylor had done a number on his self-control. He liked being near her, and her bedroom smelled so damn good, like the sweet lemony scent of her hair and the strawberry stuff she lathered on her body. Yep, he'd fully peeked into her bathroom for confirmation on the strawberry situation. Very Berry Body Wash, right there on the little shelf built into the shower.

He was so fucking pathetic.

"Vince and I set a sex date," she said emphatically, sinking down on the edge of the bed.

He sat up, wary, then scooted closer to her. "What does that mean?"

"What do you think it means?" she grumbled. "We've decided to have sex. This Wednesday. Can't wait."

Luke relaxed. "It won't happen. You know that, right? You'll be out of this city long before then."

She shifted, her big green eyes pinning him with a razor-sharp look. "You promise to keep your end of the bargain?"

He furrowed his brow. "Of course."

"Good. Then tell your team captain, or whatever you call him, to arrange the identity papers." Her expression turned fierce. "I want a new name, a new everything—for me and my mother. Anything less, and Vince will track me down."

Man. Whatever happened between her and Angelo tonight had triggered something inside her. She was broadcasting some serious anger, and what sounded like a whole lot of panic. "Olivia—"

"You don't get it," she cut in. "He'll look for me. He *loves* me, Luke. He tells me that all the time, but tonight I saw it in his eyes. I can't just move to another city and find a job and start a new life. I was fucking kidding myself, saving up money, thinking I could just move away. I'm such a fucking idiot."

Her breathing grew shallow, her eyes wild, which prompted him to pull her into his arms. "You're not an idiot, darlin'."

She buried her face in his chest. "All I wanted to do was pay for school and take care of my mother. Cora told me I'd have all the cash I wanted working at the club, and she was right—the money's good. It's really good, Luke. But then the shit in the alley happened, and now I've got this thug, a thug in expensive suits, thinking he loves me."

She sounded so miserable, he felt something crack in his chest. Fuck, this woman deserved better than this. She'd worked like a dog her entire life, and she was only twenty-five. Juggling multiple jobs, trying to get an education, taking care of a sick mother. It suddenly made him so very grateful for his own upbringing. Parents who loved him, older sisters who protected him, a nice house in a quiet neighborhood. He'd had it easy growing up, never had to work very hard, and when he'd joined the navy at eighteen, he'd had an easy ride there too.

Until tragedy had struck, but even then he'd taken the easy way out. He'd bailed, distanced himself from his family because he was too fucking grief-stricken to face them. Olivia wouldn't have bailed. Oh no, she would've clung to the only family she had left and never let go.

"When are you going to rescue that agent?"

Her change of subject made him blink. "Later tonight. One, two o'clock probably. Why?"

She glanced at the alarm clock. He followed her gaze, saw the red digits change from 10:25 to 10:26. He also saw the Glock he'd left on the nightstand, right next to his wallet and cell. She noticed it too, her expression going uneasy, but then that faded and her lush mouth set with purpose.

"Then we've got plenty of time," she announced.

He gulped. "Plenty of time for what, darlin'?"

She was already shoving her sweater over her head. His mouth went as dry as sawdust as he caught sight of her bra. A white lacy number that hugged her full breasts, with a little pink bow nestled between the cups. Oh Christ. Prim-yet-naughty lingerie had always been a helluva turn-on for him. His sex Achilles' heel.

As his body reacted, he inched away from her. Yesterday he'd told her that last night's games were far from over, but no way could he sleep with her tonight. She was too wound up, visibly upset over her impending date with Angelo.

But that didn't seem to stop her from standing up to un-button her jeans. She worked the denim down her endless legs, revealing a pair of white panties that matched her bra.

"Why are you still dressed?" she muttered.

Okay then. He wanted to point out that her glaring dag-gers at him wasn't likely to get him hot, but the bitch of it was, it *did* get him hot. His cock stiffened and strained, and his heart was suddenly beating a little bit faster.

"You don't want this," he heard himself say. "You're up-set, and I can tell the stress is finally getting to you."

Those green eyes flashed. "You're right. I'm stressed out." She blew out a breath. "So *un*stress me, damn it."

She advanced on him like a panther, graceful yet deadly. His gaze took in the tantalizing swell of her bare hips, her honeyed skin and X-rated curves, the sultry look in her eyes. He nearly fell off the bed when she climbed into his lap, straddling him with her firm thighs. She bunched up the collar of his shirt with her fist and tilted her head down-ward, her long chestnut hair cascading into her cleavage. "Kiss me," she ordered.

"No."

She practically choked him as her fist tightened over his shirt. "What do you mean, no?"

He leveled her with a steely look. "I'm not going to pre-tend I don't want you, because we both know I do." To em-phasize that, he lifted his hips so she could feel his throbbing erection. "But I'm not the equivalent of one of those stupid de-stress squeeze toys. I won't fuck you to help you forget about your problems."

He couldn't believe the words coming out of his mouth—since when did he turn down *sex*, for Christ's sake? And yeah, the notion that she was simply using him to get her mind off Angelo *was* a tad annoying, but he knew it wasn't the real reason for his holding back.

Truth was, he didn't want her to regret this.

He wanted her so damn bad he was close to exploding, but the determination in her eyes made it clear that this wasn't about sex for her. It was about amnesia, about forgetting her shit for a while via a few orgasms. From the way she'd second-guessed everything last night, he suspected she wasn't all that free-spirited when it came to sex either. She treated it with caution, with her ground rules and doubts and careful analysis. Right now, however, she was too upset to be cautious, and he didn't want her doing this only to end up with a case of *I-shouldn't-have-done-that*.

"You're actually going to turn me down?" She looked incredulous. "What happened to this only ending with you buried inside me?"

His erection twitched eagerly.

Traitor, Luke thought.

He ignored the big guy's plea for attention and said, "That'll still happen, darlin', but only when it's done for the right reasons."

She shook her head, falling into amazed silence. Then she let out a throaty laugh, completely unfazed by his rejection. "Sorry, *darlin'*, but it's happening now."

Luke's jaw fell open as she gave his chest a firm shove and got him on his back. Un-fucking-real. The *one* time he tried to be a gentleman, and what happened? A gorgeous brunette decided to sexually assault him.

God help him, but he couldn't find the will to stop her. He thought he heard himself utter a feeble protest, but then Olivia kissed him and he lost all capability of speech. Well, not true. He could still make sounds—that was totally him groaning when she slipped her tongue into his mouth. Her body was supple and warm on top of his, her lips even warmer as she kissed him with such fervor that he could barely draw a breath.

"You're wearing too many clothes," she murmured before going to work on the buttons of his shirt.

Spineless jerk that he was, he helped her out, propping up to rid himself of the clothing obstructing their goal. The goal being *naked*. It didn't take long for that to happen either. As lust turned his brain into mush, Olivia succeeded in getting his pants off, along with his boxer-briefs, socks, and boots.

"That's better," she announced.

He felt like a damn Thanksgiving feast, sprawled there on the bed while she ate him up with her smoldering gaze. He could tell she liked everything she saw, especially when her fingers circled his erection and she let out a soft sigh.

"This really isn't fair," he choked out. "I was trying to be a gentleman, and you've ruined everything."

"Tell me to stop. I dare you."

Another groan lodged in his throat as she moved her hand up and down his shaft, exerting pressure on his tip with each upstroke. His lips formed the word *stop*, but for the life of him, he couldn't make his vocal cords cooperate. Even if he could have, his cock betrayed him, weeping under her touch, a drop of pearly moisture forming at the tip.

"That's what I thought," she mocked.

Goddamn it, this woman was going to kill him.

Laughing, she bent down and took him in her mouth, and yep, he died and went to heaven. The sweet suction of her mouth had his head lolling to the side, made his breathing go ragged, and his lungs burn from the lack of oxygen. She licked him as if he were a decadent treat she was desperate to savor, alternating the featherlight strokes of her tongue with the firm pump of her fist.

Oh Jesus.

He was close to coming. Balls tight, cock throbbing, every muscle coiled like a rattlesnake. It took some serious superhuman strength to yank her mouth off him, but even then it wasn't enough because Olivia just chuckled again and continued to torture him. She brought him back to her lips and sucked him deep, her teeth nipping on the sensitive underside of his cock. She flicked her tongue over the engorged head, swirled and sucked and teased him into oblivion, until the entire world tilted and his body decided to quit fighting the rising climax.

He let out a hoarse cry, his hips jerking as his release boiled over. White-hot ecstasy slammed into him, seizing every muscle in his body, searing his blood and shorting out his nerve endings. Hot jets spurted into Olivia's wicked mouth and she swallowed every last drop, digging the fingernails of her free hand into his thigh as he shuddered in pleasure bordering on agony.

When she released him, he was still harder than stone. No recovery time needed—just the overwhelming desperation to get inside her, which only intensified when she raised her head and swiped her tongue over her glossy lips.

A wave of pure lust plowed into him. Screw it. Screw the gentlemanly approach. Didn't suit him anyway.

"Feel better?" Olivia's voice held a mocking note.

With a growl, he flipped her over and covered her body with his. She yelped in surprise, then let out an erotic moan as his mouth latched onto one breast.

Everything after that was a blur. He might have blacked out for a bit. He devoured her body, working her breasts with his hands, sucking on her nipples until she scissored her legs and made tortured sounds deep in her throat. She was sheer perfection—her satiny skin, enticing curves, mouthwatering breasts. He didn't leave an inch of skin unkissed, untasted, untouched, and yet it still wasn't enough.

Groaning, he slid down her body and buried his face between her legs. Nearly passed out when his tongue tasted her liquid sweetness. As his pulse drummed in his ears, he spread her legs farther apart and feasted on her. He didn't ease into it, didn't start off slow. He licked and sucked, slid two fingers where his erection ached to be, and gave her an orgasm that made her entire body convulse.

"Feel better?" he taunted afterward.

Her breasts heaved as she fought for air. "This . . . is kind of fun."

A laugh jammed in his throat. "Sex usually is."

"Not really." She shrugged awkwardly. "I don't think I'm very good at it."

"Huh. Because I'm pretty sure you just gave me the best blow job I've ever had."

A broad smile filled her face. "Seriously?"

"Yep."

Lord, that innocent temptress combo she had going on was

a huge turn-on. He climbed up her delectable body, thrust his fingers into her hair and kissed her, drowning in the addictive taste of her lips. Soon they were both groaning again, their legs tangled together, his erection pulsating against her belly.

"Do you have a condom?" she asked.

With a nod, he flung an arm in the direction of the nightstand and fished a condom out of his wallet. He tore the packet with his teeth, rolled on the latex, and searched her face. "It's not too late for me to be a gentleman again," he said huskily.

Licking her lips, she rolled her hips and rubbed herself against him like a restless cat. "Yes, it is. And don't bother with slow and gentle—we need this too much."

The moment he entered her, he realized she was right. The need was too great, the demand for release making it impossible to take it slow. He plunged into her, stunned by how tight she was, how wet, how eager. She met him thrust for thrust, clawing at his back as she urged him to go faster, deeper. His pulse shrieked in his ears, drowning out everything except for the sound of Olivia's moans. Another orgasm began to build, tightening his balls and gathering in his groin. He drove into her, reaching beneath her to cup her ass and lift her into him, deepening each desperate thrust.

Luke sucked in a breath through clenched teeth, helpless to stop the climax that ripped through him. Pleasure rocketed through him, hot, raw, pulsing in his veins and fragmenting his mind. And she was right there with him, unraveling beneath him, riding out her own pleasure.

Eventually they both went slack, their breathing becoming steady, heartbeats regulating.

Christ. The force of their joining shocked him to the core. There was sex, and then there was *this*.

Swallowing hard, he rolled them over so that he was on his back, Olivia curled up next to him. And then he sighed. "A part of me still thinks this might have been rape."

Her breath hitched. "What? No. I was totally into—"

"My rape," he cut in miserably. "You're the perp."

Her laughter was muffled. "I refuse to apologize. We both know you enjoyed yourself."

"Yeah, but for the record, I was trying to be a nice guy. You were too upset to be thinking clearly."

"I'm not upset anymore."

Damned if that didn't send a streak of triumph through him.

She nestled her head against his chest, and he held her, absently stroking her bare shoulder with one finger. "Can I ask you something?" she murmured.

"Ask away."

"Where do you live? The bit about having just moved here was a lie, right?"

"Yeah," he admitted. "Our compound is just west of Tijuana. I used to have a place in New Orleans, but I sold it after Katrina."

"So you live with your team now?"

"Some of the team. Holden and his wife have a place in Montana, and Trevor lives in Aspen. Sullivan crashes with us every now and then, but he prefers his boat. The rest of us stay on the compound. Not much to do, but the town has a couple of decent bars and I'm always around friends."

"What about your family?"

His throat clogged. "They stayed in Louisiana. Mom's got a new place in the suburbs, and my sisters both live near the French Quarter."

"Do you go back to visit?"

"Haven't been back since Katrina."

"Since you lost your dad," she said softly.

"I went to the funeral."

He sounded oddly defensive to his own ears. She must have picked up on it because she raised herself up on her elbow and met his eyes. Her dark hair slid onto his chest, tickling his pecs. "It must have been tough for you. Were you close with your dad?"

"Damn close." He swallowed. "He was career navy, and the reason I enlisted."

She reached for his hand and brought it to her lips, kissing his knuckles. "How did he die?"

"How else? Being a hero." His lips twisted in pain. "The entire city was in chaos after the hurricane. Dad and I hauled our old speedboat out of the garage and joined in the search for survivors. My mom and sisters were safe, bunking with a friend in Baton Rouge, but Dad refused to join them." He trailed off, his ribs aching thanks to the hammering of his heart.

Tucking a strand of hair behind her ears, Olivia gazed up at him with sympathetic eyes. "So what happened?"

Luke let out a heavy breath. "We were in the boat, saw an SOS written on a tablecloth, hanging off a roof that looked ready to collapse. A single mom and her two kids were trapped up there, and there was no way to get to them except to swim into the house. Dad and me, we were both former SEALs, so the swimming was no problem. And the family, they were brave as hell. We got all three of them out of the house and into the boat, and then . . ."

He felt the hot sting of tears and swiped at his eyes with his fist. "Their fucking dog was still in the house. We heard it whining—it must have been hiding on the second floor somewhere—and my dad decided he had to go back for the mutt. He said those two kids had already lost enough and he'd be damned if they lost their dog too. So he ordered me to stay in the boat with the family. He went back into the house alone. And the damn thing collapsed."

Olivia gasped. "Oh my God. Luke . . . I'm sorry."

He slowly unclenched his fingers. "I tried to get to him but I couldn't. There was no way in, no chance he survived the house caving in on him." His chest ached with agony. "They pulled his body out a few days later. He'd been knocked out by a beam. Drowned. The dog was floating beside him—he'd managed to get the mutt, at least."

The silence that fell was deafening. The guilt pounding into him was worse. He hadn't talked about that day with anyone, not even his family. He'd banished the memories because it was the only way to control the guilt, but now everything poured out like the floods that had ravaged his hometown.

"I should have been the one to get that dog," he burst out angrily. "But the old man wouldn't let me. Fuck, I should have tried harder to make sure he stayed in the boat."

Olivia scrambled onto his lap, shoved her arms around his neck and hugged him tight. "You and your father saved that family," she said firmly. "And your dad asked you to stay in the boat because he didn't want you risking your life. You were his son, and he wanted to keep you safe. I doubt anything you could have said would have stopped him from trying to save that dog."

Luke thought of the mutt he'd risked *his* life for and a hoarse laugh flew out of his mouth. "I guess rescuing strays runs in the family."

"Rescuing, period," she corrected. "Look at what you're risking now to find that missing agent."

As if on cue, his phone rang, and the interruption left him feeling disappointment that he couldn't explain. He hated talking about Katrina and his father, yet confiding in Olivia felt so damn right.

Sighing, he disentangled himself from her tender embrace and grabbed his cell. "What's up?" he said by way of greeting.

"We've got an extraction plan in place," Trevor announced.

"What about Olivia?"

"Isabel's already in position. She'll watch Olivia while we take care of business." Trevor's voice took on a grim note. "Get back here now. We go after Dane in an hour."

Chapter 14

"You ready?" Luke murmured as he slid his Glock from his holster.

He and D were staked out by the brick wall of the building adjacent to the warehouse. Twenty yards away, the lone guard manning the back door had halted in the middle of his perimeter sweep to light a smoke. The man was short but stocky, with a scruffy goatee and an AK-47 in his hand. The orange tip of his cigarette flared as he inhaled deeply.

Luke felt the familiar anticipation building. All they needed was Trevor's command, but the team leader was taking his sweet-ass time giving it. Holden was already in position on the roof, waiting for the word to strike, and Trev and Sully were covering the front entrance.

Next to him, D seemed unusually wired. Normally the guy was as still as a statue, unblinking, expressionless, exuding calm strength, but tonight he was acting keyed up. Black eyes blazing with purpose, fingers tapping against his thigh.

"We do this quiet," Luke reminded the other man. "Incapacitate, cut off their radio contact. No bullshit."

D lifted an eyebrow. "And you're telling me this because . . . ?"

"Because you've been itching for a fight since we got here. From before that, actually. I don't know what's going on with you, but don't fuck this up. Stick to the plan."

"Whatever you say, bro."

Static hissed in his earpiece, followed by Trevor's soft *"Go."*

They sprang into action, soundlessly advancing on the warehouse and coming up behind the guard just as he flicked his cigarette on the ground. As he became aware of their presence, the man's eyes widened, his mouth falling open. With a growl, he raised his assault rifle in a panic, but Luke kicked it out of his hand before he could pull the trigger. The AK clattered on the ground. In a flash, D got the guard in a chest lock, his forearm coming down on the man's mouth to quiet him.

Luke picked up the fallen rifle in one swift move, then leaned in to pilfer the radio sticking out of the guard's pocket. "Take care of him," he muttered to D.

He was halfway to the back door when he heard the butt of D's gun cracking down on the guard's head. There was a thud and a rustling sound as D dragged the unconscious body out of sight.

"Kangaroo out front taken care of," Sullivan's voice reported. "We're going in."

"So are we," Luke reported back. He readjusted his grip on the AK in one hand. From the corner of his eye, he noticed D removing a hunting knife from the sheath on his belt. The dude always preferred a blade if given the choice.

"Tango on the roof went down for a nap," Holden disclosed. "Going in."

Luke reached the steel door. Abby's intel said there should be two men behind it.

It was locked, but that wouldn't be a problem. They'd had an eye on this place since yesterday, and the bullshit secret knock these amateurs had come up with had been easy to figure out. Three fast knuckle punches, two long ones.

"Ready?" he murmured.

D raised his fist to the door. "Always." He knocked. *Tap-tap-tap. Tap. Tap.*

A second later, two dead bolts clicked and the door creaked open. Just a crack, but a crack was all they needed.

Luke charged inside, silencing the surprised shout of the huge goon in the doorway by barreling into the guy's chest and slamming him into the concrete wall. The guard's rifle crashed to the cement floor. They both dove for it, but Luke reached it first and kicked the weapon away before launching himself at the guard. All it took was a swift karate chop to the neck for the guard's eyes to roll back in his head, and then he was out cold.

Luke bounced to his feet in time to see D seating himself on the beefy chest of the second guard. D's shaved head gleamed under the fluorescent light illuminating the corridor, and his eyes burned with satisfaction as he brought his blade up to the goon's throat and pressed it to his Adam's apple.

With an angry curse, the guard's hand shot toward the radio on his belt, but D dug the knife deeper, drawing a line of blood. "Do it," he said softly. "Reach for the radio again."

The hand froze. Uneasiness swam in the brown eyes of D's prey.

"Do it," D said again. "Please. Just give me a reason."

Luke's shoulders tensed. He had no fucking clue why his teammate was suddenly acting like a bloodthirsty savage, but he didn't fucking like it. Keeping his gaze on D's knife, he stepped forward and uttered a low warning. "Derek."

But the guard must have seen the same thing Luke had glimpsed on D's face, because the hand hovering over the radio flopped onto the floor and the man's huge body went limp with defeat.

The rush of disappointment that filled D's eyes troubled the hell out of Luke.

"Coward," D mumbled before slamming the handle of his knife into the man's temple.

As D pocketed the radio and got to his feet, Luke's lips tightened in a thin line. "What the fuck was that?" he demanded.

D glanced from one conked-out guard to the other. "Incapacitate and take out radio contact, no?"

He was ready to call bullshit on that, but D ended the conversation by checking in with the rest of the team. "We handled the two in the back. Status?"

A grunt reverberated in their ears. "One down here. Second fucker . . . is . . . being . . . handled," Sullivan mumbled between pants.

Gunfire erupted.

At the sound of the shots, Luke all but forgot about the disturbing exchange between D and that guard. With D hot on his heels, he raced down the musty hallway, adrenaline spiking.

They reached a pair of huge swinging doors and rammed through them, emerging into a dark, cavernous space littered with empty pallets stacked up to the ceiling. Shit was happening near the front door, shadowy figures wrestling on the floor. Raising his gun, Luke sprinted across the room just as a sickening *crack* split the air.

Breathing hard, Sullivan stood up and scowled at the burly man lying dead at his feet.

"You hit?" Luke inquired sharply.

Sullivan wiped his bloody knuckles on the front of his black pants. "Nah. Idiot shot at the ceiling a few times."

Trevor stepped out of the shadows, holding a confiscated radio. He opened his mouth, but the sound of his voice was drowned out by more gunfire. Two shots, a long pause, and then the unmistakable spray of an AK-47.

Holden's urgent voice boomed into Luke's earpiece. "Second floor. Last tango is making a run for it."

Luke was the first to reach the metal staircase by the far wall. His boots pounded up the stairs, gun drawn. On the landing, he skidded to a stop at the same time a wild-eyed man dressed in black flew out of the corridor. The man took one look at Luke, then snarled and lifted his rifle.

Luke's bullet hit him between the eyes. The guard went slack. The weapon promptly fell from his hands, his big body going down right along with it.

At the thump of footsteps, Luke swept his gun up, then lowered it when Holden appeared at the end of the hall.

"I found him," the other man announced.

Shit. That didn't sound good.

Stepping over the guard's body, Luke followed Holden down the hall. They came to a stop in front of an open doorway. The room beyond it was bathed in shadows, pitch-black save for the sliver of moonlight slicing through the boarded-up window. A dark lump took residence on the cement floor in the center of the room. A body.

Trevor and the others swiftly appeared. With a resigned look, Trevor removed a flashlight from his belt and clicked it on, shining a shaft of light on the motionless figure.

"Is that Dane?" Sully spoke up.

"Don't know."

Holden stayed by the door while the others approached the body. Several more flashlights switched on.

"Two shots to the back of the head," Trevor said grimly. He knelt, got his hands under the body, and rolled it over.

Everyone grimaced. The dude's face was beaten to shit, a mangled mess of flesh, blood, and bone. Totally unrecognizable, though the hair matched the color and cut from Carter Dane's photo. The stiff wore a tattered suit that had once been expensive, which also pointed to Dane, who'd no doubt had to stock up on the Armani once he'd started wooing Angelo and De Luca.

Luke bent down and rummaged inside the dead guy's jacket. His hand emerged holding a leather wallet, which he flipped open so he could examine the driver's license in the plastic sheath.

"Kyle Barber," he said.

"Dane's alias," Trevor answered. "I guess De Luca made him."

Shaking his head, Luke stood up. "It might not be Dane. Look at his face, for fuck's sake. It's beaten to a bloody pulp. You don't do that for fun—you do it to prevent identification."

"One way to find out." Trevor went for the stiff's zipper.

"What the *fuck*, mate?" Sullivan burst out, looking horrified. "Please don't tell me you're into corpses."

"Why not? He's still warm." When Sully groaned in disgust, Trevor rolled his eyes. "Relax, man, it's all about ID." He undid the zipper and eased the corpse's trousers down a few inches, then lifted the body to sneak a peek at the top of Mr. Dead's ass.

Luke peered closer, instantly spotting the tat. It was a name, done in black cursive with a bunch of doodaddle curlicue shit around it. *Mandy*.

"Oh, Mandy," Sullivan murmured. "Well, you came and you gave without taking."

"Dane had a Mandy?" Luke asked.

"She was his high school sweetheart, died in a DUI before he joined the agency. He got inked on the one-year anniversary of her death. Dane's file said he worked Mandy into his cover story." Trevor let the body drop. "It's him."

It all felt oddly anticlimactic, but then again, wasn't this exactly what he'd been expecting? From the start, this job had felt like morgue duty. Finding Dane beaten and bullet-ridden was really no surprise.

Sullivan shrugged. "Mission accomplished, then."

"Looks like it." Trevor called out to Holden. "Contact our guy at the DEA. Tell him to send a cleanup crew."

Hours later, Trevor stepped out of the shower in the master bathroom, wrapped a towel around his waist, and strode into the bedroom in search of his phone. He found it on the dresser and headed over to the bed, sinking onto the mattress as he dialed Isabel's number.

She picked up on the first ring. "Trevor?"

He couldn't control the spark of pleasure that heated his chest. He loved the sound of her voice. If that made him a pathetic sap, then so be it.

"You get home all right?" he asked gruffly.

"Yeah. Sullivan came to relieve me at Olivia's building and I went straight home." He heard her yawn. "I'm dying to go to sleep, but I was waiting for your call."

Trevor checked the phone display, cringing when he realized it was five o'clock in the morning. The team had spent hours briefing the DEA agents who'd arrived to collect Dane's body. Guilt skated through him at the knowledge that he'd kept Isabel awake this entire time.

"Shit, I should have called you earlier," he said in apology. "We got tied up at the warehouse."

"No worries. So, are we certain the body you found was Dane?"

"Fairly certain. ID matched, and so did the tattoo, but the agency will verify it with DNA since the guy's face was unrecognizable."

"When will we know for sure?" Isabel asked.

"Hopefully a day or two, depending on how long the DNA testing takes. Morgan wants us to stick around until we get confirmation, and he wants you to keep working at the club until then."

Her voice became dry. "I was hoping to put my stripping career behind me."

"We'll pull you out soon," he promised. "But there's bound to be some fallout from Dane's body being found. Angelo will want to cover his tracks, so we need you there to keep an eye on things."

"What about the DEA's mole situation? Do they still believe someone tipped De Luca and Angelo off about Dane infiltrating the outfit?"

"They're investigating it at their own end, but frankly, even if they asked us to weed out their mole, I'd say hell no. I'm tired of this city."

"Me too." She sounded tired as she added, "I'm not sure why I even keep paying the rent on this apartment. New York offers nothing but sad memories."

He waited for her to elaborate, but the line went quiet. "Get some sleep," he finally said. "We'll talk tomorrow, okay?"

After they hung up, Trevor dragged a hand through his hair, feeling on edge. What exactly was he hoping to get from Isabel? Was he even ready to start something up with her? Gina had been gone for nearly two years, but he still dreamed of her, that same heart-wrenching dream where she appeared with a gun and tore into him for not being there to save her. And he still woke up in the middle of the night reaching for her, only to be hit by a wave of sorrow when his hand collided with nothing but emptiness. So, hell, maybe Isabel was right to keep her distance.

He stood abruptly, tired of thinking in circles. This wasn't the time to be stirring up doubts and uncertainties. All he knew was that Isabel had saved his ass six months ago. She'd given him a second chance at life.

And he'd be a fool to waste that chance by letting old fears and lingering pain stand in his way.

"It wasn't supposed to go down like that," Vince fumed. He stalked across the living room toward the floor-to-ceiling windows that overlooked the city. Even at seven o'clock on a Sunday morning, Manhattan was wide-awake and bustling. Bumper-to-bumper traffic on the streets, pedestrians rushing along the sidewalks. He had to wonder how many of those people had also woken up to bad news.

Tearing his gaze away from the flurry of activity below, Vince tightened his grip on the phone and let out a curse. "How did you let this happen?"

His associate sounded unrepentant. "Our men were caught off guard," Erik Franz snapped. "Did *you* expect the DEA to storm the place?"

"Goddamn it." He sat down on the leather couch and slammed his fist against his thigh. "Who knew the location of the warehouse? Who's the fucking canary who sang to the Feds?"

Franz sounded weary. "I don't know. Other than you and me, only the men assigned to the warehouse were in the loop. A few of the enforcers in De Luca's inner circle also knew the location, but I don't think the boss will take too kindly to us pointing fingers at his trusted soldiers."

No, De Luca wouldn't take kindly to that at all.

Hot rage exploded in Vince's gut, hardening his jaw and

making his hands tingle. In his eyes there was nothing more despicable than betrayal, and someone in his organization had just betrayed the fuck out of him. The DEA wasn't supposed to find the body until Vince *let* them, and thanks to the rat, the body had been discovered ahead of schedule.

"Are we sure it was DEA?" he demanded.

"Jimmy drove by earlier and the warehouse was crawling with Feds, crime scene tape everywhere. Five of our guys got pinched, and two were killed during the raid."

"What precinct were they taken to?"

"Seventh."

"Good. Detective O'Shea is a friend of ours. Someone needs to get into lockup and take care of the five. We can't have the death in the warehouse leading back to us."

"Already on it. I sent Dominic."

"Are we sure our man took out Dane?"

"He called me the second the shit hit the fan. I ordered him to put two bullets in the guy's head and stayed on the phone while he did it."

"So Dane's dead."

"Dane's dead."

"All right. At least that's one less thing to worry about." His eyes narrowed as something occurred to him. "We assigned eight men to the warehouse. You said two dead, five locked up. Who and where is the fucking eighth?"

Franz's heavy breathing echoed on the line. "Bruno. He was on a coffee run when shit went down. Came back, saw the cops, and bolted. He's at the safe house in Brooklyn. And before you ask, he insists he's not the rat. I'm inclined to believe him—Bruno's too damn stupid to betray you. What endgame could that idiot possibly have?"

Vince couldn't help but concur. Bruno had the IQ of a fucking Kleenex—the oaf lacked both the brains and the savvy to pull off any real attempt at treason. Nevertheless, a message needed to be sent, and Bruno, unlucky bastard that he was, would take the fall for this.

"Send Sal to take care of it," Vince said brusquely.

There was a beat. "He's not the rat. In fact, there might not even *be* a rat. One of those boneheads might have leaked the address out of sheer incompetence."

"I don't give a shit. Someone needs to pay for this fuckup. Might as well be Bruno."

"That's messed up."

"It's convenient," he snapped. "Those other motherfuckers are in lockup. Bruno isn't. So tell Sal to deal with it."

Franz paused again. "You want to give him the rat treatment?"

"Yes." He grumbled in irritation. "Slit the bastard's throat, cut his fucking tongue out, and give everyone in the organization a reminder of the consequences for snitching. And then you can keep a closer eye on the men and a tighter rein on this deal so shit like this doesn't happen again."

As disgust and residual rage coursed through his veins, he resisted the impulse to strangle someone. Namely Franz. The sole purpose of that body had been so the Feds would be looking the other way while the transaction went down. Vince couldn't afford a single fucking hiccup when it came to this deal. They were looking at almost a hundred kilograms of heroin, five million dollars of pure, grade-A shit. It was twice the size of the shipments they typically smuggled in, and the first delivery under the new agreement they'd made with the Moreno cartel.

He had brokered the deal himself, which meant that nothing, absolutely nothing, could go wrong. De Luca hadn't been keen on joining up with the Colombians—the organization already had a solid distribution deal going with the Afghans—but Vince had pushed for this, and if it went smoothly, he'd climb even higher in De Luca's eyes. If it didn't . . . well, he refused to even consider that.

"Keep me posted on the situation," he barked into the phone. "The Moreno rep is supposed to call tomorrow with a status check on the delivery, and the boat should arrive in the Miami port Monday afternoon. Make sure the crew down south is ready."

"What about the Premiere Roast shipment?" Franz asked.

"Gets in late Monday night. The cargo will be unloaded, but the crew will wait for the Dominican merchandise before loading the truck." He checked his watch. "I've got a fitting with my tailor, but I'll be at the club later tonight. Take care of those five loose ends. And silence the canary."

With that, Vince ended the call and swore out loud. How the hell had the DEA caught wind of where they'd been holding that asshole? He didn't give a damn if he was looking for a snitch or an imbecile—either way, this would not happen again.

It was also clear that he'd given Franz too much rope, and that was something he evidently needed to rectify. Delegating that much responsibility was always a bad idea.

Nothing could go wrong this time. The DEA might have found the body, but Vince would be damned if the Feds screwed up this new venture. Everything was on schedule, and he planned on being there when the merchandise arrived to make sure it all went according to plan. He couldn't afford any more fuckups. The boss already had doubts about this new partnership with the Moreno organization. If anything went wrong . . .

He banished the thought. Nothing would go wrong. The shipment would arrive safe and sound, the merch would be distributed without a hitch. De Luca would slap him on the shoulder and grudgingly admit that he'd done good.

And then Vince would earn a permanent place at the boss's table.

"Good morning," Kathleen said softly when Olivia entered the kitchen.

"Morning." She padded over to the counter to pour herself a cup of coffee, then joined her mom at the table. "Sleep well?"

"I slept better than I have in a long time." Her mother arched her brows. "I imagine you did too."

Olivia shot her a quizzical look. "Why do you say that?"

"I might be bald, but I'm not deaf." Kathleen gave a crooked smile. "So when do I meet him?"

Heat scorched her cheeks. "Meet who?"

"The man who's been sneaking into my daughter's bedroom the past couple of nights."

Oh boy. Talk about embarrassing. The two of them never spoke about Olivia's love life, but that was probably because she didn't *have* a love life. She'd only been in one serious relationship in her life, back in freshman year at NYU, but that involvement had been a fluke. Normally she was far too busy for trivial matters like dating. Or love.

Not that she and Luke were dating. Or in love.

"It's nothing," she said quickly. "Not a big deal at all."

"Really? Because I can't recall the last time you invited a man home." Her mother wrapped her frail hands around her coffee mug, pretending to think it over. "Oh, I know why I can't remember. Because you've never done it before."

"Like I said, it's no big deal."

"Does Mr. No Big Deal have a name?" Kathleen prompted.

The faint chime of her cell phone saved Olivia from having to answer. She jumped out of the chair, left the kitchen, and hurried into her bedroom, answering the phone just before it kicked into voice mail. "Hello?"

"Hey, it's me."

An involuntary streak of happiness surged through her. Luke's lazy drawl instantly had her remembering everything they'd done last night. Her mom was right—she *had* slept great. She'd gone to bed sated and relaxed, drifting off the moment Luke climbed out her window to meet up with his team and—

"How did it go last night?" she blurted out. "Did you find the agent?"

"Yeah. Yeah, we did." He paused. "The guy was already dead when we got there."

Olivia gasped. "They killed him?"

"Afraid so," he said flatly. "Either way, it's done. We

found Dane, so our job is over. Now it's time to return the favor, darlin'."

Hope skated up her spine. "You're really going to help me?"

"I promised you I would," he said gruffly. "I'm stopping by in an hour or so if that's all right with you. I need to take a couple of photographs of you and your mother so we can line up your new documents."

Her mother. Olivia's heart jammed in her throat as she realized she would finally have to tell her mom the truth.

"Liv? You there?"

God, how was she going to explain everything to her mom? She'd been lying about her job for the past twelve months, pretending to work at a restaurant on Broadway. She'd even gone into the place and asked if she could buy one of their aprons, just so she could bring it home every now and then to give her bullshit some credibility. And six months ago, she'd explained away her attack by claiming she'd been mugged on her way home from work and that the surgeon who'd worked on her face had done it pro bono.

Now she had to confess that it had all been a lie. That she was actually a stripper at the Diamond Mine who'd been attacked by a would-be rapist and had become indebted to a mobster who paid all their bills.

Tears of shame stung her eyes. "She's going to be disgusted with me."

"What are you talking about?"

"My mother." She blinked through the onslaught of tears. "She's going to hate me when I tell her everything that's been going on."

"She's not going to hate you," Luke said firmly. "And she won't be disgusted. I promise you, your mom will understand. If anything, she'll be upset with herself for putting you in a position where you had to do all this to take care of her."

"*I* put myself in this position." Olivia hesitated. "But I'm getting us out. You're getting us out, right?"

"Right." His voice became husky. "I'll be over in an hour,

darlin'. Do you want me to be there when you talk to your mother?"

The offer warmed her heart, but she knew this was something she had to do alone. "No, that's okay, but thanks. I'll see you soon."

After they hung up, she walked into the bathroom to splash some cold water on her face. When she lifted her head to examine her reflection in the mirror, she had to wonder what Luke Dubois saw in her. Yes, her face was technically flawless—high cheekbones, full lips, straight nose, and smooth skin. But her eyes . . . they were full of shadows, as Candy Cane had noticed.

Now she was about to bring shadows to her mother's eyes, and as she left the bathroom, she prayed that Luke was right and that her mother would understand.

Her mom was still at the table when she returned to the kitchen. "Everything all right, sweetheart? Who was on the phone?"

Olivia's legs shook as she lowered herself onto the chair. "A friend," she said vaguely. She took a long sip of coffee, then set the mug down and mustered up some courage. "I need to talk to you about something."

Kathleen frowned. "All right."

"We need to go away for a little wh—"

The phone rang again. The landline this time, and Olivia gritted her teeth in irritation. For the love of God.

"Hold that thought." She sighed and grabbed the cordless from the counter, answering with a quick hello.

"Is this Olivia?" an unfamiliar female voice asked.

She wrinkled her forehead. "Yes. Who's this?"

"This is Maureen. Maureen Malcolm." A pause. "Cora's mother."

Olivia's chest squeezed. "Oh. Mrs. Malcolm. I . . . I'm so sorry about Cora. I know I should have called, but—"

"It's all right, dear. I understand." The woman hesitated. "Cora spoke of you often."

"She spoke of you too." Olivia swallowed the lump in her throat. "She loved you very much. How is Katie doing?"

"She misses her mom, but she's a tough little girl. She'll be okay. Eventually."

"And you?"

"I miss my daughter," Maureen said simply. "I . . . Lord, I still don't understand any of this. Was she . . . did my daughter confide in you . . . about the drugs?"

"No. No, she didn't."

Olivia felt like someone had shoved a knife into her heart, especially when Maureen continued in a bewildered tone, "Cora was a good girl. A smart girl. I don't understand why . . . how . . . she got involved with drugs. I never knew."

The soft sobbing tore Olivia apart. She wanted so desperately to assure the woman that everything she'd believed was true—that Cora *wasn't* a drug addict. To tell her that her daughter had been murdered.

But she couldn't do it. Vince wouldn't have risked killing Cora unless he'd known he wouldn't be leaving any evidence behind. If Olivia told Maureen Malcolm the truth, she might be placing Maureen and Cora's daughter in danger.

"I'm so sorry," Olivia said.

The sobbing stopped, replaced by Maureen's dull voice. "The funeral is Friday afternoon at St. Joseph's Church. I thought you should know."

"I'll do my best to be there," she promised.

After they disconnected, Olivia turned to find Kathleen's unhappy green eyes fixed on her. "That was your friend's mother?"

She nodded. "She was calling about the funeral."

"The poor woman must be devastated. Imagine, finding out your daughter is an addict when you didn't have a clue."

But she wasn't an addict!

A rush of anger flooded her belly. These last couple of days she hadn't allowed herself to think about Cora's death, but the memory returned now in full force. Vince had killed Cora. He'd *killed* an innocent young woman just because she wasn't being cooperative during his private sex parties, and now a little girl was an orphan because of it.

And Vince was *still* doing it. Distributing his heroin, doping up dancers when his associates requested their company.

Her anger escalated, turning into an eddy of rage. And he was just getting away with it! Nobody was bothering to interfere; nobody was trying to stop him. Not even Luke, who certainly had the skills to put Vince Angelo out of commission.

"Liv?" Kathleen said cautiously, heading for the counter. "You want another cup?"

She shook her head, hoping the fury she was feeling didn't show on her face. She watched as her mother dropped a spoonful of sugar into her coffee, and was reminded of the spoon she'd seen on Cora's bedside table. The powder lining that piece of tinfoil. The fucking syringes strewn on the floor.

Another shipment was coming in. Vince had mentioned it during the conversation she'd overheard in her stairwell, and those two goons from the club had spoken of a shipment too.

It had to be drugs. More drugs were being smuggled into the city. Drugs that Vince put in the hands of dealers and in the veins of the girls he decided to pimp out.

Olivia fisted her hands so tight that her knuckles turned as white as the plastic table beneath them. She couldn't let it happen again. The thought came swift and hard. She knew she couldn't bring Cora back to life, but damn it, she could at least try to stop Vince from hurting any more of the girls at the Diamond.

"So what were you saying before the phone rang?" her mother asked, settling back in her chair.

She looked up to meet her mom's gaze. "Oh. It was nothing."

"You said something about going away?"

"No. Well, yeah, I was thinking about taking a trip, you and me. But . . . I just realized how impossible it would be to get the time off."

"A trip does sound nice, but it might be best to hold off for a while. I don't know if I'm up to traveling just yet."

Olivia reached across the table and grasped her mother's hand. "Don't worry. We won't go anywhere for the time being." She set her jaw. "We're staying right here."

Chapter 15

Luke sat on Olivia's bed, gaping as the words she'd just uttered registered in his brain. "Are you serious?"

She nodded. In her bright blue leggings and loose black T-shirt, with her long hair tied up in a high ponytail, she looked much younger than twenty-five. The youthful attire was completely out of sync with the deadly look in her green eyes.

"Why?" he demanded, shaking his head in bewilderment. "Why on earth would you stay in this city and continue working at the club?"

"I already told you—I want to stop that shipment."

He continued to gawk at her. The stubborn jut of her chin told him she meant business, yet he still couldn't wrap his mind around it. "And how exactly are you going to stop it?"

"I don't know." She shrugged. "But it'll be easier if you help me."

Disbelief pounded into him. "Are you listening to yourself? You're a college student, a *civilian*—how the hell do you plan to intercept a heroin delivery? Do you have some secret knowledge about drug smuggling that you didn't tell me about?"

She bristled. "No, that's why I need your help." Her ponytail swung back and forth as she began to pace the hardwood floor. "You've got experience with this kind of thing.

I'm sure we can come up with some sort of plan. I can't let Vince get his hands on more drugs."

Oh, for the love of . . .

Luke drew a calming breath, resisting the impulse to grab her by the shoulders and shake some sense into her. "Olivia. Be reasonable. Even if we find a way to intercept and destroy the shipment, do you honestly think you'll be winning the war on drugs? You know how many dealers are out there? How many suppliers, distributors? Are you planning on taking down every drug cartel too? Ridding the globe of the entire trade?"

She glared at him. "Of course not. I'm not interested in the global drug trade. Just this one shipment. If it doesn't reach Vince, then it won't reach anyone who works at the Diamond."

"Jesus."

"Cora is *dead*," she burst out. "Her little girl is *motherless* now! Katie's never going to know her mom. Cora won't be there for Katie's high school graduation, or her wedding, or at the hospital when she has a child of her own. Vince pumped Cora full of heroin and had her killed because she didn't do what he wanted. What if it happens again? What if another dancer dies at the hands of that bastard?"

"Fine, then we'll go to the cops. Let them handle it."

"You're the one who told me Vince and De Luca have dozens of cops on their payroll. Nobody is going to investigate Cora's death, and if I tell the police about this shipment, nobody will investigate that either."

"We'll go to the DEA then," he said in frustration.

"So Vince and his fellow mobsters can murder another one of their agents? Or so that mole you were telling me about tips off Vince?" She stopped pacing, visibly angry now. "I don't trust law enforcement to handle this. You said so yourself—they've been giving De Luca a free ride for years."

"Oh, so you trust *yourself* to take down the Mob," he said sarcastically.

"No, but I trust *you*." She marched over, sank to her

knees in front of him, and looked up with imploring eyes. "Please help me do this."

He shook his head again, stunned by this sudden turn of events. He'd come here prepared to organize the necessary identity papers for Olivia and her mother, and instead of snapping a few pictures and assuring her that everything would be all right, he was arguing with her about intercepting heroin deliveries.

With a sigh, he reached for both her hands. "Look, I know you're upset about your friend's death, but this is . . . this is *insane*. You need to leave town, now, while Vince is distracted with this drug bullshit and the discovery of Dane's body. The longer you stay, the more time you give him to regroup—and focus his sights on you again."

She yanked her hands away. "I won't let him hurt anybody else."

"But you'll let him hurt *you*?"

"He won't." She sounded sure of herself. "He told me that he won't have time for me until Wednesday. So that means the drugs will be delivered before then. Tuesday probably, since he said he has a big meeting that night. I think that's when the shipment is coming in."

Luke cursed under his breath, wondering how the hell to talk some sense into her, but she wasn't done speaking. "Ask your team to stick around. We'll figure out when and where the shipment will happen, I'll keep working at the club, and if something goes wrong, I promise I'll leave town."

"Goddamn it, Olivia."

"Please," she pleaded. "Just have my back when I'm at the club, and help me gather information. Once we have something solid, we'll turn it over to the DEA and they can handle the bust. But I won't tip them off before the delivery. If there is a mole, Vince will be warned and the delivery won't go through."

He dragged a hand through his hair, frustrated beyond belief. He could see in her eyes that she wasn't going to drop this. She would go through with her ridiculous plan, no matter what he said or did. And if he walked away, she'd do it alone. With no one to watch out for her.

But damn it, this was foolish. He had no idea how Angelo and De Luca secured their drugs, what cartel they were mixed up with, how they smuggled the shit in. And he had no desire to get involved in the drug trade. The people who dealt in drugs were bad news—they wouldn't hesitate to kill anyone who got in their way.

Like a pretty coed from the East Village.

Letting out a heavy sigh, he slowly got to his feet. "You really need to reconsider this," he said in a low voice.

"I can't. I refuse to let Vince get away with what he's done. He belongs in jail."

"Which will only happen if he's caught red-handed. What if he's not there when the transaction goes down? Did you think of that?"

"He'll be there," she said confidently. "He said so himself—there's a lot of money riding on this deal. If it goes wrong, he'll be in trouble with De Luca, and he won't leave something so important in the hands of his goons. He'll want to be there himself to make sure everything goes smoothly. And he'll be arrested right along with everyone else when the cops show up."

She moved toward him and touched the center of his chest. "Please," she whispered. "Help me."

"I . . . don't know," he said roughly. "I'd need to clear it with my boss, talk to the team. I'll be honest—I don't think they'll be on board."

"But what about *you*?" she pressed. "If your team leaves, will you stay?"

Would he? He stared into her big green eyes, then pictured her at the Diamond Mine, sticking that pretty nose into Vince Angelo's heroin business. Fuck. How the hell could he let her do this alone? If he couldn't dissuade her, he could at least make sure she didn't get herself killed.

He cleared his throat. "Yeah. Yeah, I'll stay."

A smile broke out on her face. "You will?"

Luke nodded. "Let me talk to my team, okay? I'll run this by them and see if they want to stick around too."

Olivia threw her arms around his neck and hugged him. He inhaled the lemony scent of her hair, wondering why it was so frickin' difficult to say no to this woman.

"Thank you," she murmured, tilting her head to kiss him.

As their lips met, his pulse sped up and his knees felt weak. Yep, Olivia Taylor definitely had a hold on him.

"I'll call you after I talk to the guys," he said, brushing his lips over hers one last time.

A few minutes later, he descended the fire escape, releasing the frustrated groan he'd been smothering during the entire conversation with Olivia. As he strode toward the Range Rover, he sent Sullivan a quick text telling him he was taking off and to keep watching the building. Olivia's decision to single-handedly fight the war on drugs wasn't something that should be discussed via text message, so he decided he'd fill Sully in later.

He slid into the driver's seat and started the engine, letting out another groan as a vise of helplessness pinched his insides. The last thing he wanted was to watch Olivia put her neck on the line, just so she could stop Angelo from getting his hands on some heroin. What he *did* want to do was throw her over his shoulder, force her into Morgan's jet, and get her far away from this city. Far away from Vince Angelo.

The mere thought of that bastard hurting her made Luke's blood boil. Rather than putting the SUV in gear, he reached for his phone, hit speed dial, and waited for Kane Woodland to pick up. Of all the guys on the team, Luke was closest to Kane and Sully, but Sullivan wasn't the right guy to talk to about this. Kane was far more levelheaded, and he had a lot of experience with stubborn women.

"Hey, man," he said when Kane answered.

"Hey. I heard about Dane. When are you guys heading home?"

"We're sticking around until the DNA results come in." He paused. "Listen, you alone?"

"No, I'm in the game room with Ethan. Kicking his ass in pool."

"Tell him to get lost. I need to ask you something."

Muted sounds filled the extension, then Kane saying, "Get lost."

"Fuck you," came Ethan's muffled reply.

"Okay, he's gone. What's up?"

Luke leaned back against the headrest. "Yeah. Well."

"Yeah well what?"

Swallowing, he bit the bullet and said, "How'd you know that you loved Abby?"

There was a beat of shocked silence. "For real?"

"Yeah. For real."

"Okay. Huh. Well, it wasn't something I knew so much as felt. But it probably happened when I found myself thinking about her every freaking second. And wanting to protect her." Kane laughed dryly. "Yes, I know she can take care of herself—God knows she reminds me of that every other second—but seriously, man, the thought of someone hurting her sends me into a fit of rage. If anyone touched her I'd slit their throat. And yeah, then there's the sex . . . it's out of this fucking world . . . Um, anyway. Why do you want to know?"

"I've been spending time with one of the girls at the club. Olivia Taylor. She helped us find Dane." Luke blew out a breath. "I feel weird, man."

"Weird how?"

"Like when she smiles at me, my chest goes all hot, like someone cranked the thermostat."

Kane burst out laughing.

"Hey, I'm sharing here."

"Sorry. What else?"

"I like talking to her and . . . and yeah, the thought of someone hurting her makes me want to slit a few throats too." He faltered. "So what do you think that means?"

"Might be love. Could be lust. You figure it out."

"*That's* your advice?"

"Who do you think I am, Ann Landers? I can't decode

your feelings for you. But if it helps, I don't think it's lust."

Help? Uh, it fucking terrified him. He'd called Kane hoping to hear that everything he felt was no biggie, just a common side effect of extreme lust or something.

He'd never been in love before, and truthfully, he had no idea what being in love entailed. Was he supposed to buy her a gift? Start referring to their sex life as *lovemaking*? Crap. He was totally out of his element here. Didn't know how to handle this in the slightest.

But he did know one thing—he wasn't leaving this city unless Olivia was on the plane beside him.

"No way," D announced once Luke finished speaking.

Out of everyone, he'd expected D to be the first to shoot the idea down, and the man didn't disappoint. However, when Luke focused on Trevor, he was discouraged to find that the team leader didn't look enthusiastic either.

"I'm doing this with or without you guys," he said quietly.

Holden leaned against the sofa cushions, looking resigned. "So you're going to stick around and do what? Watch her back?"

D cursed.

So did Luke. "Screw that," he said. "I won't play bodyguard while Olivia fucks around in the heroin trade, and I'm sure as hell not going to hand over the information to the DEA knowing they've probably got a few agents on the take."

Trevor narrowed his eyes. "What does that mean?"

"It means I'll track this damn shipment myself, and then I'll intercept the damn thing—myself. I'll only involve the DEA after the raid goes down."

Three pairs of eyes stared at him in disbelief.

"Jesus. You're serious," Trevor said.

"Olivia wants Angelo in prison. Hell, she *needs* him in prison in order to be safe. And she doesn't want this shipment hitting the streets." He set his jaw. "I'm going to make sure both those things happen."

"Do I dare ask how?" Trevor asked dryly.

Luke turned to Holden. "Who's that contractor we used last year in Haiti? The former DEA guy?"

"Liam Macgregor. And yeah, he was DEA, Boston field office."

"Get me his number. He probably knows a shit ton about drug smuggling." He sighed. "Look, I don't expect you guys to stick around. Once we get confirmation that it was Dane's corpse in that warehouse, y'all head back to the compound if you want."

D cursed again.

Luke flashed him a dark look. "Like I said, don't help. But me? I refuse to let Olivia get killed, and trust me, if I leave, she *will* get killed."

There was a short silence, broken by Holden's weary sigh. "I'll stay."

Luke shot the man a grateful look. "Yeah?"

"Yeah. I'll talk to Morgan and see if he can spare me."

Holden's acquiescence definitely tipped the scales in Luke's favor. The other men respected Holden and yielded to his judgment, so his involvement only boded well.

Sure enough, Trevor nodded. "I'll stay too. And I'm sure it won't be hard to twist Sully's arm."

Luke glanced over at the sliding door where D was brooding. "And I take it you're out?"

"Tell me, is the sex that good, bro?"

He stiffened. "This isn't about sex."

D gave a derisive snort. "Right, because she won you over with her personality."

Luke knew when he was being baited, and he wasn't even surprised. D had been acting like a total bastard lately, dying for a fight. Like the way he'd taunted the guard at the warehouse to fight back, to give him an excuse to kill him. Luke had no clue what was up with his teammate, but he refused to give D what he wanted.

"She's a good woman" was all he said. "And she asked for my help. End of story."

"And how's she going to return the favor this time?" D

asked with a mocking slant of his head. "She already helped us find Dane, so what now? You help her, she screws you again?"

He tightened his lips. Nope. Not gonna take the bait.

"And what about the rest of us? Will she show us some gratitude too?" D's black eyes glimmered.

A muscle in his jaw twitched.

"Toss a couple blow jobs our way?"

Luke launched himself at D, knocking the guy to the floor as his fist came crashing down on D's jaw.

"That was un-fucking-called for," Luke grunted. He jammed his forearm into D's throat. "Now, you gonna tell me what's up your ass or do I have to beat it out of you?"

An elbow shot up, slicing into his cheek.

Uh-huh. So that's the way they were going to play it.

It had been a while since he'd found himself in a good old-fashioned brawl. Except this was more than a brawl, Luke realized when D turned total animal on him. The guy was merciless, flipping Luke over, pinning him down, and it was all he could do to block the fists swinging at him. As blood spurted from the corner of his mouth, he landed an uppercut that made D grunt, then locked his arms around the guy's broad shoulders, sending them both smashing into the coffee table. Beer bottles crashed to the floor, breaking, spilling, but it didn't slow either of them down.

By the time Trevor and Holden managed to break up the fight, the living room was a mess, both Luke and D were bleeding, and the silence was so deafening you could hear crickets.

"What. The. Fuck." Trevor sounded livid, and it took Luke a second to realize the WTF had been directed at D.

D wiped the blood trickling out of his nose. "He started it," he mocked.

"Because you goaded him," Trevor snapped. "Christ, Derek. What is going on with you?"

D didn't answer.

"Forget it. Even if you agree to help with this heroin bullshit, I don't want you on it. I'm sending you back to

Morgan. Maybe he can figure out what—" Trevor halted abruptly when his cell rang. He grabbed the phone from the table and let out a curse. "Speak of the devil." He answered without delay. "What's up, boss?"

Nobody said a word, including Trevor, who was listening intently to Morgan.

Luke used his sleeve to mop up the blood pouring from his lip. His head was reeling, adrenaline still coursing through his veins. He was sorely tempted to sidestep Holden and pound D some more, but he restrained himself. No point in stirring up more trouble, and besides, he had bigger things to worry about right now. D's turbulent state of mind was not one of them.

Trevor hung up the phone. He didn't say anything for several minutes, and when he finally did open his mouth, what came out was a slow burst of laughter.

Holden shot him a quizzical look. "What did Morgan want?"

The team leader laughed again before turning to D. "Gotta love irony, right, Derek?"

D scowled. "What the fuck does that mean?"

"It means that the favor Olivia asked of Luke? The one that you shot down with a fistfight? It's just become official business."

Luke raised his eyebrows in surprise. "What?"

"Morgan's contact at the DEA checked in," Trevor said. "They got the DNA results for the body in the warehouse."

"And?" Luke prompted.

"And it wasn't Carter Dane."

Chapter 16

"I don't like this," Isabel murmured into her cell phone. Her gaze darted toward the back door of the club to make sure nobody was lurking around. She wouldn't normally have taken Trevor's call, not at the club where anyone could overhear her, but he'd sounded urgent enough that she'd had no choice but to duck outside.

And she was glad she had. Trevor had just informed her that the body in the warehouse wasn't Carter Dane after all, which meant two things—the agent was still missing, and the assignment wasn't over.

"I don't like it either." Trevor's deep voice rang with the uneasiness currently tying Isabel's gut in knots. "But the results were conclusive. The body we found wasn't Dane's."

"So he's still alive? Are we thinking double agent?"

"Possibly, but we can't rule anything out. He might still be dead, or a captive, or . . ." Trevor's voice trailed off.

Isabel wasn't buying it. If Carter Dane was dead, then why the whole production of keeping that other hostage in the warehouse? With Dane's ID, the identifying tattoo . . . someone had gone to a lot of trouble to make them *think* Dane was dead.

"Okay, there are a few options here," she finally said. "One—Dane's alive and in trouble."

"Two—he's alive and in cahoots with the people he was supposed to bust," Trevor said.

"Three—he's dead and the decoy stiff was intended to confuse us for whatever purpose. Four—"

"He's alive, faked his death, and took off for some mysterious reason," Trevor finished.

There could have been a hundred options, and she still wouldn't be thrilled with any scenario. Besides, it didn't matter whether Dane was in trouble or in cahoots with the enemy. Morgan's team still needed to find the guy, and since snooping around the club hadn't succeeded in uncovering Dane's whereabouts, Morgan had decided to shake a few Mafia branches and see what fell out. In other words—go after Angelo himself in hopes that he would lead them to Dane.

"Why doesn't the DEA intercept the shipment themselves?" she demanded.

"Because if they truly have a mole in their midst, he'll tip Angelo off and the delivery probably won't go down."

"Do you think Dane will be present for the transaction?"

"Maybe. If not, then Angelo will. And when Angelo is nabbed, hopefully he'll tell the DEA where their agent is. Dane's supervisor is also hoping Angelo will flip on De Luca if they apply enough pressure on him."

Isabel had to laugh. "You think he'll rat? No way. I know how these men think, Trevor. He'll never sell out his boss, not even to save his own ass."

"Snitches get stitches, huh?"

"They get a lot more than stitches." The image of her brother flew into her head, and she gulped, then forcibly banished all memories of Joey. "Look, I need to go back inside. But . . . I don't know if I want to be involved in this, Trevor."

His voice softened. "I already told you, you're under no obligation. Morgan hired you to go undercover at a strip club, not to mess around in the drug trade. Nobody will be upset if you decide not to help."

"Let me think about it, okay? I'll call you later tonight."

After they hung up, she headed for the dressing room to get ready for her shift. Once she'd slipped into something a lot less comfortable, she stared at her reflection in the mirror and kept her expression neutral. Behind her, the room bustled with activity. Girls changed into and out of costumes, applied makeup, chatted with one another. Isabel, on the other hand, was too busy working over this latest complication in her head.

"Can I use this?" a voice chirped.

She lifted her head to see Georgia gesturing to the black eyeliner pencil sitting on the cluttered vanity table. "I'm all outta black," the dancer explained.

"Yeah, sure," she said absently, handing the eyeliner over to the willowy brunette.

As the girl flounced off, Isabel forced herself to stick to the routine. Her shift wouldn't be over for a couple more hours, so she didn't have to reach a decision this very second. She had the rest of the afternoon to think about it. Sighing, she grabbed a tube of liquid foundation, squeezed some on her finger and began applying the makeup to her cheeks.

Trevor had told her that Olivia was determined to stop that heroin shipment from hitting the streets, and Isabel completely understood the other woman's anger. Angelo was drugging dancers and prostituting them out to clients. He deserved to be punished, not just for that but also for all the other crimes he committed on a daily basis.

But were taking down Vince Angelo and finding a DEA agent she'd never even met big enough reasons for her to go head to head with the Mob again? There was a reason she'd quit the bureau. Working the organized-crime unit had been a pain in the ass. De Luca and the other four bosses were too freaking smart to slip up.

But Angelo might. Although she hadn't encountered the guy during her government stint, she'd definitely heard of him. Eight years ago, he'd still been at the bottom of the totem pole, and now look at him—a big-time earner in charge of the boss's drug distribution. Not as big as he wanted to be, though. The man was scrambling for more solid footing in the organization, and his greed and ambition would eventually be his undoing.

Still, she didn't think Angelo would ever betray De Luca. But there was a chance he'd tell them where Dane was, if it meant reducing a jail sentence.

"Oh my God, what happened to your face?"

Georgia's shrill demand had Isabel turning to the door. Her heart sank when she saw Heaven in the doorway. The blonde shrugged indifferently as she headed for the lockers, completely unfazed by the black eye she was sporting.

"Seriously, what *happened*?" Georgia demanded, her breasts bouncing beneath her skintight corset. "Are you okay?"

Heaven didn't answer, and when it became obvious she wasn't going to in this lifetime, Georgia frowned and stalked out the door. Some of the other dancers shot not-so-covert glances in Heaven's direction, but the blonde ignored them as she removed her knee-length coat.

Isabel turned back to the mirror, following Heaven's movements in the reflection. The girl was undressing, shoving her jeans, sweater, and high-heeled boots into her locker. When she got down to her bra and panties, she walked over to the station next to Isabel's.

Isabel shifted her gaze, stifling a groan when she spotted the bluish bruising around the girl's throat. "What happened?" she asked gently.

"I don't really remember," Heaven said dully.

The revelation brought a sharp pain to Isabel's chest. Unable to stop herself, she reached out and touched the girl's bare arm. Although the dancer's eyes weren't glazed, her lips were chapped to hell, hinting at a dry mouth, and her skin felt warm to the touch. Isabel's gaze dropped to the veins on the inside of Heaven's arm.

"You can't keep doing this," she murmured.

Heaven's blue eyes flashed. "What are you, my mom?"

"Just a concerned friend."

The girl scoffed. "We're not friends. We just happen to take our tops off at the same club."

"But you do more than take your top off, don't you, sweetheart?" She shot Heaven a knowing look. "How many of those parties have you worked before, Heaven? Why do you keep agreeing to do it?"

She didn't think she'd get a response, but to her surprise, Heaven's expression turned frantic. "The money's good, Candy. It's so good. And—"

"And it supports your habit," she finished. "Right? That's why you fuck those men for Angelo. To pay for the shit you pump into your veins."

Heaven flinched as if she'd been struck, but Isabel didn't feel an ounce of remorse. Sometimes tough love was the only way to get through to people, and Heaven definitely needed a wake-up call.

"Your addiction will kill you," she said bluntly. "You do realize that, right? You're going to die if you keeping mainlining that crap." She raised her eyebrows. "Or maybe the H *won't* kill you. Maybe the next time you cater to Vince's associates in a hotel room, you'll get more than a black eye and a bruised throat. Did you think of that?"

Fear sparked in Heaven's eyes. Her mouth fell open as if the thought had never occurred to her, but just when Isabel thought she might be getting through to the girl, Heaven's mask of indifference returned.

"I don't need a lecture," Heaven mumbled. "I have to get ready." With that, the girl fumbled around on the table for a tube of lipstick.

Blowing out a breath, Isabel picked up a charcoal eyeliner pencil, removed the cap, and scribbled a phone number on a gas station receipt she found on the vanity table. Without a word, she placed the paper in front of Heaven and stood up.

The girl frowned. "What's this?"

"My phone number. Call me when you're ready to get help."

"Save yourself the trouble, Candy. I don't want or need—"

"I have connections with a good rehab clinic," Isabel interrupted. "Say the word, and I'll make the call."

Before Heaven could mount another protest, Isabel left the dressing room.

Liam Macgregor looked like a *GQ* model. Even though Luke was a hundred percent hetero, he had no problem acknowledging that another man was handsome—and Liam Macgregor was really fucking handsome. He had a chiseled male-model face, piercing blue eyes, thick black hair, a dimpled chin. In his crisp white dress shirt, fitted faded jeans, and leather loafers, the dude looked like a walking cologne ad.

Fortunately, Macgregor's looks were accompanied by a serious case of soldier. The military precision of his eyes, the predatory way he moved—he was a warrior to the core, which was probably why Morgan used his services. He was also a gold mine of information, just as Luke had suspected he'd be.

"The Five Families have a long-standing relationship with the Afghans, but they're also getting their shit from South America these days," Liam said as he took a seat on the sofa. He leaned forward to accept the coffee mug Trevor handed him. "There's been a huge increase in availability, and the Colombians are smart businessmen—they undercut their competition's prices, maintain solid pipelines, and their drugs are high quality." His blue eyes suddenly homed in on Luke. "What happened to your lip?"

"A friend and I had a difference of opinion."

The friend in question was not present for this meeting— D had been holed up in the guest room ever since their brawl, and nobody expected the guy to come out anytime soon, not since Trevor had officially ordered him back to the compound. Luke didn't envy Trevor, that was for sure. The team leader had made a tough call by pulling D out, but Luke knew that if he'd been in Trev's place, he'd have done the same fucking thing. D had been a loose cannon since this job had begun, and his presence was becoming a liability.

Now that the assignment status had reverted back to ongoing, they needed to come up with a plan of attack, which meant gathering all the intel they could if they wanted this raid to go off without a hitch. At this point, Luke had no idea what the hell to expect, not just in terms of how Angelo ran his drug operation but also regarding Carter Dane.

Because really, where the fuck *was* the guy? AWOL from the club, hadn't been spotted among De Luca's soldiers, wasn't checking in with his supervisor. Was he dead? Alive? In too deep? Working with the Mob? Too many damn questions surrounded that man.

Lighting a cigarette, Luke walked over to the open sliding door. "Any idea which cartel De Luca's tangled up with?"

"I made a few calls before I came over," Liam answered in his faint Boston accent. "They've used the Ramos outfit a few times, but rumor has it they just closed a new deal with the Moreno cartel. The Morenos used to specialize primarily in cocaine, but they're branching out."

"When did this deal go through?" Trevor asked sharply.

"A few weeks ago, according to my source. Money exchanged hands, but not the merchandise."

"That's probably why this is so important to Angelo," Holden spoke up. "New partnership, first shipment."

Luke took a deep drag of his smoke. "How do the South Americans get the stuff to the States? Air routes? Sea?"

"Both. Their methods are pretty diverse, but word is they're looking for alternative routes. With airport security tighter than ever, it's getting harder for their couriers to bring the drugs in on commercial flights. Cargo flights and vessels are also tough—there've been too many arrests and seizures the last couple of years."

"But the drugs still get here," he pointed out.

"Well, yeah. The Big Apple is one of the biggest importation and distribution hubs for South American merchandise."

"So how is the Moreno cartel bringing the drugs over?"

Liam set down his mug and ran a hand through his thick black hair. Man, he had great hair. Luke had to shake off the thought—this definitely wasn't the time to be appreciating some other dude's hair.

"They've got a deal with the Dominicans," Liam replied. "There's one group in particular, they traffic the drugs into the States through Miami. The port there is busy as hell, and corrupt to shit. The Dominicans have no problem getting the drugs into Florida."

"What happens after that?" Luke asked.

"The merch is trucked up the eastern seaboard." Liam shrugged. "I don't know what kind of fronts the New York bosses have, but the Boston outfits use certain businesses as a cover for their drug operations. They've got a bunch of import/export companies, and when the legitimate goods arrive in Miami or at the port here, the drugs are stashed in the same truck, transported to the company warehouse and then moved to various mills around the city."

Holden reached for the file folder sitting on the table. "I've got a list of businesses De Luca's involved with. Most of them are owned by dummy corps, but I've been able to trace some of them back to the organization." He flipped through the pages. "There are several import-type ventures here—coffee, fruit, textiles."

"So we need to find out if any of these companies are expecting shipments this week," Trevor said. He turned to Liam. "Can you get the intel?"

"I can try, but my contacts aren't so current anymore. Since I've gone independent, a lot of my sources have dried up."

Luke uttered a frustrated curse. "We need to know when and how this shipment is coming in."

"I'll try," Liam said again. "But no promises."

"See what you can do."

Liam propped an arm behind his head. "By the way, Morgan asked me to help out on this job. He said you might need the manpower."

Luke sighed. "Yeah. We might."

A sharp knock on the door interrupted the discussion. All four men went on the alert. Trevor, who already had his Sig in hand, relaxed when a soft voice sounded from the hall.

"It's me."

Luke snuffed out his cigarette as Trevor opened the front door to let Isabel in. She wore a black fitted coat and blue jeans, and her blond hair was tied back in a loose twist, yet Luke had a tough time recognizing her. He blinked a few times, uncertain despite the fact that he knew it was her. Isabel Roma had the uncanny ability to completely transform, and the woman he remembered from the last job looked nothing like the one standing in front of him.

But her warm smile was a giveaway, and so was her melodic voice as she crossed the room to give him a hug. "It's good to see you," she said with genuine happiness.

He leaned down to kiss her cheek. "You too. You look different."

"I always look different," she said wryly. She stepped out of the embrace and glanced over at Holden and Liam.

Holden rose to greet her. "You must be Isabel. I've heard a lot about you. I'm sorry I didn't get to meet you on the last job, but I was off rotation."

"You're lucky. That was a tough gig."

Liam stood up too, his blue eyes sweeping over Isabel's face. After a second, he nodded as if he liked what he saw. "Liam Macgregor," he said. "I freelance for Morgan."

As they shook hands, Liam held on a little too long, and from the corner of his eye, Luke saw Trevor stiffen. When the team leader rested a hand on Isabel's arm and ushered her away from Macgregor under the pretense that he wanted to take her coat, Luke tried not to raise his eyebrows. Man. Trevor totally had a thing for the blond chameleon. Was this a new development, or something that had been brewing since the last job?

Isabel sat on one of the armchairs, folding her hands in

her lap. "Sorry to show up out of the blue. I didn't think you'd mind."

"We don't mind. What's going on?" Luke asked.

She shrugged. "I was walking around SoHo, trying to decide if I want in on this gig, and somehow I wound up here."

"So what'd you decide?"

"I'll stay and help."

Luke's face broke into a smile. "Thanks, Izzy."

Instead of smiling back, she scowled at him. "But I swear to God, if I get shot again . . ."

From the couch, Liam laughed. "These jerks got you shot?" He made a *tsk*ing sound. "See, this is why the team needs me full-time. I keep telling Morgan to make me permanent."

Isabel grinned at him. "Keep me bullet-free and I'll write you a recommendation letter myself."

At that little interchange, Trevor went RoboCop again, shoulders rigid, jaw tense. Luke didn't blame him. He'd be annoyed himself if Olivia was smiling and laughing with some other man.

Not because he loved her, though. No. Because that was ridiculous. Ever since that troubling convo with Kane, Luke had been trying to convince himself that he was just overanalyzing everything. He couldn't have fallen in love with Olivia—in a week, no less. Shit like that took time, didn't it?

Pushing away the thought, he focused on Isabel, who was looking through the file Holden had left on the table. "So what do we know?" she asked.

Trevor quickly filled her in. When he mentioned that they had no clue when the shipment was coming in and how it was getting there, she tilted her head in thought. "I might know someone who can help."

"Who?" Luke demanded.

"Don't worry—they're not government."

"They?"

"A couple of guys I know. They're information dealers. These guys can find out anything, and I mean, *anything*. I've used them before a few times and they're good, trustworthy. But expensive."

"How expensive?" Trevor asked warily.

"Last time I went to them, I was out five grand. The time before it was twenty. They've got some kind of messed-up sliding scale going on—personally, I think they make up the prices as they go along. But I guess the fee depends on how hard it is to get the intel."

"Call them," Luke said. "We'll give them whatever they want."

She raised a brow. "You don't need to clear it with Morgan?"

Grinning, he gestured around the elaborate apartment. "Morgan can afford it, trust me."

Olivia was undressing in her bedroom when she heard a soft tap on the windowpane. She jumped in surprise, then relaxed as Luke's face appeared on the other side of the glass. Wearing nothing but a pair of panties and a T-shirt, she walked over to the window just as Luke climbed inside. His dark eyes instantly sought out her bare legs.

"Perfect timing," he said with a wolfish grin. "You're almost naked."

She rolled her eyes, then narrowed them. "What happened to your lip?"

He shrugged. "D and I exchanged some words."

Moving closer, she gently touched the corner of his sexy mouth. It was slightly swollen from where his lip had split, and the hint of a bruise marred his cheekbone.

"It looks like more than words went down," she said.

"D packs a mean right hook, I'll give him that."

Anger snaked up Olivia's spine. "I hope you hit him back."

"I threw the first punch, so technically all that anger on your face should be directed at me." He beamed at her. "But it's good to know you care."

She wasn't walking into *that* minefield. Nor did she want to overly examine why the thought of someone hurting

Luke bugged her so much. This thing between them was purely physical, so the urge to claw out the eyes of anyone who hurt him was totally uncalled for.

She edged backward. "I was about to hop into the shower."

"Like I said, perfect timing." He began unzipping his bomber jacket. "I'll join you."

"In case you haven't noticed, there isn't a bathroom in here. You might run into my mother in the hallway."

"It's about time we were introduced."

Butterflies of anxiety took flight in her stomach. "No," she blurted out.

His expression darkened. "Why not?"

"Because . . ." *Because this isn't going anywhere*, she almost said, but the words sounded harsh even in her own mind. Still, it was the truth. They'd both agreed this would be temporary, and they'd slept together only once, which didn't even qualify as a fling. How could she introduce him to her mom only to have to explain later why he wasn't coming around anymore?

"Because she's sleeping," Olivia finally said. Which was true. Her mother had gone into her bedroom right after dinner to take a nap.

"Well, then we won't run into her in the hall, will we?" Luke offered a lopsided smile. "So . . . shower?"

She crossed her arms over her chest. "First tell me why you're here. Did you talk to your team?"

"Yes, I talked to them. Wasn't necessary, though, since apparently we're still on the clock."

Her brows furrowed. "What do you mean?"

"The body we found at the warehouse? It wasn't the missing agent. DNA results came in earlier."

"I don't get it. Who the heck was it in the warehouse?"

"Don't know yet. They're running his profile, so hopefully he's in the system and they can ID him."

She bit her lip in thought. "Whoever he was, you were supposed to think he was your missing agent. Why?"

"Don't know that either. But none of that matters right

now, darlin'. My team's been ordered to take down the shipment."

Relief shot through her. "For real?"

"For real."

A smile lifted the corners of her mouth, and she resisted the urge to do a little happy dance. "So we're really going to bring Vince down?"

"Uh-uh, there's no *we* in this equation."

"What does that mean?" she asked warily.

"It means your snooping days are over. Leave the fact-finding to us. We'll gather the intel on the shipment and arrange to take it down. We'll deal with the Feds when the time comes. Your only job is to fly under Angelo's radar and stay alive."

Annoyance clamped around her throat. "I want to help."

"Tough."

"Don't you dare *tough* me." She glared at him. "I won't be relegated to the sidelines, and I refuse to be indebted to anyone else."

Luke gaped at her. "You're not indebted to us, Olivia. Not in the slightest."

"*I* asked *you* to help me, which means I can't expect you to do all the work and take all the risks."

"This morning it was about helping you," Luke agreed, "but now it's about doing my job. Even if you begged me at the last second to call it off, I wouldn't be able to. We've been ordered to intercept that shipment and that's what we're gonna do." His voice grew soft. "When it's over, I'm still helping you start a new life. You lived up to your end of the bargain by getting us that address, and I won't renege on that promise, darlin'."

"I know, but I still want to help," she said firmly.

When Luke's brows drew together in a frown, she decided to put an end to this bickering, and breezed toward the door. "By the way, I'm having dinner with Vince in an hour."

He bounded across the room to intercept her. "No way," he said in a deadly tone.

She should've known Luke wouldn't understand why she wanted to be involved in this mission. Why she *needed* to be involved. It wasn't just about stopping Vince, or punishing him for killing Cora and leaving an innocent girl motherless. It was about not owing something to another man. Luke might claim this wasn't about her, but she was the one who'd tipped him off to that shipment in the first place, and if she could offer something of value to the mission, then she was damn well going to.

Setting her jaw, she met his unhappy expression and said, "Yes, way." And then she gave him a little shove and peeked out into the hallway, which was empty.

"Shower?" she asked sweetly, glancing at Luke over her shoulder.

She had to give him credit—he didn't make a sound as he followed her to the bathroom. It was like sharing space with a ghost. But Olivia could tell he was furious. His facial muscles twitched and his eyes burned with frustration as she closed the door and started the shower.

"You got what you wanted," he said, keeping his voice to a low pitch. "We're going to nail Angelo. You don't need to be involved in this."

"Yes, I do." She whipped her T-shirt over her head, then wiggled out of her panties.

The air in the bathroom suddenly got thick. Luke groaned softly, his gaze devouring her naked body. "You don't play fair. This is the second time you've tried to distract me with your hot nakedness."

"It worked last time." She raised her eyebrows when she noticed the hard ridge beneath his cargo pants. "And I'm pretty sure it's going to work now."

She stepped into the shower and moved under the spray. From the corner of her eye she saw Luke stripping in a hurry. A moment later, his muscular body dominated the small space and his strong arms wrapped around her from behind. She let out a low moan when he cupped her breasts.

Had he been born with the knowledge of how to drive a woman wild, or had his expertise been honed during years of practice? She was afraid to ask, but she couldn't deny that Luke Dubois was spectacular in bed. Or, in shower.

As steam filled the bathroom, he teased her into oblivion, squeezing her breasts, playing with her nipples, and when he spun her around and sank to his knees in front of her, the teasing became torture.

Olivia gasped as his mouth found her core. He licked the insides of her thighs, then dragged his tongue over her damp folds. Her knees buckled, but he steadied her by gripping her hip with one hand and backing her into the tiled wall. Luke tugged on her left ankle and brought her leg up to his shoulder. He proceeded to ravish her with his tongue, knowing exactly how much pressure to exert, when to back off and lick her slowly, when to wrap his lips around her clit and suck hard. When she cried out in delight, he lifted his head, his features displaying the smug look of a man who was pleasing his woman and knew it. Then he resumed his ministrations, until she was gasping for air and shamelessly thrusting her hips into his face.

Seconds away from exploding, she squeezed her eyes shut and welcomed the rush of pleasure, but suddenly he wrenched his mouth away and stumbled to his feet. The water from the spray poured over him, droplets gathering on his glistening chest, working their way over the line of hair tapering down to his navel.

His gorgeous face was strained as he stood there, keeping a good foot of distance between them. "No condom," he said in a tortured voice.

"I'm on the pill." Her voice sounded breathy to her own ears. She couldn't even believe she was considering forgoing protection. She was normally far more sensible, but the pressure between her legs was so intense she feared she might die if he didn't get inside her. Now.

"And no diseases," she added awkwardly.

"I'm clean too," he said.

They eyed each other for a moment. The stall had filled with steam, and Olivia felt like she was watching him through a haze. She got the feeling he didn't like going unprotected either, which was confirmed when he murmured, "I'll pull out. The pill's not a hundred percent effective."

The matter-of-fact statistic brought a tug of irritation, especially when she realized he probably hadn't picked up the knowledge by Googling *birth control pills*. Oh no. This was a man who had sex often. Unlike her. She only got it on every other year or so.

At the thought of Luke with another woman, her irritation was transformed into a crazy rush of possessiveness. She yanked on the back of his head to bring him down for a kiss. As their tongues tangled, Luke groaned, then whirled her around like a man possessed. She purred at the feel of his erection nudging her bottom. Bracing her hands on the wall, she closed her eyes and waited, anticipation coiling in her belly. His fingers circled her waist. His lips brushed over the nape of her neck. That tempting erection slid over the crease of her ass. God, she needed him inside her. She needed—

A mind-shattering orgasm seized her body as he drove in deep.

Biting her lip, Olivia closed her eyes and let the pleasure consume her, trying to stay silent even though she wanted to announce the climax to the world. Luke plunged into her with long, smooth strokes, groaning quietly, the husky sounds getting lost in the rush of the shower spray. When she felt him pulsating inside her, she pushed her ass into his groin, taking him in deeper. His pace quickened, his fingers dug into her hips, and then he mumbled an anguished curse and withdrew. Trembling from his release, he rested his chin on her shoulder, his breath coming out in hot puffs against her bare skin.

When they both grew still, Olivia turned to wrap her arms around his neck. She stood on her tiptoes and brushed a kiss over his mouth, then reached for the bottle of body wash on the shelf. After she'd squirted the liquid soap into a bright pink pouf, she slowly met his eyes, which were no longer glazed with passion but heavy with resignation.

"You're still planning on seeing Vince tonight."

She nodded. "I have to. Please don't try to stop me."

He inched closer, resting his forehead against hers, his broad chest heaving as he released a ragged breath. "What am I going to do with you?"

"You're going to let me be a part of this," she said firmly. "I *have* to be a part of this. For Cora. And for myself."

"I don't want you to get hurt."

The water was running cold, but that wasn't the cause for the goose bumps rising on her flesh. Luke sounded so tormented, and his arms had tightened around her as if he couldn't bear to let her go. The pouf dropped from her hands and fell onto the floor of the shower. She didn't bother picking it up—she simply let Luke hold her because she knew it was what he needed. What she needed too.

"I already got hurt," she whispered. "Now it's my turn to hurt him. Please, let me do this."

"You're not going alone," he said sternly.

"We'll be in a restaurant. You can't come in with me."

"Then I'll wait outside." His eyes were fierce. "And if that bastard so much as looks at you the wrong way, I'm going to storm that fucking restaurant and rip his heart out."

And she got the feeling he meant it.

An hour later, Olivia parked the Beemer in front of the Bistro Alessio. As she hopped out to feed the meter, it suddenly occurred to her that Vince might not even be there. Truth was, she'd lied to Luke. She and Vince didn't have a dinner date per se, but after six months of "dating," she knew his schedule fairly well. On weeknights he had his dinners delivered to the club, but on Sundays he preferred Italian. He always left the club and went to Bistro Alessio, a low-key but expensive restaurant in Little Italy. He'd never once asked Olivia to join him, claiming he preferred to dine solo on Sundays, but she didn't think he'd mind if she showed up and surprised him. His ego would probably appreciate the gesture.

Unless . . . what if he'd lied about his solitary dining habits and was actually meeting his mobster friends every Sunday? The thought gave her pause, but she forced her legs to carry her to the door. If he did have company tonight then she'd just play it cool. Give him a kiss on the cheek, and tell him she'd see him when she came back to work in a couple of days.

Outside the restaurant, she smoothed her hair and gave her appearance a quick once-over. She'd worn a black scoop-neck dress paired with a brown suede jacket, nothing too fancy but nice enough for a cozy dinner. As she stood there, she resisted glancing over her shoulder to see if she could spot Luke. He'd been following her in a black SUV, but she didn't see it parked on the street. He had to be nearby, though.

She knew he wasn't happy about her coming here tonight, but she'd meant what she'd said back at the apartment. She wanted to pull her weight, and she refused to be shut out. Luke could still dig around for information about the shipment, but if she could get that same info out of Vince, and get it tonight? Why let that opportunity slip away?

When she strode into the bistro a moment later, the olive-skinned brunette at the hostess stand greeted her with a smile. "Reservation?" the young woman asked.

"Actually, I'm meeting someone," Olivia lied. "Vince Angelo?"

"Of course. You'll find him at his usual table in the back. Would you like me to escort you?"

"No thanks, I can find it myself."

She brushed past the hostess and entered the main room, letting her eyes adjust to the dim lighting. The space was cozy and attractive, boasting red velvet wall drapes, small tables with crisp white tablecloths, and servers in black-and-white uniforms. Soft piano music floated through the room, and most of the patrons were either couples or men dining alone. It was a classy place, giving off a romantic air that made her wonder why Vince chose to come here by himself every week.

Olivia finally spotted Vince at a table nestled behind a tall marble planter filled with red flowers. He was sipping a glass of white wine, a troubled expression on his face.

He looked up in surprise at her approach.

"Olivia?" His eyebrows knitted together in a frown. "What are you doing here?"

She pasted on a smile. "Surprising you. I know you come here on Sundays, and I thought we could have dinner together."

His dark eyes slitted with suspicion. "What about your mother?"

"She's sleeping. The medication makes her drowsy." She gestured to the empty chair opposite his. "May I join you?"

As he nodded, she slipped out of her jacket and draped it on the back of the chair, then sat down and met his gaze across the table. "You don't look very happy to see me." She pouted a little.

His cloudy expression dissolved. "I am. Of course I am, babe. You just caught me off guard."

"I know you prefer to be alone on Sunday evenings," she told him. "But I really needed to get out of the house."

"Is your mother feeling any better?"

"She is. Actually, I think she's well enough for me to come in to work tomorrow."

A waiter approached the table. He placed an empty glass in front of Olivia, picked up the wine bottle from the center of the table, and poured for her. When he finished, he turned to Vince. "Would you like the usual, Mr. Angelo?"

Vince nodded. "Yes, Dante. Thank you."

"And you, madam? Are you ready to order?"

Since she'd already eaten an early dinner with her mom, she had zero appetite. But she didn't want to make Vince suspicious, so she quickly picked up the menu, scanned it, and ordered a Caesar salad.

"Everyone knows you here," she remarked as the waiter disappeared.

Vince nodded absently. There was something off about him tonight. Something incredibly disconcerting.

"Why do you come here so often?" she asked softly.

He fingered the stem of his wineglass, and a faraway expression settled on his face. "Did I ever tell you about my parents?"

She shook her head.

"No, I don't imagine I did. They were garbage, both of them." He gestured to the swinging doors leading to the kitchen off to their left. "My mother worked here when I was growing up. She washed dishes in the back."

"Oh" was all Olivia said, because she couldn't think of anything else.

"My father went to the track every Sunday and since they couldn't afford a babysitter, my mother would bring me to work with her." He frowned. "I'd sit in the kitchen, watching her scrape the crap off the dishes, her hands getting all red and cracked from the hot water and that industrial soap she used."

"She must have worked very hard," Olivia said quietly.

"Not hard enough."

"Did your parents ever . . . mistreat you?" she had to ask.

"Nah. They loved me." He snorted. "Raised me in squalor—that's love, huh?" His brown eyes blazed. "We never had enough money, and whatever we did have, my son of a bitch father blew on the ponies. Meanwhile, my mother worked herself to the bone in this restaurant." He swept a hand over the room. "Cleaning the dirty plates of the assholes who could afford to eat here."

His bitterness polluted the air, and despite herself, she felt a flicker of sympathy. For his mother, that is. She knew all about working yourself to the bone.

"That's why I come here," Vince said. "To remind myself of where I came from, *who* I came from." His expression became surly. "I eat here and then my dishes are taken away and someone else washes them just like my mother used to do. I come here for the reminder, Olivia."

"To prove to yourself that you're better than your parents," she murmured.

"I *am* better than them," he snapped. "I don't need to prove that. It's a fucking fact."

"I know that," she said quickly. "Of course you're better than them."

Their food arrived and Olivia stuck her fork in her salad, forcing herself to take a bite. "Your parents didn't have what it takes to be successful," she went on. "But you do. You own one of the most profitable clubs in the city."

The ego stroking must have worked because he brightened. "I do."

"And you've got all these new investments," she added, feigning pride.

"I am doing very well for myself," he said without a trace of modesty. "And this latest investment I'm involved in— it's a big one, babe. Really big."

She pretended to be impressed. "Is that what your big meeting is about on Tuesday? Are you—what's the phrase for it? Closing a big deal?"

He offered an enthusiastic nod.

"Then we should celebrate that night," she declared as she reached for her wineglass. "That way we'll have two things to toast."

"I'm afraid I can't. Closing the deal might take all night."

She pouted again. "How late can it really go? Business hours end at six."

"This is a foreign deal, babe. The meeting won't even start until ten."

"At night?" She gasped.

He smiled indulgently. "That's how it works with foreign partners. They go by their own clocks."

"Oh." She put on a disappointed face. "Okay. We'll just stick to Wednesday night then." She cast her eyes downward. "I bought a new outfit."

Vince chuckled. "Did you?"

"Yeah." She smiled. "I want to look nice for you."

He reached across the table and clasped her hand. "You always look nice for me, babe." Then he wiped the corners of his mouth with his napkin and picked up the menu. "How about some dessert?"

*   *   *

Vince waited until Olivia's BMW disappeared around the corner before slipping his phone out of his pocket. He couldn't put his finger on it, but something about this entire evening had felt off. Maybe it was the walk down memory lane—he hated talking about his childhood. Or maybe it was the way Olivia had showed up and surprised him. She was a great girl, but spontaneity wasn't her style, which was something he'd always appreciated about her. Spontaneity wasn't his style either; he preferred careful planning, meticulous assessment. Consider every complication and think ten moves ahead.

Olivia showing up here tonight wasn't sitting right with him.

Unfortunately, he didn't have time to worry about that now. This was an important week, and he had to stay focused, keep his mind off pussy and solely on this new deal. Another thing he liked about Olivia—she wasn't one of those overbearing bitches who demanded that he spend every second with her. He didn't particularly approve of her decision to attend school—what did she need an education for when she had a man perfectly willing to take care of her? But he allowed her the independence because he knew women didn't like feeling like they were on a leash.

He wouldn't put up with it forever, though. This had been a busy year for him—becoming increasingly involved in the distribution operation, enhancing his contact network, hooking up with Moreno—but once this new partnership really got off the ground, he would focus his attention on his personal life. He had to buy his girl a ring, make this thing between them official, and the wedding would take some planning—Italians didn't do anything halfway, especially not celebrations. But all that would come in time. Business came first, as always.

Nevertheless, it wouldn't hurt to pay closer attention to his future wife's activities.

"Mikey," he said when his bodyguard answered. "I need you to place two more guards on my girl."

"Is Rocko not doing his job? Because I can arrange for someone else—"

"No, Rocko's solid. I want two men in addition to him. Get them to cover the front and rear of her building, and stay on her whenever she leaves the apartment."

"Sure thing, boss."

Vince headed for the Town Car that appeared at the curb. As usual, his driver, Paul, was efficient, but this Sunday ritual had been going on for years, so he knew the drill. Vince slid into the backseat and ordered Paul to take him to the club, then leaned his head against the leather seat. A part of him wondered if increasing Olivia's watch detail was excessive, but he still couldn't shake the feeling that she was up to something.

Probably paranoia, but Vince knew better than to second-guess his instincts. If Olivia *was* up to something . . . well, he'd find out soon enough.

Chapter 17

"I could get used to this," Luke murmured as he rolled off Olivia's flushed body.

He was still coming down from the orgasmic high, stunned by the enthusiasm Olivia had exhibited during their early-morning romp. A lot of women weren't into morning sex, so waking up to the feel of Olivia kissing his neck had been a pleasant surprise. This was the first time he'd spent the entire night with a woman, which was another surprise, but Olivia had reminded him yesterday that he'd be outside watching the building anyway, so why not spend the night warm indoors? She'd raised a good point, though they both knew he wasn't there to protect her. He couldn't even count the number of times they'd made love during the night.

Made love?

Aw, shit. He was actually thinking of it as lovemaking.

"That was very nice," she agreed, shifting closer.

He stroked her hair, marveling at its softness, its thickness. And he loved the way she cuddled beside him after sex, all warm and boneless, purring every few seconds like a contented cat.

It was official—he had it bad.

"So what do you do on your days off?" he asked, deciding that small talk was the only way to squash the strange emotions fluttering through him.

"I usually do homework. Or study. Or clean."

"Uh-oh, someone call the fun police—you're having so much fun it ought to be illegal."

She laughed. "I know, I'm a huge dork. But it's hard to make time for fun when you've got so many responsibilities."

Smiling, Luke twined a strand of her silky hair around his finger. "Okay, well, if you had the time and opportunity, what would you do?"

She was quiet for a moment. "I'd do some traveling. That was one of the reasons I wanted to be a teacher—I adore kids and love being around them, but a job where you get the summers off? That's a huge plus. I'd love to go to Scotland or England and see some castles."

"Castles?" he echoed.

"Don't make fun of me. I like castles, all right?"

He had to laugh. "All right. Traveling. What else do you want to do?"

"Not much else," she admitted. "I don't want crazy adventures. I'd prefer to cuddle on the couch and watch a movie, or go for a walk in the park or a drive in the country. I'm not into fancy restaurants—I'd pick one of those all-day-breakfast diners over a five-star restaurant any day."

"A woman after my own heart," he declared, reaching for her hand and planting a huge smack of a kiss on her knuckles.

Laughing, she snuggled closer to him, and as he continued to play with her hair, he realized just how much her answers had pleased him. His job went hand in hand with crazy adventures, and when he got back from a gig, he didn't want to do anything but take it easy. Olivia's description of what she considered a good time sounded pretty damn appealing to him. Cuddling and watching movies? Taking long walks and admiring some castles? Count him in.

Getting ahead of yourself, pal . . .

Yeah, he was definitely thinking way too far ahead here.

He had no idea how Olivia even felt about him. Hell, he wasn't sure what he felt for *her*.

"Do you have anything planned for today?" he asked.

"I need to stop by the admissions office on campus." Her voice grew pained. "I'm going to drop out."

He looked over in shock. "What? Why?"

"Because I'm leaving the city," she reminded him. "Midterms are starting, and today is the last day to drop classes. If I don't do it now, I won't get any of my tuition money back."

Luke smothered a sigh. Damn. He knew it killed her to drop out of school, but he couldn't think of anything encouraging to say. She was right. No matter how this went down, she had to get out of New York. If Angelo was arrested, De Luca might target her. If Angelo walked free, then she'd be right back where she started—under that man's thumb. Leaving town was her only option.

He dragged a comforting hand over her back. "I'm sorry, darlin'. I know how important school is to you."

The breath she released was shaky. "It is. It's very important. At NYU, I feel . . . like I have value, I guess. Like I'm more than a pretty face. When I hand in a paper or take a test, I'm judged based on my knowledge and the application of that knowledge." Anger crept into her tone. "Everywhere else, I'm judged by my looks. People expect me to be an airhead or a spoiled brat, and at the club . . . nobody expects me to be anything. Just a pair of tits and a nice ass."

Her emphatic words evoked a rush of guilt inside him. He'd been enamored of her looks too, back when she had been nothing more than Livy Lovelace, the goddess he had the pleasure of ogling at the Diamond Mine. It shamed him that he'd also assumed she'd be just another airhead stripper.

"You're more than T&A, Olivia," he said gruffly. "I'm serious—most of the things I like about you are completely unrelated to the way you look."

"Oh really?" Her dark brows lifted in challenge as she craned her neck to look up at him. "What do you like about me?"

"Your strength—" When she opened her mouth to pro-test, he gave her shoulder a playful pinch. "Don't give me that bull about not being strong, because you are. You've been working your butt off and taking care of your mom for years now—you're telling me that doesn't take strength?"

"I guess," she conceded.

"And I love your resilience," he went on. "The way you bounce back no matter what hardships life throws your way. I love that dry, subtle sense of humor of yours." He faltered, his throat closing up a little. "And your presence . . . soothes me. I feel incredibly content when I'm around you. And . . . safe."

Her breath hitched. "Safe?"

"Yeah, like I can tell you anything, and you won't judge me for it." The way he'd told her about Katrina. Fuck. He still couldn't believe he'd opened up to her about that. Not even his closest friends knew all the details surrounding his father's death.

Olivia cleared her throat. "That's quite a list you just recited."

"That was the short version. There are a hundred more things I like about you." He decided to lighten the mood. "And yes, that gorgeous, traffic-stopping face is one of them."

"My face does more than stop traffic—it sets off metal detectors too," she quipped.

Luke snorted. "Yeah, and how does it do that?"

"Here, give me your hand." She propped herself up on one elbow and took the hand he offered, bringing it to her left cheek. "Okay, feel this spot? Press down on it."

He pressed his fingers where she indicated, felt the unmis-takable evidence of metal beneath her smooth skin, and chuckled. "Gross," he teased. "What are you, the Terminator?"

"My cheekbone collapsed when I was attacked, and the surgeon had to use a steel plate and a couple of screws to fix it." She laughed. "So, yeah, I guess that does make me half robot now."

A knock suddenly sounded on the door.

"Liv?" a soft voice called. "Are you up?"

Olivia jumped out of bed so fast it was almost comical. She looked at Luke lying on the rumpled sheets, then at her own naked body. "I'm up!" she practically shouted. "I'll be out in a minute, Mom."

"I'm making breakfast," her mother said through the door. She paused. "How does your friend like his eggs?"

Busted.

Luke had to grin when the color drained out of Olivia's face. Taking pity on her, he cleared his throat and called out, "Over easy."

There was a soft chuckle, followed by footsteps retreating down the corridor.

"Why did you say that?" Olivia hissed.

He blinked. "She knew I was here. It would have been impolite not to answer."

As Olivia began snatching up items of clothing, he felt a flicker of irritation. She was acting like she really, *really* didn't want him to meet her mom, but why the hell not? He doubted Kathleen Taylor thought her daughter was a virgin, and she hadn't sounded pissed just now, so what was Olivia's problem?

Knowing that now was not the time to argue, he rose from the tangled sheets and found his clothes. He slipped into his cargo pants and buttoned up his black long-sleeve, but didn't bother with socks or boots. "Before I forget," he said as Olivia hurriedly got dressed, "I need your phone."

"But I tossed the one you gave me, like you asked."

"Not the disposable. Your real phone."

Frowning, she reached for her purse and found her BlackBerry, then handed it over. The frown deepened as she watched Luke pry out the SIM card and shove it in his back pocket. "What are you doing?"

He held up another SIM card. "Replacing it with this. This card's got a tracker embedded in it. That way we'll be able to find you if anything ever happens. Even if the phone's off, the transmitter emits a signal, and Holden can monitor it on his laptop."

"Oh. All right."

He popped in the new card. "Also, I need something you can always keep on you. Jewelry would be best—a necklace, bracelet, ring . . . ?"

Olivia walked over to the dresser and flipped open her jewelry box. She rummaged around for a moment. "Will this do?" she asked, holding up a silver chain with a small diamond-studded cross dangling from it. "It was a present from Vince, so he won't be suspicious if I wear it all the time."

Luke examined the necklace. They could easily pry out one of those little diamonds and get a tracking device in there. "It's perfect," he replied. "I'll get it back to you later. We'll bug it as well." He met her eyes. "Ready for breakfast?"

"Not really," she said with a stony look.

He sighed. "I'll wash up and meet you in the kitchen." Then he slid out the door before she could protest.

He used the head, pulled a toothpaste-on-the-finger brushing, then splashed cold water on his face and dried it with a fuzzy pink hand towel. His split lip looked moderately better—no longer swollen but still red, which meant that Olivia's mother would definitely notice it. He hoped it wouldn't ruin her first impression of him.

When he stepped into the hall, he heard murmured voices wafting from the kitchen. He followed the voices to the kitchen doorway, pausing to look around the room. It was tiny, all the appliances crammed in on one side of the space, and a small round table with four plastic chairs by the other wall.

An incredibly thin woman stood by the stove, tending to the eggs sizzling in a pan. Olivia hovered around her, trying to take over. "Come on, sit down," she was urging. "You're supposed to be resting."

Even though Kathleen was bald and downright frail, Luke could see the resemblance between the two women, especially when Olivia's mother turned to the door and eyed him with sharp green eyes the same shade as her daughter's. She had Olivia's features as well, though Kathleen's face was hollow and gaunt. Luke's heart constricted at the sight, but at the same time, a little burst of admiration went off inside him. Kathleen Taylor was a survivor to the core.

"Good morning," he said. He fidgeted for a second, then entered the room, mostly because the aroma of cooking bacon was too appealing to walk away from.

Kathleen relinquished the spatula to Olivia and slowly walked toward him. Those astute eyes swept up and down, side to side, taking in the stubble on his chin and the case of bed head he no doubt sported. Not to mention the busted lip.

"Good morning," she answered. She extended a hand. "I'm Kathleen. Liv's mother."

He shook her hand, saddened to realize he could crush those brittle fingers without even trying. Olivia's mother hadn't had an easy time with her last round of chemo; that much was obvious. "Luke Dubois," he said.

Kathleen gave a small nod. "I like that name. It's strong."

He grinned. "I probably shouldn't tell you my middle name then. It'll make you change your mind."

"Have a seat. I only made you two eggs, but from the looks of you, you probably need half a dozen."

Sinking into a chair, Luke rested his forearms on the table and glanced at Olivia's mother. "You should sit too," he informed her. "Otherwise I think your daughter might have a panic attack."

From the stove, Olivia shot him a glare, then bestowed one on her mother. "Seriously, Mom, sit down."

Kathleen settled in the chair across from his, and the two of them spent a moment sizing each other up.

"So . . . what happened to your face?" she asked briskly.

"A friend and I had a little disagreement." He flashed her a grin. "But we kissed and made up and all is good now. Nobody can stay angry with me for long."

Kathleen didn't even crack a smile. Instead, she continued to appraise him like he was a piece of meat she was considering either cooking or throwing away. As her silent inspection dragged on, Luke saw his chances of gaining her approval slipping away. At least until she asked what he did for a living.

When he replied, "Military," he won her over.

"My late husband was a marine," she revealed. "A true hero."

Luke thought he heard Olivia snort, but when he glanced at her, she was busy sliding the cooked eggs onto a ceramic plate.

"What military branch are you in?" Kathleen asked, her tone much warmer now.

"I'm former navy. SEALs. Now I do freelance work for the government." Not entirely true, but he wasn't about to reveal he was a mercenary who had no problem breaking the law if it came down to it. Besides, the team did take a lot of government contracts, like this latest gig for the DEA. So, not entirely a lie.

Olivia walked over with two plates, one for each of them. The difference in meals was astounding—while Luke's plate was piled high with bacon, eggs, toast, and sliced tomatoes, Kathleen had only a single poached egg, a scoop of cottage cheese, and an unbuttered piece of bread. Apparently chemo really did a number on your appetite.

Olivia joined them a moment later with her own plate, and the three of them dug in.

"So how did you meet my daughter?" Kathleen inquired.

Olivia's head swung in his direction. Despite her blank expression, he could hear her unspoken warning.

"At the restaurant," he answered lightly. "I was there for a blind date, but the woman never showed. Liv was my waitress, and I think she felt sorry for me. My dinner ended up being free."

Relief flickered in Olivia's eyes, while Kathleen's twinkled playfully. "I'll bet you weren't too disappointed to be stood up."

"Not after I met your daughter," he agreed. "Ten minutes in her company and I knew I'd lucked out."

Man, he *had* lucked out, hadn't he? He shot Olivia a sidelong look, but her face remained impassive. And her shoulders were kind of stiff, as if she wasn't enjoying a second of this impromptu breakfast. In fact, she didn't say much for the remainder of the meal, not even when Kathleen regaled Luke with stories about Olivia's childhood. He laughed when she told him how Olivia used to cry when she couldn't go to school on national holidays, but in truth, the story was only another reminder of how different they were.

Olivia Taylor was too smart. Too serious. Teacher, lawyer—it didn't matter what she chose to do with her life because her career was only a means to get what she really wanted: security. He saw it so clearly now, especially when Kathleen mentioned Olivia's marine father again and he saw Olivia's lips curl in distaste.

"You remind me a bit of Eddie," Kathleen said as she nibbled on the crust of her toast.

"How so?" he asked.

"It seems like nothing fazes you." She smiled knowingly. "A lot of men would have snuck out the window when their girlfriend's mother knocked on the door. In fact, I suspected you might bolt."

He decided not to even touch the *girlfriend* thing. "I never bolt," he said with a shrug. "If anything, I run toward trouble."

Olivia stiffened next to him.

"Eddie was like that too. Always running into the heart of danger. He was very reckless, that man."

With a loud scrape of her chair, Olivia stood up and carried her plate to the sink. Luke instantly knew something was wrong. He suspected it had to do with the topic of her father, but he didn't want to bring it up in front of Kathleen. Instead, he chewed his last bite of bacon and then he got up too.

"Here, let me take this," he said, gesturing to Kathleen's empty plate.

"Thank you, Luke."

He headed over to the sink and gently intercepted Olivia's hand before she could turn on the faucet. "I'll clean up."

She balked. "No, that's fine. You're the guest."

"And you need to get ready for school," he reminded her. He left out the part about dropping out, what with her mother in the room.

Although she looked reluctant, she gave a nod. "Fine. I'm going to hop in the shower then."

After she left the kitchen, Luke grabbed a sponge and some dish soap and began washing the dishes. When he felt Kathleen's eyes on him, he glanced over his shoulder and said, "Is there something you'd like to say to me?"

"Don't hurt her."

He'd figured he'd get the what-are-your-intentions speech, so her firm but gentle plea caught him off guard. "What makes you think I'm going to hurt her?" he asked roughly.

"Like I said, you remind me of Eddie. And Eddie, God bless his soul, wasn't the most sensitive man on the planet. The thing I said about his love for danger? Well, it often came before his love for his wife. I understood that about him. Sadly, Olivia doesn't."

Luke swallowed. "She doesn't want a daredevil in her life, does she?"

"Most definitely not. My daughter craves normalcy. A steady job, steady husband, steady life. I'm afraid it's her way of ensuring she doesn't end up like me."

"Hey, don't say that. She loves—"

"She loves me," Kathleen finished. "Yes, of course she does. But she thinks I wasted my life on her father, and now she's determined to have the kind of life she thinks I *should* have had."

Luke placed a clean plate on the drying rack and reached for another dish. "I won't hurt her, ma'am. I promise you."

Kathleen's expression softened. "I believe you mean that."

"I do mean it."

"Good." Now those green eyes hardened to steel. "With that said, if you *do* hurt my daughter? You'll have me to contend with, Luke Dubois."

A laugh tickled his throat. "I wouldn't expect anything less."

Rocko's call came while Vince was going over the following week's employee schedule. "What is it?" he demanded, absently initialing the paperwork.

"There's been a development," Rocko said.

Impatience rippled through him. "What kind of development?"

"There was a man at her apartment."

The blast of rage that slammed into him was so ferocious he nearly fell right out of his chair. "What are you talking about?"

"A man climbed out of her window and went down the fire escape."

"Did you see him go in last night?"

"Winters was posted at the back of the building since nine o'clock yesterday. He says he didn't see anyone use the fire escape yesterday or anytime this morning. The guy must have showed up last night before you assigned Winters and Del Vido to join me on guard duty."

Acid burned a path up Vince's throat. The thought of Olivia—of *his* girl—spending the night with another man made his vision go hazy. Red-hot fury spiraled through him. "Where is the motherfucker now?"

"He followed her when she left the apartment. He's driving a black Range Rover with New York plates." Rocko cleared his throat. "She's on campus right now. I'm on her."

"And the man?"

"He followed her to the campus, then took off. Winters has him in his sights."

"Where's Del Vido?"

"Back at her apartment, in case she gets any other visitors."

Vince slammed his free hand against the desk, sending the computer mouse toppling onto the floor. "Who the fuck is this guy?"

"I don't know, boss. He looks like a civilian, but moves like military. Not government, though, or at least I don't think so."

Vince spoke through clenched teeth. "Deliver him to me."

"How're we supposed to do that?"

"I don't fucking care how you do it. Just get it done."

Rocko hesitated. "Where do you want us to bring him?"

"The place on Riverside Road. Call me when you have the motherfucker."

Vince disconnected. He sat there for a moment. Motionless. Unblinking.

Rage twisted his insides into hard knots, and his breathing grew shallow, so shallow that his palms began to tingle. Olivia had invited a man into her apartment.

The bitch had a *man* in her *apartment*.

Suddenly his control snapped like a rubber band. With a growl, he swept the stack of paperwork off the desk, sending the papers flying. The computer keyboard was next, smashing onto the floor, a few keys popping out and bouncing around like marbles. Shooting to his feet, he sucked in infuriated breaths, then spun around and raised his fist, prepared to smash it into the wall behind him.

Might be a misunderstanding, a little voice pleaded.

His fist froze. Vince struggled for breath, clinging to any rational thought he might have left.

Olivia wouldn't betray him. She wouldn't screw some other man, not after everything they'd been through together. She was a *virgin*, for Christ's sake! She wouldn't betray him. She *wouldn't*.

But if she had?

Well, then he'd just have to kill her.

Chapter 18

Trevor and Isabel walked side by side through Central Park, close enough that their arms kept brushing. He was seriously tempted to put his arm around her, but resisted the urge.

"You sure you don't mind sticking around?" he asked as they dodged a clumsy Rollerblader.

"I won't leave you guys in the lurch," she answered. "You need eyes in the club."

"We can make do if you back out. Seriously, I wouldn't blame you. The drug business is a nasty one."

"Seems like every job I take is nasty," she said with a sigh. "At least I'm not working solo on this."

That was definitely a plus. The women Noelle employed worked alone, but Trevor didn't like the idea of Isabel on her own during a mission. She always insisted that she only did undercover work, gathering intel before Noelle or one of the others went in to do their assassin thing, but it still bugged him. He felt fiercely protective of this woman.

They wove their way through the park, which looked especially idyllic with the changing leaves and lush autumn colors. Isabel's contact had wanted to meet at the Bethesda Fountain, and as they got near, Trevor experienced a flicker of unease. "Are you going to tell me more about these guys other than 'they're information dealers'?"

She chuckled. "You don't trust me?"

"You, I trust. Strangers, I don't."

"Fair enough." She pushed a strand of blond hair off her forehead. "Their names are Oliver and Sean Reilly. I met them when I worked for the bureau."

"Are they government?"

"Freelance. They were born in Dublin, moved to America in their teens. Their father was—probably still is, actually—involved with the IRA. He trained them, and I think they were mercenaries at one point. Now they deal in information. They've got contacts all over the globe, and they can pull information out of thin air."

"Their intel is good?"

"Always. They wouldn't be making money hand over fist if it wasn't." She laughed. "You'll like them. Twin brothers, full of themselves, but pretty damn charming."

Trevor ignored the tight squeeze of jealousy in his chest. Same damn thing had happened last night when Isabel had been laughing with Liam Macgregor.

They reached their destination, and he scoped out their surroundings as they sat on the fountain's circular edge. The area probably drew more crowds in the summer, but there were still a decent number of people milling around. Reading the paper, eating lunch, chatting in small groups. Trevor didn't spot anyone that looked like an information dealer. Then again, he had no clue what an information dealer looked like.

Apparently the answer to that was *hobo*, because a moment later a tall man in a beat-up army surplus coat and ratty khaki pants came out of nowhere. He had a black wool hat over a head of blond curls, a lot of scruff on his face, and amused green eyes.

"If it isn't my favorite former Fed," the man said in an Irish brogue.

Isabel rose to her feet and leaned in so the man could kiss her cheek.

Trevor's hands curled into fists.

"Good to see you, Ollie." She looked past his broad shoulders. "Where's Sean?"

"Indisposed. He met a lovely brunette at the pub last night and I haven't seen him since." Oliver grinned broadly. "The little bird had a friend, but I was saving myself for you, luv."

Isabel laughed. "Haven't we already established that I don't date Irishmen? Your lot is far too devious."

"You're right about that. Who's your friend?"

Trevor gave the other man a long once-over before extending his hand. "Trevor Callaghan."

Oliver offered a firm shake, then slanted his head in thought. "Callaghan. Callaghan . . . why does that sound so familiar?" He snapped his fingers. "You're on Jim Morgan's crew."

Trevor frowned. "And how is it you know that?"

"I know everything." There was no arrogance in the man's voice, just complete and utter confidence. "Knowledge is my business, Trevor boy. Do me a favor and say hello to your boss."

"You know Morgan?"

"Our paths crossed in Belfast a few years ago. Tell him my ears are still open, but to quote my fellow countryman, I still haven't found what he's looking for."

Trevor wrinkled his forehead.

"He'll know what I mean," Oliver said with a wave of his hand. "Now, tell me what you need and let's see if the Reilly brothers can accommodate you."

Luke got hold of Trevor as he drove away from the corner store he'd popped into for cigarettes. Balancing the phone between his ear and shoulder, he unwrapped his smoke pack and said, "Hey, sorry I didn't answer before. I was buying smokes."

"You're not with Olivia?"

"She went to work. I asked Sullivan to cover the club because I figured you'd want me back at the apartment for briefing. How did it go with Isabel's contacts?"

"Fine. The guy's making a few calls. He said he'll be in touch tonight." Trevor snorted. "He quoted me ten grand for the intel."

"Steep. But for Morgan, it's pocket change." Luke extracted a cigarette from the pack and brought it to his lips, then plucked his lighter from the cup holder.

Just as he was about to light up, the image of Kathleen Taylor's gaunt face flashed into his mind and his hand froze. As his gaze dropped to the surgeon general's warning on his smoke pack, a curse popped out of his mouth.

"What's up?" Trevor said instantly.

He groaned. "I should quit smoking, huh?"

"Fuck yeah. We've all been telling you that for years." There was a pause. "Where's this coming from?"

"Olivia's mom has cancer."

Another pause. "I see."

Yep, Trevor was a pro at reading between the lines, but thankfully the guy didn't push the issue, which was a damn good thing. Luke still wasn't sure what his growing feelings for Olivia meant, but he did know this thing between them was quickly becoming too important to give up.

Yanking the unlit cigarette from his mouth, he tossed it in the cup holder, then signaled right and changed lanes. When he shot a quick glance in the rearview mirror, he noticed a yellow cab two cars back and frowned. Was that the same cab he'd seen at the NYU campus?

He shrugged away the thought, not bothering to remind his paranoid brain that this city was full of frickin' yellow taxis.

"Apparently these guys are worth it," Trevor was saying. "Isabel swears by them."

Luke immediately picked up on the derision in the other man's tone. "Is that a hint of jealousy I hear?" When Trevor didn't answer, he whistled. "I had an inkling last night, but now it's confirmed. You have a thing for Isabel."

"What? Of course not."

"Oh man. You're totally lying." He paused. "Does she know?"

"I'm not discussing this with you."

"Does she feel the same way?"

"Like I said, not discussing it."

Although he was tempted to keep needling the guy about it, Luke decided to cut Trevor some slack. "Did you tell our friendly information dealer about the timeline?" he asked instead.

"Yeah. Olivia's sure that Angelo's big meeting is Tuesday night?"

"She's sure." Luke continued to navigate his way through Greenwich Village, growing annoyed. All the streets around here were messed up, curving and changing direction out of nowhere. When the fine hairs on the nape of his neck tingled, he looked in the mirror and saw that the yellow cab had made the same turn. He squinted, taking note of the license plate. Yep, still the same taxi.

"So we only have one day to confirm where and when the shipment will show up. When you get back here, I want you to sit down with Holden and—"

"Shit," he muttered.

Trevor halted in mid-sentence. "What?"

"I've got a tail." He peered in the rearview and tried to get a look at the cabdriver, but the guy's sun visor was down, obscuring his face. On a whim, Luke executed a quick left onto a side street, then glanced over his shoulder. Relief trickled through him. Good. The cab was no longer—wait, still there.

"Shit," he said again. "I need to lose this asshole."

"Angelo's man?" Trevor barked.

"I don't know. The goon who keeps tabs on Olivia was at the campus, but he drives a silver Lexus."

He approached another side street and made a hard right, then an abrupt left. The cab continued to tail him.

"Are you sure Angelo didn't post more guards on her?"

Luke battled a jolt of frustration. "I don't think so, but hell, I don't know. There's only been the one guy on her this past week. He parks across the street from the building and watches the entrance. I've been going in and out through the back."

"Could he have changed it up?"

"Nah, man, he was out front this morning when I followed her to school."

The taxi stayed on him, except now the driver wasn't even bothering to hide it. As Luke stepped on the gas and blew through a stop sign hoping to thwart the dude, the cab flew right through the intersection, now dangerously close to hugging his bumper.

"This guy is persistent. Trev, I'll call you back. I need to handle this."

He shoved the phone in his breast pocket and focused on losing his tail. Fucking hell. The last thing he needed was a goddamn car chase in the streets of New York City, especially when he had no idea where the hell he was. He'd been heading south for the safe house, but now he found himself in a maze of residential streets and narrow side roads—and look at that, half the damn roads were one-way. Wonderful.

Accelerating hard, he sped down a street lined with skinny brownstones and oak trees, whizzing through another intersection and leaving several angry motorists in his wake. The taxi didn't ease up. It kept barreling toward him, tailgating the shit out of the Range Rover.

"Son of a bitch," he muttered.

A hard left, an even harder right, and then another one-way hell, this one so narrow he nearly clipped the side mirror of a parked Nissan. The driver behind him was maneuvering like a pro, pulling some real Gran Turismo shit as he pursued the SUV.

Luke yanked on the wheel again, then cursed in frustration when he realized he'd turned into a dead end. As he neared the end of the road, he slammed on the brakes, tires squealing as the car jolted to a hasty stop.

Damn it.

Looked like a confrontation was inevitable.

He was just whipping his gun out of his waistband when he noticed the taxi speeding toward him in the rearview mirror, and then the SUV pitched forward and the shriek of metal colliding with metal split the air.

The airbag exploded in his face.

Dazed, Luke blinked through the onset of stars that assaulted his vision. His ears were ringing like church bells, and the gun fell from his hands, sliding beneath the passenger seat.

"Fucking hell," he mumbled.

A car door slammed.

Pulse kicking up a notch, Luke pushed the deflating airbag away, unbuckled his seat belt, and shoved his hand under the passenger seat in a mad reach for the Glock. His fingers had barely brushed the gun when his door was thrown open and someone yanked him out of the seat. His ass collided with the hard ground, but he bounced to his feet faster than lightning—only to freeze when he spotted the barrel of a handgun pointed at his face. The man wielding it was no taxi driver. He was six feet, two hundred pounds of *thug*. And his grip on the weapon was solid. "Don't make a fucking move," he said in a cold baritone voice.

Luke sighed. "What's this about, man?"

"You'll find out soon enough. Now get on your knees."

Gritting his teeth, he did as he was told. He eyed the goon, assessing, working over his options. He could take the guy, so long as he disarmed him first, but apparently the big man wasn't trolling for a fight. With one smooth motion, the man slammed the butt of his gun into Luke's temple.

Black spots danced in front of his eyes. Fucking *hell*.

He staggered forward, fighting to stay conscious, but those black spots were damn persistent. With a jolt of defeat, Luke brought his hand to the watch strapped on his wrist and pressed a button—just as the goon's arm whipped down a second time and knocked him the fuck out.

"Son of a bitch!"

Trevor shot up from the armchair when he heard Holden's shout. He immediately took off in the direction of the back room, bumping into D in the hallway. Together, they burst into Holden's Command Central in time to see the guy stumbling out of his computer chair, a worried expression on his face.

"What's going on?" Trevor demanded.

"Luke triggered his SOS."

Trevor's back went ramrod straight. Shit. That wasn't good. The SOS meant last resort, as in *I'm royally screwed and need help big-time*. Last time they got one, it came from Ethan when the rookie had gotten himself captured by an arms dealer in Mexico after deciding it would be a good idea to check out the guy's lair—alone. Luke was no rookie, though, and this was his first alarm in all the years Trevor had known him.

"I've been waiting for him to check in," he said, unable to control his growing concern. "He was trying to lose a tail. He thought it was Angelo."

"Where is he?" D demanded.

Holden peered at the monitor, which displayed a map and an unmoving green dot. "Riverside Road. Let me see what's around there." He moved to the next computer, his fingers flying across the keyboard. "Little Italy, low-income area." He paused. "Wait. This sounds familiar. I know this place."

"Come on, man, put that photographic memory to use," Trevor said impatiently.

Holden snapped his fingers. "Angelo's childhood home was around there. Hold up. Let me find the address." He typed a few commands. "Yep, Riverside Road. Deed is under Angelo's old man's name."

"Let's go." D was already heading for the door.

Trevor didn't miss the irony of D's haste. Yesterday the guy had been clocking Luke in the jaw; today he was racing to rescue him. But since Trevor had given up on attempting to understand Derek Pratt, he decided not to question the about-face. He also decided not to mention the fact that D had a plane to catch. The surly bastard was scheduled to return to the compound this afternoon, but at the moment Trevor welcomed D's presence. Because who knew what they'd find when they tracked down Luke?

Popping into the master bedroom, Trevor quickly gathered up his gear. Kevlar vest, shoulder holster, knives in their sheaths and backup revolver in his boot. He shoved a few extra magazines in his jacket pocket, then met up with D and Holden in the main room.

"Get Macgregor to meet us there," Trevor ordered. "Sully's on Olivia, so we might need another body, depending on what we find."

As Holden got Liam Macgregor on the line, they bounded into the elevator and Trevor punched the button for the parking level.

D's lips quirked in a cynical smile. "C'mon," he said, "let's go save his Cajun ass."

When Luke regained consciousness, he found himself in a small room with lime green walls. He blinked a few times. The bright paint on the walls hurt his eyes, and when a wave of dizziness washed through him, he wondered if he had a concussion.

From what he could tell, this had to be a house, but no artwork or photographs graced the walls, no furniture save for the metal chair he was tied to. The bindings were damn problematic—his captors must have used three rolls of duct tape to secure him to the chair. They'd also gagged him, tying a piece of cloth around his jaw and jamming it in his mouth.

Damn it. This was beyond embarrassing, and he knew he'd never live it down. When the guys found him, he'd have some serious explaining to do. He'd triggered the SOS on his watch, and the goon who'd jumped him hadn't tossed his phone; he could feel it in his shirt pocket, which meant that he was transmitting not one, but two signals, loud and clear. He just hoped his boys showed up before Angelo did.

He scolded himself for the screwup. Angelo must have assigned more guards to watch Olivia, and Luke, lust-ridden idiot that he was, had been too distracted to examine his surroundings. Assumed the only watchdog he had to worry about was the one stationed out front. Now he felt like punching himself in the jaw for making such an amateur move.

As he sat there giving himself a mental ass whupping, Vince Angelo appeared in the doorway.

Shit, the bastard had gotten here fast.

Angelo was decked out in a fitted pin-striped suit, a crimson tie, and shiny loafers. His dark hair was gelled away from his face, providing a clear view of the deep crease in his forehead. "I know you," Angelo said sharply.

Luke donned a blank expression and mumbled something into the gag.

"What was that?"

He silently dared the other man to come closer, dying for the chance to bite some of the fucker's fingers off. To his disappointment, Angelo stayed put. He whistled, and the son of a bitch who'd rear-ended the SUV entered the room.

"Remove his gag," Angelo ordered.

The goon walked over and ripped the cloth out of Luke's mouth.

Angelo nodded in satisfaction. "Now leave us."

After the guard disappeared, Angelo focused those reptilian eyes on Luke. "Yes. I do know you. You got a lap dance from my girl."

Luke shrugged. "I get a lot of lap dances."

"I see." The man smiled graciously. "And do you pay late-night visits to every dancer who grinds on your thigh?"

Crap. So someone *had* seen him scaling Olivia's fire escape this morning. Luke promptly awarded himself with another mental beating. He'd let his feelings for Olivia distract him, and now he was fucked.

His best bet? Keep Angelo talking and hope the others got here soon. An SOS call from a teammate was never ignored, so the boys were undoubtedly on their way, riding to his rescue.

He also decided that he couldn't lie his way out of this, not entirely anyway. Vince knew he'd been at Olivia's apartment—there was no way out of that one. But maybe with some damage control, his slipup wouldn't get him killed. Or Olivia.

He licked his dry lips. "Olivia and I—"

"Don't you *dare* say her name!"

Luke raised his brows. "I thought you wanted to know why I went to her apartment last night."

Angelo's incensed expression dimmed slightly. "Why were you there?" he snapped.

"Olivia and I are in the same economics class," Luke explained. "That's one of the reasons I went to her for a dance. I know money is tight for her, but she's too proud to take a loan. I figured she'd pocket half the fee for the lap dance and it would be a way for me to help her without it feeling like charity. And last night, we were studying for midterms and the session ran late. I crashed there because I was too exhausted to go home."

The other man narrowed his eyes. "And climbed out the window this morning? Tell me, why would you do that?"

"Her mother fell asleep on the couch," he said smoothly. "I didn't want to disturb her by making noise on my way out—she's sick, you know—so I went down the fire escape."

Angelo seemed to absorb each word carefully, and when that crease dug into his forehead again, Luke knew the man wasn't buying any of it.

"Let me tell you how it is," Angelo said in a soft voice. "Olivia is my girl. She's the woman I'm going to marry."

"Really? She never mentioned that, but congratulations."

Angelo's mouth twisted angrily. "My man liberated your wallet."

But not his gun ... Evidently Angelo's goons hadn't thoroughly searched the SUV, otherwise they'd have discovered his weapon under the seat. That was good. Meant that he was nothing more than the man who was potentially fucking Olivia, and not one who was investigating Carter Dane's disappearance.

"Luke Dubois," Angelo went on. "New Orleans driver's license. Did you just move here?"

"Yes. For school," he lied.

Angelo offered a wide smile. "I haven't quite decided what to do with you yet, but whether I let you live or not,

I'm afraid a Manhattan education is no longer a viable option for you."

"That sounds fair," Luke said magnanimously.

Angelo's jaw went tighter than a drum. "You think this is a joke?"

"No, not really."

"Then wipe that smirk off your face."

Huh. Had he been smirking? Apparently that was a big no-no because Angelo whistled again, twice this time. His goon reentered the room, followed by a second thug with long black hair tied back in a ponytail.

Angelo scowled at the newcomers. "Gentlemen, please show our friend that I don't joke around. I'd do it myself, but I don't want to get blood on this suit. It's new."

Crap.

As the two thugs rolled up their sleeves and advanced on the chair, Angelo slid out the door and shut it behind him.

Stifling a groan, Luke looked at the two men. "Go easy on me, boys," he said with a sigh.

Chapter 19

"Can I talk to you for a second?"

Olivia fought a frown as Candy approached her station. The blonde was in her street clothes: a pair of tight black jeans, high-heeled leather boots, and a red sweater that hugged her chest. Dressed like that, Candy looked chic as hell. For a second Olivia was tempted to ask her why someone who oozed such elegance would choose to work in a place like this, but then she remembered the unsettling conversation they'd had before Cora died and promptly rejected the impulse. Luke hadn't mentioned Candy since Olivia had shared her suspicions with him. It could have slipped his mind, or maybe he simply hadn't found anything of worth. Either way, Olivia's gut continued to insist that Candy Cane was not what she appeared.

"What's up?" Olivia asked guardedly.

Candy sat down in the neighboring chair. "I wanted to talk to you about Heaven."

She blinked. "Oh, okay. I, ah, didn't peg you as religious."

The other dancer chuckled. "No, not Heaven as in Heaven and Hell. Heaven as in the dancer we work with."

Her cheeks heated. "Right. Sorry."

"I'm trying to get her into rehab," Candy confessed.

"You are?"

"Yeah, but I'm afraid she's not keen on the idea."

Olivia pictured Heaven's emaciated face, the needle marks marring her arms, and sighed. "She's pretty far gone."

"I know, but I'm not ready to write her off just yet." The blonde breathed a sigh of her own. "I think she wants to stop, but she's not sure how to do it. I told her I have contacts with an excellent rehab facility and I know if she just agreed to go, she can battle this addiction."

Olivia pursed her lips. "What do you want from me then?"

"Talk to her," Candy urged. "See if you can convince her to seek help. I figured it wouldn't hurt for someone else to have a go at it. Maybe she'll listen to you."

The look on Candy's face gave Olivia pause. Her concern was obvious, her voice strained, as if she honestly couldn't stomach the thought of another person in pain. Perhaps Olivia had been wrong about this woman. Maybe Candy really had been trying to help her that day in the dressing room, rather than digging for information.

"I'll talk to her," Olivia promised.

"Thanks. I appreciate it." Candy rose from her chair. "I'm going to wash up and get ready for my set."

As the blonde disappeared into the bathroom, Olivia turned back to the mirror and studied her reflection. God, she didn't want to be here today. The club, the city, the damn planet. She just wanted to get away from it all, and it startled her to realize that where she really wanted to be was with Luke. And not even for sex. She wanted to be near him. With him. She wanted to hear his Southern drawl and his assurance that all this bullshit would be over soon.

Loud footsteps broke through her troubled thoughts. The dressing room door flew open with a violent crash and Vince's shoulders suddenly filled the doorway. Olivia took one look at him and froze.

"Everyone out," Vince snapped.

The other girls milling around exchanged apprehensive glances, but nobody put up a fight. Whether in their costumes, street clothes, or buck naked, the dancers filed out of the room like obedient soldiers.

Olivia slowly got to her feet. "Hey," she said in a shaky voice. "What's going on?"

He moved toward her like a predator, his eyes gleaming with an odd look she couldn't decipher. "Sit back down, Olivia."

Swallowing, she did as she was told. And waited.

He didn't speak for nearly a minute. Gazed at her with that veiled yet terrifying expression. The longer he stayed silent, the more fearful she became.

What was going on, damn it?

"Vince . . ." She tried to get up again.

"Sit. Down." His smile was downright sinister. "You and I need to have a little talk, my love."

The cavalry had arrived. They didn't make a sound, didn't broadcast their presence, but one second Luke had two pairs of fists pounding into his gut, the next there were two dead bodies lying at his feet.

Groaning, he lifted his head in time to see D lower his weapon, a gleaming black Beretta with a silencer screwed onto the barrel. "If you lecture me about killing them unnecessarily, I'll shoot you too," D rasped.

Luke glanced at the puddle of blood forming around the dead thugs, then up at D. "Nah, no lecture."

"Good." D gave him a once-over. "They really did a number on you."

"Yup." He wasn't about to try to deny it. Vince's goons had graciously avoided his face, but his body had taken a real pounding. Ribs definitely bruised, kidneys felt like they were about to fail, and his abdomen throbbed like a bitch.

D removed a knife from the sheath on his hip and walked over to the chair, quickly slicing through the duct tape binding Luke's chest, hands, and feet. As Luke stumbled to an upright position, Trevor bounded into the room, his trademark Sig in his hand and a frown on his face. "You all right?"

"Just peachy."

"Good." Trevor cocked his head. "Now, do you care to explain what the *hell* happened?"

"Angelo had me jumped. His goon rear-ended the Rover." He took a step, cursing when pain shot through his chest. "The SUV's in Greenwich Village. Tell Holden to track its GPS and arrange for a tow."

His ribs ached every step he took, and Trevor took pity on him and shouldered some of his weight. "Angelo did this?"

Luke gestured to the stiffs on the floor. "Those two did, on Angelo's orders. Did you clear the house?"

"Yeah, it's empty."

"Grab their phones," Luke told D. "Angelo will expect them to check in."

"Come on," Trevor said as D collected the phones. "Holden's waiting in the car."

They exited the room and made their way along the narrow hallway. Angelo's childhood home was quite unimpressive. The place was the size of a closet, consisting of that lime green bedroom, a small living room sandwiched next to an even smaller kitchen, and a lot of peeling paint on the walls. The carpet beneath their feet was frayed and covered with stains, and the entire place reeked of mildew.

Liam Macgregor stood guard at the front door, one hand hovering over the holster on his hip. His male-model features creased with sympathy when he spotted Luke. "See, I told you Morgan needs me full-time. You boys obviously require a babysitter."

Trevor rolled his eyes. "Well, you get to babysit the stiffs, pretty boy. I'll arrange for a cleanup crew."

"Yes, sir," Liam said with barely restrained amusement.

"Make sure it's done quietly," Trevor added. "And rendezvous at the apartment when it's finished."

They left Macgregor in the house and headed to the SUV parked at the curb. The second Luke slid into the backseat, he turned to Trevor and said, "We need to get to the club."

"No, we need to get you back to the safe house and clean you up."

"Fuck that. Angelo knows I was at Olivia's apartment last night." Each breath brought a throb of agony to his abdomen. "She's in trouble."

"How did they make you?" Holden asked as he sped away from the curb.

"I fucked up, okay? He must have put a couple extra guards on her, and had someone covering the back of the building."

"And you didn't see them?" D snapped, sounding livid.

"I was distracted. I thought there was only that one tail on her." Panic clawed at his belly. "I fed Angelo some crap about being a friend from school, but I don't think he bought it. He'll confront Olivia, and if she can't talk him down, who knows what he'll do. That man is cool as a cucumber, but not when it comes to her."

Trevor swore softly. "I'll get Sullivan to handle it. You're in no condition to do anything but tape up those ribs."

"Screw my ribs. We go to the club."

"And what, shoot up the place?" Trevor shook his head. "Isabel's already inside, and Sullivan's in position. They'll get Olivia out and bring her to the apartment." His fingers flew over the phone keyboard. "I'm texting Isabel to let her know that Angelo is about to cause some trouble."

Olivia snuck a furtive glance at the door, wondering if she could make a run for it if things got ugly. Which was a real possibility, judging by the antagonistic glint in Vince's eyes. But what had provoked him? Had she sparked his suspicion by asking too many questions about his business? Or . . . oh boy, had he found out about Luke? But how? Luke had assured her that nobody would see him leaving her building.

"I've taken good care of you, haven't I, Olivia?"

Said the psycho to his captive.

She choked down her incredulity and gave a cautious nod.

"I've been generous and patient, and always nothing but honest with you." He paused. "I expect that same level of honesty in return. Is that too much to ask from you?"

"No," she said warily.

"Exactly. So, why don't we put that honesty to the test?" Vince's gaze swept over her face like a hawk's. "Did you fuck him last night?"

Her heart sank. This *was* about Luke then.

Olivia's brain quickly snapped into damage-control mode. "I have no idea what you're talking about."

"Is that how we're going to play it? Denial? I suggest you choose another strategy. I just left your gentleman caller. Alive, I should add." He smirked. "But one phone call and he dies. So now let me ask you again—did you fuck him last night?"

Panic swirled through her like a gust of frigid wind. Oh God. What the hell should she do? Lie? Vince would see right through that. Maybe play the victim and cry rape? No. She didn't have the stomach for that.

The jig is up. It's over.

It was, wasn't it? At that realization, a startling rush of relief soared inside her and she suddenly felt so utterly liberated she wanted to pump her fists in the air. Six months. Six fucking months she'd been putting up this pretense, and now she didn't have to bother anymore.

"Yes," she said in a loud, clear voice.

Vince's jaw tightened. "You fucked him."

Olivia rose from her seat. "Yes."

The temperature in the dressing room dropped at least thirty degrees. Although a thread of icy fear was slowly winding its way around her spine, she held her ground, staring Vince square in the eye. He stared right back, the contempt on his face so raw that the temperature spiked right back up as his hostility set the air ablaze.

"You . . . you . . ." His voice shook with anger. "You let that bastard be your first?"

A resigned breath slipped out of her mouth. "He wasn't my first."

Fury exploded in his eyes.

As Olivia held his gaze, all the hatred and resentment and disgust she'd harbored for this man erupted like lava from a long-dormant volcano. "That's right," she told him. "I wasn't a virgin when we met, Vince. I lost my virginity when I was sixteen."

Without warning, he slapped her across the face. Olivia's head snapped back from the force of the blow.

"You ungrateful little bitch!" Vince roared. "You have the audacity to treat me like this? After everything I did for you?"

"I didn't ask you to do a damn thing for me!" she shot back.

Her sharp tone caused his brows to fly up. "Don't you *fucking* talk to me that way, Olivia."

She ignored the warning in his voice and fixed him with an unapologetic glare. "I didn't want your help that night, you bastard. I killed that customer in self-defense, and that's exactly what I would have told the police if you hadn't covered up the attack. You made that body disappear without telling me. You paid my bills and bribed those cops when I was in surgery. You made all the fucking decisions for me without once asking me what I wanted." Disgust dripped from her every word. "And you claim to love me? You have no idea what love is, Vince."

For several long moments he didn't say a single word. His dark, reptilian eyes had gone shuttered, and he didn't move a muscle. He just stood there, watching her in silence.

When he finally opened his mouth, his soft question sent a chill up her spine. "You think you can humiliate me and lie to me without suffering the consequences?"

And then before she could blink, he pounced on her like a bloodthirsty animal, whipping her onto the floor as if she was nothing more than a rag doll. Olivia's right arm absorbed the impact of the fall. A second later, the tip of Vince's loafer connected with her side, so hard it made her eyes water. Heart racing, she tried to get up but he kicked her again, this time in the head.

She saw stars. She was suddenly thrust back to the night in the alley, when that customer had pummeled her with his fists, grabbed at her, tried to rape her.

She let out a scream, a shrill, piercing cry that went unanswered. Nobody rushed through the door. Nobody came to help. With growing terror, she realized Vince must have ordered his men to remain outside no matter what they heard.

Vince's fury whipped through the air like a bolt of lightning. He was apoplectic with rage, growling like a wild animal as he pounced on her, pinned her between his strong thighs, his heavy body pressing down on her chest, robbing her of breath.

"You think I'm going to let you get away with this? I've waited a year for you, you stupid whore! I *own* you!"

"No. You. Don't." Each word was a wheezy burst of air.

Adrenaline scorched through her veins, giving her a boost of energy that enabled her elbow to shoot up and connect with Vince's throat. He made a muffled gagging sound as his head was thrown back, and that two-second beat was all the time she needed to wriggle out of his grasp and jump to her feet.

"You fucking bitch!"

Olivia grabbed the first item she found on the vanity table—a black eyeliner pencil. Breathing hard, she curled her fingers around the pencil, then whirled and shoved the pointed end directly into the side of Vince's throat.

He stumbled a little, his eyes filling with disbelief, and then a primal cry flew out of his mouth and he lunged at her, even as he ripped the pencil out of his neck. Blood oozed from the wound, but not the gushing spurt she'd hoped for. She'd missed his artery, and that one error cost her—the next thing she knew, she was on the floor again, lying flat on her back with Vince's body crushing her chest like an anvil.

His hands came around her throat, squeezing hard. She batted at him with her fists, but that only caused him to tighten his grip. Her vision blurred and her lungs burned. God, he was actually going to *kill* her.

Vince's enraged face loomed over her, spittle flying into her eyes as he continued to fume and pant like a rabid dog. "You are not worthy of me! You hear me, Olivia? You're nothing but a cheap whore! Screwing some punk right under my nose! Who do you think you are?"

His fingers dug into her throat. No air got in, and her head began to spin, incoherent thoughts hurtling through her mind. She was going to die. Vince would strangle her to death, and then he'd get rid of her body, the same way he'd gotten rid of the customer—

"Let her go."

The cold female voice barely registered in Olivia's muddled brain, but she did notice that Vince froze. That his grip on her neck loosened.

"What the hell are you doing?" he snapped.

"Let her go. Now." A shuffling sound. "Make no mistake, I *will* use this on you. Now take your hands off her throat."

The weight on her chest eased when Vince abruptly scrambled to his feet. A burst of air promptly flooded her lungs. Coughing wildly, she welcomed the rush of oxygen, greedily sucking it in like a starved woman. As her brain began to function again, she couldn't believe what she was seeing.

Candy, standing by the lockers, holding a gun in a two-handed stance and pointing it directly at Vince's head. Vince was staring at the blonde in disbelief that mingled with the fury seething in his eyes.

"This has nothing to do with you, bitch."

"Maybe not, but I don't feel like watching one of my colleagues get choked to death." Candy's aim abruptly dipped to his crotch. "Close your mouth, Angelo. You shout out for your guards and I'll shoot your dick off. Sure, they might put a bullet in my head when they rush in, but not before I get off a shot of my own. And my accuracy is quite good, trust me."

Vince blanched, but his jaw slammed shut.

Olivia's mouth was still wide open. She stared at the other dancer, absorbed the skill with which Candy held her weapon, and in that moment she didn't doubt that Candy Cane was perfectly capable of blowing Vince's junk off.

Suddenly those sharp blue eyes were focused on her. "You okay, honey?"

She nodded numbly, reaching to rub her sore throat as she stood up on wobbly legs.

Still holding the gun, Candy dipped her free hand into the purse dangling from the locker door. She pulled out a set of keys, and, without taking her eyes off Vince, tossed them in Olivia's direction.

Startled, she caught the keys.

"Silver Honda, west side of the lot," Candy told her. "Go wait in it. I'll be right behind you."

She was about to protest, but the blonde glared at her. "*Now*, Olivia. And be careful walking out. Make sure his guards can't see into this room."

Stopping only to grab her purse, Olivia pivoted and raced to the door. She opened it a crack, took a quick peek, then slipped out and shut it behind her. Vince's guard Mikey stood in the hallway, and his eyes narrowed when he caught sight of her face. She knew she must be paler than snow, and from the way her neck kept throbbing she suspected her throat was bruised all to hell.

She caught Mikey's eye and spoke in a terse tone. "Vince is on the phone. He'll be out in a moment."

Without waiting for him to respond, she started to walk, forcing her unsteady legs to maintain a normal, measured pace when all she wanted to do was run for her life. She didn't risk looking over her shoulder to see if Mikey had entered the dressing room. She prayed that if he did, Candy would be all right.

Oh God.

What the hell just happened?

She still couldn't believe that Candy Cane had pulled a gun on Vince.

Think about that later. Focus on getting out.

Taking a breath, she moved through the employee corridor toward the back exit. Only when she got outside did she start running, breaking out in a mad sprint to the Honda Candy had described. A click on the key remote and the locks slid open, and then Olivia dove into the driver's seat. With shaky fingers, she started the engine.

She waited. A minute ticked by. Two.

God, where was Candy? She said she'd be right behind her. But what if Vince had attacked her? Or his guards had swarmed the dressing room?

Olivia's hand trembled on the gearshift. She had to go. Now, before Vince charged out that door looking for retaliation. His pride was the only thing that mattered to him, and she'd taken a damn sledgehammer to it. Now that he knew about Luke, Vince wouldn't rest until he'd punished her.

But she couldn't leave Candy behind, damn it. Not after the woman had just saved her life.

Fortunately, she didn't have to desert anyone. The back door of the club suddenly opened as if a blast of air had hit it, and Candy Cane came tearing out, her leather boots snapping as she bolted to the car.

A second later, the blonde was in the passenger seat, shouting, "Drive!"

Olivia's heart lurched. "What happ—" Before she could voice the question, the club door burst open again and two of Vince's guards ran out.

"Drive," Candy repeated.

Olivia drove. Fast. The scent of burning rubber filtered into the car as she sped out of the parking lot in a screech of tires.

"Where am I going?" she asked frantically. The residual adrenaline coursing through her blood was making her dizzy and she had to blink a couple of times to clear her vision.

"West. Make your way to Tribeca," Candy said briskly. She pulled out a cell phone and dialed a number. "Sullivan? It's Isabel."

Isabel?

And wasn't Sullivan the name of Luke's friend?

Olivia was in a daze as she listened to the one-sided conversation. Her foot shook on the gas pedal, making it difficult to control the car, especially at the high speed they were traveling.

"We've got a hell of a situation here. I got her out, but I shot one of Angelo's guys. We're making our way to the safe house. Yeah . . . yeah . . . meet us there in—"

"No!" Olivia exclaimed. "We can't!"

Candy—Isabel?—swiveled her head. "What are you talking about?"

"My mother's home alone," she blurted out. "Vince might use her to get to me."

The blonde nodded and lifted the phone back to her ear. "Change of plans. Head over to Olivia's place instead. Get her mother. No . . . try not to scare her. Make something up. Just get her out of that apartment and to the safe house . . . No . . . I'll drop Olivia off and ditch the car afterward. Okay . . . good . . . see you soon."

As Candy hung up the phone, Olivia kept her eyes on the road, speeding through an intersection before the amber light turned red. A hand reached across the seat divider, touching her arm. She flinched and scowled at the woman beside her. "What the hell is going on? What did you do to Vince?" Anger shot up her spine. "Who *are* you?"

"What's going on is that I saved your ass," the woman said bluntly. "Vince is probably hunting us as we speak, and me, well, I'm obviously not who I said I was. Any more questions?"

The Diamond Mine's employee area was in chaos. Dancers in a panic, waitstaff wandering around in shock. Vince stood outside the dressing room door, gazing down at the pool of blood on the floor.

His hands trembled in rage. That stripper bitch had shot Mikey in the leg.

Melinda, the club manager, stepped forward nervously. "Should I call the cops, boss?"

Vince bit back an expletive. "Not necessary. Just calm the girls down and make sure everybody gets back to work."

"But shootings have to be reported to—"

"To nobody," he interrupted with a scowl. "Mikey is fine. He's getting looked at by a doctor right now."

"Boss—"

"Back to work!" he snapped. "And get someone to mop up that goddamn blood!"

Stalking away from Melinda, he went up to his office and slammed the door behind him, so consumed with rage he couldn't see straight.

Candy Cane. He couldn't believe it. When she'd pointed that Beretta at his groin, the bitch had meant business. Hot waves of anger, blended with humiliation, formed a lethal cocktail in his gut. That bitch was going to pay for humiliating him.

And so would Olivia.

Oh yes, Olivia would pay for her betrayal.

His body began to shake as white-hot fury tore through him. Growling, he whipped out his cell phone and called Rocko.

"Where is she?" Vince boomed.

"I don't know, boss. All three of us went after the Honda she drove off in, but we lost her."

He closed his eyes briefly. Drew a calming breath. When he spoke, his voice was soft and deadly. "Find her. Go to her apartment, kill her fucking mother if you have to—I don't care what you do. Just *find her*."

Chapter 20

Luke jumped off the sofa when Isabel and Olivia entered the apartment an hour after he'd arrived. He ignored the agony shooting through his body and rushed to Olivia, who, despite looking shell-shocked, threw her arms around him. Their chests connected with a jolt, and when he winced, she didn't miss the reaction.

"Are you okay?" she demanded.

He offered a noncommittal shrug. "Yeah. I'm fine."

"No, he's not," Trevor announced. "Take a peek under his shirt."

Luke resisted, but she was already tugging on the bottom of his T-shirt. She rolled it up, blanching when she saw the bruises marring his abdomen. "Vince did this?"

"Yes. But I really am fine," he assured her. "I'm more worried about you. What happened?"

Her mouth flattened. "Vince attacked me in the dressing room."

She tilted her head up, and the light caught the bluish finger-shaped marks on her delicate throat.

Olivia must've noticed the murder in his eyes, because she let out a soft breath. "Don't worry. Isabel stopped him from doing any real damage."

"You inflicted some damage of your own," Isabel said in an amused voice. "Nice move with the pencil to the neck."

When he noticed that Olivia didn't return the blonde's smile, Luke offered a contrite look. "I'm sorry I didn't tell you that Isabel was working with us. It was for her protection as much as yours."

Olivia nodded. "I figured."

He glanced over at Isabel. "Thanks for getting her out, Izzy."

"I aim to please Jim Morgan and his men," the blonde replied with a faint smile.

Taking Olivia's hand, Luke led her to the couch and gingerly lowered himself to the seat, pulling her down beside him. Trevor and Isabel left them alone, the couple drifting toward the kitchen, talking softly to each other.

D and Holden were holed up in the guest room, monitoring the Diamond Mine via the security feeds, but Luke was kind of apprehensive about asking for an update. He wasn't sure he wanted to know what state the club was in. Apparently Isabel had shot Angelo's guard on her way out of there, so Vince was likely to be on a rampage. Not only had he lost Olivia, but his bodyguard had taken a bullet to the leg. He'd be gunning for both women, but Luke wasn't worried about Isabel; she could take care of herself. He was far more concerned with the woman sitting next to him.

"I'm sorry," he said in a low voice.

"What for?" Olivia asked.

"It was my fault he attacked you. I slipped up and that's the only reason he went after you."

She exhaled heavily. "No, it was bound to happen. I've been walking a fine line for the past six months, trying to keep Vince at bay, but he was going to snap eventually. I figured it would happen when I refused to sleep with him."

"Are you sure you're okay?"

"I'm fine." Her green eyes blazed. "But that's the last time that son of a bitch lays a hand on me, Luke."

"Damn straight," he said in a lethal voice.

"I'm serious. I want you to give me a gun, or show me some better self-defense moves." Her mouth set in a firm line. "If Vince or anyone else ever comes after me again, I want to be able to stop them."

He squeezed her hand, then swept his thumb over her knuckles. "I'll keep you safe, darlin'." When she opened her mouth to protest, he hurried on. "And I'll also teach you how to keep *yourself* safe, okay?"

"Okay." She went quiet for a moment, and then looked at him in dismay. "I'm worried about my mom. I called her on the way over and told her that a friend of mine was coming to pick her up. I think I freaked her out."

Trevor drifted back to the living area. "Your mother is fine. Sullivan just checked in. They're on their way here." He held two mugs of coffee in his hands and gave one to Olivia, the other to Luke.

Isabel trailed after him with two more mugs. She settled in the armchair, while Trevor perched on the arm of it.

"What did you say to Kathleen?" Luke asked.

Olivia sighed. "The truth. That she had to get out of the apartment because our lives were in danger. I'll tell her the rest when she gets here." With a grim look, she met his eyes. "What happens now? Can my mom and I stay here?"

"I think it's better if we get both of you out of the country. You can stay at the compound until we take care of this Angelo situation."

"I agree that my mom can't be here, but I don't think I should go."

"It'll be safer if you leave town too. Angelo will be looking for you. He's out for revenge, Liv."

"I know. But—"

Luke silenced her by pressing his finger to her mouth. "But nothing. You'd be taking too big a risk if you stay, and I'd feel a hell of a lot better knowing you're being protected at the compound."

Fortunately, the front door opened before Olivia could argue. Sullivan entered the main room with Kathleen Taylor, who wore a blue cotton kerchief over her head, a loose shirt, and sweatpants. She looked positively frantic—until she spotted her daughter. "Liv! Thank God!"

Olivia vaulted off the couch and hurried over to her mother. As the two women embraced, Luke heard Olivia murmuring soothing words. The sight of them spoke to something deep inside him. One so frail, the other fit, yet both women were tough as nails. It was frickin' poetic.

"What on earth is going on?" Kathleen demanded when they broke apart. She looked past her daughter's shoulders at Luke, then at Trevor and Isabel.

Olivia cleared her throat. "Is there somewhere private where my mom and I can talk?"

"Master bedroom," Trevor supplied. "Double doors at the end of the hall."

With a nod of gratitude, Olivia gently took her mother's hand and led her to the corridor.

Once they were out of earshot, Luke turned to Isabel with a somber expression. "Angelo will be hunting her," he said flatly.

"Oh yes, he will. He's furious." She hesitated. "He was strangling her. I know she said it wasn't bad, but . . . Jesus, he nearly killed her."

He gritted his teeth. "You should have put a bullet in his head."

"I couldn't. We need him alive if we want to find Dane, remember? Besides, my gun wasn't equipped with a suppressor. A gunshot would have alerted the guard outside the door." She looked apologetic. "My first priority was getting Olivia out."

His throat closed up. "You're right. That was the *only* priority."

"Mom?"

Olivia searched her mother's face, her heart breaking as the silence dragged on and on. They were sitting side by side on the king-size bed in the master bedroom, where she'd just spent the last forty-five minutes talking. And talking. And then talking some more. She'd confessed everything—about her job at the Diamond Mine, the attack in the alley, Vince's obsession with her. She'd told her mom about Luke's mission, their agreement, the drugs, Cora's death.

Through it all, her mother had listened—and hadn't uttered a single word. Now, with the chasm of silence stretching between them, Olivia was so overwhelmed with shame she wanted to weep.

She blinked back tears. "I know you're disappointed in me."

To her surprise, her mother grabbed both her hands and squeezed them. Kathleen's grip was surprisingly powerful for a woman who could barely hold a fork for longer than a minute.

"You can never disappoint me," Kathleen said with unfaltering conviction. "Never."

The tears spilled over and coursed down Olivia's cheeks. "I lied to you."

"*That* I'm disappointed by. You should have told me, Liv." Kathleen sighed. "I'm sorry, baby. I'm so sorry for putting you in this position."

She recoiled in shock. "What? No. You didn't—"

"You took that job because of me. You've been running yourself ragged all these years—for *me*. I'm sorry, Liv. You shouldn't be taking care of me. It should be the other way around."

Olivia fell into her mother's arms. The events of the past year finally hit her, and she began to shake and shudder as her mother offered the comfort she'd craved but hadn't been able to ask for. She'd kept everything inside for so long, it was like a dam had broken inside her, and when they finally pulled apart, she was hiccuping and her eyes were red and swollen.

"I'm sorry I didn't tell you," she whispered.

"It's okay, sweetheart. It's all going to be okay."

With a soft knock, Luke appeared in the doorway. "Sorry to interrupt, but I wanted to let you know we'll be leaving for the airfield in an hour." He glanced over his shoulder and beckoned to someone outside Olivia's line of vision. "D will be escorting you to our compound."

Olivia's shoulders sagged. The idea of leaving town—leaving Luke—brought an ache to her heart. But who was she kidding? They would have had to say good-bye eventually. In fact, maybe she ought to arrange for those new identities sooner rather than later. While Luke was still in Manhattan even. That way she and her mom would already be gone when he returned to his boss's compound.

It felt like a heartless move, saying a quick good-bye now instead of a proper one later when they would have more time, but what was the point in prolonging the inevitable? As wonderful as Luke was, his dangerous profession didn't mesh with her cautious approach to life. Even her mother had seen it—that adventurous streak running through Luke. The bad-boy thing he had going on.

Good-bye had always been in the cards for them. The life she wanted for herself didn't include a reckless mercenary, but a man she could rely on. Someone who came home at five o'clock and ate dinner with her, who'd be a good father to the kids she wanted to have, a dependable husband and a stable partner.

Still . . . she'd hoped they would have more time. Another day, a week. Even a few more hours.

The big mercenary with the tattoos appeared in the doorway. His visible lack of enthusiasm triggered Olivia's irritation. She wasn't sure she wanted that man anywhere near her mother.

Kathleen winced at the sight of him, but to her credit, she managed a polite smile. "Thank you," she told D, meeting his gaze head-on.

"Sure," he mumbled before stalking off.

Olivia frowned, then turned to her mother. "Did you bring your injections?"

"Yes, but I only have a two-week supply left."

"We'll get you anything you need," Luke said. "It won't be a problem."

His answer seemed to appease Olivia's mother. On shaky legs, Kathleen stood up. "Do I have time to wash up before we go?"

"You've got plenty of time." He took a backward step, then halted and sought out Olivia's gaze. "Can we, uh, talk before you leave for the airport?"

After a second of hesitation, she nodded.

"Okay. Um. Good." He took another step. Halted again. This time, his dark eyes found Kathleen's. "By the way, my middle name? It's Gustave."

Kathleen arched one brow in amusement. "Oh, dear."

"What was my mama thinking, right?"

With a little wink, he walked off, leaving Olivia staring at his retreating back with uneasiness.

"You're going to break up with that boy, aren't you?"

Her mom's blunt inquiry made her smile, as did the use of the word *boy*. "Breaking up implies we're dating," she pointed out. "Which we're not."

"But you are sleeping together."

"Yes, but that's just . . . sex."

Kathleen laughed. "Liv, we both know you're not the type of woman who does *just sex*. You wouldn't have gotten intimate with him if you didn't care about him."

She couldn't deny that. She *did* care about Luke. But that didn't mean she would sacrifice the life she wanted in order to be with him.

"Luke is amazing," she admitted. "He really is."

"But?"

"But his work is dangerous. And he *likes* the danger— otherwise he wouldn't be doing this job. I don't want a dare-devil for a partner, Mom. I don't want to be with someone like . . ."

"Like your father?" When Olivia nodded, Kathleen sighed. "Your father had his flaws, honey, I know that. And yes, he didn't always put his family first, but you know what? I wouldn't have traded him for anything."

"I don't understand you sometimes," she confessed. "You're the strongest woman I've ever met, and yet when it comes to Dad . . . you're . . . you're . . ."

Weak, she wanted to say. *Blind. Illogical.* But the words refused to exit her mouth.

Kathleen gave her a knowing look. "You think I should have left your father."

"I don't get why you didn't."

"Because I loved him." Her mom offered a gentle smile. "The heart wants what it wants, Liv."

"That's it? That's your reasoning for putting up with his recklessness and his selfishness and his—"

"Enthusiasm. Spontaneity. Laughter. Passion. Love." Kathleen's green eyes sparkled. "Eddie was the love of my life, honey."

Olivia bit her bottom lip, unsure of how to respond. The conviction in her mom's tone was unmistakable, and it gave her not only pause but an inexplicable pang of guilt. Had she spent so much time focusing on her father's shortcomings that she'd forgotten the good things about him? He must have had *some* redeeming qualities, but for the life of her, she couldn't remember.

Next to her, Kathleen's voice grew weary. "You know what I worry about, Liv?"

She met her mom's exhausted eyes. "What?"

"That when the man you're meant to be with comes along, you'll be so busy searching for someone who's not like your dad that you'll let the right one slip away."

For some reason, those quiet words sounded oddly prophetic. Olivia couldn't control the tremor of distress that skated through her. She tried to come up with a response, a way to convince her mother that those fears were unfounded, but she couldn't find the words.

In the end, she simply brushed off the concerns. "Don't worry. That won't happen." She studied Kathleen's face, her protective instincts kicking in. "You look tired, Mom. After you wash up, I want you to lie down. You need to rest."

"I'm fi—"

"No arguments. You might not like that I want to take care of you, but that's too bad. I will *always* take care of you."

"How about we take care of each other? How does that sound?"

Nearly choking on the lump that rose in her throat, Olivia reached for her mom's hand. "It sounds good." She swallowed hard, which brought a twinge of pain to her bruised neck. Hoping her mom hadn't noticed her wincing, she stood up and took a step toward the door. "I'll be right back, okay?"

Kathleen smiled. "Take as long as you want, honey. I'll be just fine."

Olivia strode into the hall, then stopped to orient herself. Male voices wafted from the living room, but when a flash of movement caught her peripheral vision, she ended up lingering in the next doorway rather than going to find Luke.

Through the open doorway, she watched D bend over a large duffel bag, then straighten up and pull a black hooded sweatshirt over his head. He rolled up the sleeves, revealing the multitude of tattoos covering his arms. Lord, he was such an imposing man.

"What do you want?"

It didn't surprise her that he'd detected her presence even with his back turned.

"Do you have a minute?" she asked.

He slowly faced her, the tightness in his cheeks hinting that he was grinding his teeth.

"You don't look happy about escorting us back to your compound," Olivia remarked.

"Gee, you figured that out just by looking at my face?" He went on before she could answer. "Seriously, what the fuck do you want?"

Setting her jaw, she stepped into the room and closed the door behind her. "To make sure your dislike for me doesn't affect the way you treat my mother," she said, the cool note in her voice surprising them both.

"I don't dislike you," he muttered.

She frowned. "You weren't exactly gracious when we met the other day. And I know the busted lip you gave Luke probably had something to do with me too. So, be an ass to me all you want, all right? But show my mother some respect. She's been through a lot."

Considering the man-of-few-words vibe he threw off, it didn't surprise her when all she got in response was a grunt and a quick nod.

Neither satisfied her.

"Your word," she insisted.

He let out a breath, then dragged his hand over the dark stubble on his jaw. "I give you my word that I will treat your mother with respect. Okay?"

Olivia nodded stiffly. "Okay. Thanks." She was about to edge to the door, but the way he kept rubbing his chin was causing his wrist to jut out, drawing her gaze to yet another tattoo.

"Anything else?" D snapped when she didn't make a move to leave.

"I, uh . . . it's today, huh?"

His head snapped up, black eyes meeting hers. "What are you talking about?"

She bit her lip. "The anniversary of . . . of whatever that date signifies." As she gestured to his wrist, she didn't miss the flicker of shock that crossed his gaze.

However, it didn't take long for the shock to transform into rage.

"That's none of your fucking business," he hissed. "And you're right—I *don't* like you. I think you're a complete fool for getting involved with scum like Angelo, and I resent the fact—no, I *loathe* the fact that Luke almost got killed by Angelo's goons all because you batted your pretty eyelashes and distracted the shit outta him. So I repeat, my tat—everything about me, for that matter—is *none of your fucking business.*"

Olivia felt like she'd been physically struck, but as she watched D's broad chest heave from each ragged breath he took, she realized he was more shaken up than angry. Had nobody else noticed the date on his tattoo? Did his teammates even know what it meant?

"Can you just leave now?" he muttered. "I promised to be nice to your mother. There's nothing else to say."

He was turning away when Olivia suddenly bounded in his direction.

And hugged him.

D stumbled back, but she simply stepped in again and wrapped her arms around his shoulders. She had no clue what had propelled her to embrace this man—all she knew was that her heart was weeping for him and her first instinct was to hold him as tight as she possibly could.

So she did. She dug her fingers into the nape of his neck, holding him so tight she herself could barely breathe. His big body was stiffer than a two-by-four, his unsteady breaths fanning over her forehead, his anger and resentment thickening the air.

And then something peculiar happened. She felt his muscles relax, felt his head drop against her shoulder. He didn't return the hug. His arms dangled at his sides, but his body language softened, sagged with defeat.

Battling a wave of embarrassment, Olivia abruptly dropped her hands from his neck.

"Yeah, so, uh . . ." She inched away. "My mom means the world to me. Please be good to her."

D's face remained utterly impassive. "I will."

"Thank you."

She hurried out of the room and tried not to dwell on what she'd just done, but the hug had left her feeling so flustered she ended up stumbling back to the master bedroom instead of searching for Luke.

When she entered the room, she saw that the door to the private bath was closed. "Mom?" she called.

Kathleen didn't answer. Probably couldn't hear her over the running water.

Olivia headed for the door and rapped her knuckles against it. When her mother still didn't respond, a tiny burst of panic ignited in her gut. She knocked once more, then turned the doorknob and peeked into the bathroom. "Mom?"

The sight she encountered stopped her heart.

"Mom!"

She dove onto the pristine tile floor where her mother lay unconscious. Kathleen's kerchief had fallen off her head to reveal the stubble-covered scalp beneath, and one limp arm was extended in the direction of the door, as if she'd tried to grab it before passing out.

As fists of fear repeatedly pummeled her, Olivia cradled her mother's head in her lap, then fumbled for Kathleen's wrist so she could check for a pulse. Relief spiraled through her when she felt a vibration there.

When both D and Luke skidded into the bathroom a second later, she was still huddled over her mother's body. She raised her head at their entrance and looked up at them with wild eyes. "We need to get her to the hospital!"

Chapter 21

"What a night, huh?" Isabel said dryly.

Trevor watched as she leaned against the railing on the terrace, her gaze fixed on the street below. They were finally alone for the first time all night and he couldn't say he minded. Isabel's presence soothed him, and after the chaos of the last couple of hours, he needed the peace and quiet.

Luke, Sullivan, and Olivia were at St. Francis Hospital, where Kathleen Taylor had been admitted. Sully had checked in twenty minutes ago with an update—looked like Mrs. Taylor had collapsed due to exhaustion. The anemia, fatigue, kidney problems . . . apparently tonight's excitement had exacerbated the woman's already fragile condition. Fortunately, the fainting spell was not an indication of the cancer returning, but Kathleen's oncologist still wanted to keep her overnight for observation.

The trio would remain at the hospital with Olivia's mother, while Holden and Liam Macgregor watched the Diamond Mine until Trevor and Isabel relieved them in the morning. And D . . . well, he was probably halfway to Mexico by now.

"What a night," Trevor echoed with a sigh. "D looked ready to kill me."

"Did you really have to send him away? I thought he was ordered to watch the Taylors."

"He was ordered to report back to Morgan. The Taylors just happened to be going to the same place." But with Olivia's mother in the hospital, that plan was shot to hell. Trevor would need to arrange for one of the contractors to take over watch duty while the rest of the team dealt with this Dane mess and the heroin shipment.

"He needs to get his shit together," Trevor added with a frown. "He wouldn't have been an asset to this mission. His head was all over the place."

"You don't have to defend your decision," Isabel said gently. "I trust your judgment."

Warmth spread through his chest. He still wasn't sure why Isabel had stayed rather than returning to her apartment, but he was glad she had. She'd seemed on edge all night, ever since she'd helped Olivia flee the club. Her body language was stiff as she absently watched a pair of teenagers stroll along the sidewalk.

This would have been a good time for a heart-to-heart—her shield was down, the easygoing front riddled with cracks, but before he could attempt to make the connection he wanted, Isabel's cell phone rang.

She fished it out of her pocket and checked the display. "It's Oliver." She quickly answered the call. "Hey, Ollie, you got something for us?" She paused, glanced over at Trevor. "Grab a pen and paper, will you?"

He popped into the living room to get a notepad and ballpoint pen. When he returned to the terrace, he handed them to Isabel, who began making notes.

"You sure?" she said into the phone. "Yeah . . . No, this is good stuff, Ollie. How reliable is the source?" She chuckled. "Right. Sorry I asked." She kept scribbling. "What about the truck? Right . . . okay . . ."

Trevor heard Reilly's tinny voice, but couldn't make out the Irishman's words. Whatever he was saying, Isabel looked incredibly pleased. "Thanks again . . . Yeah, the money was transferred into your account a couple of hours ago . . . Definitely . . . Yep, until next time."

She hung up. "All right, here's what we've got. A freighter

left the coast of Colombia earlier this week, en route to the Dominican Republic. The goods were transferred onto a cargo vessel that docked in Miami this afternoon and were being housed in a warehouse at the port until about eight p.m. this evening." She glanced at what she'd written. "There have been no deliveries in the past week from any of the companies Holden told Oliver to check, but at nine o'clock tonight, a cargo ship came in carrying a large shipment of coffee beans—recipient, Premiere Roast."

Trevor sucked in a breath. "That's one of De Luca's import businesses."

"Yep. The coffee was loaded onto a Premiere Roast truck and is being driven north as we speak. And the Dominican cargo ship has left the port."

"So the heroin came in via the Dominican and stashed on the coffee truck. Did Oliver say where it's headed?"

"Queens. That's where Premiere Roast's main warehouse is located. I wrote down the address, but Ollie's e-mailing me all the information as well. According to his sources, the truck should be arriving in the city at ten o'clock tomorrow evening."

"They're unloading it after hours, then."

"They have to, what with a hundred kilograms of heroin in it. They'd never take the chance of unloading during business hours. And Angelo will probably bring in a separate crew for this delivery. He won't risk any of the Premiere Roast workers catching wind that there's more than coffee beans on the truck."

"It'll make it tough for us to recon the coffee warehouse," Trevor mused. "If Angelo brings in a second crew, any intel we gather during the day will be useless. And we have no idea how many guards he'll bring with him for the transaction."

"I'm not sure there'll be a transaction. Oliver said the Moreno cartel usually sends one representative with each delivery, but the cash already exchanged hands when the order was placed."

Trevor shrugged. "That doesn't matter. All we need to do

is catch Angelo with the heroin. A hundred kilos is a massive amount. The Feds will nab him for possession, trafficking, maybe some racketeering violations, depending on what they find in the warehouse."

"We'll be going in blind, though," she said slowly. "Last-minute recon means last-minute surprises. Will you call in the rest of the team?"

"I already spoke to Morgan about sending Kane and Ethan out, but we'll need to bring in Macgregor and the rest of the contractors. The more manpower we have, the better." He studied her face. "I assume you'll want to be there too?"

"Yes."

"Okay. Good." He cleared his throat. "It's late. Why don't you crash here tonight? You can take the master bedroom."

"Where will you sleep?"

Their eyes locked for a moment. He was so very tempted to suggest he sleep with *her*, but he knew damn well that neither of them was ready for that.

"On the couch," he said gruffly.

With a nod, she headed for the sliding door. "So it goes down tomorrow."

He nodded. "Tomorrow."

Olivia stepped out of the bathroom and approached the hospital bed, where her mother was sound asleep on her back. Kathleen had been sedated after grudgingly admitting that she hadn't been sleeping well lately. She was also on an IV drip, and Dr. Hopkins, the chief oncologist, had insisted on running some scans, just as a precaution.

Much to Olivia's displeasure, Luke had arranged for the private room and paid for it, but she'd made him promise to let her pay him back. She knew Luke wasn't Vince, that he wouldn't use this debt as a means to control or manipulate her, but that didn't mean she felt comfortable owing money to yet another man. She'd had no choice, though. Her mother needed to be admitted, and since they didn't have health insurance and she'd left all her cash back at the apartment, letting Luke foot the bill had been her only option.

At the moment Luke was sitting in one of the two comfortable chairs next to Kathleen's bed, a pained expression on his handsome face. Olivia knew his injuries were bothering him, but when she'd tried to persuade him to see a doctor—they were in a hospital, after all—he'd shrugged off the suggestion like the macho man he was.

She, on the other hand, didn't bother trying to hide her discomfort. Her side hurt from Vince kicking her, her throat was tender to the touch, and her voice was hoarse. The memory of Vince's hands wrapped around her throat brought a trickle of fear. She'd come close to dying today. Well, yesterday, seeing as it was nearly three o'clock in the morning.

Luke could have died too during his capture, but his unfazed demeanor only reminded her of how colossally different their lives were. Yes, she was walking the path of danger at the moment, but this was a one-time deal. This was about ensuring that Vince Angelo got what he deserved, that he paid for Cora's death.

But for Luke, this wasn't a fluke occurrence. This was his job. He would continue to risk his life and throw himself into dangerous situations—and that didn't fit at all with the life she envisioned for herself or her mother.

"You're frowning," he remarked.

She sat down next to him. He immediately shifted, slinging one arm around her shoulder. She nestled her head in the crook of his neck and sighed. "I'm worried."

"About your mom?" He glanced over at Kathleen's sleeping figure. "Don't worry, darlin', she'll be okay. The doctor didn't seem to think her collapse was a sign of a relapse. She probably just overexerted herself."

"Yeah, I know."

He rubbed his palm over her shoulder. "Then what's worrying you?"

She twisted her head to look at him. "This. Us."

Luke's expression immediately became uneasy. "What do you mean?"

"I need to know we're on the same page," she heard herself say.

"And what page is that?"

"The temporary one."

"Oh right." He breathed out slowly. "I forgot."

She didn't like his tone of voice, the edge to it, the flatness. She met his dark eyes, her frown deepening. "You said you don't do permanent."

"I don't. But that doesn't mean I can't."

Panic pulled at her. "Luke—"

"Relax. I'm not pushing you to commit, okay?" His deep, sexy voice held a note of defeat. "I get it. I don't fit the perfect little life you picture for yourself."

She stiffened. "We haven't even talked about stuff like that. How can you presume to know what I want?"

His eyebrows rose. "So you're not looking for Mr. Nine-to-Five? Mr. Safe and Stable, who pays the mortgage on time and is home for dinner every night? Come on, Liv, it doesn't take a genius to figure out you've got daddy issues."

Indignation hardened her jaw. "You don't know a thing about my father."

"I know he was unreliable. You were only ten when he died, yet that was plenty of time for you to decide you didn't want to end up with someone like him."

"My father didn't give a damn about his family," she said bitterly, her gaze straying to the fragile woman lying in the hospital bed. "All he cared about was the next thrill, the next adventure."

"And you think I'm cut from the same cloth."

"Aren't you?" she challenged.

"My work gets dangerous, yes, but I'm not a hothead. I was trained to do this kind of work, and I always manage to get home in one piece—usually in time for dinner," he added with a sharpness that irked her.

"My father was trained too, but that didn't stop him from dying."

"Nothing stops people from dying. Death is a fact of life. Can't run from it, can't hide."

"Yeah, but your chances of dying increase exponentially when you throw yourself into dangerous situations. Call me a coward, but I don't want to be with somebody who's going to go out and get killed the next day."

"Enter Mr. Safe," he finished. The razor edge to his voice dulled, and he let out a sigh. "You're going to walk away from me when this is all over, aren't you?"

She was startled by the bluntness. "I told you from the start this wouldn't lead to anything."

"Yeah, you did." He hesitated. "You also told me not to fall in love with you, but I'm afraid that didn't quite work out the way you planned."

Her lips parted in surprise. She stared into his gorgeous eyes, looking for a sign that he was kidding, but all she saw reflected back at her was sheepish sincerity. "Luke—"

"Forget I said anything," he cut in, discomfort creasing his strong forehead. "Just . . . just kiss me, okay?"

She couldn't ignore the pull of attraction. Even with her sleeping mother lying five feet away, Olivia was incapable of resisting this man, helpless to stop the heat he evoked in her. The moment their mouths melted together, all coherent thought left her brain. They kissed, soft and slow, lips meeting, tongues tasting. But when she placed her hands on his chest to stroke him, she felt him flinch.

Sighing, she drew back. "This is a bad idea. You're hurt."

He touched her throat, those strong fingers skimming over the bruising. "So are you."

Ignoring the desire sizzling through her, she pushed her chair closer to his and ran her fingers through his surprisingly silky hair. "Put your head on my shoulder," she murmured. "You need to get some sleep."

That he didn't protest told her he was hurting more than he was willing to admit. Luke's dark head nestled against her shoulder, his hair tickling her chin. She threaded her fingers through those dark brown strands, petting, caressing.

When his breathing became slow and steady, Olivia knew he'd fallen asleep.

She sat there, listening to Luke's quiet breathing, feeling the rise and fall of his powerful chest. She let her gaze move freely over his gorgeous face. The dark stubble rising on his jaw, the sharp angles of his features, his wide, sensual mouth. His eyelids began to flutter as if he were in the midst of an action-packed dream, which brought a wry smile to her lips. Figured. Even in slumber he was off doing something exciting.

You also told me not to fall in love with you, but I'm afraid that didn't quite work out the way you planned.

She quickly tried to reroute her thoughts, but it was too late. Luke's confession continued to buzz in her head, following her into fitful slumber and haunting her restless dreams.

Chapter 22

The dining room teemed with huge, good-looking males. Isabel wasn't sure where they'd all come from and she was having a tough time keeping track of their names. Familiarizing herself with a bunch of mercenaries was too daunting a task for nine o'clock in the morning. And for a woman who worked solo, being surrounded by so many people—and so much testosterone—was slightly disconcerting.

A dozen men gathered around the long dining room table, which was covered with maps, files, and photographs. Trevor, Luke, and Sullivan were at the head of the table, Isabel at Trevor's left. Next to Luke were Kane Woodland and Ethan Hayes, who'd arrived earlier. It was good to see them both, especially Kane, the team's second in command and Abby's soon-to-be husband. Of all the women who worked for Noelle, Isabel was closest to Abby Sinclair, the former assassin who'd left Noelle's employment to join Morgan's team. And Abby had chosen well for a mate; with his sandy blond hair and vivid green eyes, Kane was incredibly appealing, not to mention strong and capable.

The other men in the room were contractors, soldiers Morgan called in when their services were required. They were interchangeable—big men in camo pants and muscle shirts. One stood out, however, a brown-eyed man with a buzz cut and thick stubble on his square jaw. They called him Castle, but Isabel didn't know if that was his surname or a nickname. Or hell, it could be his first name. People were calling their kids all sorts of weird things these days.

"Holden liberated the blueprints for the Queens warehouse from the zoning office," Trevor told the group. "As you can see, it's nothing fancy. One story, four thousand square feet." He pointed to the map. "We've got two entry points, front and back, with the loading dock on the side of the building."

"What are we looking at in terms of guards?" Kane asked.

"No idea."

"They'll have a guy or two on the roof," the mysterious Castle predicted.

"Probably one or two on both exits," Kane added.

"But the bulk of their power will cover the loading dock," Luke said, finally joining the conversation. He'd seemed distracted ever since he and Sullivan had returned from the hospital, and Isabel suspected he was worried about Olivia. One of the contractors, a fellow named Adam, had taken over guard duty. Although Kathleen's initial tests had come back negative, the oncologist was running a few more, so Kathleen wasn't likely to be discharged until tomorrow. Luke's edginess made it clear that he would've preferred that Olivia and her mother left town before tonight's mission went down.

It was also clear that the man was head over heels for Olivia Taylor. For some reason, it brought an ache to Isabel's heart. The tenderness she saw in Luke's eyes when he spoke of Olivia only served as a reminder of everything Isabel was missing in her own life.

Luke's voice jerked her out of her thoughts. "Loading dock's the most exposed area, and that's where the truck will be parked."

"As for the interior, we don't know what we'll find,"

Trevor said. "Angelo always travels with at least two body-guards, plus there'll be the crew, and the rep from the Moreno cartel."

"So let's say ten dudes inside," Luke hypothesized. "Maybe less, probably more."

Castle leaned forward, his piercing blue eyes studying the maps of the area. "We approach from the north and west, through this wooded area bordering the warehouse. Any other direction and we'll be spotted. The buildings are well spaced out, so they'll see us coming if we try to approach from the road."

"Two snipers," Trevor decided. "Liam." He gestured to Liam Macgregor, then glanced over at Luke. "Luke, you'll be the second sniper."

Luke bristled. "I'm going in with the rest of you."

"Are you still pissing blood?"

"No."

Luke was so obviously lying that Isabel couldn't help but grin.

"Sniper," Trevor said again, jabbing a finger in Luke's direction. "The rest of us will split off into three teams, led by me, Kane, and Castle. Snipers, you'll pick off the guards manning the front, back, and roof."

"It needs to be quick," Kane warned. "We can't give the bastards time to raise an alarm. Head shots only, and if you see one going for a radio, shoot his hand off."

Trevor nodded in concurrence. "Once the guards are taken out, one team will attack from the front, the other in the back. Third team will cover the loading dock, in case anyone tries to make a run for it. Snipers, you cover everyone."

"Simultaneous attack," Castle agreed, rubbing the stubble on his chin. "We need to pen these guys in before they know it's coming."

"The truck needs to be taken out too," Isabel spoke up. "We don't want anyone using it to escape."

At the sound of her voice, Castle turned to her with his dark eyebrows raised. "Sure you're qualified to be part of this, Blondie?"

Trevor chuckled. "She works for Noelle—what do *you* think?"

Isabel hid her amusement as several of the men shifted uneasily. Evidently Noelle's reputation preceded her. No shocker. Most people, active military or not, were aware of the legendary assassin.

"Fine. What happens inside?" Castle asked. "Take out the tangos?"

The question had a few of the others murmuring, as if they'd been wondering the same thing.

"We want them alive," Trevor said with a shake of his head. "Especially Angelo. Lethal force if necessary, but we want to restrain, not assassinate. We need these assholes to tell us where Dane is. And the DEA is hoping to use Angelo against De Luca."

"The Feds?" one of the contractors said, perplexed. "Why the hell aren't *they* leading this bust? Or at the very least supplying us with extra manpower?"

"The agency can't risk it. There could be a mole problem."

The guy who had asked, Jesse something or other, nodded. "Gotcha."

"DEA will show up when it's over," Trevor said. "After we secure the warehouse, we'll make a call, and the Feds can swoop in and make their arrests."

They went over a few more details, and then Trevor signaled that the briefing had come to an end. Luke was out the front door in a nanosecond, undoubtedly on his way back to Olivia, and as several of the other men drifted toward the living area, Trevor glanced over at Isabel. "Coffee?" he asked.

She nodded gratefully. "I'll wait on the terrace, if you don't mind."

Extricating herself from the group, she ducked outside, breathing in the chilly morning air. Her exhale released a puff of white, hinting that winter was descending on Manhattan fast. Getting colder and colder, and it wasn't even noon.

She watched the scene in the living room through the glass sliding door, the ease with which the men talked with one another, the casual back slaps and hearty laughter. She supposed she could go back inside and mingle, but she'd always been a loner. More comfortable with solitude than socializing. Which was ironic, since her job involved getting close to people to secure information.

The buzzing of her cell phone drew her from her thoughts. When she saw the unfamiliar number flashing on the display, she frowned, then accepted the call.

"Candy?" came a small whimper.

She recognized Heaven's voice at once. "Heaven? What's going on, honey?"

"I . . ." A soft sob broke through the line. "Is it okay that I called?"

"Of course it is. Are you all right?"

"No." That one syllable was laced with pure and utter misery.

"Tell me what's wrong, honey."

There was a prolonged pause. "I fucked a dealer last night."

Isabel swallowed. "Okay . . ."

"I *fucked* him. I was strapped for cash—God, I never have any money—and I was desperate. I was so desperate . . . and . . . you were right. I . . ." Heaven let out a heavy breath. "I need help. I *want* help. Can you . . . will you help me?"

A sense of relief washed over her. "Of course I will."

Ten minutes later, she hung up feeling utterly exhausted, but victorious.

"Something wrong?"

She pivoted to find Trevor standing by the door, his handsome face creased with concern. He held two steaming mugs of coffee.

Isabel shook her head. "Nothing's wrong."

"Who was on the phone?" he asked as he stepped onto the terrace and handed her a mug.

"Heaven."

"Did you tell God I said hi?" Trevor quipped.

She rolled her eyes, then swallowed the hot coffee, savoring the way it heated her belly. "Why does everyone assume I'm starting a religious discussion? I was referring to Heaven Monroe, one of the dancers at the club."

His brows knitted together in a frown. "Did she mention the shooting? Or say anything about Angelo?"

"No. She was off yesterday, and I don't think she heard about it or the part I played in the shooting. I've been trying to convince her to get help. She's got a drug problem."

"Heroin courtesy of Angelo?"

"I don't know the details, but she's in pretty bad shape. She's finally willing to get help, though. I'm meeting her tomorrow morning."

"You think that's a good idea? Just because she didn't mention anything doesn't mean she didn't hear about it. For all we know, Angelo recruited her to hunt down Candy Cane."

"It's a risk I'm willing to take," Isabel said quietly. "I already called the rehab facility and secured a spot for her. I'll drive her there tomorrow."

"And possibly walk into a trap."

"Angelo will be out of the picture tonight. After he's arrested, there's no reason I can't go to her. She needs help, Trevor."

"And it's your job to help her?" He let out a deep sigh. "You know, you're not responsible for saving the world. And you can't help everybody."

"Look who's talking. Aren't we both here to help Olivia?"

"Yes, but it runs deeper with you. Six months ago, you dropped everything to help Abby. Now it's Olivia and some dancer you don't even know." He studied her face. "And I suspect you do this often, ride to the rescue the moment someone else is in trouble."

"So I like to help people. Big deal," she said in aggravation.

Something indecipherable flickered in Trevor's whiskey-colored eyes. "But when do you help yourself?"

Fortunately, she didn't have to answer, because as was always the case when it came to her and Trevor, they were interrupted.

"Trev, the boss is on the phone," Kane said, appearing in the doorway with a BlackBerry in hand. "He wants to talk to you."

Although he looked reluctant, Trevor headed for the sliding door. Just before he reached it, he stopped and looked over his shoulder. "We'll finish this later," he said gruffly.

Isabel watched him go, wishing she could make sense of the odd emotions fluttering in her belly. She couldn't remember anyone ever challenging her need to help people or questioning her motives for doing so, and it bothered her that Trevor was perceptive enough to see that her motivations might run deeper than she let on.

It was official. Trevor Callaghan was definitely getting under her skin. Six months ago, he'd intrigued her, appealed to her protective instincts, triggered the urge to help him.

Now . . . well, now he just frightened her.

"Adam will stay with you and Kathleen until it's over," Luke said as he and Olivia sat in the waiting room down the hall from her mother's room.

She nodded. "And afterward?"

"We'll wait until your mom is discharged, and then bring both of you to the compound with us. We'll figure out the next move then."

But damn it, he wanted to figure it out *now*. When their eyes locked, Luke nearly blurted out that he loved her. Fortunately, he caught the words before they popped out. He hadn't missed her reaction last night when he'd insinuated at the L-word. Wide-eyed, uncomfortable, a touch of dread. The idea of him loving her scared her. Hell, it scared him too. He'd been a bachelor for so long he had no clue how to do the whole commitment thing, especially with a woman like Olivia Taylor. He didn't doubt that he could figure it out, though, if only she'd give him the chance.

No matter what she thought, he knew he could be the kind of man she wanted in her life—to some degree, at least. He'd love her. Cherish her. Make her laugh. Make her come. He'd give her any damn thing she asked for, if only to see that gorgeous smile of hers.

The only thing he wouldn't do was give up his work. Olivia might disagree with his choices and disapprove of the danger, and hey, maybe her fears were valid. Maybe he *did* live too recklessly. But regardless of the risks, his work brought him an overpowering sense of fulfillment that he couldn't even describe.

"I'm not a daredevil," he burst out.

She furrowed her brows in confusion. "What?"

"I just want you to know that. You think I'm like your father, that I'm addicted to danger and don't care about anything or anyone but the rush, but I need you to know it's not like that with me."

"Luke—"

"I do this work because it makes me happy. Because my skills are best used for military operations and extractions and blowing shit up." To his dismay, his voice cracked. "I *love* it, Olivia, not because of the adrenaline high—though that plays a part in it—but because I sleep better at night knowing I did some good. That I stopped a bad guy today. Or saved a life today."

She looked a bit stunned. "Because you couldn't save your father?"

Pain shot through his heart. "That's probably part of it too, at least in recent days. But I was a SEAL before I lost my dad. Saving the world is in my DNA, darlin'. I won't apologize for what I do, but you need to know that my work is only a fraction of who I am."

His gaze locked with hers. "You want a man you can rely on? A man who's steady, stable, who will put you first? Well, I can be that man. I might not show up for dinner every night, but you can damn well count on me to be there for breakfast, or lunch, or some random-hour meal that isn't scheduled. Because you know what? Schedules frickin' suck."

The corners of her lips lifted in amusement, but before she could respond, Sullivan stepped into the waiting room. "Don't mean to interrupt, but we've gotta go, mate."

Luke battled a wave of disappointment. Wonderful. Olivia was sitting beside him wearing an honest-to-God smile during a conversation that didn't have the word *temporary* in it, and just his luck they had to be disturbed.

"Now?" he said impatiently.

Sullivan's lips quirked. "Hmmm, good point. Let's go later. Why don't you call Trev and let him know we'll be late for work?"

"Smart-ass," Luke muttered.

"You asked for it."

He gave Olivia an apologetic look. "I'll be back later to pick you up, okay?"

Worry filled her green eyes. "You promise?"

He leaned in and brushed his lips over hers in a tender kiss. "I promise."

Vince paced his office at the Diamond Mine, his alligator loafers snapping against the polished parquet with each infuriated step. He'd spent the entire afternoon on the phone trying to track down Olivia's whereabouts. Now it was eight thirty, he had to head over to Queens in a half hour, and he was no closer to finding the bitch. Make that *bitches*; Candy Cane was still out there somewhere too. But Olivia remained his primary concern.

She had disappeared. Gone like a wisp of fucking smoke. Her apartment had been empty when Rocko and Del Vido broke in last night. No sign of the mother either. The old lady's medication was gone, some clothing too. Olivia's things, however, were all accounted for, and the men had discovered a cigar box jammed with cash in the back of her closet.

You didn't hoard that much dough unless you wanted to make a quick getaway. God knows he had enough cash in his safe to get him out of the country on a second's notice. The little bitch had been planning on running away from him. From *him*, the man who'd saved her life.

The notion of Olivia plotting her escape made his blood boil. And to make matters worse, he couldn't get in touch with Gino or Roy, the two men who were standing guard over the Dubois asshole. Their presence wasn't required for the transaction tonight, but he could've put them to use tracking Olivia and Candy. Except their damn phones continued to bump over to voice mail, and the only contact he'd had with them was when Gino sent a text earlier this morning to report that Dubois was still at the Riverside house and not causing any problems.

"Should I use your lover to lure you out?" Vince muttered to himself.

Definitely an idea worth considering, though the success of that plan hinged on whether or not Olivia actually gave a damn about Dubois. And using her lover as leverage didn't mean shit if he couldn't get in contact with the bitch.

Vince stopped pacing and proceeded to curse up a storm. How had everything gotten so fucked up so fast? It had all been going smoothly, and the next thing he knew, chaos erupted. Olivia was gone. Two of his guys were out of touch. And the most important deal of his life was going down in an hour, but he had no desire to be there.

He'd spent an entire year wooing Olivia. From the moment they'd met he'd known she was his other half. And she'd *betrayed* him.

How could he just disregard that? How could he focus on a fucking business deal when all he wanted to do was get his hands on the woman who'd scorned him?

But how? How the hell would he find her? His men had flashed her picture at every airport, train station, and rental car agency in the city. His contacts at the police department had assured him that she hadn't used her ATM or credit cards to book passage out of the state, which led him to deduce that she was still in Manhattan. Now it was only a matter of finding her.

As his cell phone buzzed in his hand, he brought it up to his ear with an angry "What?"

There was a pause. "Did I catch you at a bad time?" Erik Franz asked.

"Yes," he snapped. "What do you want?"

"To let you know everything's on schedule. The crew and I are already at the warehouse, and the truck arrives at ten. What's your ETA?"

"I'll be leaving shortly."

"Any word on the stripper who shot Mikey?"

"No. I've got men hunting her down, but it looks like everything she wrote on her job application was fake."

"What happened to the flawless screening system you speak so highly of?"

The sarcasm dripping from Franz's voice made Vince's gut burn. "It evidently wasn't so flawless," he spat out.

"Relax. I was kidding. Anyway, I think we need to—"

Two beeps sounded in Vince's ear. "Hold on. I'm getting another call."

He clicked over to the other line, frowning when an unfamiliar voice greeted him. "Who the fuck is this?" Vince demanded.

"It's Larry. Uh, from the records office at St. Francis."

His entire body stiffened. "What do you want?"

As the other man made the purpose of his call known, Vince's muscles began to relax, one by one. He listened carefully, a smile stretching across his face.

"Larry," he said, cutting the man off in mid-sentence, "let me call you back in a minute."

Without waiting for a response, he clicked over to Franz. "Change of plans," he announced. "You're handling this alone."

"What?"

"You deal with the delivery. I won't be able to make it."

"What the fuck do you mean, you can't make it? De Luca wants you there to oversee everything."

"You can oversee it for me. It'll do you good—you can prove yourself to the big boss, show him you've got what it takes to head up this operation."

Franz sounded flustered. "You've insisted from day one that you need to be there. What the hell changed?"

"There's somewhere else I need to be more," Vince said vaguely.

It was ironic actually. He'd spent his entire life climbing out of the gutter. Determined to prove his worth, to show those around him that he had what it took to be successful. To be wealthy. Yeah, wealth had always been his ultimate goal. Money meant power. Money meant everything.

Yet at that very moment, Vince Angelo had finally stumbled upon something that meant more to him than money.

Revenge.

Chapter 23

The Premiere Roast coffee warehouse was bathed in darkness, save for the exterior lights shining down on the pavement and the pale glow seeping out from the loading bay. Luke watched through the scope of his rifle, focusing on the two men standing by the double doors at the warehouse's entrance. Both were armed with heavy-duty assault rifles. So was the man on the roof, but along with the AK slung over his shoulder, he also had a rifle set up beneath the roof's concrete ledge, aimed at the road ahead.

Luke's trigger finger itched, but he didn't make a single move. The truck hadn't arrived yet, so killing these assholes prematurely would be a bad idea, and as much as he'd complained back at the safe house, he didn't find sniper duty as appalling as he'd let on. He genuinely enjoyed lying up here on the roof of the neighboring building, his only company the long-range rifle he'd been using for the last five years. His beloved Inga. She was Russian-made, heavier than other sniper rifles, but perfectly capable of doing the job. The guys constantly accused him of being unpatriotic for using her, but he loved this fucking gun and wouldn't trade Inga for anything.

Liam Macgregor, his fellow sharpshooter, was positioned somewhere in the rear. With his American-issue rifle no doubt, but Luke had seen Liam shoot, and he felt sorry for the guards patrolling the back. The rest of the guys, sectioned off in teams of three, were hunkered down in the woods nearby, unable to make a move until the snipers gave the signal.

Trevor's voice crackled in his ear. "Any sign of the truck?"

He shifted his aim and glanced at the long stretch of road to the north. "No, not yet."

"What do we think about the four dudes who showed up earlier?" Kane's inquiry came over the line. "Could Dane be one of them?"

"Maybe. I didn't get a good look at any of them," Luke admitted.

A couple hours earlier, a sleek black Town Car had parked near the loading dock. Four men had emerged; three had seemed distinctly Mafia with their black suits and olive complexions, but the fourth was a big question mark. Average height, tailored suit, a Yankees cap obstructing his face. He supposed it could have been Dane, but that only raised the question *why*. Why would Dane be present for this transaction? Was he still undercover or had he been lured over to the dark side?

The rumble of an engine echoed in the air. Through his scope, Luke glimpsed a truck chugging up the road. Premiere Roast's logo—coffee beans overflowing from a big red mug—was stenciled on the side of the beat-up vehicle. He spotted two men: a driver with a full beard and a passenger with his head bent downward and slightly to the side, revealing a sliver of rugged profile. Dark-skinned, the swarthy coloring hinting at South American descent. Must be the Moreno cartel's guy.

"We've got company," Luke said softly.

The truck pulled into the lot and drove directly to the loading dock. From his vantage point, he couldn't see much, but Liam speedily checked in with a visual update. "Two men getting out of the truck. Driver in a uniform. Second man looks South American. I assume it's the cartel rep."

Luke checked his watch. "It's nine fifty-eight. Where the

hell is Angelo?" He glanced at the road again. No cars in sight.

"Are we sure he's not already inside?" Castle barked through the frequency. "We know four crew members are in there, plus the four that arrived in the Lincoln. Maybe Angelo showed up earlier before anyone else got here."

"Ethan and I have had the warehouse under surveillance since dawn," Kane reported. "The employees left at five, and nobody came near the place until the crew arrived."

Luke experienced a pull of unease. Why wasn't Angelo here? He'd told Olivia he had a big meeting on Tuesday night. It didn't make sense that he wouldn't show up for such an important transaction. And according to Isabel, De Luca always sent a high-ranking member of the family to supervise new investments.

Needless to say, Angelo's absence had everyone rattled.

The creak of metal sounded from the vicinity of the loading dock. "Door just opened," Liam said. "Four men, heading to the back of the truck. Driver's unlocking it."

"Shit," Trevor swore. "We can't wait for Angelo. We need to go in while they're distracted with unloading the crates."

Luke muttered a curse of his own. This entire raid had been about busting Vince Angelo, so if the guy wasn't accounted for, what were they even doing here?

Sullivan must have read his mind. "If Angelo's AWOL, why not abort?" the Australian demanded.

"We don't know that he's not here," Luke said in frustration. "He could be the guy in the Yankees hat. The height and build are a match, and the tailored suit is Angelo's trademark."

But the guy's body language had been different, damn it. Angelo walked with his shoulders high, carrying the smug air of superiority, while the man in the cap had been slouching. Then again, that could be Angelo's way of trying not to draw attention to himself.

Isabel's calm voice entered the mix. She was on Trevor's

team, and hadn't said much during the entire exchange. "Dane could still be there," she pointed out.

"Blondie's right." Castle's voice this time. "We can't walk away now, not if there's a chance the missing agent is inside."

"Team leader?" Luke prompted.

"We go in," Trevor announced. "Two objectives—find Dane, nab Angelo. If Angelo's inside, this could be the Feds' only chance to nail him, so don't let the son of a bitch get away. Snipers, you ready?"

Luke lowered his head to the scope. "Ready."

Liam's voice joined in. "Ready."

"All right, let's do this thing," Trevor ordered.

Taking a deep breath, Luke tracked the movements of the man on the roof. As he locked in on his target, his finger curled over the trigger and squeezed. The bulky guard went down without a sound, bullet between the eyes. Rapidly rotating the rifle barrel, he took out the two guards at the front door. One shot. Two.

"Clear," he murmured.

"Clear," Liam echoed a second later.

"Let's move," Trevor said.

The next ten minutes were total agony for Luke, making him take back his earlier thoughts about sniper duty and serving as a glaring reminder of why he hated it so damn much. Being left out of the action *sucked*. He had no fucking idea what was going on, but he could hazard a guess based on what he saw and heard. As heavy footsteps and shouts echoed in the night air, he watched Castle's team swarm the loading dock, saw the Town Car sag as Liam blew all four tires out.

Heartbeat steady, Luke put the coffee truck out of commission, taking out the tires. A lucky absconder might succeed in driving the thing for half a mile before the rims collapsed, but there'd be no permanent getaways.

The sound of gunfire rang in his ears. The men inside the warehouse must have opened fire, but the din was too deafening to decipher. Shouting, demands, more gunshots.

Adrenaline spiked in his blood. His body itched for action, but he forced himself to wait patiently, to gaze through the scope and make sure nobody was fleeing the building. Castle's team had successfully gained control of the loading dock, judging by Castle's harsh command for everyone to get down on the ground.

Inside was another story. Luke heard Sullivan's distinct Aussie accent yelling for someone to take cover, and then the clamor of bullets clapping out of an assault rifle cracked through the radio. There was thumping, more shouting, another round of gunfire, until second by second the noise died, leaving nothing but the sound of his team's steady breathing in his ear.

A blur of movement flashed in his peripheral vision. He swiveled his head in time to see a panicked male flying out the front doors in a mad sprint. Brave fellow was attempting to make a run for it, only to get tackled from behind by Ethan, who launched himself onto the runaway's back, got him on the pavement, and brought a knife to his throat. A moment later, the escapee was hauled to his feet and ushered back into the warehouse.

Luke waited for a report. It finally came when Trevor grunted and said, "It's done."

"Angelo?" Luke demanded.

"No sign of him."

A muffled thud echoed through the frequency, followed by more commotion.

"Son of a bitch," he heard Trevor mutter, and then a new voice joined the mix.

"Thank God you're here!"

He didn't recognize the voice, but the others must have because the radio went eerily quiet. An instant later, Trevor's low voice said, "Luke, get in here."

Oh yeah, he definitely didn't like the sound of that.

With a burst of energy, he abandoned Inga and dashed toward the cable he'd used to scale the roof. He slid down with lightning speed, unholstering his Glock as he raced toward the warehouse. When he stumbled through the front doors, he halted, taking a moment to orient himself. The place was huge, littered with pallets containing crates of coffee with the Premiere Roast logo stamped on them. Forklifts and ladders filled up the space, and as he navigated the tall aisles toward the source of the action, he nearly tripped over the crumpled body of one of the Italian goons. Head shot. He passed three more bodies on his way, two crew members and another goon.

The team was in position by the loading dock, weapons drawn, faces hard as stone. Against one wall, five men were down on their knees, hands tied behind their backs with plastic cuffs. He instantly recognized the driver and the Colombian from the truck. The remaining trio consisted of the third goon and two of the crew who'd been unloading the truck.

No Angelo.

Luke stifled an irritated groan. After all this bullshit, Angelo hadn't even made an appearance. But why? What possible fucking reason could that bastard have for skipping out on his own business venture?

And why did Luke get the distressing feeling that it had something to do with Olivia?

Tamping down his growing worry, he ignored the five hostages and walked over to Trevor and Kane. Their backs were turned, weapons pointed at a man whose face Luke couldn't make out. The man in the Yankees cap. As he approached, Kane stepped aside to give Luke a better view.

Narrowing his eyes, Luke studied the man. "Take off the hat," he ordered.

"I've been trying to tell them, I'm not—"

"Take off the hat."

The cap came off and he found himself staring into a pair of metallic gray eyes belonging to a lanky man in his early forties. He moved his gaze over the man's face, the square jaw, faint wrinkles around a thin mouth, familiar angular features. Longish black hair fell onto the man's narrow forehead, and the black wool suit draped over his lean body looked mighty expensive.

Luke glanced at Trevor. "Did I miss the part where you checked his ass?"

The team leader shook his head, amused. "No need to. He just waltzed up and introduced himself."

"Huh. Well," Luke said, lowering his gun, "then it's a pleasure to meet you, Special Agent Dane."

Chapter 24

"Dane here claims that he's an innocent bystander," Trevor said dryly.

Luke studied the DEA agent, taking in the man's tired features and tight mouth. Dane was looking around the group with a resentful expression on his face, as if he couldn't fathom why there'd be so many guns pointed at him. Every now and then his gaze darted toward the five men lined up against the wall, but none of them met his eyes—they were on their knees, heads bent as Castle and his men loomed over them.

The rest of the team stood guard by the open door of the loading dock, where the truck had been partially unloaded. A few crates bearing the Premiere Roast emblem were scattered on the cement floor; one had been pried open and a plastic-wrapped brick of matte white powder was visible, sitting on a bed of coffee beans. Sullivan kept an eye on it, though it was unlikely the hostages would spring free and make a grab for the H.

Luke turned back to Dane, assessing, wondering what to make of the agent's presence amid this incredibly illegal affair.

"He dove for cover when we came in," Kane spoke up, looking disgusted.

"Because I didn't want to get killed," Dane snapped.

"My neck's been on the line from the second I agreed to take this freaking assignment. I begged Lewis to pull me out, but he wouldn't sign off on it."

"Is that why you faked your death?" Luke asked.

"It was the only way, damn it."

"I see."

"Look, I was in too deep, okay? And these guys are smart. I had enough evidence to nail them on the drug smuggling, but my handler said it wasn't enough. He wanted more." Dane made a bitter sound in the back of his throat. "Lewis wanted the entire organization out of commission—drugs, guns, gambling, the whole fucking shebang. He set up a joint task force with the bureau, fucking glory hunter Lewis."

Luke resisted the urge to roll his eyes. Truth was, he didn't give a shit why Dane was here. He was more concerned with why Angelo *wasn't* here. Worry gnawed at his gut as the thought settled in.

"Angelo and De Luca were on to me," Dane went on, panic lacing his tone. "I pleaded for an extraction, but Lewis refused." His eyes became wild. "And then it was too fucking late. They found out who I was! Someone sold me out and told them I was a Fed. But I managed to convince them that I'd turned."

"How'd you do that?" Trevor asked dubiously.

"By proving my loyalty," Dane said, his mouth set in a fatigued line. "I did shit I'm not proud of, all right? But it was the only way to stay alive. I convinced Angelo that my bosses had sold me out, abandoned me, and that I wanted to be a permanent fixture in the organization. I persuaded him to help me fake my death, told him that if they thought I was dead, the DEA would forget about me and abort the operation. They wouldn't risk sending in another agent if they thought the outfit had rubbed me out."

Luke sighed. "Yet here you are, greeting a shipment of heroin with welcoming arms."

"I was biding my time," Dane said miserably. "Playing along until I could find a way to skip town."

Kane chuckled. "And making a nice profit in the meantime, huh?"

"It wasn't about profit! I was trying to save my own ass! Do you know what these assholes would have done if they thought I was looking for a way out?"

"Bullshit!" a heavily accented voice spat out.

All eyes swung toward one of the hostages, the Colombian with the enraged face. The man jutted his chin at Dane and made a disgusted noise. "This partnership was his doing. He's been dealing with us for years, and he's the one who brokered the deal and brought De Luca in on the action."

Dane's cheeks reddened. "I did deal with the cartel—I spent two fucking years in Medellín trying to bring those bastards down. It was before I got assigned to infiltrate De Luca's crew. But I didn't broker anything."

"Frankly, I don't give a damn what went down," Trevor said with a shrug. "Your buddies at the agency have already been alerted and they're on their way. You can straighten this out with them."

Dane nodded grimly. "Fine."

Trevor turned to Castle. "Put him with the others until the Feds get here."

Castle hauled the agent by the arm, and although Dane followed the mercenary willingly, an unsettling feeling washed over Luke. His gaze zeroed in on Carter Dane's gray eyes. As the man stared back, time seemed to stand still, and Luke instantly recognized Dane's expression—it was one belonging to a man who knew he was defeated.

A man who had nothing to lose.

"Wait—" he started, but in the blink of an eye, Dane's arm shot toward the gun sticking out of Castle's waistband.

Luke was just raising his Glock when something hissed by his ear. Next thing he knew, Dane yelped in pain and gaped at his hand.

Everyone followed his gaze and stared at the sleek bone handle of the hunting knife lodged in Dane's palm.

Stunned silence descended on the warehouse.

"What the . . ." Trevor began, then trailed off.

Shrugging off his surprise, Luke turned around to see Ethan lowering his arm.

The rookie met his eyes and offered a sheepish shrug. "I've been practicing with Abby."

There was a soft chuckle from Trevor, a grin from Kane, and a grunt from Castle, who shot Dane a look reserved for terrorists.

"Try anything else and I'll put a bullet in your head," Castle snapped. Then, without an ounce of compassion, he ripped the knife out of Dane's hand, eliciting a pain-laced yelp from the federal agent.

As Castle dragged Dane toward the other prisoners and cuffed the guy, Luke and Kane exchanged resigned looks.

"So . . . guess he was a bad guy after all," Kane murmured.

"Looks like it," Luke concurred

As sirens howled in the distance, he holstered his weapon. "DEA's here. Finally." His gaze did one last sweep of the warehouse, resting on the crates near the truck. "Heroin accounted for?" he called to Isabel.

"Yeah, and there's a lot of it," she called back, rising from the crate she was sitting on. "This might be the biggest seizure the Feds have seen to date."

He glanced over at Dane, who was fuming on the dusty floor with his hands behind his back. "And to think," Luke said lightly, "one of their own brokered the deal." Rolling his eyes, he turned to Trevor. "Can you deal with the Feds? I want to call Olivia and make sure she's all right."

"And we need to find Angelo," Sullivan spoke up from his position by the truck. "I wonder why he didn't show."

"Join the club," Luke muttered.

His eyes met Sully's across the room, and he knew the Australian was thinking the same thing—whatever the reason for Vince Angelo's absence, it couldn't be good. At all.

Olivia set down her cards on the plastic table one of the nurses had rolled into her mother's hospital room. Kathleen was sound asleep in the bed. Sedated again, but her coloring looked better, and she'd gone for a long stroll through the oncology wing earlier, with Olivia hovering over her like an overprotective parent. Now they were settled inside the room for the night, and Adam, the soldier who'd been assigned to watch them, had spent the past hour teaching Olivia various card games.

She appreciated the company. The smell of the hospital, disinfectant and death, made her queasy, reminding her of all the days and weeks she'd spent here. Sitting at Kathleen's bedside, comforting her through the chemo treatments, reading to her while she recovered from the mastectomies, the removal of her lymph nodes, the constant checkups.

This time was different, though. Not just because her mom was here for only one more night, but because this time Olivia wasn't doing it alone. Luke had been by her side all of last night and most of today, and his presence had been comforting. She was so used to everyone else leaning on *her* that it had felt nice leaning on someone else for a change. Really, really nice.

"Ready to show me what you've got?" Adam's voice interrupted her thoughts.

"Oh, right. Two nines," she said proudly, placing her two cards beneath the five already on the table.

He stared at her in disbelief. "You went all in with *two nines*?"

She furrowed her brows. "That's bad?"

"It's terrible!"

"Then why did you fold and let me win?"

"Because you looked so confident I figured my three fours were garbage."

"I was confident because I thought two nines were good." She shook her head in aggravation. "Can we play something else? Do you know gin rummy?"

"Nope."

She sighed. "Why don't we just watch TV?"

He paused in thought. "That new chick network plays *Grey's Anatomy* reruns on Tuesdays."

"I won't even ask how you know that."

Olivia was then treated to the sight of a grown man with bulging biceps and army fatigues reaching for a remote control so he could watch *Grey's Anatomy*. Who knew?

"What, you don't like this show?" Adam asked when he caught her staring.

"I like it. I'm just surprised that *you* watch it."

"I think Meredith is hot," he replied with a shrug. He glanced up at the television mounted in the corner of the ceiling. "It's about to start."

Twenty minutes later, they were engrossed in a particularly gory episode, watching the doctors of Seattle Grace tend to patients and yet still find time to get jiggy in supply closets. During the commercial break, Olivia's thoughts once again drifted to Luke, and a swarm of questions buzzed through her head. Had the team arrived at the warehouse on schedule? Were they in position, waiting for the truck to arrive? Was Luke okay?

She prayed that they didn't encounter any nasty surprises, and as she fretfully wrung her hands, she suddenly realized that this was what her mom must have felt like every time Eddie Taylor went overseas.

I can be that man.

Luke's deep voice kept running through her mind, his declaration that he could be the kind of man she wanted. No, the kind of man she *needed*. But how was that possible? If she opened her heart to Luke, she'd be in a perpetual state of worry. Wringing her hands as she was now, wondering if he was okay.

She couldn't live that way. She already worried enough—about her mother, about school, about paying the bills. How could she let Luke into her life, knowing that she would constantly be losing sleep each time he flew off on a mission?

"Do you think they're okay?" she blurted out.

Adam's blue eyes twinkled. "You mean, is Dubois okay? Yeah, I think he's just fine. Those SEALs can take care of themselves, honey."

"You're right, he's fine. My nerves are probably getting the best of me." She bit her lip. "I'm being silly, aren't I?"

"Not at all. We always worry about the ones we love."

Heat spilled over her cheeks. "Love? No, it's not like that with Luke and me. We're ... ah ..." She trailed off.

Adam grinned. "I stand corrected. You're *so* not in love with the guy."

She was ready to voice another denial when she heard footsteps approach the door.

Adam's hand instantly lowered to the holster on his hip. A male orderly in green scrubs entered the room, holding a bedpan in his hands.

Adam relaxed.

And then the orderly slid his hand from beneath the bedpan and whipped a gun in their direction.

Olivia didn't even have time to scream. A high-pitched *pop* filled the air, and the next thing she knew, a small hole appeared in the center of Adam's forehead.

She watched in horror as his body toppled off the chair and crumpled to the linoleum floor.

Dead. He was *dead*.

With a choked sound, she shot to her feet and launched herself onto her mother's sleeping body, but the tall man bounded forward to intercept her. She opened her mouth to scream but his hand clamped over it, cutting her shriek short. As she struggled to get out of his grip, a second set of footsteps thudded on the floor, and then a familiar voice tickled her ear.

"Hey, babe, fancy meeting you here."

Chapter 25

Standing outside the warehouse, Luke tried for a third time to reach Adam, and for a third time his call was bumped to Adam's voice mail. The area around him was crawling with federal agents shouting to one another and barking orders into radios. An entire hoard of Feds was in the process of seizing the crates from the coffee truck and loading the confiscated items into a black van. Across the lot, paramedics brought body bags out on stretchers, rolling them toward the waiting ambulance and coroner's van.

Luke ignored the commotion and redialed Adam's number with increasing uneasiness. The former marine's voice mail greeted him once more. Damn it. Why the *fuck* wasn't Adam picking up his fucking phone?

Something was wrong. Luke felt it deep in his bones, in his gut, his heart, his everything. Fingers trembling, he dialed Olivia's cell number but got her voice mail too. In a last-ditch effort, he called the hospital, but after he'd been connected to Kathleen's room, the line kept ringing and ringing until he finally hung up in frustration.

"Holden!" he shouted, sweeping his eyes over the crowd. Most of the guys were milling around a pair of SUVs, chatting, smoking, looking bored. The team had no real need to stick around, but the lead DEA agent had insisted that they wait to be debriefed.

Holden extricated himself from a conversation with Sully and Liam and wandered over. "What's up?"

"Do you have your laptop with you?"

"Yeah, why?"

"Is it linked up to the GPS system?"

"Yep. Why?" Holden repeated.

He grabbed the other man's arm and practically dragged him to the Range Rover. Trevor and Isabel, who'd been standing a few feet from the SUV, quickly walked over. Luke knew his body language was screaming *panic attack* but no amount of silent reassurances could curb his growing concern.

"I can't get in touch with Olivia or Adam," he explained. "I've got a bad feeling. A really bad fucking feeling." He glanced at Holden, who was leaning into the backseat to find his laptop case. "There's a tracker in Olivia's cell phone, and one in the necklace she's wearing. See where she is, man."

Holden slid the computer out of its case and rested it on the hood of the car. "Give me a sec."

While Holden pulled up the necessary program, Sullivan and Liam approached the group. The big Australian and Mr. Male Model had been chatting up a storm during the past hour, well on their way to becoming BFFs. Now they wore matching frowns. "What's going on, mate?" Sullivan asked.

Luke ignored the question and followed the movement of Holden's fingers on the keyboard. "Come on, man," he said impatiently.

Holden studied the screen. "The phone's at the hospital. It's not moving."

"And the necklace?"

"Hold on." Holden typed a few more commands. "Shit. She's on the move."

"Where?" Luke demanded. "Heading back to the safe house?"

"No. Traveling east on the Long Island Expressway."

"What?"

"She's definitely in a car, just merged onto the Jericho Turnpike."

His heart dropped to the pit of his stomach. "Angelo has her."

Isabel spoke up, trying to sound encouraging. "We don't know that. Maybe Adam is taking her to—"

"Taking her where?" he growled. "He was ordered to guard Olivia and Kathleen at the hospital. If he was going to take either of them anywhere else, he would have checked in. Unless he *couldn't* check in. Which means he's fucking *dead* and now Angelo has her." Rage bubbled in his gut, mixed with a dose of fear so strong he nearly keeled over. "I'm going after her."

"I'm going with you," Sullivan said immediately, diving into the driver's seat.

In the end, Kane and Holden also came along, Holden so he could monitor the GPS, Kane because Trevor ordered him to—evidently Luke's state of complete and total panic hadn't gone unnoticed.

In the backseat of the SUV, he tried to control the overwhelming vise of helplessness threatening to choke him. Angelo had gotten his hands on Olivia. That's why he hadn't showed his face tonight.

"He's going to kill her," Luke mumbled.

A hand stretched out from the front seat. Kane. He leaned in to grip Luke's shoulder, those green eyes filled with determination. "He won't kill her. We're going to find her."

"He's obsessed with her, and he thinks she cheated on him. With me. It's my fucking fault he found out the truth. I slipped up, got caught by his goons, and now . . . now Olivia is going to pay the price for it."

Olivia blinked in disorientation as the trunk of the Town Car was released and her eyes adjusted to the sudden onslaught of light. Moonlight. Shining down from a starless black sky and bringing a streak of pain to her temples. Vince had knocked her out back in the parking lot of St. Francis. Her head throbbed, her brain working overtime to remember what happened.

Adam. Vince's goon had killed Adam.

Oh God.

The image of Vince's wild eyes burned through her mind. He'd threatened to shoot her mother if Olivia didn't leave with him. He'd forced her to walk out of the room, down the corridor, into the elevator, out to the parking lot. Threatened to go on a shooting spree in the hospital if she screamed. Or tried to run. She'd followed his orders only because she'd known without a shred of doubt that he wasn't bluffing. The rage shining in his eyes told her he would've slaughtered anybody in his path if he'd had to.

So she'd shut her mouth and done what he said, all the while trying to formulate an escape plan. Since her phone had been left behind in her mom's hospital room, calling for help was out, but she had planned on springing into action once they reached the parking lot and were away from anyone Vince might harm. Kneeing him in the groin, screaming bloody murder, even taking his damn driver hostage if the opportunity presented itself. But she hadn't gotten the chance. The moment they'd approached the Lincoln, the butt of Vince's gun had slammed into her right temple, and that was good night.

She'd come to about fifteen minutes later to find herself bound and gagged in the trunk of the Town Car, and now they were here. Wherever here was.

Olivia's pulse sped up when a shadow loomed over her. She blinked again, making out Vince's torso, his eerily calm face. When their gazes met, he smiled. "Good. You're awake."

As he leaned in to scoop her up in his arms, she began to struggle, batting at him with her fists, which were secured together.

Vince's brown eyes flashed. "Keep struggling and I'll cut your fucking hands off."

She went still, searching her brain frantically for a way out of this. Maybe she could talk him down, use his love for her to defuse the ticking time bomb he'd become.

Speaking through the gag shoved in her mouth, she

mumbled a protest, trying to get his attention. He ignored her, his strides long and powerful as he carried her toward a small A-frame cabin in the distance.

Olivia's gaze darted around as she took in her surroundings. They were in a deserted area surrounded by yellowing grass, flat earth, and trees devoid of leaves. The cabin was the only structure in sight, its weathered log exterior and paint-chipped front door lending it an abandoned feel.

Vince stopped on the porch and unlocked the door. It creaked open and he lugged her inside, where the scent of mold and mildew drifted into her nose. She caught a glimpse of a small room with a tattered plaid sofa against one wall and a kitchenette in the corner.

She mumbled another objection. This time Vince growled in annoyance. "Shut up," he snapped. "There'll be plenty of time for talking later."

Later? God, how long did he plan on keeping her here?

His loafers thudded against the splintered wood floor as he carried her to an open doorway across the room. Next thing she knew, she was thrown onto a bed, her body bouncing off a dirty mattress with a few of its springs exposed. A metal coil dug into her back, bringing a jolt of pain.

Vince flicked a light switch and closed the door. When he pivoted, he had a gun pointed at her, sleek and black with a silencer screwed on its barrel. In his left hand, he held a small switchblade and a roll of duct tape.

Fear crawled up her spine and lodged in her throat.

Without a word, Vince approached the bed and sliced through the rope binding her feet together. With a muffled cry, she kicked a foot up and connected with his jaw.

He grunted in anger.

And stuck the switchblade into her calf.

Olivia jerked from the searing pain, her leg involuntarily dropping to the mattress. Blood ran down her leg, soaking the cotton of her black leggings.

"What did I tell you about struggling?" Vince demanded.

She swallowed, battling the sting of tears, then gasped when he thrust her legs apart. His features reflected a combination of rage and concentration as he set his gun on the floor and proceeded to shove her right foot against the post of the rickety bed frame. He secured it with duct tape, then did the same with her left foot. He gave a satisfied grunt and went to work on her hands, and when he was done, Olivia was spread-eagled on the bed. The only upside— God, did that word even exist in a situation like this?—was that she remained fully dressed. If rape was on his agenda, it wouldn't happen yet.

"Now we talk," Vince said pleasantly, bending down to remove her gag.

"Don't do this," she croaked once she was able to speak.

"You're in no position to give me orders!" he roared. "You screwed another man! You've probably screwed *hundreds* of men during this past year, you little whore."

"That's not true," she protested. "I—"

He sprang at her and crammed the gag back into her mouth. His entire body vibrated, shuddering with icy wrath. "Talking was a bad idea. I can't listen to your fucking voice feeding me any more fucking lies."

Strands of defeat curled around her spine. Now what? If she couldn't keep him talking, what chance did she have? How the hell was she going to save herself?

"You think I'm not good enough for you, is that it?" His brown eyes bored into hers, bitterness dripping from his harsh voice. "Well, what makes you so much better than me? Your father was a weak loser masquerading as a hero. Your mother's had one foot in the grave her entire life. And *you*? Who the hell are you? What makes you better than me? Your looks? This city's full of pretty pussy! Your brains? Because as I recall, you were a high school dropout."

His chest heaved as the words poured out of his mouth like gushing water bursting through a dam. In that moment, Olivia realized just how deep Vince Angelo's insecurities ran, how skewed he'd become from what he believed to be a cruel upbringing. Yeah, *so* cruel—two parents who loved him but hadn't been able to buy him a bunch of meaningless material things.

She suddenly faltered, realizing she wasn't exactly one to talk. Hadn't she allowed her own upbringing to do the same thing to her? Skew her outlook, send her running away from any man who reminded her even the slightest of her father? Look what *she'd* been doing—keeping a wonderful man at arm's length, insisting that he was temporary, a speed bump on the road to the kind of relationship she'd always thought she wanted.

But Luke wasn't a speed bump. He was . . . God, he was the freaking *destination*.

Why hadn't she seen that?

And why was she only realizing it now, when she was tied to a bed while a seriously messed-up psycho with a gun loomed over her?

"You make me sick," Vince hissed.

Olivia squeaked in terror as he launched himself at her, the mattress creaking like a haunted-house prop as he straddled her with his strong thighs. She closed her eyes, prepared for the worst, but to her shock, she felt his hands on her face. He cupped her jaw, digging his thumbs into her cheeks, his dark eyes blazing with a mixture of anger and despair.

"Why did you have to do this?" he moaned. "Why, damn it? What the *fuck* did I do wrong, Olivia? I saved you from that motherfucker in the alley! I took care of your debts! I bought you things to show you how much I loved you! I bought you *this*, for fuck's sake!"

He tore the silver chain from her neck and held up the little cross as if that alone was the symbol of their love.

The cross!

Vince was right—the necklace *was* important. She might have left her phone behind at the hospital, but not the necklace. Which meant that at this very moment, she was broadcasting loud and clear, relaying a signal that Luke could use to find her.

On top of her, Vince was in tears now. The moisture shining in his eyes made her jerk in surprise, but nothing was more shocking than the way he dipped his head to brush his lips over hers. "You're right," he choked out, his breath fanning over her mouth. "Maybe we can try again."

What?

"I'm a fool, aren't I?" His gaze searched her face, anxious, desperate. "I know I shouldn't still love you, but I do. I love you, babe. I love you so much."

She'd never been so confused in her life. Pity and disgust vied for her attention, but the disgust proved victorious when Vince started kissing her again. He was breathing hard, shaking from head to toe. His lips were cold and wet as he dragged them over every inch of her face. He kissed her mouth, her cheeks, her eyelids, lavishing nausea-inducing tenderness upon her before moving his lips to her neck so he could kiss her there too.

She pushed aside her queasiness and attempted to find a way to use his unexpected change of heart to her advantage. She was back to toying with the idea of convincing him of her undying love when she saw a flash of movement in the doorway.

Luke!

Olivia nearly cried out in joy when she spotted the familiar dark hair and rugged features, but Luke quickly lifted his finger to his lips to silence her. She went motionless, meeting his gorgeous chocolate brown eyes as Vince continued to bestow gentle kisses on her.

Shoot him, damn it! She silently pleaded for Luke to act, but he remained in the doorway, gun in hand, a tormented expression creasing his handsome face. It occurred to her that he *couldn't* take a shot. The way Vince was leaning on her, any bullet that hit him might hit her too.

She forced herself to stay still and trust Luke, but then Vince lifted his head—and he must have noticed her looking beyond him because he whirled around and released an enraged growl.

"You!" Voice ringing with accusation, he flung his arm toward the gun he'd left next to Olivia's hip.

"Me," Luke confirmed.

And then he shot Vince in the head.

Olivia screamed into the gag as blood sprayed her face, as Vince's body toppled to the floor with a thud. Shock and horror sent her mind spinning, had her gasping for air and jerking on the mattress even as Luke hurried toward her and removed the gag.

"Olivia. *Olivia.*"

He rapidly undid her bindings and yanked her against him, his strong arms holding her tight. Her pulse shrieked in her ears, pounding in her blood. She buried her face against his muscled chest and struggled for breath, shaking so hard she feared her bones might snap like twigs.

"Look at me, darlin'," he said urgently. His hands tangled in her hair, tilting her head up. "It's okay. You're okay. *Look at me*, Olivia."

She looked at him.

The second she registered his familiar dark eyes and the deep concern and sheer love glimmering in them, her body sagged and her heartbeat steadied. Luke's presence grounded her, penetrating the haze of her mind and leaving her with a sense of pure, startling clarity.

"You all right?" he said gruffly.

She nodded, then uttered the first thing that came to mind. Make that the *only* thing that came to mind. It left her lips in a hurried rush, the words coming not from her mouth but straight from her heart.

"I love you."

It was past midnight when Isabel finally heard a knock on the door. She'd been lying on her living room couch, exhausted as hell but unable to sleep a damn wink. With Olivia missing, everyone back at the safe house had been on edge, the tension running so high that Isabel had needed to get out of there. She'd come home to shower and change, even bringing her cell into the bathroom in case Trevor called, but there'd been no word from Luke or the others since they'd left Queens.

Shooting to her feet, she hurried to the front door and threw it open, relieved when she found Trevor standing in the hall. She met his whiskey-colored eyes, fearful of what she'd find, but to her relief, his expression revealed the answer she'd been hoping for.

"Olivia's safe," he said. "Luke found her."

Isabel let out a breath. "Thank God." She gestured for him to come inside, then locked the door and led him into the living room. "And Angelo?" she asked when he didn't elaborate.

"Dead."

She nodded. The DEA wouldn't like that—Angelo could've been their ticket to nabbing De Luca—but Isabel couldn't say she was torn up about it. From the moment she'd met Vince Angelo, she'd disliked the man.

"Luke and Olivia went to the hospital to be with Kathleen," Trevor added.

He removed his coat and draped it over the arm of the sofa, then sank down in one weary motion, looking as exhausted as Isabel felt.

After a beat of hesitation, she sat down next to him and drew her knees up to her chest. "What about Adam?"

"Also dead." The emotion he hadn't expressed about Angelo's death made an appearance now. "He was a good man. A good soldier."

"You're all good men. Every last one of you."

Trevor blinked in surprise, then recovered, resting his hands in his lap. "So, the job's over."

"It's over," she agreed. "What ended up happening with the DEA?"

"Well, Dane's in federal custody, and he's going to be charged with a whole bunch of shit. Turns out Dane's supervisor suspected all along that his man had been playing both sides. And the Moreno rep, Juan Ortiz, he started singing like a canary once he realized what kind of shit he's in. He's spilling everything he knows about Dane, probably in hopes of cutting a deal."

"He'll cut a deal, all right," Isabel said dryly. "But not for info on Dane. Trust me, Ortiz will sell out the cartel in a heartbeat. If he's extradited to Colombia he'll be killed in prison, which means his only hope of staying alive is to get immunity from our government, or at the very least, a prison sentence here."

"You're probably right about that."

She leaned her head back against the cushions. "So what'd Ortiz say about Dane?"

"Dane was working with Moreno for years, feeding the DEA bogus intel and pocketing cash as an informant for the cartel. When he was recalled to the States and assigned to the De Luca case, he decided to bank an even bigger profit by hooking up the two crime syndicates and taking not only a brokerage fee, but a percentage of the drug money. He already had a whole new identity lined up—he's been using the name Erik Franz, and according to Ortiz, Dane was supposed to head back to Colombia tomorrow morning. He was going to work for the Moreno cartel full-time."

"What was the deal with the guy you found in the warehouse last week? They tattooed the name *Mandy* on his butt to try to pass him off as Dane? Do we know who he was?"

"His DNA was flagged in the system. Low-life drug dealer from Brooklyn who had the misfortune of bearing a slight resemblance to Carter Dane."

She wrinkled her forehead. "But Dane's a federal agent. He would've known that his supervisors would run a DNA test."

"I'm guessing he didn't care. I think the body was meant to be a distraction for the Feds. Angelo and Dane wanted to keep the DEA busy while they brought in the heroin shipment right under their noses—"

Isabel finished his sentence. "And by the time the DEA figured out the body didn't belong to their agent, that agent would be on a plane to Colombia and living under a new name." She smiled wryly. "So I'm assuming there never was a mole within the agency."

"I doubt it," Trevor replied. "I bet Dane only insinuated that during his last check-in so his supervisors wouldn't send in more agents once he went AWOL."

She laughed. "No, they just sent you guys instead."

Trevor fell quiet, unlacing his fingers and resting his palms on his muscular thighs. After a moment, he shot her a sidelong look and said, "So . . . what are your plans now?"

"I'm taking Heaven Monroe to rehab in the morning."

"And after that?"

"I . . ." She swallowed. "I thought maybe we'd go out to dinner."

He looked surprised again, and she didn't quite blame him, seeing as she'd tried so hard to distance herself from him over the past couple of weeks. She hadn't been able to help it, though. He always left her feeling so damn unsettled, and not just because of the attraction brewing between them. Now that he had let go of his grief over his fiancée's death, he was showing Isabel a different side of himself. He radiated strength and warmth, subtle sensuality and quiet power. Truth was, she'd never been able to relax around a man the way she could with Trevor, which was scary as hell, and the reason she'd been holding back for so long.

But tonight something had scared her even worse.

She'd glimpsed Luke's face earlier when he realized Olivia was gone. His eyes had showed such panic, such love, that she'd been absolutely floored. Seeing Luke so distraught and determined to rescue the woman he loved had made Isabel long for . . . for something. Something more. Just once, she wanted someone to feel that way about her. She wanted someone to look at her and see *her*, not the mask she wore, not the disguises she put on.

And Trevor Callaghan did. He *saw* her.

"Dinner," he echoed, his voice laced with bewilderment.

"Unless you don't want to," she said quickly.

"I want to," he said, just as quick.

She smiled. "Yeah?"

"Yeah."

And then he slid across the couch, grasped her chin with one hand, and bent down to kiss her.

Isabel gasped against his lips, then relaxed as a rush of heat filled her belly. Trevor coaxed her mouth open and nudged his tongue inside, his hands cupping the back of her head so he could drive the kiss deeper. The scent of his aftershave, the firmness of his lips, the wicked thrust of his tongue . . . it all teased her senses, making her breathless, mindless. Her fingers trembled as she dug them into his shoulders to pull him closer, taking the kiss to a whole new level, one that made them both groan.

When they finally broke apart, she felt dazed, dizzy. His magnetic brown eyes were hot and sultry, his fingertips utterly seductive as they traced the curve of her jaw.

"Now what?" she whispered.

"Now we go to bed."

Her head jerked. "We do?"

"To sleep," he corrected, a smile playing on his lips. "We're both exhausted, and frankly, I'm terrified that if I push you for anything else right now, all the progress we've made will be lost." Still smiling, Trevor rose and extended a hand to her. "What do you say, Isabel? Will you let me sleep next to you tonight?"

She reached for his hand and said, "Yes."

Chapter 26

Isabel woke up with a smile on her face. Weird, that spending the night with a man could bring this huge Cheshire grin to her mouth, especially when sex hadn't played a part in it. Trevor had been right, though—she wasn't ready for that. Her feelings for him were confusing enough as it was; adding intimacy to the mix was likely to confuse her even more.

For the moment, she was satisfied with lying next to him and watching him sleep. She rolled onto her side so she could admire his classically handsome features, the stubble rising on his strong jaw, the way his lips quirked as if he were having a seriously pleasurable dream.

As the sunlight streamed in through the curtainless window in her barren bedroom, she had to wonder what time it was. She felt like they'd slept in, which was a luxury she never indulged in. A glance at the alarm clock resting on the floor confirmed it. Eleven o'clock. Man, they must have been pretty exhaus—

"Shit!" she exclaimed, stumbling off the bed.

Trevor woke with a start, blinking rapidly. His hand shot out in search of a weapon.

Isabel quickly eased his panic. "It's fine, everything's fine."

With a yawn, he slid up to a sitting position and rubbed his eyes. "What's going on?"

"I was supposed to meet Heaven." She grabbed a pair of jeans and a cable-knit sweater, then walked over to the dresser in search of some socks. "God, I feel like such an ass! I promised I'd pick her up at her apartment at nine— I'm two hours late, damn it."

"Don't beat yourself up," Trevor said gruffly. "I'm sure she'll understand."

"I hope so." Isabel marched toward the door. "I'm going to get dressed and drive over to her place."

"I'll come with you."

"No, it'll be better if you aren't there. She's already jumpy enough. She might decide not to check herself into rehab if I show up with a strange man."

"I'm a strange man?"

Her lips lifted in a smile. "A stranger," she corrected.

Trevor grinned, and the sight brought a rush of warmth to her chest. She loved seeing this man smile. "I'll wait here then. If you don't mind, that is."

"I don't mind," she said softly.

She headed for the bathroom, where she washed up and got dressed before poking her head back into the bedroom. "The rehab facility is nearby, but it might take a few hours to get her settled. I'll probably be back late afternoon." She faltered, unaccustomed to having someone other than herself in this empty apartment. "There's no food in the fridge, but the diner around the corner is pretty good. And I don't have a TV, but I own a lot of books. I . . . uh . . . I'm not used to guests."

Trevor shrugged. "I'll manage. Go help that girl, Iz. I'll be waiting for you when you get back."

She experienced another burst of heat, feeling like a silly schoolgirl as she left the apartment. She'd never shared her personal space with anyone before, let alone a strong, sexy man she might actually have a relationship with. God. A relationship. The notion was utterly terrifying.

Dismissing the troubling thoughts, she walked down the two flights of stairs and exited the building through the back doors, sprinting toward the Mercedes she drove whenever she was in the city. The Honda she'd bought under Candy Cane's name had been ditched behind a strip mall, and Isabel didn't plan on going back for it. She was done with Candy. And, for the first time in her life, she was actually considering taking a break from her work. She wasn't sure how long Trevor planned on sticking around, but as long as he was here, she didn't want to be anyone other than herself.

She reached Heaven's neighborhood in record time, breaking more than a few traffic laws as she sped toward the dancer's apartment. She hoped Heaven was still there, and that the girl wouldn't reject her help because of her tardiness.

When she finally arrived at the seedy, low-income building, she spotted an ambulance parked by the curb.

An alarm went off in Isabel's head. As her throat tightened and her pulse quickened, she shut off the engine and slid out of the car, reaching the building's entrance just as the double doors opened and a pair of paramedics exited. Wheeling out a stretcher.

A body bag.

Her heart dropped like a lead weight. She dashed up to the EMTs and blurted out, "What happened?"

"Can't discuss that, ma'am," one of the men replied.

They brushed past her. She watched in dismay as the paramedics loaded the stretcher into the back of the ambulance.

"She's dead," a hoarse voice said from behind her. "The girl on the second floor."

Isabel pivoted and found an elderly woman with shoulder-length gray hair standing on the building's front stoop, lighting up a smoke.

"Was her name Heaven?" Isabel demanded. As an afterthought, she realized she'd never even taken the time to learn Heaven's real name.

The woman spoke in a raspy voice that hinted at too many cigarettes. "Nah, her name was Laura. Laura Monroe."

Monroe.

The air swooshed out of her lungs. *No, damn it.*

"How did she die?"

"Overdose. Girl was a raging junkie."

Isabel swallowed. "Accidental?"

"Nah, hon, there was a note. Junkie *and* suicidal. Going straight to hell, that one." The old woman gave a disgusted sneer before flicking her cigarette on the sidewalk and walking back into the building.

Feeling numb, Isabel returned to her car.

Two hours.

She'd been two hours late and Heaven had fucking *killed herself*.

God. This was her fault. She'd promised Heaven she'd be here this morning. Had Heaven waited for her? Sat there staring at the clock, slowly losing hope when Isabel hadn't knocked on the door? When had she injected that lethal dose? At ten? At eleven?

Maybe when Isabel had been lying in bed admiring Trevor Callaghan's gorgeous face.

Tears burned her eyes. Her chest was so tight she couldn't draw air into her lungs, and as she sat there with her fingers trembling over the steering wheel, she fought for breath and realized that she'd let another person down.

There's nothing you can do for Heaven now. Go home. Trevor's waiting.

Yes, Trevor was waiting, wasn't he?

But who was he waiting *for*? Isabel Roma, the easygoing, confident woman she pretended to be?

God, who was she kidding here? She could never be the kind of woman Trevor Callaghan needed. She was only capable of being other people. And Trevor, damn him, always seemed to make her lose focus, distract her from the only damn thing she was good at.

Brushing the tears from her eyes, she started the engine and pulled away from the curb. Instead of heading back to SoHo, she drove north. And watched the city disappear in the rearview mirror.

*   *   *

"So your team of mercenaries owns a private jet," Olivia remarked, glancing around the cabin of the plane. "I'm impressed."

In all honesty, she was far more impressed with the man sitting next to her. Luke still hadn't brought up the spur-of-the-moment declaration she'd made at the cabin, even though she knew it must be weighing on his mind. It was weighing on hers too, but she had yet to find the courage to address the issue.

Last night, after she'd voiced those three unexpected words, she'd promptly burst into tears, the adrenaline finally getting the best of her. Without hesitation, Luke had whisked her back to the hospital, but they hadn't had a chance to talk. They'd been too busy reassuring Olivia's mother, who'd been moved to another room after a nurse discovered Adam's body on the floor beside Kathleen's bed.

Olivia had spent an hour with a pair of police detectives, but she didn't think they stood a chance of finding the goon who'd disguised himself as an orderly and murdered Adam. After she'd given her statement, she'd stayed with her mother while Luke and the rest of his team tied up loose ends and made arrangements. Luke had returned to the hospital this morning, and he'd been an absolute rock. He stood beside her while she signed her mother's discharge papers, kept an arm around Kathleen's fragile shoulders as they walked out to the car, got them settled on the jet in the small hangar of the private airfield. Through it all, his dark eyes had studied Olivia with quiet curiosity, but he hadn't once pushed for the discussion she knew they would eventually have.

Now they were seated in the plush chairs in the jet's cabin, with the murmur of voices around them, and she still wasn't sure she was ready for this.

But apparently Luke's patience had run out.

"Are we going to talk about it?" he asked, ignoring her attempt at chatting about airplanes.

She snuck a quick peek at the others, feeling uncomfortable about having this conversation where anyone could overhear them. In the seats ahead of them, Sullivan was telling Liam Macgregor about someone named Evangeline—in a tone so reverent that Olivia decided Evangeline was a very lucky girl. Kane, Ethan, and Holden sat on the opposite aisle, discussing the pros and cons of rocket launchers. Olivia's mother was asleep on the other side of the cabin, an afghan tucked over her. That was it for passengers—the other contractors had gone off to wherever it was on-call soldiers went, and Trevor had stayed in Manhattan, which she suspected had something to do with Isabel.

Although nobody seemed to be paying any attention to her and Luke, she still felt self-conscious as she shifted in her seat so they were face-to-face.

"You said you loved me," he reminded her.

She bit her lip before answering. "I know."

"Did you mean it?" His confidence seemed to slip a little. "Or was it one of those I-almost-died-and-now-I'm-so-relieved-I'll-say-anything deals?"

She had to laugh. "Does that happen to you often?" Then she hesitated. "Last night was the first time I almost died. And . . . it was also the first time I told a man I love him."

Luke waited, his dark eyes focused on her face.

"I meant it," she admitted.

His broad shoulders sagged. "But?"

"How is this going to work? You live in some Mexican compound, I live . . . well, nowhere at the moment."

And wasn't that a scary thought. Luke insisted she needed to leave the Big Apple, at least until they gauged the kind of fallout Vince's death would cause. Apparently Ric De Luca was scrambling to cover his tracks now that his coffee import company had been implicated in drug smuggling, but Luke and the others predicted the blame would be laid at Vince's door. With Vince dead, De Luca would ensure that the burden of guilt fell on his associate rather than himself.

Even Isabel had agreed that the big boss would probably get off scot-free. The coffee warehouse was owned by a dummy corporation and couldn't be tied to the outfit, and with Vince out of the picture, the Mob boss had the perfect fall guy. The only remaining threat was Carter Dane, who was in federal custody and likely to testify against De Luca in exchange for a deal, but nobody had much faith in Dane's ability to stay alive. According to Isabel, De Luca would find a way to eliminate Dane before the double agent could do much damage.

But even though De Luca currently had his plate full, that didn't mean he wouldn't retaliate against Olivia. Luke said it was unlikely, but she couldn't take the chance, which meant staying far away from New York. Besides, she'd already dropped out of this semester's classes, so what would she do in the city? Not work at the Diamond, that's for sure. She would need to find another job, though, if she wanted to support herself and her mom.

Luke, apparently, had other ideas. "You and Kathleen could stay with me for a while." When she raised her eyebrows, he added, "Until you figure out what you want to do, and where you want to go." His corded throat worked as he swallowed. "Have you ever been to Colorado?"

She wrinkled her forehead. "No. Why?"

"Trevor has a condo in Aspen, and he mentioned that he's putting it on the market. I'm thinking of taking it off his hands."

Surprise filtered through her. "Why would you do that? I thought you liked living with your men."

"I do. Or rather, I did. But let's be honest—a compound in rural Mexico is no place for you or your mom. Kathleen needs to be near a good medical center and I assume you'll want to go back to school, right? You can finish your undergrad in Colorado, and there are some really good teaching programs there, if you choose not to go to law school . . ." He trailed off, meeting her eyes. "I only say that because I know at one point you wanted to be a teacher."

She shook her head, dazed. "I did, but . . ."

"But law offers more money and stability, right?"

"Well, yeah."

"If you had a choice, would teaching be your first pick?"

After a moment, she nodded.

"Then you need to pursue it," he said simply.

Olivia was torn between yielding to the rush of happiness that filled her and listening to the practical voice of reason in her head. As usual, the latter won. "I suppose you'll just support me and my mother indefinitely," she said dryly.

"Yes."

"I can't let you do that, Luke. I can take care of us on my own. I've been doing it since I was sixteen."

"Fine, then we'll take care of each other," he said, echoing what her mother had told her back at the safe house. He leaned close to cup her chin with his hands. "Equal partners, Liv. If you want to work while you finish school, I won't stop you. If you want to go halfsies on rent and bills, fine. But just know that you won't be doing it alone anymore. I'll be right there with you, carrying half the load."

"Why?" she whispered.

"Because I love you."

At his smoky voice, heat spread through her. "You love me."

"I know, it's weird, huh? I've never been anti-love or anything, but it's still a new feeling for me. I think I kind of like it." He slanted his head. "So what do you say? Come to Colorado with me?"

Olivia bit her lip. "I don't know . . ."

"Are you still worried about my job?"

"That's part of it."

Luke sighed. "I won't stop doing what I do, but I can promise you I'll always be careful. No matter where I am or how dangerous the job is, I will make it my goal in life to come home to you. Just give me the chance."

Indecision washed over her. God, she wanted to say yes. She wanted to give him that chance. But every time she thought about him being away while she sat at home not knowing if he'd come back, she remembered all the heart-ache her father had caused her mom.

The heart wants what it wants . . .

Those gentle words floated through her brain, followed by her mother's worry that Olivia might let the right man slip away because of her fear.

"I won't let you down, darlin'." Luke sounded so earnest it melted her heart. "You're the smartest, kindest, most beautiful woman I've ever met, and you've got the biggest fucking heart on this planet. You deserve to be happy, Liv. Let me in and I promise you, you won't regret it. I'll be everything you want me to be — and more."

Ribbons of warmth unfurled inside her, and a part of her couldn't believe she was even hesitating. Luke was saying everything she wanted to hear, damn it. Hadn't she wanted a man she could count on? A man who would be there for her? A man who loved her?

Well, here he is, you idiot!

The little voice in her head made her want to laugh. Wow. She'd known she was cautious, but this was borderline ridiculous. Maybe it was time to throw caution to the wind and listen to her heart for once.

"Okay," she whispered.

His gaze bored into her. "Okay?"

She released the breath she'd been holding. "You prom-ise you'll always be careful?"

"Always."

"And you're sure it's fine if my mom lives with us? I won't leave her, Luke. She's still recovering and—"

"You don't need to justify it. Your mother can stay with us forever if you want." His voice turned gruff. "And if you're up for it, I'd like you to meet *my* mom. Maybe we can spend Christmas in New Orleans."

Emotion clogged her throat. She knew he hadn't been home since his father's death, and that he wanted her to be there when he did go warmed her heart. "I'd love it," she said softly.

Luke's gorgeous face took on a serious expression. "So . . . we're really going to do this?"

She licked her lips. "We're really going to do this."

Their eyes locked, and the next thing she knew, his strong arms came around her and his mouth covered hers in a kiss that left her needy and breathless. As his tongue swept inside her mouth and teased her to a new level of hot and bothered, Olivia heard laughter from the front seat.

Her eyes snapped open to find Sullivan leaning around his chair to watch them. As she flushed with embarrassment, the Australian wiggled his eyebrows. "See, I was just telling Macgregor here that you should have led with the hot kiss, mate," Sullivan reprimanded Luke. "All that convincing you just did? Wouldn't have been necessary if you'd led with the kiss."

Luke rolled his eyes. "Thanks for the tip."

"No problem." Sullivan's gray eyes moved to Olivia. "Listen, sweetheart, if this jerk ever gives you any grief, come find me, all right? I'm way better at the love thing than he is."

"Said the man who's in love with a boat," Luke retorted. "Now will you turn around and pretend we're not here? Olivia and I are busy."

After a laughing Sullivan settled back in his seat, Luke drew her close again and brushed his lips over hers. PDA had never been her thing, but the feel of his mouth was too addictive, and she instinctively parted her lips to let his tongue in. She wasn't sure how long they sat there kissing, but her lips were swollen by the time they broke apart, and her hair was tousled from Luke's fingers running through it.

When she noticed his dark eyes twinkling, she gave a soft, giddy laugh. "What are you looking so pleased about?"

"I was just thinking about how I can't wait for you to meet my dog."

She stared at him. "Seriously? You were thinking about your *dog* while we were making out? Jeez. You really do need love lessons."

"With you as my teacher? I will gladly learn it all." He

leaned in and suckled her earlobe, then nibbled her flesh with his teeth. "I'm pretty sure I'll get an A too."

With the sheer emotion overflowing in her heart and the pure heat sizzling through her veins, she didn't doubt him. She got the feeling Luke Dubois could ace any lesson, tackle any challenge, slay any dragon—and yes, still make it home for dinner.

His mouth traveled down to her neck, pressing hot kisses along her fevered skin, and then he returned to her ear, his voice coming out soft and raspy as he murmured, "Want to fool around in the bathroom?"

She choked back a laugh, but the reckless glint in his eyes told her he wasn't kidding.

Luke cocked a brow, his sensual mouth quirking. "Well?"

And to think, she'd once considered reckless a *turnoff*.

Good thing she'd come around since then.

Olivia quickly unbuckled her seat belt and said, "Best idea ever."

Epilogue

Isabel sat in the corner of the large visitation room at Sing Sing Correctional Facility, her gaze trained on the door. At the neighboring table, an inmate leaned close to a female with red hair, talking in hushed whispers and gripping her hand as if he never wanted to let go. Across the room, three small children were playing on the floor while their mother argued with their imprisoned dad about car payments and refinancing a mortgage. On the surface everything seemed pleasant, unthreatening, but an undertone of menace hung in the air, in the form of the sharp-eyed guards watching the inmates and families.

Isabel continued to wait, and finally the door swung open and her father entered the room.

God, he was skinnier than the last time she'd seen him. Bernie Roma had always been lanky, but now he just looked gaunt, and his dark brown hair, once thick and lustrous, was beginning to thin. He'd turned fifty-four last month, but he looked a decade older, and his eyes were cold and impassive when he spotted Isabel. Well, at least *that* hadn't changed.

Her father shuffled toward the table and eased himself into the chair opposite hers. He didn't reach for her hand. Didn't hug her. Didn't even smile.

"Why do you keep coming here?" he asked in a tired voice.

Isabel spoke through the lump in her throat. "Because you're my father and I love you."

He didn't respond.

"How are you doing?" she asked. "Are they treating you well?"

No answer.

Her hands began to tremble, so she rested them flat on the table. "I'm doing okay, I guess. Work is good"—she didn't elaborate on that, because her father had no idea what she did for a living and had never asked—"and I'm thinking of taking a vacation, maybe Hawaii. It might be nice to lie on a beach for a while and—"

"Must we keep doing this?" her father interrupted, his features heavy with weariness.

"And I'm considering selling my SoHo apartment. I'm hardly ever there, so—"

"Can't you let me live out the rest of my days in peace?"

"—I don't see a point in keeping the place. But the real estate market isn't the best right now so maybe I'll wait—"

"Jesus Christ, Isabel!"

He slammed a hand on the tabletop, eliciting a harsh look from one of the guards.

She blinked, diverting her gaze from the cold eyes piercing into her.

Breathing hard, Bernie brought his hand back to his lap and interlaced his fingers. "I don't want to listen to your pointless bullshit and pretend we're having a chat over a cup of coffee. We're not sitting in a restaurant, Isabel. I'm in prison."

"I didn't put you here," she protested.

"No, you don't put people in prison, do you? You put them in graves."

Agony seared through her. "Dad—"

"Your brother's dead because of you. Your mother's dead because of you. Your grandparents are dead because of you." Her father barked out a cruel laugh. "Are you start-ing to see a pattern?"

The pain squeezing her throat was so excruciating it was impossible to get a word out, but he didn't give her time to regain her composure. He was already rising from the chair and signaling for the guard. "We're done here."

Isabel's legs could barely support her weight as she got up. She and her father were two feet away from each other, facing off. She didn't cry. He didn't blink.

She simply stood there and waited for it. The same sen-tence he spoke each time their visits wrapped up.

"Don't visit again, Isabel. I can't stand the sight of you."

And she said what she always said.

"I'll come back as soon as I can."

As her dad was escorted out of the visitors' room, she sucked in a breath and took her own leave. She stepped out-side a few minutes later and inhaled the cool late-afternoon air. And thought of Trevor. A fleeting image of him waiting for her in her apartment.

Sighing, she crossed the parking lot behind the peniten-tiary and headed for her car, pulling her cell phone out of her purse as she walked. She dialed Noelle's number, relief pouring into her when the boss answered.

"Hey, it's me," Isabel said. "The job for Morgan is done. What's my next assignment?"

"Sorry, honey, there's nothing on the docket at the mo-ment."

It was not the answer she wanted to hear. Stifling a groan, she said, "Nothing? Come on, there's *always* some-thing on your docket and we both know it."

Noelle went quiet for a beat. "Well, I was contacted about a job in Nigeria, but it's not your kind of assignment."

"Undercover?" she asked, unfazed.

"Yes, but this is a deep-cover gig. Three-month commit-ment, minimum, and once you're in, there's no out. You're not gathering intel, then stepping aside to let me or one of the girls finish the job. This is a kill operation, honey." No-elle continued in a dismissive tone. "So why don't you take

that vacation you were supposed to and I'll be in touch
when—"

"I'll do it."

There was a sharp intake of breath. "What?"

"I said I'll do it." Isabel's tone hardened. "Are you at the
Paris penthouse?"

"Yes, but—"

"I'll catch the next plane out. You can brief me when I
arrive."

Noelle was still protesting as Isabel disconnected the
call.

Ready for Trevor and Isabel's story?
Read on for a peek at the next thrilling novel in
the Killer Instincts series,

MIDNIGHT GAMES

Available in August 2013 from Signet Eclipse.

"He called again last night."

Isabel Roma froze. Only for a split second, but a second was all it took to tip off her boss, whose smirk widened. Crap. Noelle was a predator—show her any sign of weakness and the queen of assassins would eat you alive.

"What'd you tell him?" Isabel slowly turned around to meet those shrewd blue eyes.

"Same thing I've been telling him for the past five months. You're deep cover and can't be reached." Noelle paused, an honest-to-God grin gracing those bloodred lips.

Considering the woman only smiled right before she killed you, Isabel grew a tad worried. Gulping, she crossed her arms over her chest and said, "Spit it out, Noelle."

"He wanted me to pass along a message." That shit-eating grin got bigger. "He said he never took you for a coward."

A *coward*? The insult prickled her skin, even though she knew the accusation was Trevor Callaghan's way of evoking a reaction from her. He of all people knew that she was the furthest thing from a coward.

Bristling, she drifted toward the wet bar on the other side of the lavish living room. She was staying at Noelle's Paris penthouse until she found a place of her own, and although she was currently homeless, she had zero complaints about her current digs. The gorgeous two-story apartment was located in the Right Bank, an area known for its spacious avenues, ornate nineteenth-century buildings, and wealthy foreign residents. The enormous floor-to-ceiling windows overlooked the breathtaking cityscape, even more beautiful at night with all the lights twinkling like diamonds. Outside, the silver frost clinging to the street lamps and the layer of white covering the sidewalks created a magical ambience that Isabel would've taken more time to admire if she weren't so rattled at the moment.

With a sigh, she poured herself a glass of Maker's Mark and took a long swig. The alcohol scorched a path down her throat but did nothing to quell the uneasiness that had been rippling in her stomach ever since she'd landed this morning at the private airstrip, where Noelle had been waiting in a silver Mercedes. In that nonchalant, I-don't-particularly-give-a-fuck tone, Noelle had revealed that Trevor Callaghan had been hounding her for information ever since he and Isabel had said good-bye in New York.

Said good-bye? echoed the mocking voice in her head.

Fine. So maybe they hadn't exchanged any good-byes. Maybe she'd just left.

Left?

Gritting her teeth, Isabel tried to silence that exasperating voice by taking another gulp of whiskey, but it didn't work. Guilt continued to trickle into her, along with a pang of shame that made her chest hurt.

Damn it. Maybe Trevor was right. Maybe she *was* a coward. How else could you explain why she'd abandoned him like that?

Five months ago, she'd done some undercover work for mercenary extraordinaire Jim Morgan, which had yet again paired her with Trevor. The first time she'd worked with the former Special Forces soldier, he'd been a ravaged, grieving mess, a man with a death wish, a man she shouldn't have been attracted to but had been. The second time around, that attraction had intensified. Trevor had been a changed man. A healed man.

They'd connected during that second job, really connected. They'd *kissed*, for Pete's sake. And what had she done? She'd deserted him. Left him waiting at her SoHo apartment, hopped a plane and fled the country.

How long had he waited?

Another rush of guilt flooded her belly as the question she'd been wondering these past five months floated into her head. A part of her hoped that Trevor had figured out the score after an hour or two, but deep down she knew he wouldn't have given up that fast. He would've waited for hours, days even, and when she still didn't return ... that's when the worry would have set in. The anger. The bitterness.

But again, she knew Trevor—no matter how angry he was, he'd need to make sure she was all right, which meant he'd move heaven and earth to track her down.

According to Noelle, he'd been doing just that.

"Ditching Callaghan like that was a coldhearted move, honey," the blond assassin said with a chuckle. "Giving men the slip is more my style than yours."

Coldhearted. Was that was she was? No. No, she couldn't be. The way she'd ended things with Trevor had been callous, but she'd been motivated by the need for self-preservation, not cruelty. He'd gotten too close. Made her believe that happiness could play a role in her future, that she could actually be a normal woman who had normal relationships and a normal life—but Isabel knew better.

She wasn't destined for normalcy. The most she could ask for was professional fulfillment, and her undercover work provided that. She was good at pretending to be other people. Maybe it wasn't the most honorable profession out there, but she excelled at it. And Trevor, with his perceptive brown eyes and understated charm, with that quiet strength he exuded and his rare but gorgeous smiles ... he was too big a distraction. Each time she was around him, she lost her head and dropped her guard—and for a woman who'd spent her entire life perfecting a composed, easygoing front, neither of those responses was welcome.

"You never told me why you bailed on him," Noelle prompted.

Isabel shrugged and took another sip of whiskey.

"It's all right. I already know the answer."

Although the entire exchange was making her uncomfortable as hell, she couldn't fight that spark of wary curiosity. "Oh, do you?"

Lithe as a cat, Noelle slid off the arm of the recliner she'd been perched on and strode across the white Burberry carpet. Her tight black leggings and even tighter black tank top contrasted with the all-white color scheme of the penthouse. Isabel wondered if Noelle's interior designer had been making some sort of ironic statement. White leather couch, white armchairs, white carpeting, white walls. The place was very . . . sterile. Cold. Unwelcoming.

The penthouse suited Noelle to a T.

"You left because that man scares you shitless."

Noelle's assessment made her frown. "Trevor doesn't scare me."

Liar.

"Liar." Noelle reached for an empty glass and poured a healthy amount of bourbon into it. She curled her fingers around the tumbler, red fingernails tapping on the glass. "Callaghan was starting to get to know the real Isabel, but we couldn't have that, could we, honey? Because the real Isabel is so very damaged, isn't she?"

Her shoulders stiffened.

"Oh, don't look at me like that, *so* offended and incensed. I'm not saying anything you haven't thought a million times before." The amber liquid in Noelle's glass swished as she headed back to the sofa. With the grace of a ballerina, the blonde sank onto the cushions and demurely crossed her legs, balancing the tumbler on one delicate knee.

Isabel couldn't control the rush of indignation that coursed through her. Noelle was a bitch on a good day, but it was rare for one of her "chameleons" to be on the receiving end of that sharp, antagonistic tongue. Isabel had been working for the woman for seven years now, and this was the first time the deadly blonde had unleashed a personal attack on her.

Damaged? Christ, the woman ought to take a good long look in the mirror. Noelle was the freaking definition of the word.

"You think if he sees the real you, he'll realize how flawed you are and run in the opposite direction."

She resisted the urge to slap that amused look right off Noelle's gorgeous face.

"I left because I'm not looking for a relationship," Isabel said stiffly. "That's what he wanted from me, and I couldn't give it to him."

"Mmm-hmmm. What's the next bullshit excuse?"

Her jaw tensed. "These aren't excuses. It's the truth. Look, he clouds my judgment, okay?" Even she could hear the defensive note in her voice. "Back in Manhattan, I was supposed to help one of the girls I met when I was undercover at the strip club. I was taking her to a rehab facility, but I was late because of Trevor. I was late, and that poor girl killed herself."

Noelle offered a long, throaty laugh. "That junkie would've killed herself regardless. You think even if you did manage to get her to rehab, the program would have stuck? How naive are you, Isabel?"

Rather than answer, she raised her glass and downed the rest of her whiskey. This time, the burning sensation only made her feel nauseous. This entire conversation was beginning to piss her off.

"Enough," she snapped. "We're done talking about this."

"Meow."

"I'm serious, Noelle." Isabel took a calming breath, tried to control her rising anger. "Tell me about the fallout from the Ekala job."

Noelle sipped her bourbon. "It's playing out exactly the way we wanted it to. The media is reporting that one of Ekala's lieutenants orchestrated a coup. You did a good job."

She arched a brow, both surprised and insulted by the praise. "You thought I wouldn't?"

"I worried. You excel at short-term gigs. Deep cover was always more suited to Bailey or Abby."

"Well, I managed just fine."

"That you did. You rid the world of another sadistic fucker. Give yourself a pat on the back."

Sometimes it was incredibly hard to decipher whether Noelle was being sarcastic or not. Isabel decided to treat that last remark as sincere.

Truth was, she was damn proud of herself for the way she'd handled the Nigeria job. Her boss was right—Isabel's strength was the in-and-out gig. Transform herself into whomever she needed to be, go undercover and get the information she was asked to procure, then disappear without a trace.

These last five months, however, she'd been deeply rooted in the Nigeria mission. Posing as an American journalist, she'd infiltrated Tengo Ekala's camp and cozied up to the man who'd been terrorizing the country ever since he'd come into power. She'd even succeeded in gaining the Nigerian warlord's respect and admiration, under the guise that she wanted to tell the world about his cause.

And when the time had come to put a bullet in the bastard's head, she hadn't stepped aside to let one of the other women take over.

For the first time in her career, Isabel had been the one to pull the trigger.

"Am I officially part of the club now?" she asked dryly. "Is there a special assassin membership card I get to keep in my wallet?"

"Sorry, honey. I'm pulling you out."

"What the hell does that mean?"

"Exactly what it sounds like." Noelle set down her glass and got to her feet. "I indulged you with the Ekala job, but you're done now. You're a master of disguise, and that's the only service I require from you. You won't be assigned any more contracts."

The cool declaration brought a spark of anger and a pang of relief. Rather than dwell on the latter, she focused on the former. "I just eliminated one of the world's nastiest warlords without causing so much as a ripple of tension in the international political pool, and you think I'm only suitable for undercover work?"

"You're not a killer, Isabel. Never have been, never will be." Noelle headed for the arched doorway across the room. "Leave the killing to those of us who enjoy it."

She couldn't control her surprise. "You're saying you actually *enjoy* taking a life?"

"When it's the life of a sick fuck who deserves it? Yes." The boss's voice was oddly gentle. "You're not like me, Isabel. We've both suffered. We both came from shitty backgrounds, but, see, your crap gave you a bleeding heart. You want to *help* people. My crap crushed my conscience, plain and simple."

This was the most candid Noelle had ever been with her, and Isabel found herself speechless as she stared at the other woman. At five-two, with her long golden hair, ethereal features and pale blue eyes, Noelle looked like a damn Disney princess, yet she was the coldest, most lethal person Isabel had ever met. She'd always wondered how Noelle had gotten to be this way and now she finally had an inkling. Noelle's "crap" had crushed her conscience.

Christ.

"So we can waste some more time and keep arguing about this," Noelle said flippantly, "or you can just accept that I'm right. You're not a killer. Ergo, you're not taking on any more contracts. Now, when can I expect you back?"

Isabel blinked. "What?"

"From Jim Morgan's compound. I already alerted my pilot that you'll be using the jet tonight—he's waiting for your call. So when do you think you'll be done there? I need you on recon for Bailey in Istanbul, so don't take too long with Callaghan."

"I'm not—"

"Going to see Callaghan?" Noelle finished. Those blue

eyes gleamed. "Bullshit. That's exactly what you're going to do, and you want to know why? Because not only are you not a killer, you're also not a coldhearted bitch. That's my job, remember?"

With that, the blonde slunk out of the living room, leaving Isabel alone with her thoughts.

Once again, Noelle was right. The second Isabel had stepped off that plane this morning, her first instinct had been to pick up the phone and apologize to Trevor for the way she'd left things. The way she'd left *him*.

But he deserved more than a half-ass phone call. He deserved a real apology, and no matter how badly she wanted to put distance between them, she wasn't the kind of woman who cowered in the face of conflict. She'd always intended to see him again. To explain why they couldn't be together. Running away from him in Manhattan had really just been about giving herself some time to regroup before they had that inevitable conversation.

"You think if he sees the real you, he'll realize how flawed you are and run in the opposite direction."

Was she actually that transparent, or was Noelle too freaking insightful for her own good?

Swallowing her mounting apprehension, Isabel placed her glass on the table, dug her cell phone from her purse and called Noelle's pilot.

ALSO AVAILABLE

FROM

Elle Kennedy

MIDNIGHT RESCUE
A Killer Instincts Novel

Adopted by an army ranger, Abby Sinclaire was molded into a master of self-defense. Now, she's an assassin using raw nerve to always come out on top. Her latest assignment is to snuff out a dangerous arms dealer hiding in the underground Colombian sex trade. When the sting goes wrong, mercenary Kane Woodland is recruited as back-up. But their unexpected primal attraction could put them both at risk. Their only rule: get out of that hellhole alive.

"Fans will be eager to see what Ms. Kennedy has in store for her mercenaries."
—Shannon K. Butcher, author of the Edge Series

Available wherever books are sold or at
penguin.com

S0441

From National Bestselling Author

Shannon K. Butcher

EDGE OF SANITY
An Edge Novel

Working for private security firm The Edge, Clay
Marshall has seen it all. But the recent blackouts he's been
having are new. So is waking up with blood on his hands
and clothes, with no memory of what happened. He
knows he needs help. Dr. Leigh Vaughn has treated other
Edge employees before, but from the moment she sees
him, Clay strikes her as a special breed of man. She knows
he's dangerous, and distrustful of doctors, but is drawn to
him even as his own steely exterior gives way to his
growing desire for her. But neither can foresee the secret
danger that will soon threaten them both...

"Butcher is...phenomenal."
—*Affaire de Coeur*

Available wherever books are sold or at
penguin.com

facebook.com/LoveAlwaysBooks

S0442